TWO SISTERS

Josephine Cox was born in Blackburn, one of ten children. At the age of sixteen, Josephine met and married her husband, Ken, and had two sons. When the boys started school, she decided to go to college and eventually gained a place at Cambridge University. She was unable to take this up as it would have meant living away from home, but she went into teaching – and started to write her first full-length novel. She won the 'Superwoman of Great Britain' Award, for which her family had secretly entered her, at the same time as her novel was accepted for publication. Her strong, gritty stories are taken from the tapestry of life.

Josephine says, 'I could never imagine a single day without writing. It's been that way since as far back as I can remember.'

Gilly Middleton has been involved with fiction all her working life. She lives in Sussex, where she likes to go to the theatre and to watch cricket. She has been a huge fan of Josephine Cox for many years and feels privileged to have been asked to take on a collaborative role with this new novel.

Also by Josephine Cox

QUEENIE'S STORY
Her Father's Sins
Let Loose the Tigers

THE EMMA GRADY TRILOGY
Outcast
Alley Urchin
Vagabonds

Angels Cry Sometimes
Take This Woman
Whistledown Woman
Don't Cry Alone
Jessica's Girl
Nobody's Darling
Born to Serve
More than Riches
A Little Badness
Living a Lie
The Devil You Know
A Time for Us
Cradle of Thorns
Miss You Forever
Love Me or Leave Me
Tomorrow the World
The Gilded Cage
Somewhere, Someday
Rainbow Days
Looking Back
Let It Shine
The Woman Who Left
Jinnie
Bad Boy Jack
The Beachcomber
Lovers and Liars
Live the Dream
The Journey
Journey's End
The Loner
Songbird
Born Bad
Divorced and Deadly
Blood Brothers
Midnight
Three Letters
The Broken Man
The Runaway Woman
Lonely Girl
A Mother's Gift: Two Classic Novels
A Family Secret
A Woman's Fortune

JOSEPHINE COX

with GILLY MIDDLETON

Two Sisters

HarperCollins*Publishers*

HarperCollins*Publishers*
1 London Bridge Street,
London SE1 9GF

www.harpercollins.co.uk

Published by HarperCollins*Publishers* 2020
1

Gilly Middleton is acknowledged as the co-author of this work

A catalogue record for this book
is available from the British Library

ISBN: 9780008128074 (HB)
ISBN: 9780008128425 (TPB)

Typeset in ITC New Baskerville Std by Palimpsest Book Production Ltd,
Falkirk, Stirlingshire

Printed and bound in Great Britain by CPI Group (UK) Ltd, Croydon CR0 4YY

MIX
Paper from
responsible sources
FSC C007454

This book is produced from independently certified FSC™ paper
to ensure responsible forest management.

For more information visit: www.harpercollins.co.uk/green

For my Ken, as always

A special message from Jo

To my readers, I'd like to say how happy I am to share Two Sisters *with you. My characters and their lives have kept me company every step of the way and I hope their stories touch you too.*

Thank you for your loyalty, it means the world to me.

Jo x

PART ONE

Gina
May 1956–August 1956

CHAPTER ONE

Ellen Arnold lay back on the grass, one arm shielding her eyes from the intense brightness of the spring sky. She heard the calling of ewes to their lambs in the next field and then eventually the rustle of her sister's skirt as Georgina sat down beside her.

'You were a while closing that gate,' Ellen said, not looking round. There was a long pause. 'Gina?'

'I got the rope all twisted . . .'

They were silent and still for a few minutes.

'It's lovely here . . . so peaceful,' murmured Ellen.

'If you like peaceful. Sometimes I reckon the countryside can be a bit quiet.'

'I don't mind quiet. It doesn't have to be . . . I don't know . . . *small.* Mr Beveridge can have quiet whenever he wants to as it's his farm. Mr Stellion, at the Hall, goes all over the place on business but he's always got that lovely garden to return to.'

'Mm . . .' Gina thought of Grindle Hall, the biggest house she'd ever seen. But it was still in the village of

Little Grindle, still stuck out here on the Lancashire fells, where nothing ever happened.

'Good of Mr Beveridge to give me the afternoon off,' Ellen said.

'Yes, wasn't it?' said Gina heavily. 'Pity he was too mean to give me a little holiday as well.'

'But you took it anyway.' Ellen smiled. Her sister had the cheek of the devil sometimes.

''Course I did. I had summat I wanted to see to earlier. What's he going to do about it, anyway?'

'Well, he might give you the sack.'

Gina considered this. 'He might but I bet he won't. If Mr and Mrs B were going to sack me, they'd have done so long since.'

'Probably. Still, such a lovely afternoon. I wish every day could be like today is right now,' Ellen said. 'No hens to see to . . .'

'No water troughs to unblock . . .'

'No smelly straw to clear out . . .'

'No sheep to check on . . .'

'Oh, I like the sheep,' Ellen smiled, then laughed as a loud baa sounded from over the dry-stone wall. 'The lambs are so bonny when they're tiny.'

'You're daft, Nell – daft as they are,' Gina said mildly, turning her face to follow an oddly shaped passing cloud. It looked . . . like a dancing figure with long, spiky limbs, strangely menacing in such a gloriously blue sky. Where had it sprung from? The sky had been cloudless when they'd reached the field gate. 'I'll ask you whether you like the sheep next winter when the snow's coming in and Dad wants you to help get them down from the fell.'

'Mebbe. Might not be helping on the farm then.' Now was the time to tell Gina her news. If it all worked out, Gina would have to know anyway, and Ellen didn't want to look as if she'd kept it from her sister. She'd put off telling her long enough. 'Uncle Tom wants a new assistant – Young Lionel's left to work somewhere the other side of Whalley with Old Lionel – and Uncle Tom's asking Mr Stellion today if I could try out for it; see if it suits me.'

'You lucky beggar! I think Uncle Tom could have mentioned it to me! That's not fair. I could work at Grindle Hall. Why didn't he ask me?'

'Mebbe because I'm older,' Ellen said diplomatically. She'd guessed this might be Gina's reaction.

'And I'd rather work with Uncle Tom than Dad any day.'

'Aye, Uncle Tom's very agreeable, and I reckon I might prefer a garden to the farm. It'd be nice to grow flowers and learn how to cut bushes into those fancy shapes that they have at the Hall.'

The sisters were silent for long minutes, Ellen thinking about the garden at Grindle Hall, Gina sulking and brooding on this missed opportunity. A bee droned in the clover flowers dotting the grass around them. Ellen had her eyes closed still; Gina watched as the cloud-figure grew grotesque features before its head detached from its crooked body and formed into . . . a round and benign baby cloud.

'Oh, but it'd be grand never to have to work again at all,' Gina said after a while. 'That's what I'd really like: to have owt I wanted and never have to graft for it.'

Ellen turned to her sister to see if she were serious. 'Now who's daft? How can you have owt without working for it?'

'Stellion has.'

'It's *Mr* Stellion to you, Gina, and his family worked for years to build up the brewery business. He didn't just *come by* Grindle Hall and the lovely garden and his car and all, you know. He still runs the brewery, though I do reckon he just turns up and tells other folk what to do these days.'

'Exactly. I could tell folk what to do. What kind of a job is "telling other folk what to do" anyway, compared to real work, like being a farm hand?'

'Dad's the farm hand; we're the farm hand's farm hands,' Ellen pointed out.

They both laughed.

'But seriously,' Ellen went on, 'the brewery is Mr Stellion's family business and his work is taking responsibility. There's many a man – and some women, too – relying on his decisions for their livelihood.'

'Like Mrs Stellion, you mean?'

'Ah, poor lady. Mum was saying as how she was in bed again last week. It's a shame to live in such a grand house, warm all winter and full of nice things, time to do whatever you want, but to feel too poorly to enjoy it.'

'True.' Gina rolled onto her front and looked Ellen in the face. 'But it's all rather wasted on her, isn't it?' she said seriously. 'I reckon if I lived at Grindle Hall I'd be driving that big shiny car myself, or having parties in those enormous rooms, with dancing and a record player, and . . . I don't know . . . banquets, with *port* to drink instead of Stellion's beer.'

'Port? What do you know about port, or even Stellion's beer, for that matter, Georgina Arnold?' scoffed Ellen.

'Well, I wouldn't mind giving it a try. Mum says Mrs Stellion eats only tasteless wet stuff when she's feeling poorly – an "invalid's diet", she calls it.' Gina sounded contemptuous. 'If I were as rich as the Stellions, I'd have roast beef every single day, and Mum's roast potatoes.'

'Mebbe Mrs Stellion would like roast beef but she doesn't feel well enough to stomach it,' Ellen suggested. 'It's not right to be coveting other folk's things, thinking you're more deserving of them, just 'cos you're in better health.'

'I was only thinking about it, Nell, that's all. Just daydreaming. No need to get all preachy.'

'Everyone can dream – and it's good to have summat to lift the spirits and even to aim for, if you work hard and are lucky with your chances in life – but there's no sense in you dreaming of big houses and cars and . . . *banquets*, 'cos those dreams are never going to come true for folk like us.'

'Folk like you, you mean?' snapped Gina, suddenly angry at having the cold water of reality poured over her precious daydreams. 'Stupid little people that can see no further than a life of drudgery on some pathetic farm in the back of beyond.'

Ellen sighed. 'No, Gina, I mean ordinary people who

have to work hard for their living and mebbe don't have many advantages, that's all.'

'But, Nell, you have to dream big dreams if you want to get on in life. You have to *think* differently, think new things are possible. You may work as hard as you can, for as long as you can, but in the end you'll earn nowt but more work to do, if that's all you can see ahead.'

'No—'

'Yes! You have to dream bigger than this life, or this life is all you'll ever know. *Little Grindle* is all you'll ever know. D'you think Little Grindle is all there is . . . really?'

'Gina, I don't—'

'Look at Mum, going off to Grindle Hall of a morning to clean up after the Stellions. She must see all those beautiful things in that house – see how rich folk live – and what does she do but come home, all worn out, to our cottage – which we live in only because it comes with Dad's job on the farm – and s*he doesn't even mind.* How can she not mind? It's like she's given up.'

'Gina, that's enough. Mebbe I am a "stupid little person" in your eyes – and thank you very much but I don't want your opinion – but I hate to hear you criticising Mum. Don't you think she's got a lot on her plate, with Dad the way he is, without you getting all envious and covetous and discontented, too? In fact, I think you're beginning to sound a bit like Dad.'

'No I'm not,' Gina snapped, eyes wide with shock.

'Yes,' Ellen insisted. 'You were ranting, Gina,' she added more gently. 'Come on now . . . We were having such a lovely afternoon. Let's not spoil it with arguing.'

Gina stuck out her lower lip and looked away.

'Come on, love,' Ellen said again after a few moments' pause to allow Gina to calm herself. 'Let's go back now. Mebbe Mum will be home and have some good news for me about the job at the Hall.'

Gina sighed dramatically and rose to her feet. 'If that's what you want . . .' she murmured.

In silence they walked towards the field gate, brushing grass off their skirts.

As Gina lifted the loop that secured the five-bar gate to the post, Ellen suddenly exclaimed, 'Oh, what's this? There's summat stuffed into the gap between the stones. Looks like a little bottle with . . . mebbe some kind of thread tied around the neck.'

She reached towards the dry-stone wall but, just as she had almost grasped the find, Gina hit her hand away with a loud slap.

'Ow, that hurt. What did you do that for?'

'Don't touch it, Nell.'

'What do you mean? I was only going to look, not drink it or anything.' Ellen made to take it again.

Gina grabbed her sister's wrist and held it away from the dark-coloured phial, the stopper of which was bound with a few strands of brown hair.

'It's not safe. I mean it, Nell. It's . . . it looks like it's . . . mebbe part of a spell,' Gina said quietly. 'You mustn't pick it up or the spell could get to work on you . . . I've heard of such things.'

'A spell? What, like a witch's?' Ellen tried to keep her voice light and shrug off her sister's grasp, but Gina held on to her so tightly that Ellen realised she really meant what she said. In an instant the atmosphere became strange and foreboding.

'Exactly. Just leave it right where it is. Forget you even saw it. It's nowt to do with you.'

'Gina, you're scaring me. And what's it got to do with *you*? How do you know all this?'

Gina said nothing but let go of Ellen's arm. She knew it was safe to do so now.

'Tell me!'

'Because I put it there,' Gina said defiantly.

Ellen opened her mouth to reply but found herself speechless. She looked into her sister's violet eyes, so like her own, except now the expression in them was as hard as flint. She wanted to tell Gina to stop being silly, that this kind of trick wasn't funny and she was spoiling their afternoon, but even as she thought this, a cloud passed before the sun, the bright May day grew instantly chilly and she shivered to see the change in Gina's face as a shadow passed over it, her prettiness transformed. She looked dangerous. Worse, she looked unhinged.

Without another word, both girls passed through the gate and Gina placed the loop back over the post to secure it. Ellen avoided even a glance at the cleft in the wall. Gina strode determinedly off down the track towards the hen houses, scattering hens as she approached, while Ellen followed slowly, fearful of what she had seen and heard. It was like a bad daydream that had tainted the day.

When she reached the back door of Highview Cottage, Gina was already in the garden watering the herb bed from a heavy metal can, pointedly ignoring her, and Ellen lifted the latch and went inside alone, her mind buzzing with questions she knew better than to ask just yet.

~

Dora Arnold opened the back door to her home to be greeted with the smell of baking bread.

'Hello, Mum. All right? I thought I'd get a loaf on as Mr Beveridge gave Gina and me the afternoon off,' said Ellen, deliberately not quite telling the entire truth about the half-day holiday. She knew her mother worried that Gina would never come to any good with her poor attitude to work, and she didn't want to stir up trouble now, with Dora looking so tired.

'You're a good lass, Nellie. And is that a fresh pot of tea under the cosy? Better and better . . .'

Dora pulled off her outdoor shoes and put on the sandals she wore around the house, sighing and groaning as she eased her tired feet and then her weary back.

'Here, Mum.' Ellen handed her mother a mug of copper-coloured tea with plenty of sugar in it. 'Don't keep me in suspense. Did Uncle Tom tell Mr Stellion I wanted to try out as his assistant in the garden?'

'He *asked* Mr Stellion if he'd agree to give you a chance, yes. And he said . . . he would!'

'Ooh, I'm that glad. Thank you, Mum. And thank Uncle Tom, too, won't you?'

'You can thank him yourself when you start tomorrow morning. As the job helping your dad is little more than a casual thing, I reckon you needn't give formal notice to Albert Beveridge – they'll still have Gina helping out and it won't do her any harm to work a bit harder – but you might just want to go up to the house and mention it. It'd be only polite, like.'

'I will. And I'm to start tomorrow! We can walk to Grindle Hall together of a morning. It'll be fun.'

Dora smiled. 'I don't know about fun, lass. The gardening will be hard work, and Uncle Tom will expect you to make the same effort as if you weren't his niece, but I'll be glad of your company on the walk.' She took a sip of her tea. 'Where's Gina?'

'She was watering the garden earlier.'

'I didn't see her. Mebbe she's gone off somewhere. She'll be back at teatime, no doubt.'

'I'll just nip up to see Mr Beveridge now, Mum.'

As Ellen turned into the lane to go to the farmhouse, she looked for Gina over the hedge but there was no one in the garden. She remembered the frightening moment by the gate and that ugly, mad look on Gina's face. All that talk about witches and spells had been horrible, but now the sun was shining again and, with the good news of her job raising her spirits, the unpleasantness of the incident was receding. Already it seemed like an absurd imagined moment, almost as if it was something she'd read about in a library book.

Ellen thought about her difficult younger sister. Gina could be so wilful and immature. They were very close in age, with Ellen only fifteen months the elder, and they were very alike in appearance, both with long dark brown hair and unusual violet-blue eyes. They were also identical in height and figure, being tall and strong looking, so that they were sometimes mistaken for each other around the village. However, one subtle difference was that Gina had an odd little birthmark behind her ear, hidden under her hair. It looked like a tiny crescent moon. Ellen had long thought it must be a family thing, because Uncle Tom had exactly the same birthmark on the inside of his forearm . . .

Yes, it was very odd about that mysterious little bottle in the wall by the gate. But Gina was given to saying fanciful things and getting worked up over nothing. Ellen had once heard their mother describe Gina as 'highly strung'. She was certainly quick to anger and prone to moods. Very like their father, really . . . which was odd, as Gina and their dad were rarely at peace with each other. Mind, Philip wasn't really at peace with *anyone*, though Gina bore the brunt of his ill temper.

As if her thoughts had conjured him up, Philip Arnold came in sight as Ellen walked the turn in the lane and passed the sign that said 'Highview Farm'. Jute, Mr Beveridge's sheepdog, wandered over to greet her, circled round behind her as she approached as if gently rounding her up, then went back to sit in the shade.

'Dad, hello.'

Philip was sweeping the path into the farmyard but stopped and rested on his broom. 'What's the news? Tom taking you on, is he?'

'I'm to start tomorrow.'

'Oh, aye? So I'm to lose my help to your uncle Tom, am I?'

'You could congratulate me, Dad. It's a proper job with prospects. You'll still have Gina, and the arrangement here was only helping out anyway.'

'Ha, Gina's taken up with whatever nonsense is in her head half the time. She doesn't put in half the effort you do, and well you know it.'

'Mebbe she will now, Dad.'

'Hmm.'

Well, what did I expect? Dad's never been an optimist, Ellen thought. Or generous.

'And it'll be better when I have a proper wage. You know Gina and me only earn a little bit here,' she said, determined to jolly him along, hoping for the slightest evidence of his pleasure in her new opportunity. 'You won't miss me really, Dad. There's Edward and Mr Beveridge, and he always brings in casuals for the shearing and that. And Mrs Beveridge likes to be in charge of the hens, with Gina to help, so you never have to see to them.'

'Hens . . . bloomin' useless birds: daft. They're like sheep that way, but with wings.'

'And eggs,' laughed Ellen.

'But just as keen to be dying of one thing or another.' Philip didn't smile.

'Not your problem. I'm just going in to tell Mr and Mrs B about my job.'

'Aye. It's just her who's in.'

Ellen went round the back of the farmhouse, knocked on the open door and stepped inside. Mrs Beveridge was standing at the kitchen table, wiping eggs with a damp cloth and placing them in a cardboard tray. Ellen told her about the gardening job at Grindle Hall.

'Well, we'll miss you, Ellen, no doubt about that, but our loss is Mr Stellion's gain. And your uncle Tom's. You're a good worker and deserve a more formal job, like, after all this time, mebbe with a bit of training.'

'Thank you, Mrs Beveridge.'

'And our Edward'll be sorry not to see you about the place, too, though you'll always be at the end of the lane.'

Ellen smiled. 'Of course. We're all pleased to see Ed whenever he wants to drop by.'

'Here, take this for your pay, and there's a bit extra as thanks for your efforts. And I've a few cracked eggs here I won't be able to sell, so you can have those for your mum, if she'd like them.'

'She would, I'm sure. Thank you, Mrs Beveridge. And thanks for the pay. My regards and thanks to Mr Beveridge . . . and to Ed, too.'

'I'll tell them you said so, love.'

As Ellen walked out across the yard, carefully carrying the tray of eggs, she saw her father glance her way then disappear behind the hay barn. He was avoiding her, seemingly resentful of her new job – or maybe of her working with Uncle Tom. She sighed: nothing to do with her. Dad and Uncle Tom had never got on well. Mum was on good terms with her brother-in-law, though, and of course they saw a lot of each other, both working up at the Hall.

~

When she'd finished watering the herbs, Gina went back to the field where she and Ellen had lain in the sun earlier. At the gate she stopped to take the little phial from the recess, thinking she couldn't risk her sister coming back to investigate it. She held it tightly in her clenched fist and wished with all her heart that the spell she had conjured was real and would work. She hoped to feel something happening, experience a sign that powerful forces were at work – she was sure she'd felt the presence of some kind of power when she'd cast the spell in the bedroom she shared with Ellen earlier that afternoon – but the phial just looked like an ordinary tiny glass medicine bottle in which she'd placed a drop of blood from a pricked finger, the stopper bound round with a few strands of hair she'd combed out of her hairbrush. The exact incantation she'd recited – what a word that was: *in-can-ta-tion*; she said it aloud, liking the sound – was forgotten now, and the shabby little volume she'd filched from a second-hand bookstall and in which she'd discovered the so-called spell was hidden in her clothes drawer and not to hand. She'd moved the phial now, so she was certain the spell had lost its power.

She sat down and leaned against the irregular and uncomfortable wall to brood, still clutching the bottle.

Where was her life going? When would she ever leave this dreary little place high on the Lancashire fells? *How* would she get away? If only she had some idea of how her life would unfold, and some hope of when anything – *anything at all* – would happen to improve it. She could bear it if only she knew the end was in sight. Sometimes, on a shopping trip to Clitheroe or even very occasionally to Blackburn or Preston, she saw newspapers and a glimpse of a whole world of events that no one in Little Grindle even knew about – or worse, even cared about. It felt as if time had stopped decades ago in the village; it was certainly no place for a young woman of seventeen with her sights set on a new and entirely different sort of life.

'Come on now, *think*!' she chivvied herself aloud.

Gina hadn't hung around for her mother's return to learn the news about the gardening job at the Hall; she knew Ellen would be offered it. And Gina herself would be stuck with her father at the farm!

Miserable old sod. It's a wonder Mum puts up with him. I wouldn't. Nell's always been his favourite and now I'll be left to deal with him and his anger all day. As if I don't already have to endure the worst of his shouting and snarling, and his lashing out.

She rubbed the top of her arm where there was a greenish bruise, then looked at the phial in the palm of her hand. That would have dealt with him if he'd found it and opened it . . . if the spell were real. Which, a part of her admitted, it probably wasn't. They'd all be better off without him, and his misery and bad temper rising up like a storm cloud on a May day. Dora could marry Tom – they were well suited and obviously fond of each other – and then they'd all go to live at Tom's cottage at the gate of Grindle Hall, and who knew what opportunities would come Gina's way when she practically lived at the Hall? The Stellions sometimes had guests to stay:

people who came from all over the north, maybe even from Manchester. Once there had been talk of some visitors from London!

Well, the stupid spell – and all the fantasies she'd dreamed up around it – didn't look like it would get her to the Hall. She'd just have to think of something else. One thing was for certain: she was not going to stay in this little backwater for ever, working until she dropped, while her dreams of something better faded until they were all but forgotten. As she herself would be eventually if she stayed in the village. There had to be a way forward.

She sat thinking and dreaming, clutching the tiny bottle in her hands. Eventually . . . of course! She'd already thought of the first move, it was just the way of bringing it about that was wrong. With a shrug of contempt for her own silliness, she tossed the phial over the wall into the adjoining field. She was done with stupid spells! She needn't even have bothered to pinch that grubby old book.

Nell was going to work at the Hall, even if it was only in the garden. Mum already worked there and, though she went only to clean and help out, the Stellions knew who she was and noticed her efforts. Uncle Tom had long worked there as the gardener, of course. So Gina was already well placed to bag the next job that came up. Secure a position at Grindle Hall and the rest would surely follow.

Oh, but how long would it be before a vacancy arose? Life was passing her by, and she couldn't wait even a day longer than she had to. And what if there was a job, but someone else was recommended to Mr Stellion? The other people working there must have family who would be interested, and possibly favoured over herself.

Nell had been chosen ahead of her this time, after all. No one had even mentioned the gardening job to her! She felt another surge of anger about that, but her rising temper muddied her thinking and she closed her eyes and breathed deeply until she was calm again.

Eventually she rose stiffly to her feet, rubbing her spine where the uneven stones of the wall had pressed in. She pulled back her shoulders and lifted her head. Her mind was made up, her plan was beginning to form, and she knew exactly what her first move was to be.

CHAPTER TWO

'Mum said I'd probably find you here. Thank you for recommending me for this job, Uncle Tom.' Ellen hovered in the doorway of the ornate greenhouse.

The garden at Grindle Hall was huge – or at least it seemed so to Ellen, when compared to the neat little plot behind Highview Cottage. Grindle Hall's garden was divided up by hedges and walls with doors or gates in them, and each part was dedicated to growing different plants or seemed to have a different purpose. Ellen had arrived in good time to have a sneaky look round before anyone but her uncle was likely to be found outside.

Those sections nearest the front and back of the house were the grandest, with lawns and long flower borders. To one side was an area with about twenty of the elaborately fashioned bushes that Ellen was keen to learn to cut. At the side nearer the kitchen were vegetable beds, cold frames, and this huge greenhouse with a white-painted iron frame and complicated-looking hinges and cogs with winding handles to open various windows. Then there were potting sheds and storage sheds. It was like a tiny village of garden buildings but peopled only by Uncle Tom and Ellen herself, so far as she could see. Suddenly she felt nervous. Was this job as Uncle Tom's assistant going to be too much for her? She knew next to nothing and there was such a lot of garden!

How pleased she was to see the familiar tall, broad figure of her uncle in his corduroy breeches, tweed waistcoat and checked flat cap. Tom Arnold looked up from his wheelbarrow of compost and smiled, creasing up the laughter lines round his blue eyes.

'Nell, good to see you, lass, and so prompt, too. I'm right glad to have you come to work for me. Your mum says you're a reliable lass when it comes to responsibility, and I know you're a cheerful and honest one, of course. Plus, I gather from Mr Beveridge, who I see down at the Lamb and Flag, that you're a hard worker. I didn't tell him I was looking to poach you from him, though.' He winked at her. 'I reckon you'll do just fine. Mr Stellion likes to get to know his workers and you're to go up to the house at eleven o'clock. Oh, don't look so worried. I'll go with you,' Tom reassured her. 'In the meantime, you can get stuck in. Best to learn on the job than try to remember a lot of stuff all at once. We've these tomato plants to pot on. I'll show you how, and then you can do the rest.'

'Yes, Uncle Tom.'

'Here, I got you these. I didn't think you'd have brought any, and you'll need them.' He handed her a paper bag.

Ellen took it and pulled out a pair of leather gardening gloves. 'My, but they're good 'uns. Thank you, Uncle

Tom,' she beamed, putting on the gloves and holding up her hands to admire the fit. 'Just right.'

'And I think you should call me "Mr Arnold" while we're working side by side. It's more professional, like. Don't want the others to think I'm favouring you.'

'Others? Oh, I thought it was just us in the garden.'

'It is, Nell, and we've our work cut out to keep it looking good. I meant those employed here at the Hall, though Mr and Mrs Stellion have hardly any staff in the house now either. They tend to live a quiet kind of life these days. It's livelier when their son and daughter are home. We need to keep up the old standards, though.'

'Yes . . . Mr Arnold,' Nell replied. 'Now, what do you want me to do with these tomato plants . . .?'

~

Gina always found it easy to get out of her work on the farm, mainly by just not turning up to do it. The job was only vaguely defined and casual, the pay low, and she had long ago decided she would only work when it suited her. She'd watched Dora and Ellen set off up the lane to Grindle Hall in the early morning sunshine.

'I'll tidy up the kitchen, mebbe take the carpet sweeper through the sitting room,' she'd said to Dora as her mother and sister left. 'I'll go along then.' She did not specify where she'd be going along to.

'You do that, love, but don't keep Nancy Beveridge waiting. I know she likes those eggs collected early. Your dad's been gone up there a while.'

Gina waved Dora and Ellen off, and promptly went to put another slice of bread to toast, thinking over her plan as she waited for the bread to brown. She spread it thinly with butter – Highview was not a dairy farm, so butter had to be bought from the village shop, and even with Gina, old habits of wartime rationing died hard – but then heaped the toast with Dora's home-made raspberry jam. The supply of this delicious jam was running low now, and Philip had decreed it was to be eked out as a Sunday-only treat, but Gina didn't care to be denied, especially by her father. There was no one here to see her; she would enjoy it while she could.

When she'd eaten this second breakfast, she rinsed the evidence of the jam off the plate, set it on the draining rack, then tied her hair back with a cotton scarf of the identical blue to the one Nell was wearing this morning, and which *was* actually another of Nell's scarves made from the same fabric in her favourite colour. Nell was adept at cutting up old shirts and turning the fabric into pretty little things she could wear or use, and which Gina felt free to borrow without permission. Then Gina locked the cottage door, put the key behind the boot scraper, and set off up the lane just as Dora and Ellen had done half an hour earlier.

Grindle Hall lay to one side of the village of Little Grindle. The big house was a huge part of the village and of village life, and yet apart from it and, in both senses, above it. The lane climbed uphill, and soon Gina came to the imposing central gates of elaborately curled metal between tall stone pillars topped with perching eagles. She let herself in the little gate to the side and walked past the Lodge, which was where her uncle, Tom Arnold, lived.

From nothing more than nosiness she peered through his sitting-room window. There was his armchair, with the cushion Dora had made him as a Christmas present showing the indentation of his back, and a low table beside it on which was a small pile of books. Tom was like Nell – a real bookworm. Although he lived alone, Tom's sitting room looked cosy, neat and cheerful, like Tom himself.

Lucky Nell, going to work with him. Still, there were other ways of getting on, and Nell would probably want to stay here gardening for the rest of her life. Gina, still cross at not even being offered the chance of the job, took a few deep breaths and deliberately replaced her feeling of discontent with pity: poor Nell, this would probably be as far as she ever got in life.

Keeping a lookout for her relatives, Gina made for the side of the house where the kitchen was. She'd been to Grindle Hall on several occasions before – Mr Stellion used to host the big annual village events – and she had taken care to do a little private exploration to see what was where. You never knew when such knowledge would come in useful.

There was a chip basket of spinach on the ground beside the back door. Her confidence bolstered by this piece of luck, Gina picked it up and, without even hesitating, knocked and entered the kitchen.

The cook turned and saw the young woman dressed in breeches, a sleeveless pullover over a striped shirt and her hair tied back with a blue scarf.

'Good morning, Ellen Arnold,' she said. 'I heard you were starting work in the garden today.'

Better and better, Gina thought. She hadn't even had to explain herself to the cook, whose name she knew to be Mrs Bassett.

'Good morning, Mrs Bassett,' Gina replied. 'I've brought you this spinach.'

'Thank you. Just take it through to the scullery, there's a good lass.' Mrs Bassett indicated the inner door, which led to a corridor. 'Next down on the left.'

'Yes, Mrs Bassett,' said Gina, hardly able to believe her luck. She found the right place immediately and left the basket of spinach on the draining board. Then she crept back to the kitchen, looked around to make sure there was no one else in sight, and watched through the gap between the door jamb and the partially open door until she saw the cook go into what might be a pantry.

Immediately, Gina rushed across to the back door, opened it, called out, 'Bye, Mrs Bassett,' as if she were leaving, then closed it noisily and ran as quietly as she could across to the inner door once more and into the corridor. At the far end she'd already noticed a steep uncarpeted staircase, and she took the stairs two at a time.

At the top of the stairs there was a door covered in green fabric with fancy brass-headed nails holding it in place. Gina inched the door open and peeped through the gap: no one in sight. She swallowed nervously. It had been easy to get this far, and luck had been on her side, but the next bit was going to be altogether riskier. She had only a vague plan to seek out Mr or Mrs Stellion – she didn't really mind which one she encountered, but there was no point dealing with lesser folk, and she certainly wanted to avoid seeing Mrs Thwaite, the housekeeper – and then just ask for a job. She'd already decided she'd do anything – well, almost – and there must be plenty of work in a house this size.

She recognised the gloomy entrance hall with its dark wood panelling and dreary portraits. She could hear voices coming from upstairs and then the sound of a vacuum cleaner. It must be Mum, another person Gina didn't want to encounter: there would be no pulling the wool over her eyes.

What to do? Think, Gina!

Where would the Stellions be at this hour of the morning? Probably in the morning room. And where would the morning room be but on the east side where it would catch the early sun. Gina looked at the doors off the hall and also saw corridors leading to right and left. She chose the left, which she decided was east, and went silently down it on the soft, dark carpet. She could see there were four doors, one of which, further down, was open, but all was totally silent.

Suddenly a high-pitched and loud barking erupted, and Gina literally leaped in shock, her heart pounding. A little brown dog, no more than a puppy, raced to greet her, its spaniel ears flying and its short stumpy tail wagging madly. Gina let out a long breath of relief. Oh, thank goodness, this was no fierce guard dog, but rather a very soft dog indeed.

'Hello, you funny little fella,' Gina whispered, bending down and patting the silky head. A revised plan was already forming in her mind.

'Coco,' trilled a woman's voice faintly from the open room further down. 'Coco, come to Mummy.'

Gina saw she was standing outside a closed door. She opened it, glanced in the thankfully empty room, silently shooed the puppy in with the aid of her foot and crept in after it, closing the door behind her.

'Right, Coco, you and me are going to wait here a couple of minutes and then we'll go and find Mrs Stellion,' Gina said. 'All you have to do is be quiet.'

Coco gave a little yelp of agreement and circled Gina's feet a few times, the tail still wagging.

'Shush, you daft creature.' Gina looked around. The room was a little sitting room with deep sofas and heavy curtains at the long window.

Gina picked up the puppy and he snuggled under her chin, settling in her arms quite happily. She went to stand behind the curtains in case someone should enter the room without warning. It would be enough of a hiding place if they did no more than glance about.

Gina could hear the woman calling the dog and evidently Coco knew his name as he was listening, then gave a little bark. The voice became louder as the woman approached up the corridor . . . then faded and finally ceased. Gina held her breath, her stomach churning. It would be difficult to concoct any believable story to explain why she was hiding in this room holding the missing puppy, although Mrs Stellion would be unlikely to believe he'd managed to secrete himself behind a closed door. If only he would be quiet for a few minutes . . .

On a side table next to one of the sofas was a tray with a biscuit barrel on it. Gina, still holding the puppy, went across, grabbed it and retreated behind the curtain again, placing the tin on the window ledge and removing the lid with one hand.

'Rich tea . . . well, I reckon at least they won't do you any harm,' she whispered, giving one to the dog.

Coco had eaten three rich tea biscuits by the time Gina decided she was ready to return the lost puppy to its owner.

'Come on, let's wipe those crumbs off your whiskers. Our secret, eh?' she murmured, carefully removing all evidence of their presence in the room. She liked to think that covering her tracks was a lesson she'd learned long ago.

She opened the door, looked up and down the corridor, then set off towards where she'd first heard the voice, holding the squirming puppy tightly. The door to this room was still open and Mrs Stellion, a wispy-looking woman with fair greying hair, was sitting back in an armchair with her eyes closed. Gina knocked and Mrs Stellion opened her eyes and straightened up. She didn't look at all put out to see a stranger in her house and evidently jumped to all the conclusions Gina hoped she would.

'Hello,' she smiled. 'I see you've brought Coco back to me.'

'Good morning, ma'am,' said Gina. 'I saw the little fella taking himself off for a walk. I reckoned he shouldn't be out on his own.'

Edith Stellion held out her arms and Gina lowered the dog into them.

'Oh, thank you. Quite right. But outside, you say? How on earth can he have got outside, I wonder.'

As well you might. Gina didn't volunteer an answer.

'Naughty boy, wandering off like that.' The puppy was wagging his tail again and licking his mistress's face. She, in turn, was kissing his little head so that the puppy probably thought he was anything but naughty. 'Well, never mind, he's back now. Thank you, my dear. I take it you're the new girl working for Tom Arnold.'

'No, Mrs Stellion, ma'am, that's my sister. I'd just come over to give her a message from our dad and then I saw the puppy.' As a look of puzzlement passed over the lady's face Gina decided to move the conversation on. 'Right sweet little fella. I love dogs.' She adopted a sad expression. 'We had one ourselves until recently, but he died and I don't half miss him.'

'Oh, I am sorry. I can imagine that you would.'

So can I. There was not a word of truth in this story, but it had captured Mrs Stellion's imagination and sympathy.

'It's good of you to bring Coco safely back to me. I can see you've got a way with dogs, young lady, and he's taken a liking to you.'

Gina beamed. 'Oh, he's lovely, ma'am. If I had another dog I'd want one just like him. Spaniels are so . . . intelligent.'

'I agree.' Mrs Stellion turned to the puppy. 'Who's the cleverest boy, then? Who's Mummy's little darling?'

Clearly she doted on the puppy; she was probably a bit bored and lonely in this big house, Gina thought.

'My dear, what is your name?'

'Georgina Arnold. I'm called Gina.'

'Then I shall call you Gina, too. And what do you do, Gina, when you're not being a messenger for your father and rescuing lost puppies? Do you have to rush away to your place of work now?'

'Ah, no, that's the thing, ma'am,' said Gina, looking regretful. 'I really wanted to work here in the garden with my uncle Tom Arnold but my sister, Ellen, was given the job just because she's the oldest. Now I'm at a bit of a loose end, running messages and occasionally helping out at Highview Farm if they're really busy, which they're not just now.'

'Well, we can't have a clever girl like you wasting away without a suitable opportunity,' said Mrs Stellion. She indicated the armchair next to her. 'Do sit down and let's think what we can do for you.'

'Thank you, ma'am.'

Mrs Stellion gently patted her forehead, as if it hurt her to think too deeply. 'How would you like to come here and take Coco for his walk? I'm not much of a walker and he's a lively boy who'd benefit from running off some excess energy. I'd want you to clean him up afterwards, of course, make my lovely boy all pretty and respectable,' she said, cuddling the dog until he struggled, escaped from her knee and came to sniff around Gina's well-worn lace-up shoes.

Gina didn't think that sounded like much of a job, but

it had all the advantages she'd come here looking for. She would have a foot in the door at the Hall, and a job that was a lot easier than cleaning out those smelly old hens at Highview Farm, and all the other horrible jobs she did for the Beveridges. Who knew where this chance would lead? But one thing was for certain: it would lead somewhere. She was quite decided on that.

'I would pay you for your time, of course,' Mrs Stellion said, obviously thinking Gina was silent because she was wondering if she were to be paid and was too shy to ask. She went on to name a sum slightly greater than Gina was earning at the farm. That settled it: no need to go back there. 'And maybe, if that works out, there could be other little jobs for you to do for me.'

'That sounds grand, thank you, Mrs Stellion. When would you like me to start?'

'Well, why not now? It's a lovely day for a walk and Coco is getting a little fidgety. His lead is hanging in the boot room next to the hall. Let me show you . . .'

They reached the hall, Mrs Stellion moving slowly, the dog running ahead of them and then back again, just as the door at the rear – through which Gina had entered uninvited less than an hour earlier – opened, and Tom and Ellen appeared.

'Good heavens,' said Tom, seeing Gina looking even more like Ellen than usual today. 'That is . . . good morning, Mrs Stellion.' Even as he spoke, his questioning eyes were on Gina.

Ellen was looking puzzled and mouthing, *What are you doing here?* but Gina avoided noticing.

'Good morning, Mr Arnold. And Miss Ellen Arnold, I take it?' Mrs Stellion offered Ellen a rather weak handshake. 'I gather you're something of a gardening expert and we're fortunate to have you assisting your uncle.'

'Thank you, Mrs Stellion. I'm no expert, though it's kind of you to say. But I'll do my best.'

'Then we're doubly blessed this morning,' enthused Mrs Stellion, 'because Gina is also starting work here. I know she's going to be a great help to me with Coco.'

Gina smiled broadly at Ellen and Tom, who looked at each other, utterly nonplussed.

'Er, that's nice,' said Tom eventually. 'Well, we'd best be getting along to Mr Stellion, who's expecting us. Good day to you, Mrs Stellion.'

'Good day, Mr Arnold . . . Ellen.'

Tom and Ellen made for the corridor on the right and Gina followed Mrs Stellion towards the boot room. Ellen turned back as if she couldn't quite believe her eyes, as Gina knew she would, and Gina gave her a huge grin and winked.

~

At noon, Mrs Bassett provided sandwiches for Tom, and now for Ellen too, and on such a fine day they ate them and drank their tea sitting outside in the sun. They'd already discussed the surprise of seeing Gina earlier, and were equally at a loss to know what could have happened.

'I'm just worried that she's up to no good,' confided Ellen. 'I don't want to be mean, but she's never done owt much at the farm if she could avoid it. In fact she's *always* got an excuse to avoid it. Now, on the day I start work here, she turns up indoors and chatting to Mrs Stellion like they're best friends.'

'Well, Mrs Stellion is a good-hearted woman, Nell, not one to be standoffish, but she's also someone who knows what she wants. If she's hired Gina to help with her dog, then she'll expect her to make a thorough job of it. It won't do to be skiving off. And Mr Stellion was just as welcoming to you as Missis was to Gina.'

'Aye, he was nice. Takes an interest in the garden, too.'

'He does that. You'll see him about the place a lot, but don't speak more than a quiet "Good day, sir" unless you're spoken to.'

'Of course not, Mr Arnold. It's not me that pushes myself forward,' she couldn't help adding.

At the end of the afternoon she met up with her mother and they walked home together while Ellen told Dora about her first day and also about finding Gina at the Hall. Gina was nowhere to be seen and they decided she must have gone home long since.

'Well, I hope she's been up to the farm to tell Nancy she's not going to be there any more,' said Dora when she'd heard Ellen's whole story. 'Not that there's much difference between her going and not, the amount of work I reckon she did.'

'What do you think she's up to, Mum?' Ellen asked. 'She didn't turn up today because she wanted to take Mrs Stellion's puppy for walks, that's for certain. I don't reckon she even knew the lady had a puppy.'

'No . . . but mebbe she was a bit envious of your new job – you know what Gina can be like – and wanted to get herself a job here at the Hall too.'

Ellen remembered what Gina had said the previous day and thought her ambition lay far beyond working at the Hall, but she didn't want their mother to worry about what might turn out to be something and nothing, so she kept quiet.

When they arrived home and went round to the back door, they found a bicycle propped up against the wall. It was black and shiny, and had a very smart little basket on the front. It was, in short, a proper lady's bicycle.

They looked at each other. Then: 'Gina,' they said in unison.

'Now what, I wonder,' added Dora.

~

'Borrowed it from the Hall, didn't I?' said Gina, sitting at the kitchen table with her feet up on a chair.

She'd made herself a pot of tea, but it was tepid and stewed by now. Dora didn't waste her breath asking whether her daughter had swept the sitting-room carpet, as she'd said she would.

'Borrowed? You mean you took it?' asked Ellen. This wouldn't be the first time Gina had taken something without asking. She was still wearing her hair tied back with her sister's scarf.

'I did not! I asked Mrs Stellion and she said I could borrow it. It belongs to her daughter but she's not often at home, so Mrs S said it would be all right. It means I can pop over to the Hall to exercise Coco twice a day without having to walk there and back in between.'

'"Pop over to the Hall to exercise Coco" indeed,' said Ellen. 'What exactly is your game, Gina?'

'I don't know what you're on about,' Gina replied primly, then gave her sister a huge and very annoying grin.

'Yes you do.'

'Just 'cos you—'

'Girls, you can both be quiet now,' said Dora. 'It's what it is. The pair of you have got work at the Hall, and that's fine by me. But I'm warning you, Gina, I don't want any trouble. You know what I mean.'

'Yes, Mum.' Gina looked sulky.

'The Stellions have both been very good to me – and to Uncle Tom – and we want that to continue. In fact, it is vital to our livelihood. If you took that bike, Gina, you can take it back tomorrow and I never want to see it again, all right?'

'It was lent, honestly, Mum.'

'Well, then, you can start on those taters and, Nell, you go and get washed and changed out of those mucky clothes and then we'll get the tea on. And, Gina, if you're back before us in future you can make a fresh brew for when we get home. You know what time that is.'

'Yes, Mum.'

'*Yes, Mum. Honestly, Mum,*' sneered Ellen quietly, still angry that Gina had stolen her thunder. 'You don't know the meaning of the word.'

'Shut up.' Gina aimed a kick at the back of Ellen's legs as she passed.

'And have you been up to the farm to tell the Beveridges that you won't be there?' asked Dora.

'No, Mum, not yet.'

'Well, I suggest you get yourself up there sharpish, lass. It's a shame you're both leaving them so close together but it can't be helped. They need to know, though.'

'I will go.'

'No time like the present. Nell will help me with the tea.'

Gina heaved herself reluctantly to her feet. She was just wondering whether to take the bicycle up to the farm when Philip burst in.

Dora's smile of greeting slipped when she saw her husband's anxious face. 'Phil, what on earth's happened?'

'Bloomin' sheep, of course. That's what!' He pushed the door shut roughly and padded over in his stocking feet. 'Found three dead ewes and their lambs in the lower field just by the wall this morning. Been dealing with nowt but them and the whole sorry business all day.'

'Oh, Phil, I'm sorry. It's not foot and mouth, is it? Please say it's not. Were they looking sickly before?'

'No, it's not that plague, though that's the only good thing. And of course they didn't look like they were ailing before,' he snapped, 'or I'd've moved them into the barn away from the others, wouldn't I? Are you saying this is my fault? 'Cos I know damn well it isn't.'

'No, of course not. Sit down, Phil. Let me get you a cup of tea. Sounds bad.'

He sank onto a kitchen chair, looking tired and belligerent.

'It *is* bad. Three ewes and their lambs! Albert, Ed and me have been looking all round but we haven't a clue what's caused it. It's not foot and mouth but we're worried it's summat we haven't heard of and that the entire flock will be dead by morning.' He stood up, unable to settle, and walked about, wringing his hands.

'Do the others look ill?'

'No. Not yet, anyhow. Who knows what'll happen? I've come to expect the worst with sheep. We've fenced off that corner of the field where the dead ones were and moved the rest higher up.'

'So you think it was mebbe summat they ate, like some poisonous weed?'

'Aye, I reckon so. We didn't find owt but mebbe they ate all that there was.'

'I'll . . . I'll just go and speak to Mrs B,' said Gina quietly, sidling towards the back door. There was nothing she wanted to say to her father about the dead sheep, and she badly needed to go somewhere quiet to think. A very strange idea was nagging at her head.

'Yes, just go,' said Dora dismissively. 'Say we're all sorry to hear about the sheep.'

'Yes, Mum.'

Gina went, putting her shoes on outside and deciding she'd rather have the space the walk afforded her to think than take the bike. She wandered up the lane a little but stopped before she came within sight of the farm. There was hawthorn in bloom in the hedge, but the pungent sweet-sour scent of the May blossom repelled her today, and she found a grassy place away from it. She sat down by the hedge, resting her chin on her knees.

Philip had said the dead sheep were in the lower field, and near the wall. That was the field next to where she and Ellen had been lazing about the previous afternoon. Gina recalled hearing the ewes calling as she'd watched those strangely formed clouds. She thought about how she had made the excuse of fastening the gate as a chance to hide the little bottle she'd used for the magic spell in the gap between two stones, a place both noticeable but also reasonably discreet. Then, after Nell had seen the bottle, she'd thrown it away, thinking it was a waste of time . . . or perhaps that it wouldn't work once she'd taken it out from its hiding place . . . She wasn't quite sure what exactly she had thought. She didn't really believe in it, yet she had believed completely when she'd cast the spell earlier that afternoon. She felt confused now, and worried. She'd definitely thrown the tiny bottle over the wall without a thought, though.

But what if the spell was like a weapon – which she'd intended to use against her father – and then she'd thought she'd made it safe by moving it, but she hadn't? Perhaps it was like a gun that she hadn't successfully unloaded, or like a bomb. Yes, supposing it was like a time bomb, resting in its hiding place until its victim withdrew it and set it ticking? But then *she* had taken it from the gap in the wall and *she* – the one who had cast the spell – had 'set it ticking' and the poor sheep and their lambs had been the victims!

Could this possibly be what had happened? It seemed such a strange idea on this beautiful sunny evening, thin white clouds high above, all the usual innocent sounds of the fields around her.

But she had cast the spell, she had believed it was for real then, and the intent to cause harm had been in her mind.

She closed her eyes and curled up so that her forehead rested on her knees, trying to think through what she had done. All she knew was that she hadn't wanted to kill the sheep and their lambs – if, indeed, she had.

And if she had killed them . . .?

That meant the spell was real, that the book of spells she'd stolen was real. It meant that she had cast a spell. She had that power! What yesterday had seemed at first real and desperate, then silly and even a bit mad, now assumed a certainty. It had gone wrong this time because she'd been careless and not realised what she was doing. Nor had she understood the power she had conjured up. She vowed not to make that mistake again. She didn't want to hurt any more animals.

When she cast the next spell, she'd be sure to be very, very careful. Because she knew there would be a 'next time'.

With this strange new power that she didn't really understand, and a job at the Hall in the personal employ of Mrs Stellion herself, how quickly her life had changed, and for the better, in just a day. It was a shame about the sheep but it couldn't be helped. Who knew what tomorrow would bring? Gina could hardly wait to find out.

CHAPTER THREE

Ellen was tired after her first day at her new job. Her father had cast a pall over the remainder of the day, lamenting over the mysterious deaths of the sheep while the family had their tea and washed up, so she was glad to use the excuse of her weariness to go up to bed early and read one of her library books in peace. She had hoped he might ask about her first day working in the Hall gardens, but he was too focused on his own problems to show any interest in her news, so – though she felt rather hurt – she kept quiet.

Gina, who'd had a peculiar look on her face all evening, soon followed her sister upstairs and got into the twin bed on the other side of the room they shared. She too had been unable to bear the atmosphere, with the misery her father was spreading, and no one had mentioned her new job either. That was definitely a subject that could wait.

'Damn! I forgot,' Gina cursed mildly, the thought of her work at the Hall reminding her. 'I meant to tell

Mrs B I won't be going to the farm any more.' The words were out before she could think better of them.

'I don't suppose she'll miss you, Gina,' said Ellen, putting her book aside and preparing to go to sleep.

'Well, no. Farm work didn't really suit me, I reckon.'

'So, what did you do?'

'What do you mean?' Gina asked sharply.

Ellen frowned. 'When you went out before tea, of course. You were supposed to be going to see Mrs Beveridge and you were gone long enough. So where were you if you forgot? Wasn't that the whole point of going out?'

'Oh, I just went for a walk up the lane a bit; got some fresh air.'

'Won't you get enough fresh air "popping over to the Hall to exercise Coco"?'

'Give over, Nell. Can't you be pleased about my new job?'

'I could if you were more pleased about mine. You only went up to the Hall because you were envious I was starting work with Uncle Tom.'

'So? What's it to you if I just happened to meet Mrs Stellion and she just happened to need someone to walk her dog?'

Happened to meet? Happened how? Ellen thought there was no limit to Gina's nerve but she felt too tired to argue now.

'Oh, you're right,' she conceded. ''Course I'm pleased for you. If you want to work at the Hall and you've got a job walking the dog, who am I to complain?'

She managed to sound generous but also slightly superior, though Gina didn't rise to it.

'One thing, though . . .' Ellen continued.

'Mm?'

'Yesterday. That odd business with the tiny bottle . . .'

Why is Nell mentioning that now? Has she made some connection between that and the dead sheep Dad was on about all evening? Surely not!

'What about it? It was nowt.'

'But what did you mean about a spell, Gina?'

'I've just said, it was nowt.'

'You didn't look like it was nowt at the time. You looked . . . I don't know . . . like I've never seen you before. It was strange and a bit scary.'

'Nell, it was just summat silly, a game. I wanted to see if I could frighten you without doing owt.'

'Frighten me? Why?'

'Just to see if you'd be scared. I made a bet with myself. It was just a bit of nonsense. I don't know why I did it. But it's all right, there was nothing to be scared about. It was a daft game, that's all.'

'You can be very unkind, Gina. Can you at least try to be nice now you've got the job at the Hall? New start and all?'

'Yes, all right. New start, new me,' Gina said, hoping to end the conversation by turning off the overhead light on her side of the room with the switch on the flex beside her bed. Thank goodness Ellen hadn't voiced a connection between the little bottle and the death of the sheep. Of course, Gina would have dismissed any such idea, but she still didn't want anyone even thinking along those lines.

Her thoughts turned to Mrs Thwaite, the housekeeper, and their encounter that day. Gina had brought Coco from his first walk back in through the door to the downstairs corridor and there was Mrs Thwaite with a face that would sour milk.

'You'd better not have that puppy walking dirt all over the house, girl,' she said.

'Good morning to you, too,' said Gina. 'Mrs S says you'll show me where to clean his feet.'

'She did, did she? And it's Mrs Stellion to you, young madam.'

Gina didn't reply, just stood and waited while Coco sat leaning against her leg. Eventually she spoke again: 'Mrs Thwaite, are you going to show me, or shall I go and find a bathroom upstairs?' She made to move off and Mrs Thwaite stepped in front of her, thinking she really meant it.

'No! I forbid you to do that!' She held up a hand as if to prevent Gina's progress.

'*You* forbid me, do you? Well, Mrs Thwaite, Mrs Stellion has asked me to bath the dog and she said you'd show me where. If you can't do as you're told, then I'll sort myself out.'

'*Can't do as I'm told?*' The woman looked ready to explode with indignation.

'That's right. You've got it,' said Gina, smirking.

Mrs Thwaite turned puce and led the way silently to the scullery where Gina had left the basket of spinach earlier.

'Thank you, Mrs Thwaite,' said Gina pleasantly. 'That will be all,' she couldn't help dismissing the housekeeper, unwisely as it happened.

Mrs Thwaite turned even redder, if that were possible, and came to stand up close to Gina, raising her chin so that she was looking her straight in the eye.

'I don't know how you've got the nerve to turn up here,' she hissed, 'after what happened in the village shop. Some folk round here know all about you and the missing money, and those that don't – well, we might think it our duty to warn them about the kind of girl you are, Georgina Arnold. If it wasn't for your mother, who we all respect, I'd make sure everyone in Little Grindle and everyone in this house knew as well.'

Gina turned white. Would that wretched business with the till money at the Fowlers' shop always come back to haunt her? She hadn't even taken very much . . .

Attack was the best form of defence with someone as pathetic as Mrs Thwaite, she decided. It was no use trying to bring her round; she wouldn't understand, and besides, Gina was too furious to attempt anything but a threat.

She leaned in to the housekeeper, who was slightly shorter than she was, and said slowly, in a low voice, 'Mrs Thwaite, if you so much as mention owt about me to anyone, you can be sure I will make your life a misery.' She neither moved nor shifted her angry gaze, and the housekeeper shrank away, visibly shaken.

Even Coco was frightened by the tension in the room and began to whine.

Gina took several deep breaths until her fury had passed. Then she turned to the cowering puppy and, with a not quite steady hand, patted his head.

'There, there, Coco. Nowt to be scared of – not for you, anyway. But Eliza Thwaite had better beware, or I might be trying out an incantation on her. What do you say, boy? Shall I give it a try? Nowt for me to lose; everything for her . . .'

~

The next morning Philip was up as soon as it was light. Dora got up then, too. There was no point in staying in bed – nor had there been much point in actually *going* to bed as Philip had been sighing and fidgeting all night, throwing the blankets off and then pulling them roughly over his head, turning over and over on the sagging mattress, cursing and muttering.

'Shush now, love. It wasn't your fault,' Dora had whispered at about one o'clock, reaching out to calm him, but she might as well have saved her breath.

'I wish I'd never started working with sheep,' he muttered. ''Course it's not my fault, but sheep have a death wish like no other creature and they bring nowt but misery. I don't doubt I'll find the rest have followed the first to their Maker by morning . . .'

There would be no bringing him round that night, so Dora left him to stew in his own pessimism and tried to find a comfortable spot on her side of the bed where she couldn't hear him fretting quite so loudly.

When she woke in the morning, her husband was nowhere to be seen.

'I'll cook you some of these eggs,' she said, when she came down to find Philip was pacing the kitchen, waiting for the kettle to boil. She was bone tired and her back ached, but she was determined to show a brave face. He looked wrecked and was making the most of it.

'No, I'd best get up there and learn the worst,' he said pitifully.

'I don't expect it'll be the worst, Phil, but even if it is it can wait while you come,' she replied stoutly, and started breaking some of the eggs Mrs Beveridge had given her into a bowl.

In the end Philip saw sense and stayed to eat his breakfast.

When the girls appeared, damping down their excitement at their new jobs in the face of their father's black mood, they found their parents sitting silent and weary over cups of strong tea.

'Give us a fill-up, there's a good lass,' said Dora, and Gina obeyed while Ellen cut bread to toast and broke eggs into a bowl to scramble.

'Not for me,' said Philip. 'I'm away to the farm to see what disaster has struck this morning.'

His wife and daughters exchanged glances.

'Might be all right, Dad,' Ellen ventured.

'Aye, but I have my doubts, the way my luck's playing these days.'

'Oh, for goodness' sake,' muttered Dora, glad to see

the back of him. 'Off you go, Phil, and then you'll know how it is and you can stop imagining the worst.'

Philip put on his cap and jacket and left without saying goodbye, shutting the door noisily behind him.

'Good grief,' Gina muttered.

'He didn't even ask how I got on yesterday,' said Ellen.

'No, love, but he will when he comes round,' Dora assured her. 'There's no reason to think all the sheep will be dead, but you know what your dad's like.'

'Aye, we all do,' said Gina heavily. 'It was nice to get away before tea yesterday. I wish I'd stopped out longer.'

'Was Nancy Beveridge all right about you not working there any more?'

'Fine . . .'

Ellen gave Gina a hard stare but she just shrugged and concentrated on eating her breakfast.

'What time are you due up at the Hall?' Dora asked her.

'Said I'd be there about nine o'clock.'

'Perhaps you really could sweep the sitting-room carpet before you go, then.'

'Yes, Mum,' Gina answered, thinking she'd *really* better go to the farm to tell Mrs Beveridge she wouldn't be back. She also wanted to find out if any more sheep had been found dead. She wasn't sure what she'd do if they had, but at least if the news was good she wouldn't have to think about the stupid sheep again.

After she'd waved her mother and sister off, she rode the bicycle up to Highview Farm. Edward Beveridge was just coming out of the back door as Gina propped the bike against the farmhouse wall. He was a good-hearted, tall, big-boned young man with a ruddy complexion, the apple of his parents' eyes. He was particularly friendly with Ellen, and Gina thought, first, that he was a bit in love with her, and second, that he was a bit stupid.

'Gina . . .' he greeted her brusquely, but the smart bicycle caught his attention and made him pause.

'Ed, hello.' She couldn't help herself: 'What do you think of the new bike?'

'It's right smart. Pinched it, did you?'

'No I did not! Mrs Stellion lent it to me. It belongs to her daughter.'

'Does she know?'

'Who, Diana Stellion? I doubt it. She's not there.'

'No, I meant Mrs S. Does she know she's lent it to you?'

Gina gave Ed a long look. 'It's nowt to do with you anyway,' she muttered.

'If you've come to work you're wasting your time. Mum says she can't rely on you and she'd rather not be wondering whether you're going to bother to turn up of a morning.'

'Oh, but I came to tell her I won't be here no more.'

'I've already told you that, Gina, didn't you hear me? She's giving you the sack.'

'What . . .?'

'You might want to collect your pay for the few hours you've worked this week before you disappear, though.'

'I might. Or I might not bother,' said Gina, furious,

'seeing as I've a new job up at the Hall. Mrs B can't sack me if I've already left.'

'True,' said Ed slowly, as if considering the point. 'But I reckon it's good riddance whichever way she looks at it.' He walked away, saying over his shoulder, 'I'll see you about, no doubt, Gina.'

'Not if I see you first,' Gina flung at him.

This was not going to plan. Gina had wanted to arrive on the shiny bike, show off about her new job, working personally for Mrs Stellion, and collect her pay. It hadn't occurred to her that the farmers would be only too pleased to see the back of her. She didn't fancy starting the day with a difficult encounter with Mrs Beveridge, but neither did she want to forgo her pay, even though it would be no more than a few shillings.

She thought it over and pride won out over pay. *Good riddance, indeed!* She grabbed the bicycle and rode out of the farmyard and away down the lane.

She hadn't gone far, though, before she straightened her back and raised her head high. Good riddance worked both ways! Soon she was pretending this was her own bike as she pedalled round the ruts and the patches of grass growing down the centre.

What do I care about Nancy Beveridge and her smelly old hens? Or those sheep? Onward and upward.

She rode on with renewed high spirits towards the Hall . . . towards a whole world of new opportunities.

~

Tom Arnold was in the drive tidying up the camellias when Dora and Ellen arrived for work. He looked up when he heard their footsteps on the gravel. Dora looked pale and tired. It must be hard work for one woman to keep the Hall spick and span. The Stellions' housekeeper, Mrs Thwaite, brought in extra help for the annual spring cleaning, or if there was a 'do' to prepare for, but the general appearance of a clean and tidy house was Dora's work. She took a pride in it and had done it for several years, but maybe it was getting too much for her. Or maybe there was another reason she looked all in. Probably something to do with his miserable brother, Tom thought.

'Morning, Dora . . . Nell.'

'Morning, Tom.'

'Morning, Mr Arnold.' Ellen beamed at remembering to be formal, even though all those present were family. She was learning already that appearances were important at the Hall.

'You ready to get started, Nell? You could take over here, clearing up these dropped blooms and generally tidying the drive while I go and see to the lawn mower. Be sure to get up all these brown flower heads, pull out any weeds from the gravel and then just rake it over lightly.'

'Of course, Mr Arnold,' Ellen smiled willingly. She took off her old Fair Isle cardigan and hung it over the handles of the wheelbarrow. Her gardening gloves were in her bag – her school satchel, which was proving useful years after she'd left school – because she'd proudly taken them home to show her parents. In the end, only Dora had admired them.

'Thank you, Nell. I'll come and see how you're getting on in a bit.'

He and Dora moved on towards the house.

'You all right, love?' asked Tom when they were out of Ellen's hearing. 'Only you're looking a bit tired, like.'

'Aye, I am a bit weary,' said Dora. 'I'll be all right once I get polishing.'

Tom smiled. 'Have you time to tell me about it while I see to the lawn mower?'

'Five minutes then, but we'll stay outside. I don't want anyone getting the wrong idea: you and me in the shed together.'

Tom threw back his head and laughed. 'Aye, lass, that would never do.'

They walked round to what Ellen had thought yesterday looked like a little village of garden outbuildings and Tom opened the big shed and wheeled out the lawn mower. Then he and Dora sat down behind it on a couple of large upturned plant pots, where they could see anyone approaching.

'What's the matter? Is it that brother of mine?'

'Well, I can hardly blame him for worrying,' said Dora, loyally. She told Tom the sorry tale of the dead sheep and lambs.

'So he was fretting and worriting all night? I can imagine. Not a thought that you might need a good night's sleep before another day's work. Selfish bugger. Typical: if he's got summat on his mind he makes sure everyone else shares the worry.'

This seemed to Dora a fair summary of Philip's attitude

throughout their marriage, and he was getting worse as he grew older. She was too tired to find any loyal words to contradict Tom. Suddenly tears sprang to her eyes and she brushed them away hastily before he saw and misunderstood.

'Hey, chin up, lass,' he said. 'I'd be willing to bet there's no more dead sheep today and the whole business will remain a mystery until everyone forgets about it.'

'Aye, I'm hoping so.'

'And Phil'll go on about it for a few days, just to eke out the bad news, like, and then even he will have to shut up.'

Dora gave a watery smile. This also was a pretty accurate account of the pattern of Phil's gloomy moods.

'You never know, he might even remember he has two beautiful daughters – in addition to his remarkably fine wife – and be glad for them about their new jobs. It'll do him no harm to think of summat beyond himself.'

'You're right, of course, Tom, though I know there is cause to be anxious about the sheep, with everyone fearing foot and mouth these days. Phil takes his work at the farm very seriously – of course he does – but if it wasn't the flock it'd be summat else causing him fretting or fury, and often it's a trifling matter. It's hard work bearing the weight of all his pessimism, and the girls shouldn't have their home life cast under a black cloud and be tiptoeing round their father's ill temper all the time. I worry they'll be off at the first opportunity – and I could hardly blame them – and then it'll just be me trying to cope with Phil alone. I don't know if I'd be able to manage. Sometimes it's like he's sucking all the joy out of my life.'

Tom reached out and took Dora's hand where it rested in her lap, and she didn't resist when he raised it to his lips and gently kissed the back of it.

'Oh, Dora,' he murmured, 'if only—'

'—it had been different,' she finished. 'But it is what it is, lad, and I'd best get on and tackle that sitting room before Mr and Mrs S want to be in there.' Reluctantly she pulled her hand away, stood up, brushed off the seat of her thin coat and straightened her shoulders. She never allowed herself more than a minute or two alone with Tom, yet she relished that brief time as a thirsty insect might devour tiny drops of water on a petal. She must never look for more than that, she knew; she could not trust herself.

'And I'd best oil this beast and make the first cut of the season,' said Tom, also getting to his feet but not taking his eyes off Dora.

'How did Nell do yesterday?' she asked, stepping away and adopting the tone of Mrs Arnold, the Hall's reliable domestic. 'She seemed to think it went all right.'

'It's early days but I think she'll be grand,' said Tom Arnold, the gardener. 'Oh, but, lass, we need to be extra careful with both the girls here,' he added quietly.

'Huh, Gina! I don't know what she's playing at, but I've had a word about the kind of behaviour I expect – or rather, don't expect. I don't want her giving the Arnolds a bad name. We have our reputations to think of,' said Dora pointedly, then smiled and turned for the house.

'As if I'm not thinking of your reputation every day,' Tom murmured, watching her go. 'Why else would I be feeling this way about you and doing nowt about it?'

~

Gina pedalled down the drive of Grindle Hall. Ahead she could see her sister bending over a pile of dead flower heads she had raked together.

'Morning again, Nell,' Gina called as she passed, and managed, with a well-timed kick, to tip the wheelbarrow onto its side, spilling the soggy brown debris of spent flowers onto Nell and the gravel, and casting her cardigan and satchel onto the ground. 'Whoops, sorry!' Gina called as she rode on, not looking back.

She continued round behind the kitchen and left the bicycle in one of the outbuildings. Then she went into the house via the kitchen door. Even Gina knew it wasn't her place to use the front door when she arrived, though already she dreamed of a time when it would be. As she'd said to Ellen, you have to dream big dreams if you want to get on in life. And now she had this strange, new and rather frightening power that she didn't yet understand. It couldn't just be a coincidence that the sheep had died, could it? Gina questioned herself once again and came to the same disturbing conclusion: she had killed the sheep by mistake. No one need ever suspect, so her secret was safe. She had already resolved to be more careful in future.

Mrs Bassett was at the kitchen table, rolling out pastry.

'Good morning, Mrs Bassett,' said Gina.

The cook looked up. 'Good morning, Ellen Arnold. Would you get me some taters, please, and I think there's a bit of salad ready under those cloches. Mr Arnold will show you.'

'Oh, I'm not Ellen,' said Gina, laughing, but politely. 'I'm Georgina.'

Mrs Bassett looked puzzled. 'But I thought your name was Ellen. Aren't you working in the garden with Tom Arnold?'

'Oh, no. The garden's nowt to do with me, Mrs Bassett. I'm working for Mrs Stellion,' said Gina, and went through the door into the corridor, then up the stairs to the green door and on into the hall, amused at leaving the poor woman plainly confused.

She quickly collected Coco's lead from the boot room and then went to find Mrs Stellion and her puppy in the morning room, where she'd met the lady the previous day.

See, only one day in, and already you're going about your business in the house quite happily.

When she thought of the previous day and how Nell and Uncle Tom had come bowing and scraping up the back stairs, she almost laughed aloud.

She knocked on the closed door, heard the call to enter, and in an instant the little dog was yapping and panting around her feet. He was a bonny young fella and it would be easy to become fond of him, she decided, and if she meant to make herself indispensable, Coco could be a real asset. She bent to greet him with almost equal enthusiasm.

'Gina, good morning,' said Mrs Stellion. 'How prompt

you are for Coco's walk. I do like people who are reliable. You've even got his lead handy. Now, if you walk him around the garden for twenty minutes, clean his feet, then back up here for biscuits, that will be fine.'

'Yes, Mrs Stellion,' said Gina, hoping there would indeed be biscuits, though she suspected Mrs Stellion meant for the dog.

She fastened the lead on the puppy's collar and walked him down to the hall, then slipped out through the front door and down the steps to the gravel. This was, after all, Coco's home, even if it wasn't hers.

She led him round the house to the back, meandering in and out of the different parts of the garden, opening doors and gates to see what was what, memorising which areas were most suitable for the dog and which were of more interest to herself. When they got to the back they played a while on the grass with a stick Gina had found.

Soon Tom appeared wheeling a gigantic green lawn mower.

'Hello, Uncle Tom,' Gina called.

'All right, lass? Looks like that dog needs a ball to play with.'

'You're right. I don't know if he's got one. I'll have to ask Mrs Stellion.' She laughed at the idea of Mrs Stellion running about on the grass throwing a ball for the energetic puppy. Of course, that was the very reason she was here.

Tom bent to fondle the puppy's ears and he barked delightedly, loving the attention. 'Nice little dog,' Tom said. 'I may know where there's summat he can play with. Come and find me later.'

'Thank you, Uncle Tom,' said Gina, and scampered after Coco, who was now heading for the flowerbed. 'Coco, come here, you little beggar . . .'

Tom watched her go. In some ways she resembled the carefree and undisciplined puppy, he thought. Gina was all right, but not steady like Nell. He had to admire the way she'd got herself this dog-walking job, though. However she'd managed it, it had been fast work. He made a mental note not to underestimate his niece Gina.

~

Edith Stellion looked out of the morning-room window at Coco playing with the stick the Arnold girl had found for him. Her husband, George, came to stand beside her and they watched together in silence. George glanced at his wife and saw that she was smiling at the antics of her little dog running around with the new girl – what was her name? Not Ellen . . . Gina? – but at the same time there was sadness in her eyes. He knew what she was thinking.

'She'd have been about that age now, wouldn't she?' he said. 'Clarissa.'

Edith nodded. 'Seventeen next week.'

'Of course.'

They stood quietly watching for a few more minutes.

'Looks like Coco is going to be a handful, Edith,' said George. 'Are you sure such a lively puppy was a good idea?'

'No,' laughed Edith, throwing off her sadness at the thought of their little daughter who had died long ago, 'but he's very sweet-natured and amusing, and if Gina Arnold is taking him out most days, then I think he'll not be too boisterous for me.'

'Hmm . . .'

'She can help me with his obedience training. And it's nice to have a young face about the place, don't you think?'

'I agree. I know it's a bit quiet for you when I'm out on business, and with Diana and James away now most of the time, though I admit to being confused which of the Arnold girls is which. Suddenly there's two of them here, and at first glance they do look surprisingly alike.'

'They do indeed, though I think we'll all soon learn. Mrs Thwaite says Mrs Bassett was all at sea about them earlier.' They exchanged amused glances.

'Mrs Bassett is a dear, and a wonderful cook,' said George, then lowered his voice, 'but not especially clever in other regards.'

Edith was thinking. 'George, I know it's early days, but if Gina Arnold works out well with Coco, you wouldn't mind if I gave her a few other little tasks to do for me, would you?'

'No, darling, if you think she's the right person. What have you in mind?'

'Oh, just keeping me company, really. It's a big effort to go out if I've got one of my headaches or I'm in a sad mood.' She sighed. 'I can hardly ask Mrs Thwaite, can I?'

'Of course not.' George thought of the elderly and

humourless housekeeper. She had been at the Hall for several years and, really, with Diana and James in London much of the time, there was little for her to do most weeks. She was only kept on out of kindness because she was a widow, but Edith had never been especially fond of the prickly woman. 'But Gina Arnold – I'm assuming she's a village girl through and through, if she's anything like her sister. Though of course their mother is Dora, and she has her own dignity, for all she's had very few advantages, nor, I imagine, lived anywhere but Little Grindle. But do you really think Gina Arnold would be the kind of young woman to amuse you when you're feeling low?'

'Ah,' said Edith. 'There you have me. But I think I might find out as time goes on. I suspect that a lively, reliable and good-natured girl about the place will probably do me no end of good.'

~

Ellen had had a trying day. After Gina had knocked over the barrow, she'd had to shovel up all the dead flowers and the weeds again, and then there'd been a sudden shower of rain while she was tying up some roses and she'd got uncomfortably wet. Now, this afternoon, Gina was queening about on the lawn, playing with the puppy while she, Ellen, was standing on a plank in the damp herbaceous border next to it, weeding with a long hoe.

Coco came snuffling round to see what she was doing and, instead of calling him away, Gina encouraged him to make a nuisance of himself.

'Can't you just go away while I'm working here?' Ellen said eventually.

'Are you talking to me or the dog?' Gina asked innocently.

'Well, the blessed dog, obviously,' Ellen snapped. 'I wouldn't expect an intelligent reply from you.'

'No need to adopt a tone,' said Gina. 'I'm just doing my job, same as you.'

'Job! What kind of a job is it, for goodness' sake, gallivanting around with a puppy?'

'Same as yours. You answer to Uncle Tom and I answer to Mrs Stellion, so I reckon that makes it a proper job, Nell, so you can get down off your high horse.'

Ellen bit back her retort and took a deep breath. Surely Gina and the dog wouldn't be out here for long. She'd just ignore them. But it proved hard to ignore a mischievous and playful puppy when he started chewing the gloves Ellen had taken off and left on the newly cut grass because her hands were hot. Gina just stood watching and giggling.

'Just go, can't you, Gina? Why do you have to play here?'

'All right, we're going. No need to get all worked up. We've enough of that at home with Dad,' she said. 'Come on, Coco . . .' She fastened his lead back on his collar. 'We've got the rest of the garden to play in, haven't we, boy? Let's go and see how those strawberries are getting on.'

'Don't you dare let Coco go among those strawberry plants,' said Ellen. 'He'll only wee on them and ruin them.'

'I was only joking, Nell. You should see your face, though,' said Gina, and, laughing loudly, led the puppy away.

'How did you get on?' asked Tom when Ellen had finished a good area of the border and come back to the sheds for a cup of tea.

'All right, I suppose. I've done about a third, but I could have managed better without Gina and that dog messing about round me.' Ellen wasn't a habitual tale-teller but she didn't want to have to put up with Gina and Coco every morning and afternoon. Gina had a cruel streak and knew instinctively how to wind people up.

'I'll have a word,' said Tom.

Ellen hoped that would be the end of the matter. Both girls liked and respected Uncle Tom, and even Gina would do as he asked. But Ellen felt uneasy about having Gina around at the Hall, as if Gina had somehow pushed into her life, which was unfair when she considered that both had started working there on the same day. Maybe it was the suddenness of Gina coming here that was unsettling. Ellen had to admit that she hadn't felt quite at ease since Gina had slapped her hand away from that little bottle hidden in the wall and then started talking some rubbish about witches' spells. It was hard to forget about that and the mad look she'd seen on Gina's face. Despite what Gina had said the previous night, she couldn't really believe she'd heard the last of it.

CHAPTER FOUR

'NELL, YOU'VE GOT a visitor,' Tom announced.

Ellen looked up from pricking out seedlings on the greenhouse bench. It was hot behind the glass in late May; she had her sleeves rolled up and was feeling rather clammy.

'Ed! What a nice surprise.' She brushed a strand of hair away from her flushed face with her forearm. 'We haven't seen you at the cottage for a week or two. Is everything all right?' She put down her dibber and wiped the soil off her hands on an old towel.

'I won't keep you long, Nell; just wanted to say hello as I was here anyway.' Edward Beveridge turned to Tom. 'If that's all right . . .?'

Edward felt slightly overheated himself. For one silly moment he didn't know whether to remove his cap on entering the greenhouse. He'd thought to look Ellen out when he came up to the Hall to deliver some meat that Mrs Thwaite had ordered. Now, seeing Ellen working in this imposing place, setting what looked like hundreds of tiny plants, he realised he knew nothing of her life since she'd left the farm nearly two weeks ago and he felt overawed. With her eager face and untidy hair, she looked very young and very pretty, an attractive combination with the confidence and self-possession she was displaying in her new work.

'Nell knows what she has to get done,' said Tom, smiling.

'Thank you, Mr Arnold.'

Tom went off to tend the vegetable plot and Ed turned to answer Ellen. 'Aye, thank you, we're all fine. Mum says you're to drop in any time.'

'I'll do that. It'd be lovely to see her. I was right glad to hear no more of the sheep died. It must have been a terrible worry for you.'

'It was, but that's behind us now.'

They stood awkwardly for a moment, Ellen keen to get on but not wanting to seem rude to her friend, Edward reading that thought in her face and beginning to wish he'd gone straight home. He must think of something to say, and quickly.

'Would you like—'

'Well, I really must—'

They both spoke at once.

'Please, you first,' said Ellen.

'I'm just wondering if you'd like to come for a walk up the field this evening – after you've finished work, of course. Mum could pack up a tea for us.'

'Thank you, I'd love to,' said Ellen. 'It'd be nice to catch up on everyone's news. I've been so busy since I started here.'

Edward took the hint. 'Come over whenever you're ready, then.'

'I'll look forward to it.' Smiling, Ellen picked up her dibber to resume her task while Edward turned to leave, grinning.

At midday Tom reappeared and told Ellen it was time to stop working.

'Oh, the time just flies by when I'm busy,' she said. 'I didn't realise it was so late.'

'Well, it's library day,' Tom reminded her, 'so we'd best get a move on if we don't want to be fined next time for late returns.'

'I hadn't forgotten,' said Ellen, and went to the shed to collect the books she'd brought with her.

Tom and Ellen walked down the drive to the main gate together, meeting Mrs Thwaite coming the other way carrying a small pile of books, and found the van parked neatly up against Tom's cottage. Tom nipped inside to fetch his books while Ellen mounted the steps and presented hers, opening them at the pages with the date stamps and the little cardboard pockets.

The usual librarian, Mr Shepherd, wasn't there today. Instead there was a younger man with round wire-rimmed glasses and a severe haircut, which could not disguise that he was very good-looking.

'Mr Shepherd not well?' asked Ellen. She'd grown fond of the kindly librarian with his gentle manner and knowledgeable reading recommendations, even about light fiction.

'Mr Shepherd's been assigned to the archives,' said the new man.

'Oh . . .' Ellen was worried. Was that a discreet way of saying he'd been forced into retirement? He was getting on in years but he hadn't said anything about retiring when he last came by. 'And does he . . . is he quite happy about that?'

'I wouldn't know,' said the man abruptly. 'Why do you ask?'

Goodness, what a rude man! 'Well, it's only . . . well, Mr Shepherd's been the librarian for a long time and . . . folk are fond of him.'

'Aye, in Little Grindle we care about folk,' said Tom, coming in with his books. 'We're like that round here.' He gave the new man a stern look but it didn't soften his manner.

'Indeed?' he said dismissively. Then barked at Ellen: 'Name?'

He took the tickets under her name from his card index box, placed them in the books and then closed the volumes to put on the 'Returned' shelf, glancing at the titles.

'Romances down at the end,' he said with a slight sneer, pointing.

Ellen shuffled away, feeling as if her taste were being judged and found wanting.

As she was returning with her chosen books, she noticed there was a shelf of practical kinds of books: handicrafts, woodworking and gardening. She hadn't thought to look there before, never venturing beyond light romances, which she and Dora both read in the fortnight they were lent out. There was a picture book of beautiful gardens and she wondered if it was worth a look, if only to compare the photographs – which were, disappointingly, mainly in black and white – with Grindle Hall, so she took that to the librarian's little desk too.

'The rule is you're allowed only three volumes,' said the new librarian.

Ellen knew this and felt foolish for forgetting to put one of the novels back when she'd found the gardens book. She was starting to apologise when Tom interrupted, approaching with a couple of hefty novels from the classics section.

'I'll put one of yours on my ticket,' he said.

'No borrowing is allowed on another reader's ticket,' said the librarian, not looking up from his card index.

'I'm not borrowing on Miss Arnold's ticket,' said Tom mildly. 'I'm borrowing on my own ticket.'

'It's all right, Uncle Tom, I've decided not to have this book after all,' said Ellen, and put one of the novels to one side. 'I'll take the gardens book instead.'

'It would be helpful if you didn't take books from the shelves that you don't wish to borrow,' said the librarian, snatching up the novel and putting it on the 'Returned' shelf.

'But *I* want to borrow it,' said Tom, taking it carefully off the shelf and adding it to his pile of books.

The librarian stared at Tom for a long time with raised

eyebrows. Tom returned the look and the librarian blinked first.

'See you next time,' Tom said in a friendly tone as he and Ellen descended the steps, clutching their stamped books.

Ellen couldn't help bursting out laughing, although she suspected the librarian could hear her.

'Oh, Uncle Tom, you are brilliant,' she giggled. 'Thomas Hardy, Charles Dickens and *The Fickle Heart of Lady Blanche*.'

'I shall enjoy that one no end,' said Tom, deadpan, handing it over to Ellen. 'Whoever Lady Blanche is. Make sure you bring it back next time, love. I don't want my wrists slapped by that jumped-up little stand-in for our Mr Shepherd.'

'I wonder what's happened to Mr Shepherd. He'd surely have told us if he was expecting not to be round in the van any more. That rude man said he'd been "assigned to the archives", but I don't really know what that means.'

'Oh dear, I wonder if that's a euphemism for being pensioned off. I'll make some enquiries . . .'

~

Gina enjoyed going up to the Hall twice a day. She didn't mind exercising Mrs Stellion's puppy, but being at the Hall was, to her, the whole point of her employment. She always eked out the tasks of cleaning Coco's paws and tidying away his lead and the old tennis ball Tom had found for him so that she could spend as long as possible around the house.

This morning Mrs Stellion was in good spirits and was sitting writing letters with a fountain pen, quickly covering thick sheets of paper from her desk stand in neat writing, so that when Gina returned the happy dog to his owner, Mrs Stellion was too occupied to chat for long. Nor was there tea and biscuits laid out on a tray for Gina and her employer, as there sometimes was.

'Oh, thank you, Gina,' said Mrs Stellion, looking up and smiling at the dog. 'Good boy, Coco. *Sit!*'

Coco obediently sat down beside his mistress's chair at her leather-topped desk, a vase of fragrant early roses on it.

Gina felt proud of her pupil. 'He's coming on well, isn't he, ma'am?' she said, looking for praise.

'Indeed. He's a clever young fellow. Coco and I will see you this afternoon, then, thank you, Gina.'

'Yes, Mrs Stellion. Goodbye for now.' Gina knew she was being dismissed.

It was a beautiful morning and she didn't fancy cycling home to do household chores until it was time to return here. Maybe she could just stay if she didn't get in anyone's way.

She went back to the gloomy entrance hall but, instead of leaving through the green door at the back, she decided to do a little exploration. Gina had seen Mr Stellion driving away in the big car earlier, so she knew only the morning room was occupied. She also knew that Dora was cleaning upstairs today and Mrs Thwaite was doing something in the kitchen. It was a good time to have a little look around.

Gina took the other corridor from the hall. There were four doors off it, mirroring the arrangement of rooms at the far side, and she opened the first slowly and peered in. It was filled with bookcases and the window blind was pulled down to keep the light low. She moved on.

She saw light was pouring in at the far end. The door on that side must be glass. Of course . . . it was a conservatory; she'd seen it from the outside. She approached, glanced quickly behind her to see that the coast was clear, then crept in and closed the door quietly.

It was quite a big room, with a high glass roof and stone floor, which was damp in places, as if the many plants in pots had recently been watered. It was very warm and the air smelled green and lush. Gina sat down in one of the basket-like chairs set between the pot plants, arranged the cushions and closed her eyes . . .

'And what do you think you're doing, young woman?' asked a severe voice.

Gina opened her eyes and saw Mrs Thwaite standing in front of her.

'Oh, Mrs Thwaite, I'm afraid I got lost and then it's so warm in here that I—'

'Lost? Really? You didn't look like you were making much of an effort to find your way out,' said Mrs Thwaite.

'No. As I said—'

'I heard enough of what you said, Gina Arnold. You may have business here playing with Mrs Stellion's puppy, but let me remind you, that is *all* the business you have here.'

'I was only—'

'I can see exactly what you "were only" doing. I hope I don't need to remind you that you are not a resident of this house. Your *job* – if "job" it can be called – is to entertain the dog, make sure he's clean enough to be inside on the furniture and then to leave.'

Gina felt herself turning pink with fury. *Entertain the dog!* That made her sound as if she were the dog's servant. Mrs Thwaite had clearly plucked up the courage to take some pathetic revenge for what Gina had said to her on that first morning. Most days they managed to avoid each other – and certainly that suited Gina, who would rather the episode about the missing money at the village shop were well and truly forgotten – but Gina knew she had overstepped the mark by being here today. Simmering with anger though she was, she bit back the insult she was about to fling at Mrs Thwaite and decided to retreat with what dignity she could.

'Yes, Mrs Thwaite,' she said quietly. 'It's all right, I'm leaving now.' She went to the door, but the housekeeper was there before her and opened it, so that Gina knew she was literally being shown out, as if she wasn't to be trusted. She walked back up the corridor and Mrs Thwaite followed behind her like a gaoler escorting a prisoner. In the hall, Gina forgot herself for a moment and stepped towards the front door, as she did when she walked Coco.

'Back stairs,' barked Mrs Thwaite, pointing the way. Then, as Gina passed in front of her to reach the green door, she hissed, 'And don't you ever forget your place in future, Gina Arnold.'

Gina didn't answer or look back, but went through the door, glad of the cooler air on the staircase against her burning face. She went down the corridor, past the kitchen and to the door at the end, which opened into the courtyard where the outbuildings were. She wheeled out the bicycle and pedalled away, not looking round, knowing she'd been well and truly bested by the housekeeper this time.

Mrs Stellion was usually very friendly – less so today because she was busy – but now Gina felt as if she'd had a wake-up call. She had thought she had a way into the lives of those at the Hall, only to have it brought home to her that she was merely the girl who walked the dog – the dog's servant, as Mrs Thwaite had implied. Dora had the run of the house and was trusted, after many years of service, and Ellen was learning a proper trade and, from what Gina had seen of her in the garden, was going about it in a very competent manner. But she . . . oh, it was too bad: sacked by Mrs Beveridge and now practically thrown out of the Hall by the housekeeper. For a moment she wondered if she would bother going back this afternoon, but it was Mrs Stellion she answered to, and it was possible that the lady neither knew nor cared that her dog walker had sat down in her conservatory. Gina decided it would be worth returning to see how the land lay.

In the meantime she had a few hours alone at the cottage until it was time for Coco's afternoon walk. She had avoided taking the little book of spells out from its hiding place since the incident with the sheep. Events had run away with her then, and she had felt unsettled by the suspicion that the power she could muster was not entirely under her control. Now, though, passing time had blunted her fear, and she decided she needed a little help if she were to teach Mrs Thwaite the lesson she deserved. She arrived at the cottage, unlocked the door and rushed upstairs to consult her book.

~

'Good grief, Gina. What on earth is that awful smell?' asked Ellen. 'It's like a singed perm, but it doesn't look as if you've burned your hair,' she said, staring at Gina's long brown curls, which looked just the same as usual.

'It must be bleach,' said Gina, thinking fast. 'I got a mark on my shirt and I've been trying to get it off.'

'Mm . . .' Ellen opened the window of their room to let in some fresh air. 'I'm off out with Ed in a minute, when I've got changed. We're just going for a walk and a packed tea. Do you want to come?'

'No fear,' said Gina. 'I'm not playing gooseberry to you two.'

'Don't be daft.' Ellen changed out of her shirt and breeches and put on a cotton frock, first time on this year. It looked shorter and was definitely tighter than it had been on its last outing, and somehow the fabric had faded on top of the skirt gathers since she'd put it away in September. Strange how clothes changed when you didn't wear them for a while. Sometimes they came out looking better; mostly they were worse.

'What do you think of this? Does it look too tight?'

'A bit,' said Gina.

'Ah, well, it'll have to do. I've nowt else and I only wanted summat cool to wear. It's been hot today, potting up seedlings. How did you get on "popping over to the Hall to exercise Coco"?'

Gina rolled her eyes; the joke had lost its sting with frequent repetition. Instead of answering she asked, 'What do you think about Mrs Thwaite?'

'I don't have owt to do with her really. She's all right whenever I do see her, though. Why?'

'Nowt . . . Just wondered.'

'I know she takes her books to the mobile library, same as me and Uncle Tom. We met her on her way back. Mr Shepherd – you know, the old librarian who's always so friendly – he wasn't there. He's always been there before now. Funny that Mrs Thwaite didn't mention it when we met her.'

'Mebbe she doesn't get on with Mr Shepherd.'

'No, Mr Shepherd gets on with everyone. Uncle Tom's going to try to find out what's happened. What if he's ill? Folk in Little Grindle would want to do what they could for him.'

'Nell, I've really no idea,' said Gina.

Ellen took her brush through her hair and tied it back with her home-made blue scarf knotted in a bow above her ear. 'Right, I'm off to the farm. See you later.'

Gina listened to her sister's feet descending the stairs, then Ellen was saying something Gina couldn't hear to Dora, and then there was the sound of the back door closing.

She pulled the shabby little volume of spells out from under her bed, with a candle, a box of matches and a saucer, a bottle of vinegar, various bits of plants she hoped she'd identified correctly, and some scraps of paper on which she'd written various wishes for the intervention of whatever power she'd hoped to conjure up before she'd gone to walk Coco that afternoon. Whether it had worked or not, she didn't know. Mrs Stellion hadn't mentioned the conservatory and Gina had seen nothing of Mrs Thwaite. So far as Gina was concerned, that was a good result to be going on with. Time would reveal whether the short-tempered housekeeper had met her match.

~

Ellen and Ed took the well-worn path past the hen houses, up through the gate into the field where the girls had lazed on their afternoon off, and on up higher. Ellen remembered about the silly business with the little bottle, but whatever Gina had been up to, nothing had come of it and Ellen's fear of that mad moment had faded until it was almost forgotten.

'Such a lovely hot day,' she said. 'Like midsummer. The air's a bit fresher up here, though.'

'Aye, it is, but look over there.' Edward pointed to the west. 'Those clouds mean rain, though I think we'll be all right for this evening.'

'Shall we stop here for our tea?' asked Ellen after a few more minutes. 'The view's amazing this high up.'

Edward laughed. 'Yes, a rare sight to be able to see so far. Look, there's the Hall over there, and the village street stretching away. Half the year the clouds are down to the ground and all you can see up here through the fog is tragic-looking sheep clinging onto the fell.'

'Don't I know it! I was helping with them until a few weeks ago, don't forget.'

'It feels as if you've been gone for ages,' said Edward, sitting on the dry cropped grass.

'Yes, funny, that. I feel the same,' smiled Ellen.

'Do you miss it?'

'Oh, no, not at all. It was nice working with you and your parents, but I think I like gardening better than farm work,' said Ellen. 'And I'm learning all kinds of new things. You can understand why I'm keen on that, can't you, Ed?' She was anxious not to offend by mistake.

'Of course.'

'I want to learn all about gardening, get to know everything Uncle Tom knows – and he knows so much I think it will take me years to catch up – so that one day mebbe I can be in charge of a garden. I'd like to learn to cut those bushes into shapes like chessmen, though I'd settle for trimming a box hedge straight for now,' she laughed. 'You don't think it's daft, do you, that I should want to learn and mebbe even be a head gardener somewhere?'

''Course not. Why would it be daft?'

'Well, I'm just Ellen Arnold, who lives in a tied cottage in Little Grindle and hasn't much of an education. It's not like I live in a place where there's lots of different things happening and opportunities to do them.'

'You never know, you might still get to do all sorts,' said Edward. 'If you work hard enough, I reckon you can do whatever you want. It's not about where you come from, is it, Nell? It's about where you're going: all the things you're going to do in your life. When I saw you this morning you looked as if you knew exactly what you were doing with all those little plants. That's a start, isn't it?'

'Thank you, Ed. There's so much to learn that I sometimes feel as if I'll never get anywhere with it. I am trying hard, though.'

'I know you are. And think how much you've done in the time you've been at the Hall. I reckon Mr Arnold wouldn't be putting up with anyone who was a hindrance and not a help. He wants the best for the Hall garden, and he won't waste time with you if you're no good to him, even if you are his niece.'

'True,' Ellen conceded. 'He's kind, but I know he'd say if I were hopeless. And you're kind, too, pulling up my spirits like that.'

'Aye, well, just don't be setting off down the road to success and forgetting who your friends are, will you?' Edward said. 'And I'd really miss you if you went away to be head gardener at some other big house. We all would – Mum and Dad as well as me,' he added, shy about his feelings and safely diluting them by bringing his parents into it. 'I'm a farmer's only son so I shan't be going anywhere. My future was mapped out at birth.'

'Well, I'm here for now, and for at least the next ten years if I'm to learn everything about gardening from Uncle Tom,' smiled Ellen. 'Now, I'm starving and I expect you are, too. What's your mum packed in that picnic basket? It's heavy enough for a feast.'

'I reckon she's feeding us up,' said Edward, pleased Ellen had no real plans to leave Little Grindle. He admired and understood her ambition, but he certainly didn't want her to go away. He had, at the back of his mind, plans for his own life that might well include Nell Arnold.

CHAPTER FIVE

'We're all set for summer, I see,' said Philip, casting a disgruntled look through the kitchen window at the rain teeming down. 'It'll be like this for weeks now, you mark my words.'

'You don't know that, Dad,' Ellen said. 'It was that hot yesterday it felt like midsummer. Could be as quick to change again.'

'I doubt it,' said Gina, recklessly imitating her father's voice and pulling a long face. 'Cheer up, Dad, we might all be dead by July.'

'Gina, shut up.'

'Gina—'

'You're not too old to feel the back of my hand,' threatened Philip as Ellen and Dora tried to shush her. They all knew that, Gina most of all. He took a step towards her with his arm raised and she stepped quickly out of reach, the smile gone from her face immediately.

'Sorry, Dad,' she muttered, then quickly said, 'I think I'll take Coco for a run around the outbuildings; save us both getting wet.' She watched ribbons of rain cascading down the windows.

'You'd better ask Mrs Stellion,' Dora suggested to her. 'She might want her dog to have a proper walk, rain or no rain.'

'He won't shrink in the wet, Gina,' said Ellen.

'No, but I might. Perhaps we'll even play inside and not go out at all,' Gina mused.

'Well, I think it's time you got yourself a proper job, like our Nell, and stopped "playing" with puppies,' said Philip. 'Just 'cos you got the sack from the farm doesn't mean you can't make a fresh start. After all, you got the sack from the shop but it didn't stop you working again. You need to make the effort, Gina, if you even know what that means. Playing with puppies'll get you nowhere in life.'

Like you've got somewhere, you mean? Gina intended to go an awful lot further in her life than the farm at the end of the lane. Her job at the village shop had been a short-lived disaster. Gina still maintained publicly that it wasn't her fault the money in the till didn't match the receipts.

'You got the sack from the farm?' asked Dora. 'You never said.' She, too, recalled the unpleasantness at the village shop. For a while she'd been reluctant to go there, which had been awkward, though the Fowlers were good people and hadn't blamed her for the incident at all.

'I hear they need someone for general labour at Fellside, that farm on the way to Great Grindle,' Philip went on. 'They grow vegetables and have a little dairy herd. Even you can muck out cows and pick taters, Gina. They needn't know you were sacked if you don't tell them – I know you're good at keeping secrets; you have a good teacher – and you could work full time and earn your keep for once in your life. It's time you started paying your way, and playing with puppies won't be doing that.'

Ellen frowned, wondering what exactly he was referring to about secrets, but she knew better than to say anything, so instead she went to look out her wellingtons from under the stairs, keen not to get drawn into this kind of low-level argument that seemed to run perpetually between her father and sister, and which would occasionally erupt into physical violence.

'General labour! Muck out cows and pick taters!' Gina was horrified. She thought of Mrs Stellion's pretty morning room and how she had the run of almost the entire garden to play with the dog. No way was she going back to filthy farm work! She had hardly begun to get her plans under way yet, but she meant to forget she'd ever seen a farm, never mind worked on one.

'Why don't you just get off to work,' said Dora to her husband, keen to damp down the full-scale argument brewing between him and Gina, 'before you get the sack, too?'

'Aye, I'm going, woman,' he said, and left, grumbling to himself as he buttoned up his coat.

'What was he on about?' Gina asked.

'About you getting a proper job instead of "popping over to the Hall to exercise Coco", as you know very well,' said Ellen. 'Still, at least you seem to be doing that all right. Just keep that dog out of the vegetables, though, and anywhere I'm working.'

'What, outside? On a day like this? And I meant what did he mean about me being good at keeping secrets?'

'I've really no idea,' said Dora dismissively. 'Now, Gina, tidy the kitchen before you leave for the Hall, please, and if you see Ellen working you're not to disturb her.'

Dora and Ellen gathered their mackintoshes, hats, umbrellas and wellingtons, and went out, exclaiming at the fierceness of the downpour.

For a moment Gina stood staring out at the driving rain. It was tempting not to leave the cottage at all, but what Philip had said about going to work at Fellside Farm had unnerved her. She needed to make sure of her role at the Hall and there was no time to lose.

~

Dora shook out her wet coat and hung it on a hook in the downstairs corridor, then pulled off her wellingtons and put on the shoes she kept at the Hall. Not a good start to the day: rain running down the back of her neck, despite her rain hat and umbrella and, even more annoying, Phil in another of his black moods, and making snide remarks about her.

She would never forget his jealousy and suspicions about her so-called secret on the night Gina was born. She'd put up with it for years, although he'd never referred to it before in front of the girls. Dora hoped this was not the start of a season of blacker moods and worse temper in her difficult husband. Was that when their marriage started to go wrong, or had it been failing even before then? It was hard to remember a time when they were happy, before this darkness descended on Philip . . .

~

Dora held her newborn baby in her arms. She was a beauty, with fine dark hair and the softest skin on her perfect little body.

'A lovely girl,' said Betty Travers, the midwife. 'All the right limbs in all the right places and a good weight, too. A wonderful start to the New Year: a baby born just on the stroke of midnight.' She opened the bedroom window just a crack so that Dora could hear the church bells in Little Grindle ringing in 1939, then quickly closed it again. Betty didn't believe in fresh air for her new mothers and babies, especially in January.

Dora smiled tiredly. It was wonderful to have a second daughter, a sister for Nellie to play with. Nell was little more than a baby herself, a clever little thing, walking and trying to speak, though she wouldn't be two until the autumn. Dora had hoped for a daughter but kept this to herself because Philip had said he wanted a son. Well, he had a second lovely little girl and she just had to hope he'd come round to the news when he saw her.

Dora smoothed the baby's damp hair. *Oh!*

'Betty, she's got a little mark just here . . . look. Is

summat wrong? It won't get bigger, will it? She won't be scarred?'

Betty took the baby in her arms and looked closely. 'Oh, bless you, Dora, it's just a tiny birthmark. It might even fade as she gets older, but it certainly won't get bigger. And she's lucky it's behind her ear: by the time this dark hair has grown it'll be completely hidden. Don't you fret, love, there's nowt to be worriting over.'

Philip thought very differently, though, when he came in to see his new child.

'What's this, then?' he asked, seeing the tiny birthmark straight away. 'It looks like a little crescent moon, same as the one our Tom has on his arm.'

'So it does,' said Dora, feigning surprise. Of course, she had already thought this. 'Mebbe it's just summat that runs in families, like,' she said, then realised this was leading her husband to entirely the wrong conclusions.

'Well, I've got no birthmarks and I'm the child's father,' he growled. He looked pointedly at Dora. 'Aren't I?'

Dora caught Betty's eye with a desperately tired look.

'And Baby has your dark hair,' the midwife joined in. 'There's a strong resemblance between your beautiful new daughter and yourself, I'd say, Philip.' Betty and Dora had been good friends for years, but even Dora thought Betty was laying it on a bit thick with that.

'But what about this mark?' Philip persisted. 'I've not got one, but Tom has.'

'It really is of no account, Philip,' Betty said. 'Some babies have birthmarks and most don't, and that's all there is to it. Now, why don't you go and make Dora a cup of tea? I'd say she was ready for one and I think I could manage one, too. We've been hard at work up here.'

'Aye, I heard the fuss,' Philip grumbled.

'Well, you can be thankful you were out of it then,' Betty replied shortly.

When Philip had retreated to the kitchen, Dora sighed deeply.

'She's a bonny little thing but my Phil does get some daft ideas,' she muttered. Tears were now springing to her weary eyes. 'After all that birthing, you'd think he'd be pleased to have his child delivered safe and sound. I wanted another little girl, though I didn't say owt and I didn't really mind. Little Nellie's been such a good baby that I feel I know how to cope with girls. But as Phil wanted a boy, I reckon he's disappointed.'

'Fellas get some queer ideas sometimes, love,' said Betty. 'All these years I've been a midwife, and I'm still surprised why anyone wouldn't just be glad to have a healthy child, regardless of whether it's a girl or a boy.'

'And bringing Tom into it,' said Dora, determined to make sure Betty knew the truth. 'He's always been envious of Tom. For goodness' sake, Tom's my brother-in-law, but I can't exchange a few pleasant words with him without Phil flying into a jealous sulk.'

'Aye, Tom Arnold's got a lot going for him and, with him being the elder, and so agreeable, like, I can see that Philip might reckon he was playing catch-up when they were boys,' Betty chatted on. 'But they're both grown up now, and Philip is the father of two beautiful children, whereas poor Tom has never married, nor found anyone else, so far as I know, after that girl from Great Grindle he was engaged to was killed – what was her name?'

'Sarah . . . Sarah Swaine.' Of course Dora knew the woman's name. They'd have been related by now, had she not died.

'Aye, I reckon you're right. Sarah Swaine; looked like an angel, God bless her. It's a shame, but there we are. Life doesn't always deal us the best cards . . . although there's some have a good hand and don't even know it. It's time your Phil grew out of feeling inferior to Tom, bucked up and thanked the Good Lord that he has a beautiful wife and two lovely daughters.'

Philip came up the stairs with two cups of tea on a tray.

'Oh, you've managed that,' said Betty without sarcasm. 'Well done, lad. Now I'm off when I've had this cuppa, but I was just saying, you've much to be thankful for with a good woman like Dora and now two lovely babes. Think on it and don't be starting no more of your nonsense . . .'

Philip, cowed by the efficiency of the forthright midwife, with her plain speaking and her knowledge of the mysteries of women's matters – and, it was said, other mysteries – retreated downstairs once more. When Betty had gone, he went to view his new daughter again, but though he tried to see a resemblance between himself and the baby, whom Dora suggested they call Georgina, he could not warm to her. The crescent-shaped birthmark looked prominent on the baby's soft skin, mocking him, identical to the one he'd seen all his life on his brother's arm.

'Georgina it is, if that's what you want,' he shrugged. 'The girl's name's nowt to do with me. I'll be off up to the farm first thing to collect my little Nellie and bring her home. For all she's taken to young Edward Beveridge, she'll be glad to be home with her dad.'

'And her mum, and her new baby sister,' said Dora, but Philip had turned away and didn't answer her.

~

Dora rubbed her eyes and sighed. *Oh, Tom . . .* It was her joy to see him on the days she was working at the Hall, and also her torment. She wanted to pretend they were just in-laws and old friends who had known each other for years, yet in all honesty he meant so much more than that. She wanted to be a loyal wife to Philip, yet how could a loyal wife be in love with her husband's brother?

If only it had been different. If only . . . No, don't even think of it! She was married to Phil and that was that. They had two lovely daughters and at least one was a credit to them.

That got her thinking about Gina. If Gina could just manage to behave herself . . . Such a worry, that girl. Sacked from the shop and now sacked from the farm, though Nancy and Albert Beveridge had kind hearts and almost limitless patience! Dora decided it must be the miserable weather this morning that was causing her to dredge up all these gloomy thoughts.

Still feeling low, she took her floral-print crossover pinny from its hook, tied it on and went to fetch her dusters from the cleaning cupboard. With a deliberate effort she put her worries out of her mind, assumed the smiling face of Mrs Arnold, the competent domestic, wished Mrs Bassett a cheery good morning as she passed the kitchen and ascended the stairs to begin work.

This morning it was the turn of the rooms on the west-facing corridor to get a clean. She enjoyed her work, for all it was physically hard and menial. She was proud of keeping the Hall looking good, proud that the Stellions relied on her and appreciated her efforts. She had no education to speak of, so domestic work suited her just fine, and she couldn't envisage life outside Little Grindle. She had everything she wanted. Well, almost.

~

Dora finished cleaning the little library, leaving it smelling of lavender polish. She was taking the vacuum cleaner down the corridor to Mr Stellion's study when she thought she heard the sound of running water. That must be the rain falling. It had continued unusually heavily this morning. She thought Tom would have found Nell something to do under cover, and Gina was quite capable of disobeying any instructions to go out if it didn't suit her.

Now she could hear quite a loud splashing sound. It would be irresponsible not to make sure everything was all right. She left the vacuum cleaner outside the study door and continued down the corridor in the direction of the watery noise, which by now she could tell was coming from the conservatory. She opened the door and . . .

'Oh, good heavens!' she exclaimed.

Water was pouring through the roof! A huge puddle had formed on the floor and was flowing – actually *flowing* – towards the door, threatening to flood into the corridor.

Dora shut the door and ran as fast as she could to find Mrs Thwaite.

~

Gina was playing with Coco in the dry of one of the outbuildings, encouraging him to jump over a little hurdle she'd made of a broom handle between bricks, when Ellen arrived at the door, rain running off her mac and sou'wester.

'Gina, you're to take Coco inside now and come and help us. Mrs Stellion says so. The conservatory's flooding and we're all needed to help clear up before the water gets in the house.'

'What? A real live flood?' This was exciting news in so many ways.

'I said so, didn't I? Don't stand there looking pleased about it, you daft bat. Take the dog inside and come now!' Ellen ran off, leaving Gina to do as she was told. Normally Gina would have taken her time to follow any instructions Ellen gave her, but she was eager to see the flood and hurried Coco in through the door to the downstairs corridor, quickly towelling him dry and wiping his feet.

'Come on, Coco,' she said, running up the stairs to the main hall. 'This is something I can't wait to see.'

She ran along to the conservatory where her mother, Ellen and Uncle Tom, all wearing wellingtons and macs, were sweeping what looked like gallons of water out through the French doors into the garden, while, almost as quickly, rain poured in through the roof to replenish the flood.

'Heck . . .' said Gina, admiring the chaos.

'Gina, take the dog away, and go and put on your mac and wellies,' said Tom calmly. 'Then come back as quickly as you can and you can help Nell to move these chairs and the pots out of the way.'

'Yes, Uncle Tom.'

She turned to go and almost bumped into Mrs Thwaite.

'Out of my way and do as you're told, girl,' snapped the housekeeper, which made Gina decide not to hurry. 'I've telephoned the handyman in Great Grindle,' she said to Tom. 'He should be here soon to assess the job of making the roof watertight again.'

'Good. We'll get rid of as much water as we can and clear a space for him to work in,' Tom replied. 'No, Mrs Thwaite, don't you come in here, in those shoes . . .'

But Mrs Thwaite had foolishly tiptoed into the conservatory in her leather-soled shoes, intent on taking some chair cushions to safety, and at once her feet slipped from under her.

'Aah!' She went down hard on the floor, a gigantic splash of rainwater making a mini tidal wave around Tom, Dora and Ellen's boots. 'Oh, my arm! My arm!' she screamed, rolling onto her back in agony in the flood waters.

Tom, Dora and Ellen left their brooms and buckets and rushed over to help the wailing woman, trying to get her to sit up.

'I'll get Mrs Stellion,' said Gina, and ran off to the morning room, Coco, on his lead, racing beside her, barking excitedly.

Oh, but this was amazing! Gina wished she had a moment to think it all through, but she needed to act quickly and do as she was told, while events were playing entirely into her hands.

Edith Stellion was in the morning room as usual, keeping out of the way of the flood.

'Ah, Gina, there you are. Bad news, I'm afraid. Rain is coming in through the conservatory roof. I've just telephoned my husband to tell him and he's coming home straight away.'

'Yes, Mrs Stellion. Ellen told me to bring Coco back and to go and help. But there's worse news. Mrs Thwaite has slipped on the wet floor and I think she may have broken her arm.'

Mrs Stellion stood up, putting a cooling hard to her forehead in her accustomed manner. 'Oh, but this is terrible. I must go to her.'

'Uncle Tom, Mum and Nell are there seeing to her,' said Gina, settling Coco in his basket.

'If her arm is broken she will need to go to hospital at once,' said Mrs Stellion. 'I must find out.' She made for the door.

Gina thought quickly. 'Don't go and slip on the floor too,' she said. 'Let the others bring Mrs Thwaite safely out into the dry and then you'll be able to see how bad she is. I couldn't bear it if you were hurt too.'

'Dear child . . .' Mrs Stellion touched her hand to Gina's cheek in a motherly way. 'Get your waterproofs and wellies on, Gina, and then at least you'll be quite safe. I'll go and see what I can do and I promise not to get my feet wet.'

They left the room together, shutting Coco in, and then parted ways in the hall, Gina to fetch her coat and boots and Mrs Stellion to tend to her ailing housekeeper.

She found Mrs Thwaite lying wetly on the corridor carpet, holding her arm and moaning in pain.

'Do you think you could stand, Mrs Thwaite?' she asked. 'Come and lie down on the sofa in my husband's study.' She moved the vacuum cleaner out of the way and opened the door. Then Tom and Dora helped the housekeeper to her feet, careful to avoid touching her arm, and manoeuvred her into the room.

'Such a stupid thing to do,' wept Mrs Thwaite, her bedraggled hair dripping down her soaking back and the hem of her skirt clinging and heavy with rainwater. 'I'm so sorry, Mrs Stellion. I was only trying to help.'

'Sit down and let's look at that arm,' Mrs Stellion said.

'No, don't touch it!' screeched the housekeeper.

'I think it must be broken and you must go to

hospital,' said Mrs Stellion. 'I shall go and telephone for an ambulance.'

'No need,' said a voice from the corridor. George Stellion appeared, still wearing his motoring gloves. 'I shall drive Mrs Thwaite to the hospital myself. It will be quicker.'

'Oh, George, thank goodness you've come.'

'I can see what's happened, Edith. Come along, Mrs Thwaite, let me help you to the car,' he said. He assisted the groaning woman through the house and out of the front door. His enormous shiny car was parked at the foot of the steps.

'Lean on me, Mrs Thwaite,' he offered, holding an umbrella over her.

Everyone crowded round the front door to watch. Gina, in her mac and sou'wester, ran out and took the umbrella, while Mr Stellion opened the door and very carefully helped his housekeeper into the front passenger seat. Then, while he went round to get in the car on his side, Gina folded the umbrella and stood it in the footwell where it dripped on Mrs Thwaite's feet, then closed the car door firmly.

As the car pulled away, Gina gave Mrs Thwaite a big smile and waved her off.

~

The clean-up took a while but eventually a row of galvanised buckets was placed under the leaking seam in the glass roof, the water was swept outside and the handyman from Great Grindle arrived and assessed the repair needed.

'Good work, girls,' Tom said to Dora and his nieces. 'We'll need to keep emptying these buckets, but I think the rain is easing off now. I'm right proud of you all.'

'Aye, it takes an Arnold to resolve a crisis,' said Gina cheekily.

Or to make one! She was by now desperate to have some time alone to think through what had happened. The spell she'd cast the previous day had read confusingly in the old book, and she wasn't sure she'd understood what she had to do, or if the elements she'd gathered to cast it were even the right ones, but she had known what she wanted to achieve. The book of spells had instructed Gina to write down on a small piece of paper what she wished for and she'd written down that she wanted Mrs Thwaite taught a lesson for her rudeness. Now it seemed her powers had not failed her. And how! A deluge, no less, had dealt the necessary blow to the interfering housekeeper. Mrs Thwaite would not be troubling Gina for a while if her arm really was broken. It was a lot to take in. Could she really have conjured up this vast amount of rain – with all its consequences – just from the spell she'd cast in her bedroom?

Tom and Ellen left through the conservatory when the drama was over, and Dora and Gina came back along the corridor.

'Well, that's put me behind,' said Dora. 'Let's just see if Mrs Bassett can find us a sandwich while we dry off. It's hardly worth you going home in this rain, just to come back in an hour or so to walk Coco.'

They met Mrs Stellion in the hall, keen to thank them.

'And yes, I've asked Mrs Bassett to prepare you lunch. Such a long morning for you both. Thank you for staying on to help, Gina. You really are such a sensible girl. Coco will need a good walk this afternoon at the usual time – if the rain isn't too heavy – but come and find me a few minutes early. I've been thinking, and I may have some news for you.'

'Yes, Mrs Stellion,' grinned Gina.

The implication was that this was news to Gina's advantage. She just hoped it meant she need never go anywhere near Fellside Farm and its potato fields.

CHAPTER SIX

GINA HAD TIME to kill between eating the sandwiches Mrs Bassett had made and going to hear what Mrs Stellion had to say. Tom and Ellen were in control of the ever-filling buckets, so Gina tacitly opted out of helping with those and, when she saw Dora disappearing into Mr Stellion's study, decided to take the opportunity to have a look upstairs. There was no danger of encountering Mrs Thwaite that afternoon.

She quietly went up and looked into the silent bedrooms one by one. The first was Mr and Mrs Stellion's, with books on little tables at either side of the bed, dressing gowns hung on the back of the door, and scent bottles, medicine bottles, brushes and a little vase of roses on the dressing table. From the threshold, Gina inspected the bright room with floral wallpaper and a floral carpet, then quietly closed the door and moved on. How could they sleep with all those flowers busily blooming all around them? No wonder Mrs Stellion often said she was exhausted.

Next Gina found what she decided must be the children's rooms, although the Stellion offspring were no longer children, of course.

James's room was plain and rather dark, with a lot of big furniture and a huge model of a Spitfire suspended from the ceiling. When he stayed here, did he wake in the morning and think he was about to be strafed? There were books on shelves and on a stand by the bed. What a lot of books the Stellions had. So much time must be wasted just getting through them all.

Diana's room was, like her parents', papered in a flowery pattern, but the carpet and curtains were plain pale blue and the whole atmosphere was light and pretty, rather like Diana herself. Gina went in, closing the door behind her, and sat down at the dressing table. There was little on the surface – Diana must have taken her hairbrush, scent and jewellery to London with her – but Gina opened one of the drawers and found some thin pairs of leather gloves folded very flat, and a couple of pretty silk scarves. She took one out, unfolded it and wrapped it around her neck, looking at herself in the mirror. The scarf smelled of something wonderful, like roses but even rosier. The reflected sheen of the material brightened her face and, despite her old jumper, which was worn through at one of the elbows, and her awful breeches, she felt transformed. She lifted her ponytail and wound it up in a bun, admiring her reflection. She'd once seen Diana with her hair in such a style and she'd looked lovely.

For a moment Gina was tempted to help herself to the scarf, but when would she be able to wear it? Dora would be furious if she saw it and Philip would half kill her. It had been bad enough when she'd had to leave the job at the shop. Unconsciously she eased her shoulder where Philip had belted her. It was the hardest he'd ever hit her and it still felt stiff though it was months ago now. For days afterwards a tense silence had hung over the cottage, Dora and Ellen subdued by the fierceness of the punishment, as well as Gina. She folded up the scarf and put it back in the drawer, then opened another one.

This one had an untidy assortment of things in it: a train ticket dating from Christmas-time, a stiff card inviting Diana to a party last February, a couple of blunt pencils, a stray button and, most interesting, a little green leather coin purse. Gina opened it and shook the money out into her hand. It was mainly coppers but there was a florin. She took that and put the rest back.

Briefly, she inspected the bookshelves, which held some hardback novels, several in yellow dust jackets. Gina wasn't really interested in the books and she turned away, lay down on the big bed and thought about what had happened earlier.

The book of spells was real after all. There was no doubt of that in her mind now. When she'd cast the spell with the little bottle, she had wanted it to work but she wasn't entirely sure that it would. Then she'd thrown the bottle away into the field and the sheep and lambs had died. She wished they hadn't, but it wasn't as if they had names or anything; they weren't *loved.* Then she'd directed the second spell at Mrs Thwaite, and what a result that had been! Gina laughed quietly to herself: it was possible Mrs Thwaite wasn't loved either. She was a widow, her husband having been killed in the war, and Gina didn't know if she had any living relatives. Gina was excited to think she could have conjured up the unusually heavy rain, but the flooded conservatory had not only seen off Mrs Thwaite, it had resulted in Gina being cast in an even more favourable light than usual with Mrs Stellion. Gina didn't care at all that the house could have been flooded. The Stellions had lots of rooms to live in and lots of money to mend the roof. Oh, but it was fitting that it was the very room where Mrs Thwaite had told off Gina for sitting on the chair that had flooded. It was as if there was a pattern and, though she couldn't see it at the time, everything that happened was connected. Exciting it may be, but it was also a little bit frightening. She must be very careful what she wished for when she next cast a spell. These incantations were like sparks to a powder keg.

Just now, however, she didn't need to work any magic to get what she wanted. She had only to prepare and then listen to what Edith Stellion had to say.

There was a little gold-coloured bedside clock and Gina saw it was time to move. She slipped out into the corridor, made sure the coast was clear, and crept along to see what else there was. The next three rooms were all completely empty except for the furniture; the beds were bare, awaiting making up for guests. After that there was a nursery with a cot, a toy box, a rocking horse and shelves with boxes of board games and picture books. It was strange that the Stellions hadn't got rid of all that stuff by now. Diana and James must be in their early twenties. Still, in a place this size you could keep as much old rubbish as you wanted and never be in your own way.

Gina marvelled at the bathroom and lavatory she found next. Oh, the luxury! If only they had upstairs plumbing at the cottage, instead of having to trek out through the kitchen to the bathroom Mr Beveridge had added at the side, which was infested with spiders in autumn and freezing cold in winter. Before that they had had only the outside privy, a tin bath and the scullery. Mum had been very proud when her bathroom was built. Really, it was pathetic.

Around the corner at the end, as she'd hoped, there were more stairs, which also led down to become, she guessed, the ones she'd seen going up from the bottom corridor. Gina went up them and found a row of small attic rooms. One was used to store suitcases, a trunk with brass fastenings, and a wooden box with the initials 'J. A. S.' on the top. What could that be for? There were old hatboxes, too, and a brass bedstead. The next two rooms were plain and empty but for a narrow bed and chest of drawers in each: servants' rooms from the days when there were more staff here. Now, so few people worked here. Mrs Thwaite had a couple of rooms off the downstairs corridor, Mrs Bassett came in daily from the village, and Tom lived in the Lodge at the main gate. These attic rooms looked habitable, though. Gina tried the beds, looked at the views from the windows . . .

When she had completed her look round to her

satisfaction, Gina crept downstairs again. In the hall she saw her mother approaching, carrying her bag of dusters and polish and dragging the heavy vacuum cleaner behind her.

'Let me help you with that, Mum,' said Gina. 'I've been giving Mrs Bassett a hand. I'm going to take Coco out for his walk but I've time to take this down.' She pushed open the green door and took the vacuum cleaner down the stairs to the cleaning cupboard.

'Thank you. You're a good lass, Gina,' said Dora. 'It's been a tiring day. I wonder what the news is of Mrs Thwaite. Mr Stellion isn't back yet.'

'No doubt we'll hear soon,' said Gina. 'I'd best get on . . .'

She rushed away, back up to the hall, then opened the door and stepped calmly through. Mrs Stellion moved her activities – or lack of activity – to the sitting room in the afternoons. Gina went along and knocked.

'Come in, Gina. I knew it was you,' Mrs Stellion smiled. She was lying on the sofa with her feet up on the arm, reading a magazine. 'What a morning that was; I'm quite worn out.'

Gina came in and Coco gave a little bark, jumped out of his basket and came fussing round her feet, eager for his walk.

'I'm sorry to hear that, Mrs Stellion. Can I do anything for you?'

'No, dear, I have everything I need, thank you.' Mrs Stellion lowered her feet to the ground and sat up tentatively. 'Sit, Coco. *Sit.* Good boy. I just wish I knew how

Mrs Thwaite is. Such a horrid accident. If she has broken her arm, she may well be out of action for weeks.'

Or even longer, with a bit of luck. Though Mrs Thwaite had made it clear that Gina wasn't welcome in the house, Gina meant to make herself not only welcome but indispensable. If Mrs Thwaite was gone – if not for good, then for a good long time – then Gina's path onward and upward would be so much easier.

'I'm sorry to hear that,' said Gina.

'Well, it's about that possibility that I have a little plan, if you would agree to it? Oh, please sit down, dear. You're making my poor neck ache, looking up at you like that.'

Gina went to perch on the edge of an armchair and Coco, never a faithful puppy, went to sit at her feet, gazing up at her adoringly. Gina couldn't have wished for more at that moment.

'The thing is, Gina dear – and you must say if this doesn't suit you because I can always think again – if Mrs Thwaite is unable to work I shall need someone else to help me organise the house. It isn't a difficult job, but it does mean remembering to do lots and lots of little things: telephoning people, making sure letters are posted and things are ordered in time, seeing that the people who work for us in Little Grindle have what they need when they need it and are paid promptly . . . Do you see?'

Having lived in the village all her life, Gina knew several people who did some work for the Hall, washing and ironing, sending up orders of meat and vegetables and other goods.

'Yes, of course, Mrs Stellion,' said Gina, trying her hardest to look serious and professional, and not break out a huge grin.

'Now, I wouldn't expect you to step into Mrs Thwaite's shoes – that would be much too much to ask as I know you have no experience – but you're a willing and thoughtful girl, and so sensible. If you just kept things going while Mrs Thwaite recuperates, do you think you could manage? Do please tell me if I'm asking too much of you, dear. It would be unfair to overwhelm you. I could always get someone in from an agency, just temporarily, but I'd rather have you, whom I know and trust. What do you think, Gina?'

I think I can't believe my luck. It's just what I wished for but didn't really expect. That was powerful magic indeed. I've got rid of Mrs Thwaite, even if only for a while, and now I'm taking on her role! That'll show her, the spiteful old crone.

'Thank you, Mrs Stellion. It's kind of you to give me the chance, me being a beginner and all, and I know I've got a lot to learn.'

'You're a good girl, Gina. Maybe you'd like a little longer just to think it through, though?'

'Well . . . mebbe just while I take Coco for his walk? It's such a big thing I can hardly get my head round it.'

Mrs Stellion laughed and agreed. 'Off you and Coco go, then. The rain seems to be easing off a little and I think Coco needs a good walk this afternoon.'

'Yes, Mrs Stellion. Thank you. Come on, Coco.'

Gina got up and the little dog followed her out of the room. Once in the hall she picked him up and hugged him.

'Soon I shall be living here, Coco,' she whispered into his silky ear, 'and there'll be no more shabby cottage and Dad snarling and hitting out at us, spreading gloom and smelling of sheep all the time. And I shall have a room of my very own and get to meet all kinds of folk when they come here. And if Dad is so keen on the work at Fellside Farm, he can go and pick taters there himself.'

Laughing, she went to fetch Coco's lead from the boot room and then went down the back stairs to put on her coat and boots. If Mrs S wanted Coco to have a good long walk, then that is what he would have. Gina was careful to make their route go past the sitting-room window a couple of times.

~

'So what did you say?' asked Ellen, handing her mother and sister mugs of tea, barely able to believe her ears.

'I said I'd do it, of course. I'd be daft not to.'

'But you know nowt about housekeeping. You can barely lay the table.'

'Mrs S knows I know nowt but she's asked me to do it anyway.'

'You've done well, Gina, but I still can't think why she asked you,' said Dora. 'You did tell her the truth, didn't you?' she ventured anxiously.

'I told her no lies, Mum. She said she knew and trusted me, and she'd rather have me than someone from an agency while Mrs Thwaite's broken arm mends.'

'Ha! Knows and trusts you, my eye,' said Ellen. 'You've pulled the wool, haven't you?'

'I have not! She decided herself and then asked me. Just 'cos you're jealous, digging out in the wet garden while I'm the new housekeeper.'

'I'm not jealous of you, you little madam! At least I came by my work honestly—'

'Girls, be quiet, the pair of you. We've all had a trying day and I won't have the evening spoiled by you sniping at each other.' Whatever Dora's suspicions, she had to take on trust Gina's account of how her new position had come about, though she secretly felt put out that Gina was now her superior at the Hall.

'So Mrs Thwaite's arm *is* broken?' Ellen asked.

'Yes. Mr S came back while me and Mrs S were talking about my room at the Hall and told us both so.'

'*Room at the Hall?*' gasped Ellen.

'Yes, I'm going to have two empty rooms in the attic, where it will be nice and peaceful. One will be a bedroom and the other will be turned into my sitting room,' said Gina, beaming at her sister. 'I have the use of Mrs Thwaite's bathroom downstairs.'

'Good grief,' said Ellen flatly. 'I think I've heard it all now.'

'Of course, I couldn't have Mrs Thwaite's comfy rooms just yet, in case she comes back.'

'What do you mean?' asked Dora, looking stricken.

'The poor woman's not at death's door, is she? I thought you said it was just a broken arm.'

'It is, but badly broken. She's going to be in hospital for a few days and then she's going to stay with her sister, who lives in Great Grindle, Mr S said. He wonders if Mrs Thwaite might want to retire. She's getting on in years and it'll mebbe be a while before she fully recovers.'

'Well, you needn't sound so pleased about it, Gina,' said Dora. 'It's not decent to be glad about other folk's misfortunes.'

'Whose misfortunes?' asked Philip, coming in on the tail end of the news, dripping rainwater and smelling of the farmyard.

The three women related to him the story of the flood, Mrs Thwaite's accident and Gina's extraordinary promotion from dog walker to housekeeper.

'Well, I'm blessed,' he declared when they'd finished.

That's a first, thought Gina.

'And how much are they paying you?' he asked. He didn't sound at all happy about her news and perhaps hoped to catch her out.

Gina was pleased to name a sum that she'd guessed straight away was more than any of the rest of her family earned. 'But it's all right, Dad, I'll send some of it home,' she said graciously, 'what with my room and food being all included.'

For a moment Philip was speechless, but then he looked gloomier than ever. 'Just mind you do, Gina. You've never paid your way yet so I reckon you owe us quite a bit.'

'Don't be daft, Phil,' chimed in Dora. 'We don't expect our children to pay us to bring them up.'

'I didn't mean that, you soft woman,' he snapped. 'Just she's never earned owt much and paid her way before, that's all.'

'Well, that's all about to change so let's be glad for her,' said Dora, bringing the subject to an end. 'Now, we need to get our tea on the table. Gina, you can scrub those taters and put the oven on.'

'Yes, Mum, and then I'm off up to pack my stuff. I'm moving into the Hall tomorrow.'

'Good thing you've got the loan of the bicycle then,' said Ellen, 'because I shan't be lugging your bag over there.'

'Thanks, Ellen,' said Gina sarcastically. 'I'll remember that when I take the things over.'

It sounded like a threat, but Ellen was too tired to care after a day dealing with the flood. She felt sure the sound of water dripping into buckets would haunt her dreams that night. Still, there was a bright side to all this. At least she'd have the bedroom to herself for a while.

~

Next morning the rain had ceased but the sky was dismal and overcast. Ellen and Dora set out for the Hall at the usual time, leaving Gina to finish packing up her things and transport as much as she could in the bicycle basket. If there was too much, she'd have to make a second journey.

'I'd best go round to the back straight away and see how those buckets are,' said Ellen to her mother as they walked up the long drive towards the house. 'I think Uncle Tom will have been up all night emptying them.'

She was nearly right.

'Well, it stopped raining about midnight, and the dripping had slowed right down at about one o'clock,' Tom told her when she found him inspecting the buckets. He sounded surprisingly bright considering he'd been up half the night, but then he'd always been a cheerful sort. 'The good thing is, Mr Smithers from Great Grindle is coming over this morning with his fellas to fix it, so I'm hoping we've seen the last of the flood mess. Apart from the garden, that is.'

'Oh, no! What's happened?'

'You didn't think that much rain would have no effect, did you, Nell? Go and take a look at the rose garden. I'd like you to work on that today, please, but keep your mac on – it'll be a wet business. And take a wheelbarrow with you.'

'Sounds bad.'

'It is bad, lass.'

The rose garden was Ellen's favourite and Tom had given her plenty of responsibility to keep it looking good since she'd started working there. Her heart sank but she couldn't go without telling Tom about Gina's temporary new job as housekeeper.

'Before I go, I've some news that you'll be amazed by.'

'Well, I never,' said Tom, when she'd imparted all the details. 'And living in, you say? There's a turn-up . . .

Still, I expect Mrs Stellion knows what she's doing.' He didn't sound as if he meant it, but neither did he openly criticise. 'Right, Nell, off you go to see to those roses and I'm about the herbaceous. Come and find me if you need help.'

The rose garden was a disaster, the full blooms balled and heavy with rainwater, heads hanging down, petals that had been so perfect and fragrant two days ago now scattered and browning on the paths. In a couple of places the mature bushes, heavy with new growth and flowers, had been pulled away from their supporting trellis by the weight of water. The place looked a wreck.

Tears sprang to Ellen's eyes. What a mess! What a waste! All that work feeding and spraying, and just when the flowers were getting to their very best, this happened. Mrs Stellion was especially fond of her rose garden and she would be upset by this, too. Such cruel weather for the end of May, causing so many bad things: the flood, poor Mrs Thwaite with her broken arm, and now this . . .

Still, if Uncle Tom managed to put on a brave face then so would she. But it was with drooping shoulders and a grim face that Ellen went to fetch the wheelbarrow and her secateurs.

~

By the end of the day, Ellen had removed the ruined flowers that had dropped and pruned back any damaged bushes. She and Tom had tied back strong loose shoots between them and the rose garden looked tidy but depleted, while two days ago it had been lush and gorgeous.

Ellen viewed the wheelbarrow heaped with sodden, discoloured flower heads and suddenly she could contain her emotion no longer. Her shoulders heaved as she sobbed openly.

'Don't fret, lass,' said Tom, coming along between the rose beds. 'It's not spoiled for good. It'll come through this – and worse – and still be a credit to all your hard work.'

'Aye, I know, Mr Arnold,' said Ellen. 'But it just seems such a shame. I was that proud of what we'd done, and I wanted Mrs Stellion to enjoy her lovely garden at its best. I think she hardly saw it. I suppose that was pride before a fall, and it serves me right.'

'Nonsense, Ellen. First, it's nowt to do with you that it rained so hard, and why shouldn't you be proud of a job well done, anyway? And second, I happen to know that Mrs Stellion sometimes comes out here of an evening, when it's fine, and sits on that bench and has a little think or a little read of one of her books, and very much notices her rose garden. She may not do owt in terms of digging it, but that's what we're here for, and don't forget we get to enjoy it while it's looking good too.'

Ellen wiped her tears away and gave a wobbly smile. 'Of course, you're right, Uncle Tom . . . er, Mr Arnold. It's not our garden but we're lucky to be able to share in it a little.'

'Now you're thinking straight, lass; thinking like a proper gardener. And while Nature can destroy, it can heal too. And if it does the first then, in turn, it will surely do the second. There'll be another flush of roses later and, you never know, they could be all the stronger.'

Ellen nodded and lifted her head. 'Yes. Thank you, I feel better now.'

'Now off you go home. I'll tidy up here. I saw your mum a minute or two back waiting at this end of the drive for you. It'll be just you and her when you first get home tonight.'

Funny how Uncle Tom instinctively understood her, thought Ellen, gathering her gloves and making for the shed where she'd left her bag, before joining her mother in the drive.

'Tom says the garden's a mess,' said Dora, putting her arm round Ellen's weary shoulders.

'Aye, it was awful, but we've both been working on it and we're getting it nice again,' said Ellen.

'Are you all right, love? Looks like you've been crying.'

'A bit, Mum. It was like all our hard work had gone to waste, but Uncle Tom says it will sort itself out, with our help, in the end. He's such a kind man, isn't he? He makes me think that everything will be all right after all.'

'Oh, yes,' said Dora. 'Sometimes he makes me think that, too.'

~

Dora extracted the key from behind the boot scraper and unlocked the door.

'Right, just us till Dad gets home,' she said, stepping

inside. She pulled a greaseproof-paper parcel from her shopper. 'And look what I've got. Mrs Bassett said they were left over and I could take them.' She opened the bag to show Ellen some pieces of shortbread.

'Oh, what a treat. We haven't had cake for days . . . weeks, even.'

'Makes a nice change to have summat special with our tea. I'll put the kettle on, love, and you go and change out of those mucky breeches.'

Dora busied herself making a pot of tea while Ellen disappeared up to her room. Dora had just put the knitted cosy over the brown pot when there was a furious cry from upstairs. She rushed over and shouted up.

'Nellie, are you all right? What's the matter, love?'

'Oh, Mum,' wailed Ellen, appearing at the top of the stairs wearing her ancient petticoat with nothing over it. 'Gina's taken my frock and my skirt. She's even taken the only cardi I've got without holes in the sleeves. She's left me with nowt to wear!'

CHAPTER SEVEN

GINA LIKED PLAYING at being housekeeper. That's how the job felt to her: that she was playing the role. It had all the fresh appeal of novelty, but there was a constant thought at the back of her mind that the position wasn't a permanent one and that she'd be demoted back to dog walker as soon as Mrs Thwaite returned. That prospect was very disheartening. In the week since the rainstorm, she'd heard only that Mrs Thwaite was out of hospital and had gone to stay with her sister in Great Grindle.

'How is Mrs Thwaite?' she asked Mrs Stellion one morning in early June, hoping to hear bad news for Mrs Thwaite and good news for herself.

'I gather she's finding it quite difficult to manage with her broken arm,' Mrs Stellion replied. 'It's kind of you to ask. I think I should go and visit her. Her sister hasn't got a telephone, so I'll have to write and suggest a day. I'll do that now, so please would you post my letter for me when you take Coco for his walk?'

'Of course, Mrs Stellion.'

Gina considered not posting the letter, leaving Mrs Thwaite feeling abandoned by her employers, but then she herself would not learn whether Mrs Thwaite was recovering, and how quickly. She realised she needed to know how the land lay. Before she went out with Coco, she made a note of the address at which Mrs Thwaite was staying. Depending on the news, she might even visit the lady herself . . .

~

'I have news of Mr Shepherd,' Tom told Ellen as they set dahlias in the herbaceous border.

'Oh, is he all right? I've been thinking of him and, what with him being quite old, I'm worried that we won't be seeing him in the library van any more.'

But Tom's mind was first and foremost on the job in hand. 'This one's got a bit pot-bound. Here, let me show you how to tease the roots out . . . There, now I'd dig a bit deeper if I were you . . . He's got a bad hip and he's been finding driving the van and sitting at the desk all day very painful, so he's had to give it up.'

'That's a shame. So what that rude fella said about Mr Shepherd being "assigned to the archives" was a load of rubbish.'

'Yes, I'm afraid it was an unkind sort of joke.'

'It *was* mean – as if we wouldn't care about Mr Shepherd. I hope that awful man hasn't taken over Mr Shepherd's job as librarian, though I fear he might have.'

'Me, too. Let's see on Monday. How's *The Fickle Heart of Lady Blanche*, by the way?'

'Marvellous. Mum loved it, too.'

'Aye, your mother always did love a bit of romance. Nowt wrong with that, either . . . Now, this one comes up shorter – make a note of the name, Nell, and then you'll remember next time – so we should put that nearer the front so it's not hidden.'

'I saw in the picture book I borrowed how they planted the different heights in a border,' said Ellen. 'It's tricky to get both the heights and the colours to best advantage.'

'It can be, but if you keep noting things down in that exercise book of yours, and remember to use your eyes as well as your brain, you'll be all right.'

Ellen smiled and held up her book, showing Tom the soil-stained cover and handprints on the pages. 'I'm doing my best. I even drew a sketch of my favourite planting from one of the photos in the book, but it's hard to guess the colours in black-and-white.'

Tom laughed. 'It certainly is. Just think about what you're working with, Nell, and don't mind too much about photographs,' he advised. 'If you keep at it, you'll get there.'

'Yes,' agreed Ellen. 'I know you're right. Look at the rose garden: last week I thought all was lost, but after what we did to tidy it up, already it's beginning to look better. I'm right glad.'

'I told you Nature finds a way, with the help of a little nurture. And I reckon you've got the makings of a good gardener,' said Tom.

Ellen beamed. Tom was always ready to encourage and

to praise, though she thought it would take her a lifetime to learn everything he knew.

'So how did you hear about Mr Shepherd?' she asked.

'In the Lamb and Flag, of course. Reggie Travers told me Betty has made up an ointment for Mr Shepherd to try to ease the pain in his hip.'

'Betty's so clever. She knows about all sorts of cures, not just delivering babies. Where does Mr Shepherd live? Only if it's near I could go and see him; I don't want him to think his old readers don't care about him.'

'Or his young readers,' joked Tom. 'He's in Great Grindle, so you could get the bus, or walk if you've got the time. Hand me your notebook and I'll write down the name of the cottage . . .'

~

Gina liked the complete set of black clothes that Mrs Stellion had supplied as her uniform. They made the position of housekeeper seem as if it really was hers.

'I think you'll want to keep your own things for when you're not working,' Mrs Stellion had said kindly, eyeing the dress and cardigan Gina had presented herself in on her first day. Gina knew they weren't really right for the job, but they were Ellen's, and after Ellen had been so nasty about the housekeeping position, and unhelpful about lending a hand to move her things, Gina thought it only right to take them and teach her a lesson.

Dora had collared Gina soon after she'd arrived that first morning.

'You take those clothes back to Nell,' she'd ordered. 'That was a right mean thing to do, Gina.'

Gina had looked mutinous.

'Gina, you heard me, and you can do as you're told for once.'

'All right, Mum, I will,' Gina had said, but she'd kept the clothes until she had the black uniform, and then decided not to send any of her pay home until she'd bought herself a couple of new frocks.

It was typical of Nell to make a fuss about a shabby old frock and a hand-knitted cardi. It wasn't as if anyone important was looking at her anyway, digging in the dirt in the rain and then spending her free time with Ed Beveridge mooning over her, or else with Sally Mason, who was Nell's best friend and had been since infants' school, and who had been given the job at the shop when Gina herself was sacked over the missing money.

After a few days at Grindle Hall, however, it occurred to Gina that no one was looking at her there either. She'd thought life at the Hall would be fun, people coming and going all the time – interesting people who knew life beyond this half-dead corner of Lancashire – but no one exciting had visited so far. Mrs Bassett dealt with most of the deliveries at the back door: farmers and shopkeepers with food orders. Gina could meet farmers and shopkeepers in Little Grindle any time, and had no wish to do so now at the Hall.

Occasionally Mrs Stellion went out in the car, her husband driving, to see people Gina knew only by name, with no idea of who they really were: Mrs Peters, Mrs

Lampton, Miss Stanwick. So far, though, they had not visited in return, and after an afternoon out paying calls, Mrs Stellion often succumbed to a headache and went to lie down, leaving Gina with no one to talk to except her own mother, who was usually busy getting ready to go home by then, or Mrs Bassett, in whom she had no interest.

An awful thought crept into Gina's mind: *It's just as dull here as it was at the farm. Nothing ever happens! I thought I was getting on in life and instead I'm stuck in another dead end. And Mrs Thwaite might yet come back.*

It was a Friday afternoon and Mrs Stellion was out visiting her friend Miss Stanwick, who lived just outside Clitheroe. Gina was at a loose end and went into the garden to think things through.

She sat down on a bench on a sheltered side of the vegetable garden, leaned back and let her mind wander over the possibilities of her situation.

It had been quite a few days since Mrs Thwaite's accident; it was high time Gina found out whether the woman was intending to return to the Hall.

But you're just going to let her walk back in and do nowt about it, are you? a little voice in Gina's head asked. *You'd do well to make sure she doesn't come back at all.*

How was she to do that? Gina thought of the little book of spells in her attic room, hidden away, but the magic had proved to be very powerful, and with a little careful planning it might not be necessary to unleash its force, especially if Mrs Thwaite wasn't coming back anyway. Just a little nudge in the right direction might persuade her that life with her sister had a lot more to offer than resuming her work at the Hall. After all, everyone had a secret that they might not wish other folk to know about . . .

An idea was forming in Gina's head and she was just about to get up to follow it through when she heard voices close by. It was her own name that caught her attention.

She kept quite still and listened. Soon she realised it was her mother and Tom Arnold; they must be just the other side of the hedge, next to the shed where Tom kept the lawn mower.

'Aye, she seems to be making an effort this time,' Dora said. 'I haven't heard of anything going wrong yet. Or going missing, either.'

Tom gave a short laugh. 'And what does Phil make of Gina's success?'

'Oh, you know Phil. Every night he comes home and asks if she's been sacked yet. Poor Gina, it's no wonder she's left home to live here. She's always looking to get just what she wants and she doesn't mind how she gets it. I've tried to tame her wildness with a mother's love, but it's not enough when the only attention she's ever got from her own father has been him expressing his disappointment or anger or serving up some punishment.'

'He's a miserable bugger,' said Tom. 'I don't know how you girls put up with him.'

'He's hard work, and no mistake,' said Dora. 'He's a difficult man to love.' She sighed again.

'Then leave him,' said Tom suddenly.

'What?'

'Leave him. Come and live with me at the Lodge.'

Gina, now with an ear pressed close to the hedge, held her breath, and there was a long silence, so she guessed Dora was probably holding hers too.

'Don't be daft,' she said eventually. 'You know I can't. It's not like you to make an unkind joke, Tom.'

'I'm not making a joke, lass. But you're right: forget what I said. It wasn't the right thing at the right time. I would never mean to upset you.'

'You haven't,' Dora said, but she sounded teary.

'Here, love, dry your eyes.'

'Thank you.' Dora's voice was now muffled, by Tom's handkerchief, Gina guessed. 'Oh, Tom, I do understand what you're saying, and I feel the same, but I can't go back on my marriage vows. I made a promise before God and that can't be undone.'

There was a long sigh.

'I respect how you feel, lass,' said Tom heavily, 'but I live in hope that one day I'll be able to "love and honour" you. I'd never raise a hand to you nor waste our time together with grumbling and moaning and being angry.'

'I know . . .'

'We could make each other so happy. We only have one life, love, so why waste it being miserable because of the mistakes we made long ago?'

'I've told you why, Tom. I just wish . . . But it's too late. I've made my bed and I must lie in it,' said Dora unhappily.

'Oh, Dora, love, that sounds so bleak. Promise you'll think on what I've said.'

'I'll think on it, Tom – I reckon I'll be unable to think of owt else – but I can't promise owt either. I'm still married to Phil and I still made those vows.'

They were silent for a few moments and Gina thought they might be kissing.

'Poor Phil,' said Tom, then. 'Nobody loves him. I almost feel sorry for him. Almost.'

But not as sorry as he feels for himself, thought Gina.

She sat quite still, hardly daring to breathe. She'd known her mother and Tom got on well, and were friendly and agreeable in each other's company, whereas with Dora and Philip the relationship was always marred by tension, and by Philip's violent temper and black moods. But to hear this! Tom's hopes were what Gina herself had dreamed up when she'd cast the spell to get rid of Philip: Dora and Tom would live happily at the Lodge, and there would be room for her and Ellen, too. Now Gina lived at the Hall, but her mother and sister were stuck at the cottage with Philip casting a black cloud of misery over their lives, not to mention resorting to violence against them if he felt especially out of sorts.

Well, she'd keep quiet about what she'd learned – for the time being. If Dora and Tom didn't bring this about themselves, Gina might reveal what she had heard in her own time, when the moment was right, and spur them on their way to a future together. That would serve her father right!

Gina grinned as she imagined for a few moments life

after her father had been completely abandoned by her mother. She'd never have to go back to the cottage and find him there again, because Mum and Nell would be at the Lodge with Tom. She herself would just avoid him if she saw him heading her way. She wouldn't have to feel the force of his slap if she answered back, nor have to endure the joy being sucked out of every home situation, nor see Mum and Nell subdued and tense, tiptoeing round him to avoid his sulks or, worse, his fists. Sometimes she'd speed past the Lodge in a big shiny car – she hadn't decided whose car it was yet – and see, in the soft light of the uncurtained window, Mum and Uncle Tom sitting together, smiling companionably, in the little sitting room. Then, one morning, Dad would turn up at the back door of Grindle Hall, a broken man without Mum, repentant of his past harshness to his wife and daughters, begging for a job – anything, even scrubbing the floors – and Gina would say, 'There's nothing here for the likes of you. I hear they want someone to pick taters at Fellside Farm. Try there, and don't bother us here again.' And Mum and Nell and Uncle Tom would all be standing there laughing . . .

Gina pulled herself out of her reverie to listen again.

Dora said she must go, then Tom said something Gina couldn't hear, and there was the crunch of gravel as one or both of them walked away.

Gina made herself very small on the bench in the hope that if either of them came past she wouldn't be noticed, but the garden on this side of the hedge remained empty. Eventually she felt it was safe to get up and go back to the house, her mind full of what she had heard.

It wasn't until she was inside that she remembered she had been about to do something. Now, what was it? Oh, yes, Mrs Thwaite . . .

~

'You get yourself off home, if you want, Mrs Bassett,' said Gina. 'I can dish up Mr and Mrs S's tea.'

'That's good of you, Gina. I'll put it in the bottom oven, and it'll be ready when they are. Just warm that tureen and ladle it in carefully. Are you sure you can manage the potatoes?'

'Yes, I'm sure,' said Gina drily. *Taters are about the one thing I can cook!*

'There's enough for you to have a helping, too, of course.'

'Thank you, Mrs Bassett.' *Will the woman never stop fussing?*

Then Mrs Bassett took an age to change into her outdoor shoes, and then had to look into the oven to be sure all was well, then thought of something to write down on her shopping order before she forgot, then had to check the oven again. Then she wasn't sure whether one of the lamps on her bicycle was working properly and had to take it apart and put it back together again, although, this being June, it would be light enough for her to cycle all the way to Preston without lamps, Gina thought. All was done at a pace that made Gina gnash her teeth.

She'd no sooner waved Mrs Bassett away and taken the

key to Mrs Thwaite's sitting room from the hook in the kitchen than she heard the sound of car tyres crunching up the drive and round to the garage.

Damn it! And I'm left with their tea to finish getting ready, too.

Mrs Stellion came in through the back door, as she often did when the car was round the back, and Coco rushed in with her, barking and grinning as only a spaniel can.

'Gina, hello, my dear. I've had a lovely time at Mildred Stanwick's but I'm so tired now. Coco isn't a bit tired, are you, my darling? Good boy, Coco, *good boy*. Gina will take you for a nice long walk while Mummy puts her feet up. Have you had a good afternoon, Gina? Did you get everything done?'

'Not quite everything, Mrs Stellion, but, yes, it's been a very interesting afternoon. And I'll get the rest done just as soon as I can.'

~

The following Monday saw the mobile library parking by the Lodge at the front gate. Ellen trooped down the drive carrying her books, but she no longer felt the delightful anticipation of a few minutes browsing the shelves. Mr Shepherd's charming manner and generous sharing of his knowledge were as important a part of the library visits as the books themselves, she now realised, and the surly young man who had taken his place put a dampener on the whole event.

Tom, as usual, went to fetch his books from the Lodge, while Ellen presented hers at the desk.

'How are you returning four books?' asked the librarian. 'You know the rules permit only three per person.'

'This one is on Tom Arnold's ticket, if you remember,' said Ellen, handing over *The Fickle Heart of Lady Blanche.*

'I remember no such thing,' the librarian said. 'The library lends out hundreds of books – I can't be expected to remember who borrows every trashy potboiler. That's what the card index and ticket system is for.' He said this last sentence very slowly, and with unnecessary emphasis, as if Ellen were slow-witted.

'Then I think if you look under Tom Arnold's card you'll find the ticket for this novel,' Ellen said with quiet dignity. 'I am simply returning this book for my uncle while he fetches the others he borrowed.'

She resisted the temptation to look away and instead drew inspiration from Tom's actions the last time, and gave the librarian the benefit of a questioning raised eyebrow. Really, she thought, I shouldn't have to face an ordeal every time I want to borrow or return a few books.

He hurriedly turned to his card index, knowing he had overstepped the mark.

Tom appeared with his heavy classic tomes, both of which he had read in the fortnight, and he and Ellen browsed the shelves, their backs to the rude man. Ellen tried to relax and pretend that it was Mr Shepherd at the desk, but she knew if she chose the frivolous romances that she and Dora liked, she would be faced with the young man's superior attitude as he stamped the books.

All the joy had been well and truly removed from library day.

Tom chose a couple of books and saw that Ellen hadn't found anything.

'Choose summat you and your mum would like, lass,' he said softly. 'Yon fella probably doesn't know a rose bush from a cabbage, so why should you care what he thinks?'

Ellen nodded and quickly picked three titles, but she didn't really feel engaged with the treat of selecting new books now. She half hoped Tom would swap them for his own choices at the desk and stare down the man's sneer but he didn't. Tom was clearly letting her fight her own battle today.

The books were stamped in a tense silence between Ellen and the librarian, though Tom looked quite relaxed as he scooped up his books.

'See you next time,' he said cheerily as he stepped out of the van.

The librarian cleared this throat. 'There is one thing,' he said, looking uncomfortable. 'Mrs Thwaite borrowed some books last time and I need them back. That is, I wondered if you would get them . . . as I know she's not well, like, and she won't want to be running up a fine.'

'A fine, you say?' said Tom, turning back and looking interested. 'Well, I reckon she won't be fined unless you fine her.'

'Yes, that's true.'

'And since you know she's not well, why would you be imposing a fine?'

'It's the rules,' said the librarian sullenly. 'I have to impose the fine if the books are late back.'

'Do you?' asked Tom, as if he were fascinated by this information. 'But who's to know? After all, the lady's circumstances are no fault of her own, as you seem to be aware, and I think I'd be right in saying she always returns her books on time normally as she's a library regular. Would it not be an act of kindness, then, to forget the fine, as Mrs Thwaite is away recovering and can't give you the books herself?'

'But I need to keep to the rules. I'm not allowed to make exceptions. You could get them, couldn't you? As you work here?'

Tom looked at the librarian for a long time until the penny dropped.

'Please?' the young man added.

'I don't work in the house and I can't get the books for you,' said Tom.

'Oh, but—'

'But I can ask for Mrs Thwaite's books to be brought out to you.'

'Thank you,' the librarian muttered.

Tom and Ellen slipped through the little gate, Ellen waited while he put his books inside the Lodge, then they walked up the drive together.

'What was that all about?' said Ellen. 'The man's obsessed with his rules, but why is he so bothered about Mrs Thwaite's books? I doubt he'd care about *us* running up fines.'

'Oh, I think he must know Mrs Thwaite,' said Tom.

'He was new to the library last time but he knows her name and seems to care, in his own strange way, that she shouldn't be fined. Anyway, I'll take your books and put them in the shed while you go and find Gina and ask her if she'd mind dealing with Mrs Thwaite's books.'

Gina didn't mind at all. In fact she was surprisingly chipper about running the errand for Mrs Thwaite.

'I'll see if I can find them,' she said, and went to fetch the key to Mrs Thwaite's room from the hook in the kitchen.

~

Mrs Thwaite's room was neat to the point of severity, Gina was pleased to see. Straight away she saw three books on a little table in the sitting room and a quick inspection showed them to be from the mobile library.

Gina decided to allow herself three minutes to see what useful facts she could find out about Mrs Thwaite. Quickly she opened the drawers in a little sideboard to one side of the fireplace: letters and stationery. Then she looked in the wall cupboard, but that was just crockery and, interestingly, a selection of glass tumblers.

Promising. And what does she drink out of those glasses, I wonder.

There was no obvious place to hide any bottles, so Gina ran into the bedroom and quickly searched under the bed, finding only a pair of worn slippers and a stray handkerchief. So now, the wardrobe or the chest of drawers?

She flung open the wardrobe door and the odour of mothballs enveloped her. Reaching in low, she pulled out a handbag from the floor of the wardrobe and felt about behind at the back. Hurray! A bottle of gin and, better still, a half-empty bottle of gin. Gina recognised the shape and the label from the bottles that the Stellions had on a tray in the sitting room.

I bet she's stolen them. And this awful smell of mothballs covers up any smell of the drink on her.

There was no time to contemplate Mrs Thwaite's Achilles heel any longer: the library van was waiting and Gina had been quite long enough 'finding' the books in a pristine room.

The mobile library was parked by Tom's house and there was no one else around. Nell sometimes spoke of an old fella called Mr Shepherd, so Gina envisioned an elderly, grey-haired and wrinkled librarian at the desk. What she saw was a darkly handsome young man just a few years older than herself. Not Mr Shepherd, then.

'Are those Mrs Thwaite's books?' he asked, looking carefully at Gina's face.

Both Gina and Ellen were used to people remarking on the likeness between them, and so Gina knew why the man was gazing at her.

'Who's asking?' she said.

'I am the librarian,' he answered unhelpfully.

'Yes, I can see that,' Gina replied, 'but who are you to Mrs Thwaite that you should be so keen to have the poor lady's books returned . . . to save her being fined, I gather?'

'Mrs Thwaite is my aunt,' the man disclosed reluctantly.

'Oh . . . so you must be Mrs Thwaite's sister's son,' ventured Gina. 'And Mrs Thwaite is staying at her sister's recovering?'

'Yes,' said the man, wondering how this pretty young woman knew so much. 'Aunt Eliza is at our house until she's better.'

'And how is Mrs Thwaite?' asked Gina. 'I was that sorry to hear that her arm is broken.'

'It's a bad break but she's mending slowly.'

'Well, it's right decent of you to ask for her books back, Mr . . .?'

'Hillier.' The unfriendly man was shaking Gina's proffered hand before he knew it.

'Mr Hillier, a pleasure to meet you. So, here are your aunt's books back.' She took her time opening them to the date-stamped pages, chatting all the while. 'And so is it just you and your mother, and now your aunt at home? I know Mrs Thwaite's husband was killed in the war . . . such a tragedy to be left alone. Except she's not alone now, of course.'

'Yes, my uncle died in the war, and my father, too.'

'That's a shame. Leaving you and your brothers and sisters to be brought up by your mum.'

'Just me. I have no siblings. It was just me and Mum.'

Mummy's boy, I expect.

'She must be so proud of you, running the mobile library, taking this big van out every day.'

'Oh, I don't run the library, exactly, but, yes, it's a lot of work . . . long days.'

'Mm, I should think so. Do they ever give you a day off?'

Mr Hillier brightened. 'Saturday afternoons and Sundays,' he disclosed.

'Oh, yes . . .?'

'What about you, Miss . . . er, Miss Arnold?'

'Yes, that is my name.' Gina was enjoying herself.

'I meant, do you get a day off?'

'I do indeed,' said Gina. 'Now are you going to take in these returns or not?'

As Gina walked back up the drive to the Hall she felt well pleased with herself. If she played her hand carefully, the housekeeper's job was hers for good and Mrs Thwaite would not be returning. What she needed after that was a plan to liven things up at the Hall and make sure Mrs Stellion knew just what a treasure her new housekeeper was.

CHAPTER EIGHT

IT WAS GLOOMY that Wednesday and looked like rain.

'Take the afternoon off, if you want, Nell,' said Tom as they tied some runner beans to a lattice of canes. 'We'll be done here shortly, and I wonder if you'd like to go and see Mr Shepherd. I'd be glad of some news of him.'

'Thank you, Mr Arnold. I'll see if I can persuade him to return to the mobile library,' Ellen said with a smile.

'Do, if he's feeling better. We'll be glad to see him and so, I gather, will a lot of his regulars, though I reckon he's probably retired for good. He must be nearly seventy.'

'Mebbe so. Do you think I could take a few flowers for him, please? I know they're Mr and Mrs Stellion's, of course, but they let us cut some for ourselves so p'raps it would be all right if I gave Mr Shepherd what I might have taken for myself?'

'I think on this one occasion it would be fine,' said Tom. 'Don't take owt in bud, though.'

Ellen decided that she'd like some company on her visit to Great Grindle, a walk of about two miles if she cut across the fields. She went to see if her friend Sally Mason was available and willing to accompany her. It was half-day closing at the village shop in Little Grindle, so Sally might well be at home by now.

Moments after Ellen had knocked on the cottage door, Sally opened it, and the noise of a young and lively family burst out to greet Ellen.

'Nellie! Them flowers for me?'

'Go on with you. They're for Mr Shepherd. I thought I'd go and see how he is now he's retired with his hip from the mobile library. D'you want to come too? He lives in Great Grindle. I thought I'd walk but get the bus back if it comes on to rain.'

'I'd love to. You can tell me all your news while we go. Come in while I finish giving our Polly her dinner and get my shoes on.'

Ellen followed Sally inside to a chaos of infants, their half-eaten food, and their toys and clothes strewn around. One of the babies was bashing his dish with the end of his spoon while the other was singing raucously and tunelessly to himself. Polly, meanwhile, was telling off her teddy, with whom she shared her high chair, in a loud and bossy fashion.

'Mum, it's Nell. We're off to see Mr Shepherd, if that's all right?'

'Hello, Nell. All right, love? Aye, you go, Sal. Just spoon the rest of that down Polly and I'll see to the little 'uns. Give him my regards, won't you?'

Audrey Mason's twin babies were about a year old, and Polly was not yet three. Sally and her elder brother, Roger, were the children of her first marriage. Audrey's first husband had been in the navy and had been killed in the war, leaving her struggling, but then she had married Mr Mason, who had adopted Sally and Roger as his own children and given his adored and adoring new wife three more. Sally and Roger loved their new father and were overjoyed to see their mother happy at last.

Ellen always felt a little pang of regret about her own home life when she observed her friend's. The Arnolds had been married for years and should have been equally happy, in her view, but she felt her father's violent temper and bleak outlook on life had sucked the joy out of their lives. Truth be told, she preferred it at home when her father wasn't there.

'There you go, Poll. Last spoonful, big wide gob . . . and all done.'

Sally lifted Polly and her teddy out of the high chair and set them on the floor to play, then cleared away the dish that was now scraped clean of rice pudding, kissed her mother and the babies, tied on her lace-ups, grabbed an umbrella from by the door and pulled the door to behind her and Ellen, abruptly shutting off the noise.

She paused to enjoy the moment. 'I love 'em to bits but, oh, it's nice when the row they make stops,' she laughed.

Ellen and Sally set off along the village main street, turned down a lane that cut off a big corner from the journey by road, then skirted some hilly fields via a series of stiles, keeping close to the dry-stone walls.

Sally asked how Ellen was getting on at the Hall and Ellen told her how the rose garden was recovering from the rainstorm and that her uncle Tom had given her responsibility for looking after it. Then they talked about who had been in the shop and what news Sally had learned from the customers this week.

'Gina's getting very grand, isn't she, ordering in by telephone for Mrs Stellion?'

Ellen laughed. 'Aye, she seems to have got the hang of using the telephone and taking over from Mrs Thwaite. I don't know how she's learned to do it but she has.'

'Mr Fowler isn't keen to deal with Gina after . . . you know,' Sally lowered her voice, though there was no one around to hear her, 'that business with the money, but of course he wants to keep the Stellions as customers and it's Gina who does the ordering in. I don't mind taking the orders from her. If Gina's turned over a new leaf, surely it's a good thing and nowt to be bearing a grudge about. Good luck to her, I say.'

'Well, I can understand Mr Fowler's point of view a bit,' said Ellen. 'Still, it's a huge relief to see Gina getting on at the Hall. I admit it's a welcome surprise.'

'Between you and me, I don't think it's a difficult job, Nell,' Sally said. 'I heard from Mrs Bassett that Mrs Stellion doesn't really need a housekeeper at all, with there being only the two of them living there now, and Mrs Bassett cooking their meals and your mum keeping the house nice. Mrs S only keeps on Mrs Thwaite because she's been there for years and wants to continue working.'

'Then why would she replace her with Gina, even though it's only temporary? Surely she'd have no one if she could do without.'

'Aye, well, there you have it. Mum reckons Mrs Stellion just likes to have someone about the place to talk to. Apparently she had a baby that died and this child would have been about Gina's age by now. Mebbe she likes to have a young person around now James and Diana aren't living at home and she thought she'd bring Gina more . . . kind of into the limelight, if you know what I mean.'

'Goodness, that's very sad. Poor Mrs S. She must be lonely, I suppose, with Mr S out quite a bit and her children not there much, and her feeling poorly. Well, I think it's nice for Gina to be appreciated . . . so long as she behaves herself.'

They both rolled their eyes, remembering numerous occasions when Gina had very definitely not done so.

Great Grindle came into sight and the girls were relieved it was a downhill walk all the way to the little town. Clouds were gathering on the fells and Sally's curly hair was forming increasingly tight corkscrews on her fair head.

'I think I'll be glad of this umbrella,' she said. 'Now, where does Mr Shepherd live? Don't tell me you don't know?'

'Uncle Tom gave me the address. Bookworm Cottage,

would you believe? It's on Main Street, so I reckon we'll find it easily enough.'

They walked along past shops until the street became residential and they found the right name on a little wooden gate leading to a tiny front garden and a neat and very old-looking little house.

Ellen knocked, they waited, and then the door opened and there was Mr Shepherd. His face lit up when he saw his visitors.

'Ellen, Sally, come in, come in. Oh, it's so good to see some young and friendly faces.'

The door opened into a very low-ceilinged sitting room, the beams visible, bookcases lining the walls. Mr Shepherd showed them in, then hobbled over to an armchair, relying heavily on his walking stick.

'Sit down, ladies.' He indicated the sofa with his stick.

'These are for you, Mr Shepherd,' said Ellen, handing over the flowers wrapped in newspaper. 'Oh, perhaps you'd like me to put them in water for you?' Feeling silly, she took them back.

'Thank you, Ellen. So kind. There's a vase on the windowsill in the kitchen.' He pointed to a door at the back.

When she returned with the flowers in a vase, Sally and Mr Shepherd were laughing about something. Ellen now noticed there was a kind of bunting along the low central beam of the ceiling, made of old book jackets stuck up with drawing pins.

'I was just telling Sally,' Mr Shepherd said, seeing where she was looking, 'it's to remind visitors to duck their heads.'

'Duck or grouse,' giggled Sally, and the other two groaned at the old pun.

'My, but those flowers are grand,' said Mr Shepherd. 'Thank you.'

'Mrs Stellion allows Uncle Tom and me to take a few when we're tidying up,' Ellen explained, anxious that the elderly librarian shouldn't think she'd pinched them.

The girls asked after Mr Shepherd's health and then Sally said, 'Mr Shepherd, you must tell us about your books.' Her eyes were wide as she took in that there were many hundreds in the room. 'Have you read them all . . .?'

And so the afternoon passed in wonderful bookish talk.

When it was time to go, the girls left with a list of reading recommendations, Mr Shepherd's good wishes to pass on to Sally's mother and Ellen's uncle, and an invitation to the girls to call again as soon as they could.

'I'm so glad to see you,' Mr Shepherd said, reluctantly showing them out late in the afternoon. 'It's good to see young people, and to exchange some views and learn how folk are doing.'

'Don't you have many visitors?' Sally asked, while Ellen dug her discreetly in the ribs, but Mr Shepherd didn't seem to mind the question.

'A few. Folk round here are good souls, but it's not like going all over in the library van every day. I used to meet all sorts in the villages around here, but I reckon

I won't see some of them again. It's amazing what you get to know about people from the books they borrow and the pleasantries exchanged over the years. You get to care, like.'

He looked sad and Ellen noticed how his shoulders drooped and the lines of arthritic pain were etched in his friendly old face when he let down his guard.

'We'll let any regulars of yours we see know that you'd be pleased for them to visit, if you like?' she suggested.

'Yes, Ellen, thank you. I'd be glad to see any who're prepared to drop by,' Mr Shepherd said, 'what with me finding it difficult to go far myself now. And I'll see you both again soon, I hope?'

'Yes, please,' they chorused, and waved as they went to the gate.

It wasn't raining yet and they decided to walk home to save the bus fare.

'It always seems more uphill going back from Great Grindle,' said Sally. 'It can't be, though, can it?'

'It's 'cos the really steep bit is at the beginning this way. I'm so pleased we decided to go, though.'

'Your idea. Thanks for asking me. He's such a lovely man.'

'I wanted to ask about the new librarian, but he made a mean joke about Mr Shepherd being "assigned to the archives", which Uncle Tom and me think was heartless, so I didn't like to mention the new fella and spoil the afternoon.'

'No, I reckon it was telling that Mr Shepherd didn't ask about him or mention him either,' said Sally.

'I don't even know what he's called, and I'm not sure I want to.'

'I do 'cos Mum just asked outright, but I won't tell you if you don't want me to.'

'Oh, go on then.'

'Lucas Hillier.'

'Lucas? I don't know anyone called Lucas.'

'You do now, Nellie. What happened was this. Mum took the babies into the library van and of course they began making a noise – not yelling or anything but just being babies – and this Hillier fella started on about silence in the library, as if people don't go and chat in there. So Mum said summat like, "Let me introduce you to the little 'uns and you can address your concerns to them. This is David and this is Frank. And your name is . . .?" And the fella was so startled that he said his name like he was speaking to the twins so now we know what he's called. Then Mr Fowler came in and started making a fuss of the babies, and Mum said, "Mr Fowler, this is Mr Lucas Hillier, our new librarian, and he's just about to tell David and Frank the rules about visiting the library." Of course, that shut up Lucas Hillier, and serves him right.'

'Your mum's brilliant,' laughed Ellen. 'My mum will be amused by that story, and so will Uncle Tom.'

Ellen said goodbye to Sally at the Masons' cottage and walked on to the lane that led to Highview Cottage and, ultimately, Highview Farm. As she went, swinging her satchel, she thought of how pleased Mr Shepherd had been to see his visitors, and she wondered if – as Sally's mother had suggested to Sally – Mrs Stellion felt like that about Gina and that was why she employed her. She clasped her hands together and muttered a kind of prayer-wish that the lonely lady would not regret her decision.

~

Edith Stellion had gone to see a private doctor in Preston about her headaches and exhaustion that Wednesday afternoon, leaving Gina with the task of going to buy the special rose-scented soap she liked to use from the smart chemist's shop in Great Grindle.

Until a few weeks ago, Gina would have taken the short cut over the fields on foot but, wearing her shiny new black shoes, and with the fare to spare, she decided to take the bus.

Gina knew the name of the chemist's and exactly where it was, but she had never been in before. A bell tinkled loudly as she opened the door and the scent that greeted her was comforting: talcum powder, something vaguely medicinal and a sweet floral soap smell.

Gina circled the shop, looking at the displays of goods in pretty and expensive-looking packaging: soap in boxes, face powder in round cardboard tubs with satin bows decorating the lids, lipsticks in gold-coloured tubes. She looked to see where the sales assistants were. It all looked so tempting . . . Then she went over to the counter in front of a huge chest of glass-fronted drawers, each with a handwritten label above it in a tiny brass frame.

'Good afternoon, miss. How may I help?' asked the middle-aged man in a white coat, standing behind the polished wooden counter.

'Good afternoon,' replied Gina. 'I'd like two boxes of the special rose soap that Mrs Stellion of Grindle Hall always buys, please.'

'Of course,' said the man, and went across the shop to fetch them from a shelf devoted to fancy soap.

'And is this for Mrs Stellion herself?' he asked.

'Yes,' said Gina. 'She asks that you charge it to her account, please.'

'Of course, miss.'

The man wrapped the boxes in brown paper, which he tied with string and sealed with a paper sticker with the name of the shop printed on it in gold. He wrote out the bill in triplicate, then placed a copy of it and the parcel in a thick paper carrier bag and came round the counter to put it into Gina's hands.

'Thank you,' said Gina, smiling politely. 'Good afternoon.'

She left, the doorbell jingling merrily behind her. What a nice shop, she thought. She would not extract from her jacket pocket the lipstick she'd stolen until she got back to her rooms at the Hall. You never knew who was looking – or, in the case of the chemist's shop, not looking.

Her errand for Mrs Stellion accomplished, Gina decided it was time to pay a visit to Mrs Thwaite.

She'd made a note of the address of Mrs Thwaite's sister's house from the letter she'd been asked to post the previous week: 17 Lloyd George Road. She had no idea where that could be, but Great Grindle was quite a small place, so it surely wasn't far. She walked along Main Street, saw a newsagent's shop and went in to ask.

The man behind the sweets counter gave her directions.

For a brief second Gina thought of helping herself to a tube of Smarties as she left, but she knew newsagents were constantly on the lookout for people filching the sweets so she smiled and went out empty-handed.

She walked down Main Street, passing houses both big and small towards the end, then turned left, walked along a few hundred yards, turned left again and found the road she wanted. Number 17 was on the right-hand side, a stone-built semi-detached house with a straight tiled path to the front door and a single bay window on the ground floor.

Gina paused on the pavement to gather herself. *Come on, it's only stupid old Thwaite, with a broken arm. She's not going back to work at the Hall and now all you have to do is tell her that.*

Gina straightened her back, opened the gate and marched up to the front door. She rapped on the knocker and waited. Would it be Mrs Thwaite who answered, or her sister, Mrs Hillier? Either way, Gina had her visit planned.

It was Mrs Thwaite who opened the door.

Promising so far.

'Good heavens, Gina Arnold, what do you want?' said Mrs Thwaite, her face betraying that she thought this was a nasty surprise. She stood with her good arm on the door latch, the other in a bulky plaster cast supported in a sling.

'I've come to visit you, of course,' said Gina in a friendly tone, and was over the threshold with the door shut behind her before Mrs Thwaite could stop her. 'And Mrs Hillier, if she's in?'

'No, my sister's out at work this afternoon,' said Mrs Thwaite before she realised she'd played into Gina's hands.

'What a shame. So it's just us, then?' Gina's voice now had a dangerous edge to it and Mrs Thwaite looked even more unhappy. Since her accident she'd lost her appetite and appeared drawn and shrunken: a little old lady. Gina deliberately stood tall, knowing she towered over her.

'What have you come for?' Mrs Thwaite asked, fear in her eyes despite her bossy tone.

'I told you: to see you; to see how you're doing. I thought we might have a little talk, Mrs Thwaite; discuss how things are.'

'What do you mean, Gina Arnold?'

'I think, Mrs Thwaite, that you might want to sit down. I've got some bad news for you.'

Mrs Thwaite turned paler. 'W-What news? What do you mean?'

'Shall we go in here, then?' said Gina, seeing a door ajar off the narrow little hall. Obviously it was the sitting room. She propelled Mrs Thwaite by her good arm into the room, where she sank fearfully into an armchair. This allowed Gina to stand over her, which was exactly what she wanted.

'What news?' asked Mrs Thwaite, tremulously. 'Is someone dead?'

Gina laughed. The old woman was in a right flap now. 'Oh, no, nothing like that. At least not yet,' Gina added daringly, enjoying herself. 'No, the news is that you won't be returning to Grindle Hall.'

'But Mrs Stellion said—'

'Mrs Stellion may have said one thing, but she'll be saying quite another when she hears what is hidden in your wardrobe.'

Mrs Thwaite gasped and her hand went to her mouth. 'No . . . Oh, no . . .'

'Oh, yes, Mrs Thwaite. Seems you've been found out and that's sealed your fate.'

'But . . . but it isn't much to her. Such a small sum. Mrs Stellion can afford it. She never even missed it,' said Mrs Thwaite.

Gina kept quiet. It was quite clear to her that Mrs Thwaite wasn't talking about the gin. She thought quickly.

'Ah, but you see she has missed it,' she said.

'After all this time? I don't believe you. You said she doesn't know it's been found yet.'

'She doesn't, but I do. And as housekeeper I feel it's my duty to tell her, Mrs Thwaite.'

'You? Housekeeper? I don't believe that either. That's my job. You're just the dog walker.'

'Not any longer, Mrs Thwaite. You've not kept up with the news from the Hall lately, have you? So much has happened and that's why I'm here: to put you in the picture, so to speak. About the missing money, and the bottles of gin found in your room.'

'But it's only twenty-five pounds or so, and I only took a little at a time, and they would have said something before if they'd noticed it had gone.'

Got you!

'Twenty-five pounds, seven shillings,' said Gina, improvising with confidence now. 'That, and the bottles of gin, which you also stole from them, and drank while you were supposed to be working.'

'I never—'

'Yes, you did. That's how you slipped and fell in the conservatory that day, wasn't it, Mrs Thwaite? Drunk and falling over. Mrs Stellion will realise that at once when I tell her you stole the gin as well as all that money.'

'No!' wailed Mrs Thwaite. 'I never drank while I was working.'

'Do you think anyone is going to believe you when you took the money as well?'

Mrs Thwaite was sobbing now. 'Since my Robbie died . . . in the war . . . it's been so difficult . . . and I was so lonely . . . so glad of the job at the Hall. And then . . . and then lately I couldn't sleep, and I just thought if I tried a little . . . a little nightcap it might help . . .'

With an expression of distaste, Gina watched the old lady break down. She'd come here with one aim and she wasn't going to be sidetracked by pity. She stood over Mrs Thwaite in silence until the sobs subsided.

'Don't you worry yourself, Mrs Thwaite,' she said gently then. 'Because I don't think Mrs Stellion need necessarily know that you robbed her. And mebbe she suspects you're a drinker, but I reckon she doesn't need to find that out for sure. After all, you won't be coming back to work at the Hall, will you? You're going to write to say you've decided to retire. So it's all done with. I'll keep your nasty little secrets and in return I continue as housekeeper and you can live here happily with your sister and never set foot in the Hall again. Mrs Stellion gets to keep her money and her gin in future, so everyone's happy.'

She looked around the little sitting room for the first time, seeing old-fashioned, slightly damp-mottled wallpaper and yellowed paintwork, the patterned curtains at the bay window faded in stripes, the hearthrug threadbare. There were a couple of dead flies on the windowsill and dust on the mantelpiece. 'Mebbe Mrs Hillier needs a housekeeper,' she suggested drily.

Mrs Thwaite began to cry again.

'Well, Mrs Thwaite, it was lovely to see you. I'm sorry your arm is giving you so much pain that you won't be able to return to work. Still, Mrs Stellion isn't too upset about that because I can manage the job that used to be yours – but isn't any longer – walk Coco, as well as keep the lady amused when she's bored. Yes, Edith and I are becoming very close,' she added.

'Go! Just go,' said Mrs Thwaite, both tearful and furious now.

'Yes, I'll see myself out,' said Gina cheerfully. 'And don't worry, I shan't tell a soul that you robbed your employer of her money and her gin. Not unless I'm forced to. You get busy writing that letter, eh? It's best that she isn't upset by learning what you're really like.'

'That's rich, coming from you,' gasped Mrs Thwaite, rising up from her chair. 'Let me remind you I know all about the money that went missing from the village shop in Little Grindle, and that it was you that took it.'

'It's odd you should mention that,' said Gina, temper flaring. 'You see, I'm the one with the job of housekeeper at the Hall, while you are a thief who's been found out and will not be going back there.'

'Thief?' snarled Mrs Thwaite, struggling with the word despite having been so completely exposed. 'Well, all I can say is that it takes one to know one.'

'Exactly!' snapped Gina, who went out, slamming the sitting-room door in Mrs Thwaite's face, then hurried down the hall and out of the house.

She strode along the little front path to the street, trying not to run, then walked back the way she had come, glad to turn the corner.

She stopped then and covered her face with her hands, breathing deeply. Oh, but that had been horrible. When that awful old woman turned on her and mentioned again that business with the money from the shop! It was months ago – why would anyone feel the need to bring that up now? So unfair . . . It was all over . . . all over now . . .

'Excuse me, love, are you all right?' It was a woman in her fifties asking, wearing a brown overall as if she had just come from work. 'Only you look a bit heated, like.'

'No . . . thank you. I'm . . . yes, I'm quite all right,'

said Gina, pulling herself up, shoulders back, breathing deeply.

The woman patted Gina's arm in a motherly fashion. 'You take care, love,' she said kindly.

'Yes, thank you. It'll all be all right now,' said Gina, and turned towards Main Street as the woman continued along into Lloyd George Road.

~

When Gina got off the bus in Little Grindle, she could see Ellen ahead of her, just waving off Sally at the Masons' cottage. The girls were smiling widely, then Sally called something and Ellen laughed. Gina stood quite still, watching. She knew that if she moved then Ellen would probably notice her and wait for her to catch her up, and Gina didn't want to answer questions about her afternoon and have to endure Ellen's chatter.

Sally went inside and Ellen walked on, swinging her satchel, and looking, from her bearing, very pleased with life. At the lane end, Ellen turned towards Highview Cottage. Gina, following at a distance, came to a halt at the turning. If she went after Ellen she'd find Dora at home, and there would be strong tea, and the inevitable potatoes to peel while they exchanged their news. There would be the familiar comforting smells of the farm cottage – the scent of home – and Dora's strong arms to hug her in greeting now she no longer lived there. Then, later, there would be Philip, with his long face and some story of the latest sheep death or mishap on the farm, prophesying disaster and spreading gloom over the family, short-tempered and snarling at anyone who tried to jolly him out of it. The evening would be ruined.

Gina watched as Ellen stopped walking and bent her head, her hands clasped, seeming to say a little prayer. Perhaps she was praying for a peaceful evening.

Gina set her face towards the Hall and strode on just as the sky opened and the long-forecast rain started to fall.

CHAPTER NINE

EDITH STELLION WAS exhausted after her trip to the doctor in Preston and took to her bed the whole of the next day. Gina wasn't alarmed: her employer often said she was tired and went to lie down. But even the following week, Edith was listless and inactive, staying in bed in the mornings and hardly wanting to bother to tell Gina what it was she required.

Mrs Bassett tried to tempt her to eat with sweet milk puddings, but Edith wasn't very interested in those either.

'Do you think she's seriously ill?' Gina asked Mrs Bassett when she returned the breakfast tray to the kitchen one morning, the coddled eggs and thin slices of toast barely touched. 'That doctor in Preston doesn't seem to have made her any better.'

'I don't think she's dying—' said Mrs Bassett.

'That's a relief.'

'—but she suffered a loss when she was younger and it's at this time of year that she remembers it especially.

I don't like to gossip, but it made a difference to her, like, and she's not been the same since.'

Gina, who was feeling impatient with the invalid and also bored, was not sympathetic, but it seemed a good idea, if life were to buck up at the Hall, to try to get Mrs Stellion back on track.

'Perhaps I should speak to Mr S, see if he has any ideas,' she said. 'In the meantime there's been a letter from Mrs Thwaite this morning. She's not going to come back to the Hall. She's intending to set up home with her sister in Great Grindle. I'm told to pack up her things and send them on, then move myself down to those rooms.'

About time, too. I thought she'd never write the bloomin' letter. At least I didn't have to go back there to persuade her, or help her on her way with a suitable spell.

'Oh dear, that is bad news. That is, it's lovely to have you here, Gina, dear, but Mrs Thwaite was part of the furniture almost, if you know what I mean.' The cook sounded regretful and Gina wondered how close the two women were. She'd better be careful not to confide anything in Mrs Bassett.

'Well, it seems she's not any longer,' said Gina, trying her best to sound sorry about it. 'I'm going to ask Mum to help me pack up Mrs Thwaite's things and see to the rooms. Mrs Stellion doesn't like the sound of the vacuum cleaner upstairs when she's in bed feeling fragile of a morning, so it'll be summat for Mum to do.'

'Good idea, Gina. Right thoughtful of you . . .'

~

Gina took Coco for his walk around the garden. It was looking very pretty and she remembered the conversation she'd had with Ellen all those weeks ago on their half-day holiday from the farm. Really, Mrs Stellion was not enjoying her lovely garden at all, and her house remained quiet and empty. The place was completely wasted on her, with her moping about feeling sorry for herself. But now Gina herself was here to enjoy it, and after Coco had been exercised this morning, she'd be moving to far nicer rooms than those she currently occupied in the attic.

Things were looking up: easy work to do with regular pay, her own rooms in this grand house, lots of good food to eat that she didn't have to help prepare, and the favourable opinion of her employer, with little effort on her own part. All she needed now was to liven the place up a bit and meet some useful people who could help her to better herself further . . .

She saw Ellen in the distance, bending over some white flowering things in the big border. Ellen straightened up, saw her and waved, and Gina went over. She knew Ellen wasn't one to bear a grudge, and once the stolen clothes had been returned, Ellen had never mentioned them again.

'Hello, Gina. Hello, Coco.' Ellen bent down to fondle the dog's ears and he gave a cheery woof of greeting.

'*Sit*, Coco. Nell, you'll never guess what's happened.'

'Probably not. Tell me.'

'Mrs Thwaite isn't coming back. I'm to pack all her stuff up and move mine into her rooms downstairs.'

'Poor lady. Her broken arm has finished her job here for her, but I'm glad for you that you've stepped into her shoes – and her rooms.'

Gina grinned in reply.

'How's Mrs Stellion this morning? We haven't seen much of her in the garden lately.'

'Ah, miserable. I'm trying to think of summat to cheer her up, make her forget herself, like.'

'Gina, that's really kind of you,' said Ellen, looking at her quizzically. 'While you're being kind—'

'I'm always kind.'

'—Dad was in a terrible temper last night: summat to do with some walls that needed repairing, right up on the tops, and some sheep had strayed – and he was being especially horrible and turned on Mum when she said summat to try to snap him out of it. As if it was her fault! I kept quiet and went to bed early, but I could hear him going on.'

'He's getting nastier, I reckon,' said Gina. 'I'm glad I see you and Mum here and don't have to go home and look at his miserable mug ever again, though I reckon it's 'cos I'm not there to take the brunt of it that you and Mum are getting it in the neck more often. But don't worry, I'll look out for her. I'm going to ask her to help me pack up Eliza Thwaite's rooms. That'll be fun.'

'Fun? How?'

'Well, interesting, at least,' said Gina. 'Now, Coco, I'll race you to the front. Bye, Nell.' And she ran off with Coco, on his lead, dancing along beside her.

Ellen watched them go. Maybe her hopes were being answered and Gina was just what Grindle Hall – and Mrs Stellion – needed.

~

Gina took the key to the housekeeper's rooms from the hook by the kitchen door and went down the corridor to open up. The sitting room was exactly as she'd seen it when she'd come to look for the library books. What a fruitful little search that had been!

Dora and Mrs Bassett were drinking tea and having a sit-down in the kitchen, and Mrs Stellion and Coco were enjoying each other's company in the morning room. Gina had not gone into Mrs Thwaite's rooms since that library day because she didn't want to be caught where she had no business. Now, at last, she had every reason to be here.

Quickly she crossed the room to the bedroom door. The bedroom was musty with the smell of mothballs and felt somehow sad. There was little time to lose surveying the scene, though. Gina opened the window, then the wardrobe. She knew the money Mrs Thwaite had stolen was somewhere inside because she'd inadvertently told her so. She moved the handbag from the floor of the wardrobe and felt all over as best she could, but there were just the two gin bottles at the back, which she left where they were.

Where? Must be . . . in the bag, of course!

She opened the snap fastening of the black handbag,

which was lined with what might have been a kind of paper that felt like cheap, brittle suede. A handkerchief, a little coin purse – one and tuppence inside – a zip pocket . . . empty.

But she told me the money was in the wardrobe . . .

Any moment now Dora would appear to help and the chance to find the money unobserved would be lost.

'Gina, are you there, love?' Dora was calling from the corridor.

Gina put the handbag in the wardrobe, closed the door and hurried back to the sitting room.

'In here, Mum. It smells of old lady in here and I've opened the bedroom window.'

Dora appeared carrying a lot of empty cardboard boxes.

'Mothballs. They might repel moths but they repel other folk, too. Let's get this window open as well . . .'

She put down the boxes and reached up to the window catch. Gina saw a large bruise on her arm as the sleeve of her blouse rode up.

Dad's work. Hateful man. How I wish—

'Now, we'll take all Mrs Thwaite's things from here and put them in these boxes. Be careful, mind. Then we'll do the same with the bedroom. There are more boxes in the corridor.'

'Yes, Mum. And we mustn't forget the bathroom down the corridor, though you know I've been using that anyway and I've put all her stuff in a box already.'

As they worked, Gina wondered how she could find the money but keep the find to herself, while leaving her mother to 'discover' the bottles. By the time they'd cleared the sitting room and Mrs Thwaite's meagre belongings were packed up, she had a plan.

'Mum, if you pass the clothes out of the wardrobe, I'll fold them and put them in a box.'

They started their tasks. Mrs Thwaite's clothes were mostly black. It seemed she had no dresses for life outside her job. Probably she had no life at all outside her job – the thought passed through Gina's mind. Well, what did she care?

Dora handed each garment, still on its hanger, to Gina, who laid it down on the bed. As she folded each one, she quickly and discreetly felt in the pockets for the money.

Soon the number of garments left hanging up was sparse and Dora bent down and removed the handbag from the floor of the wardrobe.

'She'll be needing this, poor lady,' said Dora. 'I feel bad that I never thought to send on anything she might want since she came out of hospital.'

'Not really your job, Mum. She could have asked. Anyway, she'll have it very soon.'

Dora passed Gina another garment, then: 'Oh, my goodness!' She lowered her voice. 'Gina, there are bottles at the back – gin bottles.'

'Gin? Are you sure?'

''Course I am. They look the same as the ones in the sitting room upstairs.' Dora pulled out the two bottles, one half empty. 'Oh, my word, do you think Mrs Thwaite was a secret drinker?'

Gina couldn't help laughing so she decided not to

pretend to be shocked. 'Who'd have thought it? And she so strict and respectable!'

'Shush, Gina, it's not funny.'

Gina was laughing aloud. 'It is, Mum. It's brilliant. Mrs Po-faced Thwaite and her secret love of mother's ruin.'

Dora fought for control of her face, then gave in to her own, more moderate, laughter. 'Oh dear, I reckon she might have *helped herself* to these, either from the sitting room or by ordering in more than Mr and Mrs Stellion asked for. Why else would she have the very same make with this fancy label?'

'Aye, Mum, I know nowt of gin but I reckon this isn't the cheapest. Thing is, though, we don't know for certain that she pinched them. If we said owt and we were wrong it wouldn't be fair to Mrs Thwaite.'

'But if we didn't, but they do belong to Mr and Mrs Stellion, we'd be helping in the theft, wouldn't we?'

Gina pretended to ponder the dilemma. 'Well, we both *think* she pinched them, so why don't we just put them aside somewhere safe and out of sight for a couple of days and if Mrs Thwaite wants them she'll ask for them? If they're not hers, she won't have the nerve to ask us to send on stolen goods, will she?'

'Clever girl, Gina. I don't really want owt to do with them, but I'll put them at the back of the cleaning cupboard, just till the end of the week, mind. You're to remind me about them if Mrs Thwaite doesn't ask. And if anyone were to find them and think that I'd stolen them, you're to back me up.'

'Oh, Mum, of course! Why don't you go and do that now?'

Dora found an empty paper carrier and stuffed the bottles in, wrapped in a clean pillowcase to cover them and also to stop them clinking as she went.

As soon as she'd gone, Gina went to look through the pockets of the few clothes left in the wardrobe. One was a jacket of suiting material and she saw from its size and the position of the buttons that it was a man's. At once she knew her search was over. Sure enough, in the secure inside breast pocket was a neat bundle of one-pound notes and a handful of shillings. She grabbed the cash, stuffed it into her dress pocket, then ran quickly out to the corridor where her mackintosh hung ready for rainy dog walks. She had just transferred the money safely to her coat pocket when Dora appeared.

'Just getting my hanky, Mum,' said Gina, sniffing. 'Those mothballs are making my nose run. Did you manage without being seen?'

'Nowt to it,' said Dora, looking pleased with herself. 'Mebbe I'm a born gin smuggler.'

Gina laughed. 'Oh, Mum, anyone less like a criminal would be hard to find.'

'Just remind me they're there on Friday, love,' Dora fussed. 'I don't want anyone to think those bottles have owt to do with me.'

They continued with their work. When Dora passed the man's jacket to Gina she looked stricken, and all the humour of the gin find evaporated.

'I reckon this must have been Mr Thwaite's,' Dora said

sadly. 'Why else would she have a man's jacket? She must have kept it all these years since he was killed as a memento of him. Fold it up nicely, Gina, love. There's some tissue paper in the other room – use that and let's respect her memory of him. She must have loved him very much.'

Gina did as she was asked, and if, for a moment, she wished she had been a little kinder to Mrs Thwaite, she quickly shrugged the thought away.

~

'Mrs Stellion, how are you feeling this morning?' asked Gina, coming into the morning room with the daily newspaper. She'd tried a few suggestions to get Edith interested in life over the weeks – playing the piano, doing the crossword, reading the glossy fashion magazine she had delivered but which was left unopened, telephoning her friends – but with only moderate success. June had been unusually cool and overcast, but today the weather had improved, and that seemed to have affected the lady's mood.

'Perhaps a little better than yesterday, thank you, Gina.'

'As it's such a lovely day, Coco and me wondered if you'd like to go out with us for our walk this morning.'

Edith bent over the arm of her chair to stroke Coco's head where he sat in his basket. 'Did you, Coco? Good boy. But, I don't know, Gina. I'm not much of a walker, as I think I told you.'

'But Coco would love you to come,' insisted Gina. 'Wouldn't you, Coco?'

The little dog got up and went to lay his head on Mrs Stellion's knee as if he understood.

'See?' said Gina, laughing.

'I'm not sure . . .'

'Please, Mrs Stellion. We'd both like you to come.'

'Oh, all right then. But you're not to walk too fast, Coco, or Mummy won't be able to keep up.'

'Coco will do exactly what his *mummy* tells him when you take his lead,' said Gina confidently. 'Now, Mrs Stellion, I reckon you should take your cardi, just in case, and we'll go and have a look at your roses, if you like?'

'Yes . . . yes, all right, Gina, dear, let's do that. Perhaps a walk is just what I need.'

Honestly, it's like dealing with a child.

They set off, walking slowly, Edith wearing a very smart pair of brogues and holding Coco's lead, Gina in her sensible black housekeeper's shoes.

'Let's go across the front lawn,' said Gina. 'It's Coco's favourite route.'

She knew Mr Stellion was in his study this morning and she wanted him to see them. As they approached the study window, she started telling Edith something amusing the little dog had got up to and Edith laughed, which was exactly the desired effect. Gina bent down to tie her shoelace more securely, telling another tale of Coco's talents, taking her time just in case Mr Stellion hadn't noticed them.

They moved on to the rose garden, where Ellen was deadheading.

Edith stopped to speak to her assistant gardener and ask something about one of her favourite varieties, then walked on, stopping to smell the flowers every so often.

Gina found herself smiling: it was good to see the lady enjoying what was hers instead of lying about alone in her big, empty rooms, and it was sweet the way Coco kept looking up at her as if seeking approval.

They walked on, next viewing the topiary garden, which Tom was constantly snipping away at, maintaining the strange shapes that cast interesting shadows, and then back to the big border, which was magnificent with colour in all its summer splendour.

Mr Stellion came out of the doors at the back of the house and down the wide steps.

'Edith, my dear, it's so nice to see you out.'

'It was Gina who persuaded me to come for a walk with her and Coco,' beamed Edith. 'And, do you know, I feel a lot better for it already? I feel as if my head has cleared for the first time in weeks.'

Gina smiled and George Stellion put an arm around his wife's shoulders and kissed the top of her head.

'Gina, would you like to walk Coco a little further while we go back to the house?' he suggested.

'Of course, sir.' Gina took the lead and went on with the little dog by her side.

'Now, I've been thinking about what we discussed, Edith, and I can see that maybe now Mrs Thwaite has retired it's time to reorder our household a bit. I know she hasn't been at the Hall long, but Gina Arnold has been a godsend and, frankly, we'd be silly not to give her more of a rein in entertaining and occupying you. It's lonely for you when I'm so busy with the brewery, and of course it's been so hard for you since Cassie . . . since we lost Cassie.'

'Yes, George. I think of her and miss her every day. It's a long time ago now but it doesn't get any easier. I know you feel the same. But having Gina around – well, I think she helps. She's got a no-nonsense attitude but she's also very kind.'

'It was Gina who came to me last week and suggested I brought you that bouquet of your favourite roses from the garden to raise your spirits. "If Mrs Stellion doesn't feel up to going out, you could bring the garden in to her," she said, and so I asked Ellen to cut me the best ones in bud and it was lovely to see your face when I gave them to you, my darling.'

Edith laughed softly. 'And there I was thinking you had decided to bring me the flowers all on your own.'

'With three Arnold women working for me, I hardly need to think a thought, never mind lift a finger,' he replied.

'Yes, and we've got Tom Arnold, too, of course.'

'He's a sound man,' said George. 'He's bringing on Ellen to be very useful about the garden. I like to keep abreast of how they're getting on, and I couldn't ask for better from either of them. So, shall I tell Gina that we've decided to alter her duties a little, or will you?'

'I think I should like to, George, if you don't mind?'

'Excellent. I'm so glad to see the roses coming back

in your cheeks after your walk this morning. I suspect Gina Arnold is just what you need.'

'Thank you, George. I think so, too.'

~

'So more than just the housekeeping duties?' asked Gina. 'And walking Coco, of course.'

'Yes, it would be nice for me if we could have our meals together when Mr Stellion is out, and we'd also do more things together during the day so I wouldn't be bored by myself.'

'But what about the housekeeping?'

'I think we both know there's not much to it, with only my husband and me living here; just making sure the house runs smoothly. It isn't a lot of work for you, is it?'

'Not at all,' said Gina.

'And, in all honesty, you've become much more than a housekeeper over the weeks anyway. I just think it's time to acknowledge that. So do you agree, Gina?'

'Yes, please, Mrs Stellion. That is, thank you for asking me,' grinned Gina.

As soon as Gina could, she went down to her own little sitting room and thought through the surprising news. Since she'd cast that first spell all those weeks ago, her life had been transformed – and so quickly that she found it hard to believe. It was almost as if the magic power was in her and she'd somehow tamed it so that all she had to do was want something and it would happen. It was strange and wonderful.

She looked up and saw the shabby old book of spells on her shelf. It was the only book there, sitting beside her little basket of knitting, but small enough to be discreet; no one coming in would even notice it. It was comforting to know it was there whenever she might need it.

~

Ellen and Sally, on their way back from visiting Mr Shepherd in Great Grindle, parted as usual outside the Masons' cottage, Sally joking about the chaos and the noise that awaited her inside.

'By heck, those twins can make a mess for one-year-olds,' she laughed. 'Mum says she's thinking of keeping a pig; it can follow them around, eating up all the dropped food.'

'You know you wouldn't be without any of them,' Ellen replied.

'Aye, I remember what it was like before our dad came on the scene and it's better now,' said Sally, making a rare understatement. Some memories were too raw to be allowed into the light. 'Family's everything.'

Ellen thought of her own family: Dora bullied by Philip's temper; Gina, never coming home these days and, for all the Stellions were a different sort of folk, more a part of life at the Hall than the farm cottage. And herself – how did she fit in? Highview Cottage was a place where she went to eat her tea but tried to avoid her father; her real life was in the garden, knowing Gina and their mother were working close by, and she herself learning her trade with Tom.

Maybe the Arnolds were just at a different stage of family life than the Masons, with the little ones. As quickly as she had the thought, she dismissed it. The Masons were happy at home, the Arnolds were not.

'Thanks for going with me, Sal.'

'Wouldn't miss it, Nell, though I'm finding it hard to keep up with all these reading suggestions of Mr Shepherd's.'

Ellen nodded in agreement. 'Aye, it's difficult when Lucas Hillier will allow "no borrowing on another reader's ticket".' She did a very good impression of the unpopular librarian and they both burst out laughing.

Sally turned to open the cottage garden gate and saw Edward Beveridge coming along the road behind them.

'Ah, you have company, Nell.'

'Mebbe he wants to speak to you, Sal.'

'No chance. He has eyes for only one of us and it certainly isn't me. Hello, Ed. All right?' she greeted him with a wave and a smile, then went up the path, opened the front door and was gone.

'Hello, Nell,' said Edward, hurrying up to her. 'I've been taking some eggs down to Mrs Slater. Are you going straight home? I'll walk with you if you are . . .'

They strolled along slowly in the July afternoon, exchanging news. Edward had got a new young sheepdog of his own to train up and his father had promised him a little flock of Herdwick sheep once the dog was ready.

'It's the first step towards making the farm my own, Dad

says. He's not ready to hang up his boots for a few years yet, but he wants everything to be ready for when he does. He's generous enough to let me have my own way about where the farm's going, what we'll be doing in the future, but he's seen a lot over the years and he always puts me right if he thinks I'm moving owt in the wrong direction.'

'That's lovely for you, Ed. I'm right glad. You're on your way, so to speak.'

'On my way but stopping here,' Edward laughed. 'What about you?'

'Same. I feel quite at home in the Hall garden these days, and that's down to Uncle Tom's generosity. He takes the time to show me and explain things.'

'Not still thinking of moving on to a garden of your own, then?'

Ellen blushed. 'Oh, I was being a bit silly, I reckon. I'd hardly started at the Hall when I said that and I didn't realise how much there was to learn. The more I know, the more I see there is to know. It was daft to think of going anywhere else – not for years, anyway.'

They had turned off the road into the lane to the cottage and the farm, enjoying the cool breeze and the sound of a few birds singing in the hedges. Already hawthorn berries were forming, hard and green. It would be autumn soon enough, then the long, dark northern winter. They both stopped walking, as if they sensed a change of mood, a melancholy in the air. No one else was about.

'I'm right glad about that, lass,' said Edward softly. 'I don't want you to go away.' He bent his head and kissed her softly on the mouth. 'Please don't ever go away, Nellie.'

Ellen found herself kissing him in return. She reached up and removed his flat cap with one hand, then ruffled his thick straight hair with the other.

'Too early for promises, Ed,' she whispered, 'but I'll not be going if I've a good reason to stay.'

CHAPTER TEN

'DON'T FORGET YOUR brolly, Nell, love,' said Dora, as the last of the whist players left Little Grindle village hall and Reggie Travers switched off the lights and locked up.

'I seem to have needed it so often this summer I think I should tie it to my hand,' Ellen sighed.

'Perhaps you could just stand on the leeward side of that lad of yours and he'll keep any rain off,' Mrs Fowler said.

Everyone laughed and Edward looked down affectionately at Ellen. 'I would if I could,' he said.

'Night-night, everyone,' called Sally, and there was a chorus of replies.

She, Betty and Reggie Travers and Mr and Mrs Fowler set off for their homes on the village main street, while Ellen, Dora and the Beveridges turned the other way, towards the lane that led to Highview Cottage and Highview Farm, taking out their pocket torches and pulling their coat collars up. It was often cold in this bleak corner of Lancashire, and the summer so far had been exceptionally dismal.

Nancy and Albert walked ahead, Dora between them, chatting, while Ellen and Edward lagged behind, holding hands and exchanging discreet kisses. It had been a lively, friendly evening of card playing, the whist drive organised to raise money for the repainting of the village hall's windows and doors. So many places had become shabby and neglected-looking since the war, and the people of Little Grindle felt it was time to make improvements.

At Highview Cottage the Arnolds and the Beveridges parted, and Dora and Ellen went to the back door.

'Looks very dark,' said Ellen, puzzled, as Dora opened the door. 'Dad? Are you there?'

Dora tried the light switch, half expecting the power to be off or the light bulb gone, but the kitchen was illuminated immediately to reveal Philip sitting in his chair with a furious scowl on his face.

'Phil, what on earth's the matter? Why are you sitting in the dark?'

'Why shouldn't I sit in the dark if I want? There's nowt to put the light on for this evening, is there?'

'What do you mean?'

'What I say.'

'But what's the matter?'

'Nowt.'

'All right, then. If there's nowt the matter, I'll get on and get ready to go up.'

Dora and Ellen each had a sinking feeling. They'd

seen this kind of sulk many times before and already it was shaping up to spoil what was left of the evening. If Phil was out of sorts he made sure everyone else suffered. It would be best to bring what remained of the day to a close as quickly as they could.

'No one here to make my tea and not even a note – that's what's the matter, as you know full well. How was I to know where you'd gone or how long you'd be gone for? You could have been anywhere.'

'Like I'd be gone "anywhere". Of course I left you a note. Your tea is on the side under that teacloth there, see?' Dora bent down and picked the note she'd left from off the floor. 'Must have got wafted off the table in the draught when you opened the door, but I thought you'd have been able to heat up a bit of food.'

'You know where we were, Dad. Mum told you this morning about the whist drive. We had to get there early to help set up the tables and chairs, remember?'

'I remember no such thing, Nell.'

'But, Dad, Mum did say—'

'Do you think I'm stupid?' he snapped.

Ellen, knowing what that aggressive tone could lead to, tried to defuse the situation. 'No, Dad, I'm not saying you're stupid. I'm just saying you've forgotten,' she said quietly.

'Well, if you two didn't go off gallivanting of an evening and stayed in and cooked my tea like decent folk, then there'd be no need for notes or remembering what rubbish you'd talked this morning.'

'Phil, it was perfectly decent. It was a whist drive for

the village hall fund. There was no *gallivanting*,' Dora defended herself.

'So now you've got money to spend on the village hall, have you?' Philip snarled. 'And where are you getting all this cash you seem to have to splash about on stuff that's nowt to do with you?'

'Oh, Dad, it was just a little fundraiser – just a bit of fun, that's all,' said Ellen. 'Lots of our friends were there.'

'Friends? You mean my employers – yes, I heard them making a row outside just now – and no doubt mad Betty Travers and that daft fella she's married to.'

'Betty's my friend and has been for years.'

'Mr Travers isn't daft.'

Dora and Ellen both spoke together.

'Well, why don't you go and spend all your evenings with them, then? Leave me here with nowt to eat and no idea when you'll be back. You obviously prefer their company to mine.'

Ellen knew better than to answer that. She'd had a lovely evening in the company of Betty and Reggie. They were always good for a laugh. There weren't many laughs when Philip was home.

'Phil, come on, now. You're talking nonsense. I'm always here to cook your tea and I expect I will be in the future.' Dora tried to placate him though her stomach was already knotting with anxiety.

'I didn't see you here this evening.'

'Mum did leave you something to eat,' Ellen said. 'And the note.'

'Do you think a working man wants to come home,

having slaved away all day, and have to make his own tea of an evening?' Philip raised his voice, determined to be unreasonable. 'Do you?'

'Mum works too,' Ellen pointed out quietly.

'Shut up! Who asked you?'

'Phil, don't speak to Nell like that. She's worked hard all day, too. We all have,' Dora said. 'Now why don't you simmer down and I'll just take off my coat and heat this through for you? It'll be done in no time.'

'I don't want it now.'

'Nell, love, you get your father a plate out and I'll pop this in a pan.'

'Leave it. I'll do without.'

'It won't take a moment.'

'I said leave it!'

Philip pushed Dora out of the way, picked up the basin of stew from under the cloth and hurled it to the floor.

'There! I said I don't want it, but would you listen? Now do you believe me?'

There was a shocked silence as they all surveyed the splatter of stew across the floor and the shards of the broken basin.

'Phil—' Dora began, trying to hold back her tears. She'd had such an enjoyable time playing cards with her friends, but the memory of the happy evening was fading fast.

'It was you made me do that,' Philip shouted at her. 'It's your fault, with your gallivanting, and free-spending of an evening instead of behaving like a proper wife. You try me to the end of my patience.'

It had usually been Gina whom he claimed tried his patience, but these days Dora and Ellen found themselves entirely in the firing line. But, even so, Ellen was determined to counter his unfair accusations.

'Dad—'

'Shut up, Ellen, or I'll make you shut up.'

He raised his hand to strike her but Dora, knowing Ellen spoke only out of fairness to herself, grabbed hold of his arm and he turned on her instead, delivering her a swift, hard slap to the side of her head with his other hand. She recoiled, clutching her face, and tears sprang to her eyes.

'Mum!' Ellen rushed forward. 'Let me see. Let me look where he hit you . . .' She turned her back on her father and gave all her attention to Dora. 'Sit down, Mum. There, now.' She dug in her coat pocket for a handkerchief, ran it under the cold tap and pressed it gently to Dora's red ear, then hugged her mother to her. 'Don't cry, Mum, don't cry . . .'

Seeing his wife and daughter were ignoring him, Philip became even angrier.

'Shut up, the pair of you. You're like a couple of daft old hens, fussing about.'

Ellen made shushing noises and Dora's weeping subsided, but neither of them paid him any other attention.

'Come on up to bed, Mum,' said Ellen. 'You haven't even taken your coat off yet. There, let me help you. Why don't you sleep in my room, in Gina's bed tonight?'

'Aye, love, I think I will,' said Dora, rising to her feet.

'Oh, no you don't. What about this mess?' yelled Philip.

Ellen turned to him at last in disgust. 'You made it, Dad, so you can clear it up.' It took all her courage to stand up to him, having seen him punishing Gina for little more than cheek in the past, but she could not allow her mother to fight this battle alone.

'Don't you use that tone with me, Ellen Arnold, or I'll—'

'You'll what? You'll hit me, too?'

'Aye, like that.' He gave her a hard slap to match the one he'd given Dora. 'Only harder.'

'Right, that's it,' said Dora, as Ellen now clutched her throbbing face. 'I've had enough. I'm fed up of you hitting us, like we were beasts of the field being kept in line. We've done nowt wrong, we've just been out for the evening with our friends, and if you had any friends yourself you might have wanted to come too. You're in a stupid rage because you had to heat your own tea for once in your miserable life. A child could have managed it, but you had to get all mardy about it and spoil the evening, just because you're jealous that we had a nice time and you're feeling left out.'

'Jealous? *Mardy?* Your place is here, getting my tea after I've been working all day, not making a spectacle of yourself at the village hall, giving away money like Lady Muck.'

'Spectacle of myself?' Dora, outraged, shrugged off wise caution. 'What on earth are you on about now? I sat and played cards with my friends and drank a cup of tea. Then I came home. That's when the *spectacle* started.

The only person making a spectacle of themselves is you, Phil. As for giving away money, it was a fundraiser. The *whole point* is to give money.'

'My money—'

'No, *my* money. Wages that I earned working at the Hall, the bit I keep to have my hair done at Christmas or get a bit of wool to knit up. You wouldn't even have noticed it was gone because it wasn't ever yours to start with.'

'Mebbe I'm allowing you to keep too much if you can afford to give it away like some spendthrift,' snapped Philip.

'You've a daft answer for everything tonight, haven't you?' said Dora. 'I can do nowt right.'

'You said it, woman.'

'Come on, Nell,' said Dora, putting her coat back on. 'We're off. Don't forget your torch.'

'Where do you think you're going?' shouted Philip as his wife and daughter made for the door. He tried to get to them to bar the way, but the spilled stew and the broken basin impeded his progress. Seeing that, Dora gathered Ellen close and they stepped quickly aside just as Philip kicked a large, deadly-looking shard of the broken basin at them. It missed Dora's ankle by half an inch and hit the foot of the dresser, coming to rest like an unsheathed knife.

'Away from here,' she said. 'I'll see you tomorrow, and I just hope you've snapped out of it by then.' As she spoke she rushed for the door, pushing Ellen out ahead of her, then slammed it behind them, turned the lock and put the key in her pocket. 'Come on, love. It'll take him a minute or two to find the spare key.'

Philip was hammering on the locked door and shouting like a madman.

Dora and Ellen switched on their torches and hurried up the path to the lane, their breath coming in gasps of fear.

'Oh, Mum, where are we going?' asked Ellen, anxious to get away before her father unlocked the door and pursued them. She suddenly had a monstrous vision in her mind of him hunting them down and beating them both senseless in the dark of the lane.

'To the farm,' Dora answered.

Oh, how she wanted to say they would go to Tom, but she knew if once she sought his protection, then she would never go back to the cottage again and her marriage would be over.

But wasn't it over already? What was left of the promises she'd made when these days she seemed to be married to a madman? Where was the love? It had long since died under a battering of sulks and black moods, anger and violence.

For a moment she hesitated outside the cottage, but Ellen took her arm and steered her to the left.

'Quick then, Mum, before he comes after us.'

Holding their torches before them in the pitch-dark, they ran as fast as they could manage towards the safety of the Beveridges' farm.

~

This was the first spell Gina had tried since she came to work at the Hall. In the quiet of her sitting room off the downstairs corridor, the house all silent around her with Mrs Bassett long gone home and the Stellions in bed, the act of casting the spell took on a solemnity and importance that it had never achieved while she was hastily and surreptitiously conjuring her magic in her shared bedroom at the cottage.

She read the words very carefully – the language was old, the spelling unfamiliar – and lined up on her table the artefacts and ingredients she had gathered ready: various plants, which she suspected might be poisonous, a kitchen knife and a saucer, the inevitable candle, a charcoal pencil and some writing paper. She lit the candle and wrote her father's name on a piece of paper, then folded it with some sprigs of the plants inside and burned it in the candle's flame, dropping the glowing remains into the saucer, where the flames died and it finally smouldered into ash. Some of the words in the book she recited aloud, others she customised into a wish in her head.

The candle flame seemed to surge higher and burn brighter after she'd burned the paper. She knew she had to leave it for a while for the spell truly to take hold before she should blow it out. She sat in silence, trying to exclude from her mind all other thoughts but her wish, and to concentrate on empowering her spell. Her eyes started to close and her breathing slowed . . .

Suddenly the silence of the room was shattered by the sound of a door slamming. It was very loud and sounded nearby. Gina's stomach flipped and her heart was instantly pounding.

Who could that be? What?

She listened intently, trying to silence her ragged breath, but heard no more. Gradually she relaxed. She must have been mistaken; it was nothing.

When she felt the spell had had time to . . . to what? To cook? – She laughed to herself at this. Time to be born, maybe? – she blew out the candle and enjoyed inhaling the smoke.

There, that will teach Dad to hit Mum and Nell and kick up so much that they have to seek refuge at the farm.

They'd gone back home next morning, Dora had told her when Gina had insisted on hearing exactly how Dora's face had come to be bruised, and Mr Beveridge promised to have a very strict word with Philip.

'Next time, Mum, I think you should go to Uncle Tom's,' said Gina, looking her mother hard in the eye.

'I'm hoping there won't be another time, love,' said Dora, looking away and shrugging the incident off. 'I reckon your dad was just anxious about summat at work and it made him short-tempered, like.'

'Mum, why do you make excuses for him? Uncle Tom will deal with him once and for all if you go to the Lodge.'

'And that's why I won't be going, Gina,' Dora said. 'And I went straight to Tom this morning and told him he's to do nowt either. I can't be responsible for more violence.'

'There shouldn't be any violence at all,' said Gina. All her life she'd been on the receiving end of physical punishment by her father, but she'd always been a naughty girl, too, and she almost regarded it as the cost of being found out. But now, with her living at the Hall, it seemed Philip had turned more violent towards Dora and Ellen, who surely were blameless.

It was then that Gina decided she needed to seek the help of her magic powers to deal with her father. Let the magic do the work for her, and for Mum and Nell.

~

It was raining hard and Edith was plainly bored.

'Let's take Coco to the outbuilding and he can show you his tricks,' suggested Gina. 'I know it's good for him to have some exercise outdoors, but the poor boy will be washed away today, and I might be too.'

Edith sighed. 'All right then. This oppressive weather is starting to make my head ache.'

'You'll feel better if you get some air, Mrs Stellion. Don't you always? And you'll be amazed at Coco, I promise,' said Gina, who'd been teaching the little dog several entertaining moves.

In the empty outbuilding, Gina set up the broom handle between two low piles of bricks and Coco performed beautifully. Then she raised the bar by another brick at each side, and then another.

'It's higher than he is! What a clever boy you are, Coco,' said Edith, marvelling at her puppy's antics. Coco barked excitedly and did another leap just to show his talent wasn't a fluke. Edith and Gina laughed together. Then

Gina had him jumping up on his hind legs for a biscuit as his reward.

Diana's bicycle was propped up at one side of the place and it caught Gina's eye as Edith was fussing around her little dog.

'Does Diana ever come home?' she asked.

'Not often, I'm afraid. She's so busy with her life in London. She works in an office, typing. It's in Whitehall, in London, a government place. I think she's got important things to type,' said Edith.

'That's a shame for you not to see her. And what about James?'

'No, my son is also very busy in London.' Edith looked sad. 'Let's go back inside, Gina,' she said. 'It's cold for July. Come on, Coco. There's a good boy.'

Gina closed the outbuilding door and ran across the courtyard to the back door, which Edith was by then holding open for her. Edith went to ask Mrs Bassett to make a pot of tea while Gina dried off Coco's paws and then they followed her upstairs.

'Why don't you ask them, Mrs Stellion?' Gina said when they were all back in the morning room. 'If you write and ask your son and daughter to come and see you, I reckon mebbe they might.'

'But wouldn't they think something was wrong if I suddenly write to them like that?'

'Wrong? Not if you just say you'd like to see them. Tell them you miss them and you'd love them to come home for the weekend. They could bring some friends mebbe; show the folk from London what it's like up north.'

They both looked through the window at the pouring rain, the clouds obscuring the view at a low level.

'Tell them to bring their macs,' said Gina, deadpan, and they both burst out laughing.

~

Gina was very busy suddenly, preparing the Hall for the visitors. Diana had written back to her mother that she'd come for a weekend some time next month and she might ask one of her friends if she'd like to come with her. Why didn't her parents suggest hosting the village fête at the Hall, as they had done years ago? James telephoned and said he'd see if he could find the time, but he wasn't making any promises and he'd let his parents know.

'I remember you and Mr Stellion holding the fête on the back lawn,' said Gina. 'It's a few years since. Would you like to do it again?'

'I'll ask Mr Stellion what he thinks. I expect when he sees from her letter that it's Diana's suggestion, he'll be all for it,' Edith smiled. 'It'll be a lot of work for you, though.'

'Oh, I don't know about that, Mrs Stellion. I'll just make sure the gates are open! Mr Travers and Mr Mason can organise all the stalls in the usual way. I shall be busy getting the rooms ready for Diana and her friend, and James, of course, if he comes.'

Sure enough, Mr Stellion agreed to Diana's suggestion, the fête committee were consulted and delighted to move the event back from one of the farms to the beautiful venue of the Hall garden. Tom consulted Mrs Stellion and decided to rope off some of the garden as private but allow visitors to view other parts, and he and Ellen turned their attention to making the public parts as perfect as they could.

Suddenly the Hall, far from being silent and dull, was buzzing with activity. Mrs Stellion appointed herself in charge of 'lists', and the sitting room became the headquarters of 'Fête Day'. The difference in her was a joy to see, Mr Stellion told Gina gratefully.

'No more headaches and exhaustion. It's amazing. I'm so glad Diana thought of the weekend,' he added.

Gina felt a bit put out. Inviting Diana and James home had been her idea, but there was the prospect of meeting some new people, which to Gina was the entire point of the event, and in the meantime the Hall was livelier and busier.

Mrs Bassett was in her element, suggesting menus and trying out new recipes.

'It'll be just like the old days, Gina,' she said. 'I loved it when the children were home for the school holidays and there were cakes to bake and picnics to pack up. It's nice to cook a great big lunch for a lot of people and see everyone enjoying it, and then hardly able to move in the afternoon.'

Gina couldn't imagine eating that much food. Even on Christmas Day the chicken was eked out to last through Boxing Day and beyond. And the idea of eating so much you couldn't move was rather horrible. Mrs

Bassett, being a cook, however, must take it as a sign that she was appreciated.

'I can see it's more fun for you than preparing the invalid menu that Mrs Stellion used to eat,' Gina suggested.

'Aye, but it's not about me, love, it's about Mr and Mrs Stellion, and I can see it's more fun for them now Missus is feeling better and has plenty to think about.'

And more fun for me, too.

Gina could hardly wait to meet Diana and her friend, and James.

CHAPTER ELEVEN

DIANA AND HER friend arrived at Grindle Hall on a Friday evening in early August. The fête was to take place on the following Monday, a bank holiday, and they intended to stay for that.

George Stellion went in his big shiny car to fetch his daughter and her friend from Clitheroe station. Gina was just as excited as Edith about their visit, though of course for different reasons. They talked about Edith's plans for the weekend while they waited, though they kept getting up to peer out of the window to see if the car was returning. To Gina, Mrs Stellion looked younger, livelier, and her eyes were shining at the prospect of seeing her daughter for the first time in months.

Gina looked forward to having new people in the house, people who knew life beyond Little Grindle, even beyond Lancashire.

At last they heard the car crunching along the gravel drive. It drew up in front of the house.

Diana leaped from the front passenger seat and George

was out and opening one of the rear doors for her friend in a moment, as if he were a chauffeur.

'Come on, Piggy. Come and meet Mum,' said Diana, all slender legs and high-heeled shoes below her generously pleated skirt.

Piggy?

The figure that had emerged from the car couldn't possibly be anyone's idea of a pig. What a ridiculous name, thought Gina, seeing a slim young woman of about twenty-two or -three, wearing a neat little hat perched on pretty dark hair and a very smart costume – a matching jacket and dress. They weren't the kind of clothes people round here wore. Even Edith's fine jumper and well-cut skirt lacked the flair of Diana and Piggy's outfits.

Coco rushed out to be introduced, wagging his tail and exercising his winning ways, and Diana and Piggy bent to fuss and admire him.

Edith was laughing and embracing Diana, and then was introduced to Piggy, who turned out to be called Penelope Turner.

By this time Gina was helping to carry the women's cases from the car to the house, and when Edith introduced her gushingly as 'Georgina Arnold, housekeeper and general all-round helper, and an absolute godsend', Gina had to put down the two little weekend cases to shake hands.

'Oh, lovely. Mum mentioned you in her letter. Georgina, would you mind just popping those in our rooms? Thank you. Mum, I'm gasping for a cup of tea, if Mrs Bassett can provide?'

'Mrs Bassett has stayed to see you, Diana, though she doesn't usually work this late.'

'I'll go down now, then, and say hello to my favourite cook. Any sign of James?'

'He's turning up at some point "if he can manage it",' said George heavily. 'I don't expect he'll arrive this evening now.'

Diana pursed her lips and said something to her mother that Gina didn't catch. Then she said, 'Come and meet Mrs Bassett, Piggy,' and led Penelope Turner away.

Mrs Stellion couldn't stop smiling as she closed the front door and gathered Coco into her arms for a hug, while Mr Stellion took the car round the back.

'Oh, Gina, it's so nice to have her home. If only James would hurry up and get here, everything would be quite perfect.'

~

It was Sunday before James showed up. He arrived just before lunchtime. The family were about to sit down to a feast of roast beef, which Mrs Bassett had taken all morning to perfect, when there was the roar of a car engine and the crunch of tyres on gravel. Gina, who had brought up a jug of water for the table, was able to observe the arrival from the dining-room window. A very sporty-looking car pulled up in front of the house and a tall, fair, well-built young man got out, took a small case and some bags from the back seat and strode up to the door just as Edith opened it and rushed out to greet him.

'James, my darling!'

'Hello, Mum . . . Dad.'

'James. We've been expecting you for a while now. We're just about to start lunch,' said George.

'Good-oh. I'm starving.'

'Come on in – leave your things there; Gina will take them up – and you can meet Diana's friend Piggy over lunch. They've been here since Friday,' George added pointedly.

'Well, you're here now,' beamed Edith, to offset her husband's tone. 'But for goodness' sake, go and wash your hands and comb your hair.'

James laughed and ruffled his already dishevelled fair hair. 'That's the car, I'm afraid, but I couldn't pass up the chance to put the top down . . .' Gina was by now standing silently to one side in the hall, and he winked at her as he passed as if she was in on some kind of subtext to his words, though they hadn't even been introduced. Then he mooched off to the downstairs cloakroom with his hands in his pockets.

Edith and George went back to the dining room, where Diana and Penelope remained, and Gina hurried down to the kitchen to tell Mrs Bassett that there would be one more for lunch, then came back up to set another place at the table. There would be no seat at the table for her, she realised. Instantly, she had assumed her old role of 'staff': the housekeeper, the dog walker. Diana had treated her like a servant from the outset, and presumably James didn't even know who she was. Well, she'd see if she could change that over the next few days.

Gina was helping Mrs Bassett with the food while there were guests. She'd learned a lot about cooking over the months she'd been at the Hall, where there was a wider range of dishes to prepare than were ever eaten at home. She had the foresight to realise that these new cooking skills could be useful in life, although she had no intention of ending up working as a cook herself. They might, however, help her on her way to better things.

'So James has arrived at last,' said Mrs Bassett, her tone hinting at disapproval.

'In a tiny little sports car,' said Gina, round-eyed. 'I've never seen owt like it before.'

'Aye, there's not many sports cars in Little Grindle,' said Mrs Bassett. 'Not the weather for sports cars up here. I'll give them a minute and then take up the joint. You can follow with the taters in that tureen, please, love. It's hot, mind.'

'You don't sound like you care for sports cars – or James,' ventured Gina.

'Neither's owt to do with me. Would you pour that gravy into the jug, please, Gina?'

'Looks grand, Mrs B. Do you think James will stay long?'

'I couldn't say. He'll do as he wants.'

'I think Mrs Stellion would like it if he did. She was that pleased to see him.'

'Then let's hope she's not disappointed,' said Mrs Bassett. 'Right, I think we'll go up now . . .'

~

After lunch, which Gina ate with Mrs Bassett after she had taken upstairs the cook's magnificent trifle, Gina went out to help with the final fête preparations. There were little marquees set up on the lawn and a big one along one end for the vegetable show. The table-top stalls were to be put in place the next morning in case of overnight rain. The forecast was, as ever that summer, for cool and changeable weather.

The fête committee had brought in several helpers, who were noisy and relaxed, having met up in the Lamb and Flag beforehand. The Stellions and Penelope were all outside helping, which seemed mostly to take the form of encouragement and cheerleading, though George took a practical role, measuring distances and lending a hand with tent ropes. He addressed everyone by name and did a lot of back-slapping. When Gina went out, the girls were laughing loudly at something Tom had said; he was standing on a ladder, hammering a pole into the edge of the lawn.

'We can hang the bunting, if you like, Mr Arnold?' said Diana.

'Thanks, Miss Stellion. That'd be a help,' said Tom. 'Just secure it to the nail at the top of the pole and it'll do nicely.'

'Gina, you can give us a hand, too, if you like? There's miles of it,' said Penelope.

Penelope Turner was very friendly, and she and Diana had asked her opinion on various aspects of the fête. Both a few years older than Gina, they rather took her under their wing, expressed admiration of her housekeeping role at such a young age, and thanked her very nicely whenever she did anything for them. Gina knew they were merely being kind although they were also quick to dismiss her when she'd done as they'd asked, especially Diana. Gina still didn't understand why a pretty young woman like Penelope would put up with being called Piggy, though.

'How many poles are there, Mr Arnold?' called Diana.

'Fifteen all told,' said Tom. 'I've three more to put up.'

'So, let's see. If I measure the bunting and we divide it by fifteen, then we'll know how loosely to hang it.'

'But if there are fifteen poles, there are fourteen gaps,' Gina pointed out. 'We need to anchor it to the first pole, then the first stretch goes to the second pole.'

'Good grief. You are clever,' said Diana, raising an eyebrow. 'I shall bear that in mind.'

'I think you should be in charge and we'll just do as we're told,' said Penelope, smiling at Gina with genuine admiration. 'I don't think I'm clever enough to be able to divide by fourteen.'

'Neither am I,' said Gina. 'Never mind, we can always adjust it when we've got it up. As long as the end reaches the last pole, I reckon no one'll be measuring.'

'Mm, I can see why Mum says you're a godsend,' said Diana drily. 'Oh, no, can you stop Coco? He's got the end of it and it will be all over the garden in a minute.'

'Coco! Coco, come here, lad. *Bad* boy. *Sit!*'

The excitable young dog was brought under control and disaster averted. Gina went inside to get his lead and then took him over to Mrs Stellion, out of mischief and harm's way. When she returned to the bunting, however, she saw Diana and Penelope were disappearing off to look at the rose garden and she was left alone. Everyone seemed very busy with other tasks so there was nothing for it but to make a start by herself.

She was halfway round, balancing on a set of kitchen steps, when she smelled cigarette smoke. She looked down to see James standing with one hand in his pocket and a cigarette at the corner of his mouth, gazing up at her.

'That's a pretty sight,' he said.

'It'll look good when it's finished,' said Gina, though she half thought he wasn't referring to the bunting. She secured the flags to the nail and was descending the steps when she felt a hand on her arm, another arm round her waist.

'Here, let me help you. Can't have the indispensable Gina falling and hurting herself, can we?'

'Thank you, I can manage,' said Gina, stepping away from him, not keen on his tone. Was he being sarcastic? If so, why?

'We'd have to cancel the festivities, wouldn't we? Everyone would be so disappointed.'

Gina looked at him hard. What was his game? She decided he needed keeping in order. There had been boys like him at school; if she gave as good as she got, they soon left her alone.

'There's plenty to do over there, if you want to help,' she suggested, pointing to where James's father and Tom were putting up the last of the little tents with a couple of men from the pub, Reggie Travers instructing them from a diagram on a sheet of paper.

'Oh, I think the old boys can manage without me. But I do love work,' said James. 'I could watch it all day.'

Gina laughed.

'Not an original line, I'm afraid,' he said. 'But I rather think I've a talent more for bunting than tents, and you look like you need some help.'

'Oh, go on with you,' said Gina. 'If you really want to help you can stop being clever and grab the end of this length.'

'*Jawohl, mein Führer.*'

Gina gasped. People didn't make light-hearted references to the war in Little Grindle. It was – even now, over ten years after the end of the conflict – too uncomfortable a subject, and jesting about it was thought to be in poor taste.

'Just a joke. No need to look so shocked.'

'Not a funny joke,' said Gina. 'If you're not going to help, just go away and let me get on, please.'

'How about I hold the steps?'

'How about you get lost?'

'All right, all right, no need to snap. I'll go up the steps, you pass me the bunting and show me what to do.'

Gina looked at him for a very long moment. Then: 'Fine,' she said. 'But for goodness' sake keep the flags away from that cigarette. We don't want them catching fire.'

By the time the bunting was all in place, James had stopped trying to be clever and Gina had decided he wasn't too dislikeable after all.

'Looks lovely,' she said, standing back to admire the pretty flags fluttering along two sides of the lawn.

'Does indeed,' said James, looking straight at her. 'I'm just wondering, what is there for a girl like you to do in the evenings at Grindle Hall?'

'You mean after I've cleared the tea . . . er, the dinner things? Well, when your dad's out, as he sometimes is on business, I play cards with your mum, or we do a jigsaw or the puzzles in a magazine, or listen to the wireless. And I'm teaching your mum to knit. It seems she never learned but she's coming on nicely.'

'Sounds fascinating,' James said flatly.

Though Gina privately agreed that the evenings could be long and boring, she had grown fond of Edith, despite her peevishness, and she knew better than to express even a hint of discontent, especially to anyone in Edith's own family.

'I think your mother is pleased to have you home,' she said, trying to change the subject. 'How long do you plan to stay?'

'Oh, I'm not a great one for making plans, Gina. I prefer to see how things work out. That way I can just go whenever I want and not feel I'm letting anyone down. Anyway, we were talking about you. You were telling me all about your entertaining evenings with my mother.'

'Was I?'

'You were just about to say that now the girls are here you are, regretfully, completely at a loose end. Then I was going to take pity on you – all alone with no jigsaws to do and the knitting lessons suspended for the duration

– and offer to take you for a drive in my car, if you would like.'

'I was? Were you?'

'Certainly I was. So what do you think? Are you free for a little spin about the countryside in the beautiful Lancashire twilight, or is there a play on the Home Service you simply have to catch this evening?'

'I reckon there is,' said Gina. 'You see, James, I don't care for folk "taking pity" on me, especially when I'm just doing my job. Now, I see Mrs Bassett there with a tray of tea, so I'm off to give her a hand. Thanks for your help with that bit of bunting.'

She walked away without looking back, though the temptation to do so was almost overwhelming. What an annoying man, she thought, smiling to herself. Good looking, though.

~

'But, Dad, we're all going to the fête. We always go. It's just that it's at the Hall this time, like it used to be years ago. Please go with us,' said Ellen.

She wasn't especially bothered whether Philip was there or not, but she knew if he stayed away he'd only be making a martyr of himself, and probably be in one of his sulks by the time she and Dora got home, spoiling their day.

'You can help Mr Hardcastle with the Splat the Rat. There're always little lads trying to get a free go. You'd keep them in line, like.'

'You'd get to see what our Nellie's been up to in the gardens. It's really lovely,' encouraged Dora. 'I'm that proud of her, and you would be too if you just took a look.'

'And there's a tea tent, Dad. If nowt else you'd get summat nice to eat. Mrs Fowler's been baking for days. I hear there's chocolate cake,' Ellen added.

'All right, all right, stop going on at me. I'm not a child, to be bribed with a bit of cake,' grumbled Philip.

'Well, please yourself,' said Dora. 'But I'm not putting up with any bad moods when we get back. It's supposed to be a nice afternoon for everyone to join in, so if you're not joining in then that's your choice. But I wish you'd come with us, I really do.'

'I'll think about it,' Philip mumbled. 'Now shut up about the blessed fête and give a man a bit of peace.' He flapped open an old copy of *Farmers Weekly* and held it up in front of his face, cutting off the sight of them.

Edward and Nancy came to call for Ellen and Dora on their way past, and the four set off to the Hall without Philip, who said he might go later, though his wife and daughter didn't expect to see him. Dora was carrying a tin of flapjacks and Nancy had a Victoria sponge. Cake was a big feature of the event.

Edward had a huge cucumber in a string bag, which was his entry in the vegetable show. This was traditionally, with one exception, an all-male competition, and heavily contested by the gardeners and allotment holders of Little Grindle. Tom Arnold entered the vegetables he had grown at the Hall under the name 'Mrs Stellion', but although they were often plainly the biggest and best, they never won, and Mrs Stellion herself would graciously present the little silver cup for 'Best in Show' to one of her rivals.

Ellen and Ed walked ahead, joking about the giant vegetables of past years and speculating on Ed's chances of winning in his class.

'First prize is a three-shilling postal order, so it's worth having,' he said.

Dora and Nancy shared their cake-baking secrets as they went. Mrs Fowler was the acknowledged queen of cakes, but the rivalry for her crown was fierce in a friendly sort of way.

'And Betty's doing her fortune-telling again,' said Dora. 'She's looked out that spangled frock she got last year and a shawl to pull over her head. We all know it's Betty, though.'

'Are you going to have your fortune told?' asked Nancy. 'I never know whether to believe it – like reading your horoscope in the magazines: you want the good bits to be true, but then after a day or two you forget about it anyway. I expect Betty makes up summat and folk come away pleased.'

'Oh, I don't know as it's made up,' said Dora, Betty's best friend. 'She's got a crystal ball and everything.'

Nancy considered this seriously. 'Well, she's certainly a wise woman and knows all sorts, so I suppose there's no reason why fortune-telling shouldn't be another string to her bow. Mebbe I'll have my fortune told, after all. Perhaps I'll meet a tall dark stranger.'

'If there's a stranger round here you can be sure we'll all know about him within a day, and most of us will have met him within two days,' Dora laughed.

'Which reminds me, have you seen James Stellion's back home? Arrived yesterday, apparently. Mrs Fowler saw him zooming past in a flash little car, disturbing the peace of a Sunday dinnertime.'

'Mrs S will be pleased. She thinks the sun shines out of that one. 'Course, I'd prepared his room for Friday, same as for Diana and the friend she's brought with her, but I didn't know he'd got here. Gina will tell me all the news if I can catch her. She's been that busy this week . . .'

The fête was not yet quite under way when the four of them arrived. Ed went to place his cucumber to best advantage in the vegetable show, and Ellen had a quick look round before she took up her position at the gate to the rose garden. She'd got a chair there and a little table with a toffee tin to hold the money, and Tom had agreed with Mrs Stellion that visitors were to be charged tuppence to enter, the fee to go to the war veterans' charity that the fête supported every year. He also warned her to keep an eye out for visitors with secateurs.

'One year – oh, it was a long while back now, when the fête was held here every time – we had a couple of women coming away with bouquets of blooms they'd helped themselves to. There's no end to folk's cheek, you know.'

At half past two Mr Stellion declared the Little Grindle

Village Fête 1956 open, and the crowd – which had gathered to hear him exhorting them to spend generously – quickly dispersed to do so.

'And what are your duties today, Gina?' James asked, appearing at her side.

'Oh, I shall be that busy . . .'

'Doing . . .?'

'Enjoying myself, mostly.'

'May I ask, would you care to enjoy yourself with me?'

'Thank you, but I know everyone here and I don't need to be escorted round.'

'But I do, Gina. I can't remember the names of half these people, though I'm sure I ought to know them. Please, take pity on me and whisper their names in my ear so I don't look a complete ass.'

'I doubt I can save you from making an ass of yourself,' she replied.

'Oh, Gina, don't be hard on me. Help me out here. Who's that, for instance?' He pointed.

'Mrs Beveridge from Highview Farm.'

'And that?'

'Reggie Travers.'

'And that?'

She giggled and slapped his hand down. 'It's your mother, of course.'

'I thought I recognised the little dog she's holding. See, I'm hopeless without you.'

'Come on, then,' said Gina, sighing dramatically. 'I fancy having a go at the coconut shy.'

They went off to the far side of the lawn where a queue

of people was forming to hurl wooden balls at coconuts on stands.

James managed to throw and smoke at the same time. He had a cricketer's speedy action and felled one of the coconuts at the second attempt.

'Here you are,' he said, presenting it to Gina.

'What am I supposed to do with this?'

'I've no idea. Is it edible?'

'It might be if I ever got into it. Mrs Bassett will know what to do with it, I expect.'

Gina carried it around for a bit and then left it behind on purpose at the white elephant stall.

'Oh, fortune-telling. Now this I've got to try,' said James, when they reached a little tent with a flap over the entrance and a lot of red and black bunting festooning the outside.

'Madame Bettina Predicts Your Future' read the sign.

'Shall I come in with you?'

'No, better not. I think the readings are meant to be private. Maybe I'll tell you when I come out – depends, though, what I learn.' He waggled his eyebrows theatrically.

James went inside and Gina decided not to wait for him to reappear. It wasn't as if he wouldn't tell her later what had happened. And did she care anyway?

She decided to go to look at the vegetable show, which had just been judged. The tent was crowded as people waited to hear who had won 'Best in Show'.

'Dad, what are you doing here? I thought this wasn't the kind of thing you like.' This was not a good start,

Gina reflected. Still, at least if he was here he wasn't at home getting worked up about other folk enjoying themselves. There had been other occasions she'd rather not remember . . .

'I can come if I want, can't I?'

'It's just . . . Well, never mind. Here you are. Have you entered owt in the competition?'

'Nah, it's daft, isn't it, growing those great monsters of veg? Who'd want to eat those?'

'Shush, Reggie Travers is reading out the names of the winners.'

'. . . And the winner of "Best in Show" goes to Fred Hardcastle for his display of onions.'

Fred came forward, blushing and holding his cap, to receive the little cup from Edith.

'Gina, hello again,' said Penelope as she and Diana appeared. 'This is fun. I've never been to a village fête before.'

'I'm introducing Piggy to all our neighbours,' said Diana. 'It's a great turn-out.'

'Yes, so difficult to remember who's who with so many people,' beamed Penelope. 'Though, of course, I do remember meeting your father yesterday, Gina. I saw him just now taking over from your sister in the rose garden.'

Puzzled, Gina half turned to Philip, but Penelope was gushing on.

'Now you've got your hair up I can see you've got the same little mark as he has on his arm, and there's definitely a family resemblance— Ow, Di, that was my foot.'

Gina turned to introduce Philip and put right the mistake, but he was already barging his way through the crowd to the marquee entrance.

'What's the matter?' asked Penelope, seeing Gina and Diana's faces.

'Sorry, Gina,' said Diana. 'Piggy didn't mean to upset your father.'

Penelope looked confused. 'Your father? Oh dear, I've said the wrong thing, haven't I?'

'No . . . no, it's all right,' said Gina, vaguely. The birthmark was old news in the family so why was Dad making such a fuss about it now? Really, he was impossible to fathom sometimes.

'Come on, Piggy, let's go and get a cup of tea,' said Diana, taking her friend's arm and leading her away. 'See you later, Gina . . .'

The crowd in the vegetable marquee was slowly dispersing now the results had been announced. For a moment Gina stood and wondered if she should go to find Philip, but she knew he'd be in a bad temper and she couldn't face that today. Besides, she'd had enough to do helping to prepare for the fête; let Mum and Nell deal with him.

'Gina? You all right?'

It was Ellen, holding on to Edward Beveridge's arm as if they were Siamese twins.

'Oh, it's just Dad. He was here and Diana's friend said summat about me looking like Uncle Tom, except she thought Uncle Tom was our dad, and Dad stormed off.'

'Oh Lord, he's always been queer about the birthmarks

– it was the birthmarks, wasn't it? – and now he'll be all the wrong side out for days.'

'Can I do anything?' asked Ed.

'Er, I don't know. I don't want our day spoiled, but neither do I want Mum to get it in the neck when we get home.' She sighed. 'Oh, this is exactly the kind of thing I didn't want to happen today.'

'Let's go and see if he's still here and mebbe we can talk him round with a cup of tea,' said Ed.

'It'll take more than a cup of tea, I reckon,' said Ellen. 'But thank you, Ed.'

They followed the crowd out of the marquee and Gina put her hands over her face for a moment to gather herself. When she looked up, the first thing she noticed was an enormous cucumber with a red rosette next to it and Ed's name on a card. She'd always thought Edward Beveridge was a bit dim, but now she acknowledged that he was, more than anything, considerate. He hadn't even mentioned his first prize and had immediately volunteered to take on the job of talking Phil out of his mood.

Lucky old Nellie! They were so obviously in love and maybe she'd got herself a fine man there, after all. Nell's future was pretty much mapped out: she'd marry Edward and eventually he'd inherit the farm and Nell would be a farmer's wife with a farm of their very own. Nell had spoken about wanting to be a gardener, but she'd probably forget all about that if she married Ed Beveridge. They'd take their place in the generations of Beveridges at Highview Farm, in Little Grindle, and be quite happy about it.

And where would she, Gina, be? What was there for her?

Maybe she'd better visit 'Madame Bettina' and try to find out. It was time to have some more fun. Maybe then she and James could compare the futures that Betty Travers and her crystal ball had invented for them.

CHAPTER TWELVE

'COME IN, DEAR,' said Madame Bettina. 'Sit down here.' She indicated a chair on the other side of the little round table from hers. The table was covered with a billowy cloth on which stood a crystal ball on a polished wooden stand. The little tent felt stuffy and humid.

'Thank you, Madame Bettina,' said Gina, entering into the spirit of the fortune-telling. 'Do I have to cross your palm with silver first?'

'No, love. It's thrupence, that's all.' Madame Bettina indicated a pudding basin in which there were a good many thrupenny bits and Gina added one from her purse. 'Thank you, love. Now, let me concentrate and the images will come before me,' she said, leaning over the crystal ball and looking hard at it without blinking. She sat like that for a long time and Gina was impressed at her technique. Betty must have been practising, she thought.

'What do you see?' she asked eventually, unable to bear the suspense any longer.

Madame Bettina was frowning. 'I see a journey.'

That sounded exciting. 'Will I go far?'

'Where you go will be different from here.'

'Who will I go with? Will I be alone?'

'You will never be alone, dear,' said Madame Bettina. 'You will always have someone special and very close to you looking out for you. Whatever you do, you need not fear that you will be alone.'

That sounded both comforting and perhaps a little bit frightening at the same time. Still, no one wanted a life in which nothing happened. And this was only Betty Travers with a headscarf on. The crystal ball looked shiny and solid, though; quite an impressive prop for a village fête.

'Will I go on this journey soon?'

'Sooner than you expect.'

'Will I be rich?'

Madame Bettina gazed into the ball for a long while again. Eventually she said, 'Your life experiences will be rich and varied.'

That sounded good. It was just a pity Betty wasn't a real fortune-teller.

'Do you see anything else, Madame Bettina?'

The so-called clairvoyant waved her hands back and forth above the crystal ball, as if wafting away obscuring clouds. Gina was amused: Betty had all the right mannerisms.

Suddenly Madame Bettina's face changed to an expression that combined anger and anxiety. She looked up and fixed Gina with furious eyes.

'What?' gasped Gina. 'Tell me what you've seen.'

'The special gift of a wise woman is not to be treated lightly,' Madame Bettina said angrily. 'Those that have the knowledge must use it only for good. Those that are ignorant should not try to engage with what they don't understand. There is great harm to be done in such foolishness.'

Gina was taken aback; this was supposed to be fun. 'W-what do you mean?' she said faintly.

'You know!' Betty yelled, rising to her feet and looming terrifyingly over Gina. 'Now go, and put your nonsense behind you!'

Gina leaped to her feet and rushed out of the tent, her face burning and her heart pounding. She walked away from Madame Bettina's tent as quickly as she could without actually fleeing. She urgently needed to go somewhere quiet and think about what had happened. As a part of the Hall household, she was free to go anywhere in the gardens, so she made for a part closed off to visitors, where she could sit quietly and recover herself.

'Gina! There you are.'

It was Ellen calling after her, but Gina didn't look back. She dodged into the topiary garden and hid behind one of the giant sculptured bushes. This part of the garden was famous locally and there were several visitors here admiring the strange shapes. Gina waited a minute or two, then, keeping a lookout for anyone she knew, slipped away through the gate today marked 'Private' at the far end, and went to sit in a secluded corner of the vegetable garden to contemplate the horrible fortune-telling experience.

Gina had no doubt that Betty had been talking about the magic spells Gina had cast – what else could she mean? But how did she know? Could she really have learned about that through looking into the crystal ball? It seemed too far-fetched, but then Gina believed she herself had cast the spells, so why wouldn't she believe that Betty could see such strange things? Oh, it was so confusing and yet it made a weird kind of sense.

Betty had been very angry, too. *There is great harm to be done in such foolishness* – was she a foolish person who could do great harm? She had accidentally killed the sheep and the lambs, but then she had successfully rid the Hall of Mrs Thwaite and stepped into her shoes, so maybe that business with the sheep was just a beginner's mistake. She was still awaiting the result of the third spell, and was beginning to think that nothing would come of it. Since Gina had assumed the role of housekeeper at the Hall, and also keeping Edith company when she was lonely, Edith had been a lot happier, and it was down to Gina that Edith's children had come home to visit her now. How was that doing harm? She had got much of what she'd set out to do so far, and everyone else was better for it.

Maybe Betty Travers enjoyed her unique reputation as a woman with rather unusual talents for healing and, in a village fête kind of way, predicting the future, and didn't like any competition in the realm of strange powers. Now that Gina thought about it, that sounded plausible. If, by following the instructions in a book, Gina could cast spells, then anyone reading the book and performing the strange rituals set out in it could do the same. Betty Travers wouldn't hold a special place in the village if everyone knew how easy it was.

Satisfied that Betty's anger had been because she was

jealously guarding her own position, Gina closed her eyes and took some calming breaths. *Better now* . . . In a minute she'd be ready to go back to the fête as if nothing had happened. But she'd avoid that old baggage Betty Travers. And she wouldn't be taking any notice of what she'd said, either.

~

A series of sharp showers brought the fête to a prompt close. By five o'clock the garden was deserted of visitors and the committee were already taking down wet tents and gathering up props and garden furniture. George Stellion, wearing a mackintosh, helped by lending a hand and voiced encouragement and thanks.

Gina was taking some crockery back into the kitchen when she saw James coming downstairs with one of the bags he'd brought in from the car the previous day.

'Are you leaving already?' she asked.

'Why, Gina? Would you mind if I were going?'

'I'd know your bed needed stripping, that's all I meant,' she said.

'Well, I'm sorry to disappoint you but I'll be staying, at least tonight. But I thought I'd go to the pub.'

Gina looked at the bag but he didn't explain. Instead he said, 'Would you like to come – that is, if you aren't too busy?'

'As it happens I'm not busy at all this evening, once I've plated up the cold food Mrs Bassett put by earlier for your family. Can you give me a few minutes, please?'

'Ten,' he said seriously, looking at his watch.

Gina rushed off with the crockery and hurriedly put the cold food on platters in the larder. Then she ran to her room to apply the lipstick she'd stolen from the chemist's in Great Grindle and to comb her hair.

When she came out of the front door, she half expected to see James had gone, but he was standing by his car, smoking a cigarette.

'That's what I like, a woman who can tell the time,' he said, and opened the passenger door for her.

Gina slid into the seat feeling that she'd earned a treat and a little attention. Diana had treated her rather too much like a servant, she thought, but perhaps James understood what an important role she had in his mother's life at the Hall these days.

He had the top up on the car this evening, and it felt very small inside, with not much room for Gina to stretch out her legs.

'Good thing you're slim,' James said, getting in beside her and seeing her trying to make herself comfortable. 'Imagine old Ma Bassett sitting there.'

Gina laughed. 'I don't think you'd have got the door closed,' she said.

'Cruel, but true.'

He started the engine and sped off down the drive. The gates were open to allow the fête committee access, so James drove straight through, past Tom's house and out onto the road into the village.

'Oh,' said Gina as they passed the Lamb and Flag, 'I thought you said we were going to the pub.'

'We are, just not that one.'

'Where then?'

'You won't know it,' said James, and put his foot down as they headed off south and west, a watery sunset forming on the horizon ahead of them.

~

Ellen and Dora stayed to help pack up the leftover cakes, of which there were very few, take down the bunting and fold the tablecloths.

'We spend all that time preparing for the fête and it's all over in a single afternoon,' said Dora.

'A bit like Christmas,' Ellen smiled. 'Mum . . . I hope Dad's not still in a mood when we get home. Ed was working hard at trying to bring him round, but I don't think he really managed it and we all know Dad's quite capable of keeping up a bad temper for ages.'

'Aye, I haven't seen him for the last hour or so, and he certainly hasn't stayed to help pack up. Not that that means owt. Still, as you say, there's no knowing what we'll find.' She sounded anxious.

'Shall I ask Uncle Tom to come home with us, just to make sure we're all right, like? It was horrible about the stew that time,' she lowered her voice still further, 'and hitting us.'

'It might be worse if Tom's there, love. I think we'll have to brave it ourselves.'

'Mum, we shouldn't have to "brave" going home to our own house. It's not right.'

'No, Nell, it isn't,' said Dora thoughtfully. 'Well, let's see what happens. Mebbe it'll be all right.' She gathered herself, put on a courageous face, and Ellen tried to suppress her worries.

They finished helping to pack up, said goodbye to their friends and then set off down the drive.

'Tom's the fête treasurer,' Ellen reminded Dora, 'so I'll just nip into the Lodge and leave him the garden money. I think we did quite well, considering the showers. Go on ahead, if you want.'

'All right, love. I'll just call out good night and you can catch me up.'

She did this and continued on her way, while Ellen left her toffee tin full of pennies with Tom, then ran after her.

When they arrived at Highview Cottage, Philip was sitting in his chair scowling.

'Put the kettle on, love,' Dora said to Ellen. 'Phil, would you like a cup of tea?'

He ignored her as if he thought her beneath speaking to.

Ellen and Dora exchanged worried glances and Ellen's eyes were wide. This looked to be exactly the situation she had been anxious about, but how could they avoid it? They had to come home.

'Make a pot, love, and we'll see,' said Dora quietly. 'So how much do you reckon you made from the garden visitors?' she went on, trying to behave as if nothing was wrong; as if the atmosphere wasn't tense with Phil's temper ready to explode.

'Between seven and eight shillings, I think. We were quite busy.'

'That's good,' said Dora, distractedly. Even to her own ears the conversation sounded stilted and unnatural.

'And at least this year no one tried to steal the flowers.'

'Steal the flowers? I've never heard owt like it.'

'Yes, Uncle Tom told me—' Ellen stopped abruptly, her hand over her mouth. How could she have been so stupid?

Of course, Philip leaped on her slip-up. 'Uncle Tom, Uncle Tom . . . all I ever hear is Tom this and Tom that. You'd think he lived here, not me. It's like he's haunting the place – or mebbe I am. Mebbe I'm the one who's the spare fella, what with Tom making his presence felt all the time, even when he isn't here.'

'I'm sorry, Dad, I didn't mean to upset you. It was just summat he said this afternoon.'

'Oh, aye? Well, I heard some stuff myself this afternoon. I've no doubt Tom's full of interesting stories to entertain you and your mum. How you must hate coming home and finding it's only me here and not Tom, with his winning ways, and his handsome face and his charm. So tall and so clever and so popular, and a job in the posh garden at the Hall, not up to his neck in sheep—'

'Phil, calm down,' said Dora tiredly. 'I don't want to hear any more about it.'

'I'm sure you don't. And we all know why that is, don't we?'

'Oh, Phil, don't be talking nonsense. We just want to spend the evening here like civilised human beings. We've had a lovely afternoon with our friends, and we've raised some money for a good cause and now we just want to have a sit-down and a cup of tea and talk about it.'

'Shut up about your "lovely day", you daft woman. A lovely day with Tom, was it? Gina's father?'

Dora sighed. 'Not that old story again. You know that's not true. You've been fretting about that since the day she was born. It's rubbish and you know it.'

'But everyone can see Gina looks exactly like Tom. Even that daft girl at the fête saw it straight away.'

'Dad, Gina looks exactly like *me*,' said Ellen. 'Everyone knows that. It's only 'cos her birthmark looks like Tom's that anyone would make that silly assumption at all.'

'Yes, Phil, some babies have birthmarks and most don't, as Betty told you on the night Gina was born.'

'But how can I believe you?' shouted Philip. 'You've always been friendly with Tom, Dora, and . . . why wouldn't you prefer him to me?'

'What?'

'All I hear is what a great fella Tom Arnold is. There he is, holding court at the Lamb and Flag, and half the village in there laughing at his jokes and buying him drinks. Of course you prefer him to me.'

'But I don't!' insisted Dora, aware that she was lying. 'It's you I'm married to.' That at least was true, unfortunately. 'So what if Tom has plenty of friends? You'd have friends if you ever went down to the pub and spoke in a friendly way to anyone, or sat on the fête committee.'

'Don't you patronise me, Dora. I'm sick of you trying to jolly me along like a child.'

'Then stop behaving like one! You're just like a little boy who hasn't got picked for the football team and is feeling resentful,' said Dora. 'If Tom's popular it's because he makes an effort to be pleasant, and if you were to make even half that effort, you'd be doing better.'

'You see, that's exactly what I mean,' shouted Philip. 'You're always comparing me to Tom and finding me wanting.'

'I do not.'

'You do. You're doing it now. How can a man live like this – his wife always comparing him to someone better? Someone she sees every day at the Hall?'

'Oh, shut up with your self-pity and your envy,' Dora retorted, knowing there was no point in trying to placate him any further. 'All I wanted was a nice quiet evening at home after a busy afternoon. Is that too much to ask?'

'Please, Mum . . . Dad . . . please stop shouting,' said Ellen.

'Shut up, Nell,' yelled Philip. 'You say you and Gina look alike—'

'Everyone says we do. It's obvious.'

'—so mebbe you're Tom's daughter as well.'

'No! Why are you saying this? Dad, that's a mad idea. Why on earth would you say such a thing? Mum, tell him.'

'What's the point? He wouldn't believe me,' said Dora.

'He? *He!* You even speak of me as if I'm not here.' Philip started wringing his hands and looked ready to burst into tears. 'I can't bear it any longer. You and Tom have ruined my whole life between you.' He lashed out and swept the empty mugs off the kitchen table.

There was silence as the three of them looked at the shards of broken crockery, Dora and Ellen with eyes wide with shock. Luckily, the teapot full of tea was still behind him.

'Phil, please, stop before you hurt someone,' said Dora.

'Mebbe you deserve to be hurt,' he snapped. 'I've put up with you flirting with my brother all my life—'

'That's not true and you know it.'

'—and mebbe I've finally had enough.'

'No, Dad, stop it. You're behaving like a madman,' said Ellen.

'Then it's her that's driven me mad,' Philip roared, pointing at Dora as he pulled the belt from off his trousers to give her a lashing.

'No, Dad, no!' screamed Ellen.

Suddenly the back door opened. 'Phil, put that down now or, by God, I'll grab it off you and give you the hiding you deserve,' Tom said.

For a moment Philip and Dora froze. Ellen gave a silent sigh of relief. She'd told Tom of her fears when she took the garden money to him – indeed, leaving the money had been an excuse to speak to him – and he had promised to follow her up the lane and listen outside to make sure she and Dora were all right.

'What are you doing here? Come to see my wife, have you?' snarled Philip, holding the belt between his hands.

'No, Phil, I've come to see you,' said Tom.

Dora stepped back to put some distance between herself and Philip's belt, and Ellen rushed over to wrap her arms around her.

'What do you want? Why are you here?'

'Well, it occurred to me, Phil, when I saw a big bruise on Dora's arm one time, that you are a cowardly wife-beater. Dora told me she had banged it on a door, but I didn't really believe her and so I asked Nell. And Nell told me the truth. Then a few weeks ago both Dora and Nell had bruises on their faces, and Nell told me what had happened, and how they had had to escape from their own home and seek refuge with Nancy and Albert. So that got me thinking. I thought if I ever saw you raise a hand to either of them, I would do exactly the same to you – blow for blow. And if it happened a second time, I'd give you two blows for every blow, and three for each on the third occasion, and so on until you got into your thick skull that beating innocent women is a mug's game. If I had to beat you to within an inch of your miserable life to teach you that lesson, it would be no less than you deserved.'

'Mind your own business and get out of my house,' said Philip, advancing on Tom with the belt, ready to lash out.

'Or what, Phil?' Tom asked calmly.

'Why, you smug bastard, how dare you come round here interfering in my marriage?'

'What marriage would that be, Phil?' said Tom. 'The one in which you promised to love, comfort and honour Dora? 'Cos I reckon you're in no position to get all righteous about that now, are you?'

'Aah!' Philip swung out with the belt, the heavy buckle flying through the air like a mace.

Tom ducked to one side and the belt made contact with the dresser with a loud crack, leaving a deep gouge in the pine. In a second Tom had grabbed Philip as he leaned forward behind the weight of the blow, and propelled him back against the wall, one hand around his neck, under his jaw, his feet almost leaving the ground with the speed of Tom's move.

'You try that again, Phil, and I promise I shall make you very sorry, you snivelling little coward,' hissed Tom in his ear while forcing his head back. 'Only a bully would take his temper out on his wife and daughters.'

Philip struggled to get away, but Tom was a bigger, stronger man and pinned him to the wall all the tighter.

'You don't deserve them, Phil. You're not man enough to take care of them as you should. I'm disappointed in you, Phil, because I thought you could do so much better, but you can't get over your own inadequacies and treat these gentle women as they deserve to be treated – with respect and love. It's always been all about you, hasn't it: your sulks, your temper, your selfishness; how you wanted to punish them if they had a good day or something nice happened? You always wanted to spoil it, didn't you, to show that your feelings were more important than theirs?'

Philip was sweating and gnashing his teeth as he tried to escape. Tom adjusted his grip and held on tighter.

'But, you know what, Phil, they don't have to put up with that any longer. You've shown your true colours, so after all these years of putting up with you, it's only fair to allow Dora and Nell to decide if they want to continue their lives here with you. Shall we ask them, Phil? Eh?'

Philip tried to speak but Tom was now gripping his jaw too tightly for any sound to come out.

'I don't hear you, Phil. Was that a "yes"?'

Dora and Ellen were standing at the other side of the kitchen, fixated by the sight of Philip reduced to a helpless victim, a position in which he'd placed them all on numerous occasions. Ellen tried to feel sorry for him but could find no mercy in her heart. She hoped Dora wouldn't crumble when she faced the inevitable decision.

'Let him speak, Tom,' Dora said, tears in her eyes.

'Mum—'

'Shush, love. Let's see this through.'

Tom lowered his hand sufficiently to let Philip speak, though he was still pinned to the wall by Tom's gigantic arm against his chest.

'Ask them, Phil. Go on.'

'Dora, w-will you stay with me?' Philip's eyes were pleading. 'Please . . . stay.'

Tears were running down Dora's face unchecked as she looked at the man she had tried so hard to live with. Now she recognised that was impossible if she wanted to keep herself and her daughter safe. She had tried and she had failed, and the failure felt like hers as much as his. Yet if she stayed and gave her moody, ill-tempered, violent husband one more chance, then she feared there would be one more chance after that, and another after that, and so on for the rest of her life.

'I can't stay, Phil,' she said. 'I can't go on like this. You'll never change. I thought at first I could make you happy, but now I don't know if you even *want* to be happy.

It's easier for you to be the underdog, the one who's hard done by, the one who prefers to think his younger daughter is not his own. You've chosen that road and I don't want to be on it with you any longer.'

She put her hands over her face and wept pitifully for a few moments. Then she swiped the tears from her face and straightened her back.

'Tom asked me to go to him a bit since, but I wanted to give our marriage another – yet another – chance. Now you've had your chances. I've done nowt wrong today that you should take your belt to me, and Ellen hasn't either. I'm done with you, Phil.'

She turned to Ellen. 'Go and get what you need, love, and we'll come back for the rest.'

'If you go to Tom you are never setting foot in this house again,' Philip snarled. 'Either of you.'

'Then we'll take what we can tonight and lose the rest. What are a few bits of stuff compared to being beaten? Nellie, go and do as I ask, please.'

'Yes, Mum,' Ellen whispered, her eyes full of tears. She went heavily upstairs and Dora, Tom and Philip waited without speaking, hearing drawers and cupboard doors being slammed. In a few minutes she returned downstairs with two bulging bags.

'We're going now,' said Tom. 'If you make any trouble, I promise you I shall tell everyone how you've treated Dora and the girls. It's quite possible the Beveridges are only keeping you on at the farm out of respect for Dora and Ellen. I'd think on it, if I were you.'

Dora and Ellen put on their macs and boots and carried

their shoes and umbrellas while Tom took up a bag in each hand. Silently, in the gathering twilight, a watery pink sunset behind them, they set off up the lane like a little party of refugees.

'You'll be back!' yelled Phil.

No one even turned to acknowledge him.

CHAPTER THIRTEEN

James drew up by a pub called the Duke of Clarence on the outskirts of Preston.

'Why have we come all this way for a drink?' Gina asked. 'We've passed quite a few other pubs.' She had noticed every painted sign and hoped at each that James would stop. She had cramp in one leg from being squashed into the little car, and James drove so fast that she felt queasy.

'A friend told me it was a good one,' James said, and came round to help her out of the car. Then he opened the tiny boot and took out the little canvas bag.

'What's in the bag?' Gina asked.

'Never you mind,' James said lightly, tapping the side of his nose, and held open the pub door for her.

The air inside was thick with cigarette smoke and the smell of beer, and the heavily patterned carpet felt as if it were coated in grease when Gina walked on it. This place was nothing like as nice as the Lamb and Flag in Little Grindle. Why on earth had he brought her here?

'What would you like to drink, Gina?'

Gina didn't know. She'd never had a drink in a pub before, and only knew how clean and welcoming the Lamb and Flag was because village events were sometimes held in the back room there.

'Er . . .' she remembered Mrs Thwaite's tipple and smiled. 'I'll have a gin and tonic, please, James.'

Gina sat down at a table stained with ring marks while James went to the bar and got the drinks. There were only a few people in the pub, despite the miasma of smoke, which Gina suspected never cleared, and he came back quickly with a pint of beer and Gina's gin.

'There's no ice, I'm afraid,' he said.

She didn't mind; she hadn't expected ice.

'James, why are we here?' she asked.

'I told you, it was recommended.'

Gina looked around at the horrible interior – she noticed smears on her glass, too – and didn't believe him. Whatever he was here for, it was something to do with what was in the bag, which he'd tucked away under his chair. He kept looking round discreetly as if he expected to see someone he knew. She decided to go along with whatever he said and see what happened.

They talked about the fête, which to Gina felt as if it was days ago now, and James laughed about his experience with Madame Bettina.

'Oh, she was full of warnings about behaving myself,' he laughed. 'Worse than my father! Good thing I don't believe a word of it. What about you?'

'Much the same,' said Gina, shrugging. 'Perhaps she says that to everyone.'

James laughed. 'Maybe she's the self-appointed guardian of Little Grindle's morals.'

'Summat like that,' agreed Gina.

Suddenly James stood up. 'If you'll excuse me a moment, Gina, I'm just out for a breath of air and a smoke.' He picked up his cigarettes from the table and went towards the rear of the pub without looking back. Gina saw that a rough-looking man was standing by the door and he went out ahead of James. James, she noticed now, was carrying the little bag.

She sat and waited for his return, her mind racing. What was this all about? Did James know the man by the door, or was it just coincidence that they went out at almost the same time? It was clear that if James wanted to smoke he had no need to go outside. The whole place smelled like an ashtray.

A horrible thought then came to her. What if James just drove off in his car and left her here? Why would he do that, though? But no matter how much she tried to suppress that idea, she still felt anxious.

James had been gone about three minutes. Should she follow him out to see if he was round the back, smoking? Some half-formed warning in her mind told her not to do this: there were too many unanswered questions about this whole evening, and if James wanted her to know he would have told her right out at the beginning. So it was a secret . . .

With a glance at the back door just to make sure he wasn't returning right then, Gina got up and quickly went out through the front door. The car was still parked by the roadside. At least that laid to rest one of her fears.

She walked to the corner of the building and peered round to see if anyone was there. There was no one. Then she stole up the side and looked round the back corner. James and the other man were standing facing each other, talking and smoking. The man was holding the canvas bag now and he reached inside his jacket, pulled out something and gave it to James. Gina couldn't see what it was. Nor was she near enough to make out anything they were saying. Some of her questions had been answered, but many more had been raised. She rushed back the way she had come and was just settling at the table when James re-entered alone.

'All right, Gina?' he asked.

'Fine,' she smiled.

'Shall we go?'

'Aren't you going to finish your beer?'

'No, I reckon this isn't much of a place after all.'

I could have told you that the minute you opened the door. As if I believe a word of that story of a recommendation . . .

'All right, then. Let's go.'

They went out, got back into the car, and James drove off the way they had come. They were about halfway back to Grindle Hall when he spotted a pretty inn with lanterns lit outside. It looked cosy and welcoming.

'Must have missed this one on the way past earlier,' he said.

'But you told me some friend of yours recommended the Duke of Clarence,' Gina pointed out innocently.

'Wasn't that why we went all that way?' She looked at him for a reaction at being found out lying, but he just chuckled and shrugged.

'So I did. You're a clever girl, Gina. I'll have to remember that,' he said, and parked the car round the side of the pub, which was called the Painted Maypole. 'Let's hop out and see if this one's any better. Gin and tonic, is it . . .?'

~

The gates of Grindle Hall were open, so James drove through and Gina offered to get out and close them behind him.

'I can walk down the drive. There's no need to wait,' she told him.

'There is! I'll see you safely in,' he insisted, which Gina thought was considerate. She hadn't had him down as considerate at all until then.

As she swung the gates closed, she saw the lights on downstairs in the Lodge and she couldn't resist a quick glance inside. Good grief, there were Mum and Nell! Why were they there at this time? What could have happened?

Gina was torn between going to find out – fearing some row with her father after the temper he'd flown into at the fête – and having a peaceful end to the evening. The latter option won; Dora's news would still be news in the morning, and she and Ellen would be safe at Tom's house.

Gina got back in the car and James drove to the house, then round the back into the courtyard of outbuildings. When he'd locked the car, they walked together to the back door.

'Thank you for your company, Gina. I'm sorry about the first pub, but never mind, we did better at the second.'

'We did. Thank you, James. The Painted Maypole was right smart and the food was lovely.'

Gina remembered hearing the landlord saying the cook had just finished for the evening, but James produced some banknotes and just happened to mention – as the landlord went 'to see what he could do' – that his name was Stellion. The Painted Maypole sold Stellion's beer, and Gina saw for the first time in her life just how commerce and influence worked hand in hand. It had been quite an eye-opening experience.

The food was served by the landlord's daughter, who was about Gina's age, and she all but curtsied at their table. Gina felt what it was like to be respected, even if that respect was bought by the money of the man she was with.

The food was delicious and she and James chatted and laughed about Little Grindle and life at the Hall. Gina asked about his life in London.

'Oh, it's not so exciting, Gina,' he said. 'The air is filthy and the fogs in winter are terrible.'

'I'm not bothered about bad weather,' she replied. 'I've lived up here all my life and I reckon I know all about that. Tell me what it is you do and the kinds of places you go to.'

'Well, I deal in things,' he said vaguely. 'Buying and selling.'

'What kind of things?'

'Oh, just little pieces: sometimes jewellery, watches . . .'

'Goodness, that sounds grand. Do you have a shop?' asked Gina, to whom a shop in London represented the height of business success.

'Oh, no,' said James, looking amused.

'What then?' *How can you sell owt if you don't have a shop?*

'I have contacts. I know people, see?'

Gina nodded, though she didn't understand at all. She didn't want him to think she was an ignorant country bumpkin.

'Right, well, I'd better say good night,' said Gina now, unlocking her sitting-room door in the downstairs corridor.

'It was a good evening . . . very interesting. I was glad of your company,' said James softly, and then turned her towards him, bent his head and kissed her on the mouth. 'Good night, Gina,' he whispered, smiling, and then walked away, leaving her standing watching him, her hand to her kissed lips.

~

The next morning was all bustle at Grindle Hall. Diana and Penelope were going back to London and Edith was fussing about their departure, whether they'd remembered all their things and what time the train was. George drove the big car round to the front and the two girls and their luggage were installed inside.

'Thank you for making our stay so nice and everything you've done for us, Gina,' said Penelope smiling and shaking Gina's hand.

'Yes, I think Mum's much jollier with you as housekeeper, Gina,' said Diana. 'And you've done well with Coco's training.' She gave a little laugh. 'Housekeeper and dog walker – my parents know how to get good value from their staff, it seems.'

'Thank you, Diana.' *Making sure I know my place, I reckon.* 'Have a safe journey,' said Gina, turning to smile at Penelope. Despite Diana's slapping her down, Gina thought life at the Hall much livelier and more interesting in the few days Diana and her friend had been there.

There was a lot of waving as they were driven away.

James had made the effort to get up in time to see them off, standing on the front steps with his hands in his pockets. He winked at Gina as he turned to go back in and sauntered off to his father's study, saying he had to telephone someone.

Dora arrived at the back door to start her work soon after that, with Tom accompanying her.

'I know Mr S has taken the girls to the station and I didn't like to come first thing,' he said to Gina, 'but I've some news and I reckon Mr and Mrs Stellion should be told it as well as you.'

'I'll go and make a start and you come up when you're ready,' Dora said to Tom. 'We'll talk later, love,' she added to Gina.

'Come into my little room,' said Gina to her uncle, 'and then you can tell me. It's about Mum and Dad, isn't it?'

'Who told you?'

'No one. I knew there was a row brewing yesterday, and then I saw Mum and Nell at the Lodge in the evening as I went by. So I guessed. I am right, aren't I?'

'Yes, your mum and Nell are staying at the Lodge. She's left him.'

'For good?'

'I reckon so. I don't think she'd dare go back.'

Gina nodded, looking grim. 'I don't blame her!' she said. 'I hate him. I hate the way he hurts her and how he can't ever be nice and kind to her. I hate it that he drags the life out of everything and makes it all dreary and horrible with his sulks and his silences. I know he's your brother and that, but I'm sorry he's my dad.'

'Did he hit you too when you were there, Gina?' Tom asked, angry and concerned.

'Yes, he hurt all of us, though he bashed me the most. He was horrible to us and I reckon now I'm well out of it he's made up for that with Mum and Nell. He beat us with his belt, sometimes for nowt at all but summat he imagined we'd done, or summat we said that he took the wrong way. He took everything the wrong way, though, so in the end Nell and me almost gave up trying to have a normal pleasant conversation with him and we avoided him when we could, though Mum still tried far harder than he deserved. I promised myself I'd get away and find summat better, and here I am, though I know I haven't gone far yet. At least, living here at the Hall, I'm safe from him. It's my greatest wish never to have to set eyes on that bully again, Uncle Tom, and if I could just get rid of him for good, I'd be all the happier.'

'Oh, Gina . . .'

'I'm glad you and Mum are in love – I know you are – and you must keep Mum safe and make sure that Dad never harms her again. Or Nell.'

Tom put his arms around Gina and held her close.

'Don't worry, lass, I'll make sure your mum and Nell are safe. But you must understand that Mum is still married to Philip and it looks bad, her living with me, like she was my mistress or summat,' he looked uncomfortable, 'though she isn't. I don't want folk who know nowt about it judging her and jumping to the wrong answer.'

'You could ask Mr Stellion if she could stay here for the time being. There are the two attic rooms I used to use, now empty. Nell and Mum could both fit in there and it'd satisfy the gossips,' suggested Gina.

'Gina, that's a grand idea, although I mustn't assume that Mr Stellion will say yes.'

'I'll ask Mrs S now. She likes Mum,' said Gina.

Mrs Stellion was very upset to hear about the end of Dora's marriage and that she'd had to escape and seek the protection of Tom Arnold. She asked Dora to come to see her, and Ellen, too, and she listened to their story. Then she agreed to let Dora and Ellen have the attic rooms and made a lot of fuss about whether they were all right after the violence they'd suffered over the years, and whether they'd be comfortable enough there. She had Mrs Bassett making tea for everyone, and could not have been kinder, though the whole business was such a strain on her that she then had to go and lie down on her bed with the curtains drawn.

~

Gina saw James drive away mid-morning. This was what she had been waiting for. Since the previous evening when she'd seen him give the bag to the rough fella lurking at the back door of that awful pub, she had been almost bursting with curiosity, and James's reluctance to tell her anything had only fuelled her desire to find out.

Carrying a large pile of clean towels as a cover for her actions, she went into his room and shut the door. Everyone was at work and Mrs Stellion was lying down.

It was odd, now Gina had met him, to think that this room was where James slept when he came home. With the Spitfire suspended from the ceiling, it was like a little boy's perfect bedroom, not a man's room at all.

His things were lying around untidily. Gina knew she needed to cover her tracks, so she decided to make a note of where anything was before she moved it. She couldn't see a bag like the one he'd given to the man in the pub, though she thought he'd taken a couple out of the car on his arrival. However, she hadn't actually seen him leave the house and he might have taken the second one with him. Nor could she see anything that might have been what the man had given him in return.

She went over to the wardrobe, remembering Mrs Thwaite's hiding place for the stolen gin, and opened the door. There was a shirt and a jacket hanging inside, and that was all. Of course, the first thing she did was search the jacket pockets, but they were empty. The little pigeonholes at the side had only a few small items of clothing in them.

Gina drew out the bottom drawer and found it empty.

She looked around and saw James's little weekend case, which she remembered seeing him take from the car, tucked not quite under the bed. She kneeled down and carefully drew it out. She tried to slide the locks across at the front but they would not move.

Damn . . .

Why would he feel the need to lock his own case under the bed in his own room? The answer was simple: because he had something hidden in it that he didn't want anyone else to see.

Fearing that she'd been here quite long enough, Gina looked around in the vain hope that she would see the key left lying about. Nothing. He probably had it on his keyring and had taken it with him when he went out.

Half-heartedly she opened the bedside cabinet drawer, expecting to find that empty; instead she discovered a key that might well fit the little case. In an instant she was on her knees, trying it. The two little locks turned, she slid them back, and the catches shot up, each with a click.

In the case were a few items of clothing, and underneath a brown manila envelope. This might well have been what she had seen the rough man handing to James the previous evening. She picked it up – it was fat and well filled – and looked inside . . .

Banknotes! Gina gasped. She had never seen so much money in her life – why would she have? Most of it was green one-pound notes, but a quick glance told her that there were very many red ten-shilling notes, too, and, at the back, a few folded white pieces of paper, which she took to be five-pound notes, though she couldn't remember when she had last seen one of those. This was far more than the little hoard of stolen funds Mrs Thwaite had accumulated.

She couldn't resist, there was just so much of it that she thought it wouldn't be missed: she took one of the ten-shilling notes and slipped it into her pocket, then put the envelope back exactly as it had been, under the clothes. She quickly locked the case, pushed it back under the bed and put the key in the drawer where she'd found it. She was just picking up the towels she'd brought to provide her cover for being here, when the door suddenly opened and there was James.

'Gina?'

'James! I was just changing the towels. I'll leave you a couple of clean ones.' She put the top two on the bed.

James gave her a quizzical look. 'Fine . . .' he said, distracted. He took off his jacket and laid it on the bed where it fell heavily.

Gina risked a glance and saw there was the slightly bulging shape of a flat rectangle outlined on the front. A brown envelope with more cash? Possibly.

'Will you be staying for lunch? Mrs Bassett would find it helpful to know.'

'Tell Ma Bassett I wouldn't miss her lunch for anything.'

Gina smiled. 'I'll tell *Mrs* Bassett.'

She went out with the rest of the clean towels, which she took back to the airing cupboard now they'd served their purpose.

Whoo, that was close.

That afternoon, when it was quiet, Gina added the money she'd stolen from James's case to her stash stolen from Mrs Thwaite, who'd stolen it from Mrs Stellion. It passed through her mind to wonder where James had got the money from, and if that, too, had been stolen, but apart from his secretiveness she had no real reason to think so. And anyway, he was the Stellions' beloved son – why would he be a thief?

~

'Do you never stop petting that little dog, Gina?'

'His name's Coco, as you know, James, and he's your mother's little darling – unless that's you,' laughed Gina. 'It's my job to take him for walks, make sure he's all nice and clean, and restore him to your mother so they can have a little nap together in the sitting room of an afternoon.'

'Lucky old Coco. Would Coco mind, d'you think, if I came for a walk with you?'

'I'll ask him,' said Gina, seriously. She bent down, lifted one of Coco's long silky ears and pretended to whisper. 'He says he'll have to show you his best tricks, though.'

'Can't wait,' James replied drily.

'We'll do that first, then,' said Gina, and led Coco on

his lead, and James, from the front of the house round to the outbuildings to show off the dog's high-jumping trick, then had him begging for a dog biscuit.

James was amused. 'I'm not surprised Mum dotes on the little fellow.'

'Now he's used up some spare energy we can have a nice quiet walk,' said Gina, and set off for the big lawn at the back.

It was three days since the village fête and the grass was showing signs of recovering from the tents and visitors.

'I'm surprised to find you still here,' said Gina. 'Don't you have business in London?'

'I do indeed,' said James, 'but I've had a few things to see to up here, too, though a lot of my business can be arranged with a telephone call or two to the right people.'

'Yes, I do that, too,' Gina said. 'Ordering stuff in from the shops for your mother.'

James laughed loudly at that, which Gina thought rather rude. She felt foolish.

'Anyway, I may be going back very soon.'

Gina nodded. She'd expected as much. 'Where do you live in London?' she asked.

'Oh, I've a place in Pimlico,' he said. Then, seeing she looked blank: 'South of the Houses of Parliament.'

That sounded grand, as did the words 'a place'. Grindle Hall was 'a place', and Gina thought James must have a big house with a garden all round.

'Just wondered if you'd like to come out with me this evening – if my mother can spare you, of course, now she hasn't got the girls to amuse her?'

'Well, I'm sure your mother can spare me if *you* ask her,' said Gina. 'Besides, I understand your father is at home this evening, so I shan't be needed for company.'

'And *would* you like to come out for a jaunt?'

'Yes, please.'

'I've got a couple of people to see, but when I've done that we'll have the evening to ourselves.'

'That's all right, James. You did say you'd business to do up here. But you won't be going to that horrible Duke of Clarence pub again, will you? 'Cos if you are, you can go by yourself.'

'No, Gina. As I said, that was a recommendation that I won't be taking up again. Put on your prettiest frock and I'll square your outing with Ma. I'm sure she won't mind you going out with me for a little jaunt before I go back to London if I ask her. I'll have the car out the front at six thirty.'

Gina beamed at him. James knew lots of people and lived in a grand place in London. Who knew what opportunities would be opened up if she played her cards right?

When Gina had finished her work and returned to her room that evening to get ready to go out, she decided to take a quick look in her little book of spells. If she kept in with James, who had a place in Pimlico, so many opportunities would appear, she was sure. Maybe there was an incantation she could try to help things along . . .

~

Ellen and Dora took a paper carrier bag each and strode down the drive to the Lodge. Tom had cooked their tea for them since they'd escaped Philip's violence at Highview Cottage a few days ago, but Dora had said she would cook this evening. She'd walked into Little Grindle earlier and bought a few things from the village shop that she thought he might like to eat. That had been a very enlightening visit.

Ellen had apprised Sally of the news that she and her mother were now living at the Hall when they had gone to see Mr Shepherd the previous day, and she had sworn Sally to secrecy. Sally was to be trusted and, though one or two people had heard rumours, she expertly batted away their questions as she served them in the shop.

But people will gossip, and when Dora entered the village shop late in the afternoon, a hush fell, and the two customers there suddenly had nothing to say. Dora waited her turn behind Mrs Slater and Miss Birch, who usually had an opinion about everything and everyone.

When they had left, Mrs Fowler and Sally were the only ones there.

'I heard about your trouble, Dora, love,' said Mrs Fowler quietly, leaning over the counter. 'You know you can allus turn to me if you need to – you and Ellen both.'

'Thank you, Renee. That's kind.'

'It's all round the village, I'm afraid. Philip's been telling anyone who'll listen, bad-mouthing you and the girls, calling you all sorts of disgusting names. Ranting like a madman, he was, I'm sorry to say.'

'Oh . . .' Tears sprang to Dora's eyes. 'That's so unfair,'

she lowered her voice even though no other customers were there, 'after all we've put up with. We had to escape for our own safety. Why must it be the women who always get punished?'

'Well, you won't be punished by me and Jack,' said Renee Fowler stoutly, 'and I reckon no one's listening to Philip. Everyone likes you, Dora, and no one thinks badly of you here. It's him that's come out wearing the dirt he's been chucking. Think on it, love: who are they going to believe, you or him? When did he ever do anything for the village or for his neighbours? Can anyone in Little Grindle name one single act of kindness with his name on it? I don't think so.'

'It's true, Mrs Arnold,' Sally joined in. 'Folk in Little Grindle look out for their friends, and you and Nell have plenty of friends here.'

'You'll not be alone, love,' said Mrs Fowler. 'I gather you're staying at the Hall, but if you need to find somewhere else, you'll soon learn there's plenty of us happy to have you.'

'Thank you, Renee . . . Sally,' said Dora, wiping her eyes. 'That's right good of you. I don't know what's going to happen 'cos I'm still married to Philip, but I don't want to have to move from here to get right away from him.'

'Nor should you have to, love. It's him that's the bad 'un, and if anyone's going it should be him. Anyway, if you're out and need someone to walk back with and see you safely home, me and our Jack will be happy to do that.'

Sally laughed. 'Aye, Fred Hardcastle was saying the same thing earlier. He said if he saw that Mr Philip Arnold threatening you in any way, he'd beat him with his skillet – and I'm amazed Mr Hardcastle can even lift his skillet, he's that skinny. But he looked like he meant it.'

'Bless him,' said Renee, and the other two nodded.

'So, just to warn you what Philip's saying, that's all, love. There's none that believe it nor think badly of you for turning to Tom in your hour of need. We all like Tom and we all like you, and I reckon it'll soon blow over and there'll be summat else to interest folk before long.'

'Thank you, Renee.' Dora reached across tubes of peppermints and a plate of scones sitting on a doily and hugged her friend, then did the same to Sally.

When she left the shop with her carrier bags, Mrs Slater and Miss Birch were standing chatting on the path outside.

'You all right, Dora?' asked Mrs Slater.

'Yes, thank you, Mrs Slater.'

Miss Birch patted Dora's shoulder. 'You take care, love,' she said kindly. 'Us womenfolk stick together.'

'All right-thinking folk stick together, Florence,' amended Mrs Slater.

'Shall I see you home, Dora?' asked Miss Birch, who was very proud of being 'eighty next year', as she reminded everyone regularly.

'That's so kind of you, thank you, Miss Birch, but I think I'll manage,' said Dora and, as she turned towards the Hall, she thought she'd manage all the better for the support of such kind folk as the villagers of Little Grindle.

CHAPTER FOURTEEN

'WAIT IN THE car. I won't be a minute,' said James, and got out before Gina could ask any questions. Without another word he locked her in and strode away.

He'd driven the short journey to Blackburn and stopped in a cobbled street of sooty-looking terraced houses. He crossed the road and went to the scruffy door of number 16. Someone must have been looking out for him because the door opened to admit him before he knocked, then closed behind him.

Gina hoped he wouldn't be long. The car was already attracting attention. A fella of about her own age came out of another house further up; he stood on the pavement, smoking a cigarette and looking straight at the car. Then he was joined by another youth. Gina was feeling self-conscious, though she knew it was the car that they were looking at, not her. Still, she wished James would hurry up.

She glanced away, out of the side window, and noticed a grubby net curtain twitching aside. The door of the house next to that one opened, and a woman wearing a crossover pinny came out; it was like the one Dora wore to work, but matched with a pair of grubby and misshapen carpet slippers on her feet such as Dora, who was herself a thrifty dresser, would scorn to possess. The woman stood with her arms folded, staring at Gina in the car.

Gina hunkered down in the little seat, her legs bent uncomfortably in the tiny footwell, and prayed for James to hurry up with whatever business he had in the house opposite. The passenger seat of the low-slung car had been agony to sit in as he'd driven over the cobbles. Now the inside was steaming up as Gina sat and waited, and the air outside was grey and felt damp with smoke from the numerous chimneys. She looked around for something – anything – to distract her while she waited, but there was nothing but a dog-eared copy of *Sporting Life* wedged down beside her seat.

Was a drive out here why he'd asked her to put on a pretty frock? Surely not. Even the Duke of Clarence pub in Preston seemed like luxury compared to this filthy place.

Gina closed her eyes and tried to conjure up an alternative scene in her mind. She imagined she was sitting in the garden at the Hall, with Coco curled up on the bench next to her. Deliberately she breathed more slowly and pictured the beautiful flower border running the length of the lawn at the back: all the pink and mauve flowers, the white and pale yellow, the smell of roses and the newly mown grass . . .

The car door opened abruptly, Gina's eyes flew open and she caught her breath as James got back in.

'You scared me,' she gasped shakily. 'This is your idea of an evening out, is it? Some sooty backstreet slum with gawping idiots eyeing up your car while I sit nearly squashed under the glove box for half an hour?'

'Nothing to be scared about,' said James, slamming the door.

'Says you. You weren't the one sitting here, wondering if any of those rough types were about to break in and make away with me. And me with my nice frock on, looking for an evening of fun and half expecting to end up kidnapped instead.'

'Ah, Gina, I would never have left you in danger,' James replied. 'You're far too pretty and, I suspect, far too much of an asset for me not to take proper care of you.'

She looked at him sidelong. 'You'll have to do better than that,' she said. 'This is the second time you've taken me to some hellhole.'

'Oh dear, it's not looking good is it, my dear Gina? I shall have to make it up to you.' He smiled into her eyes and she thought again how handsome he was. 'But I'm all done in Blackburn and now I have in mind something of a treat for you.'

'At last,' said Gina, crossly. 'Then we'd better get on our way.'

'That's my girl. Chin up – let's go and have some fun.'

With a grin James put the car into gear, executed a rapid three-point turn and drove back the way they had come. Providence Street – Gina saw the sign on the wall of the last house as James turned right and pulled away. Surely it couldn't be more misnamed. Ahead in the distance was the most enormous chimney Gina had ever seen, dwarfing everything else, like some structure from a world of giants.

'Something to do with waste disposal,' James said, seeing where she was looking.

'Heck, there must be a lot of waste in Blackburn,' she marvelled.

'A lot of wasters, at any rate,' laughed James. 'At least the people I deal with.'

'Was it all right . . . the business you had to see to there?' she asked tentatively. She was longing to know what it was all about.

'It was fine,' he said, making it clear that was the end of the conversation.

He continued driving in silence for a while, turning west towards Preston, then on towards Blackpool.

'Are we going all the way to the seaside?' asked Gina, seeing the signposts.

'It's all right, you won't need your bathers,' James answered. 'I thought you'd like a walk along the Prom, dinner, maybe a visit to a club. What do you think?'

Gina beamed. 'Thank you, I'd love it. You can make up for earlier.'

'I intend to,' promised James.

Gina had only ever been to the seaside once before. It was quite a long journey from Little Grindle to Blackpool, the nearest seaside town, by bus or train, and Philip had never understood why anyone would want to have a little holiday and some fun on the beach. Gina remembered the day – when she was about eight and Ellen nine, not so very long after the war – being an outing that mainly consisted of restrictions rather than treats; wanting to try new things and being told they couldn't, that it 'costs too much' or 'it's a waste of money' or 'What do you want to do that for?' Dora had tried to make it a happy day for her girls, with a fish-and-chip picnic on the Prom, but it hadn't really been the fun that a day at the seaside was reputed to be at all.

A visit to Blackpool with James Stellion would be far more enjoyable, Gina decided. Or at least she hoped it would. So far the trip was not looking promising, but the prospect of the seaside raised her hopes.

By the time they arrived and James had parked his car in a side street off the front, Gina was excited and quite prepared to put up with the pain in her back and the cramp in her legs from being squashed in the tiny car seat.

'What would you like to do first, Gina?'

'Oh, I'd like to see the sea. I'd love to just walk on the beach for a bit, breathe the fresh air. Blackburn is well named, I reckon. I feel as though I have smuts of soot on my face and I didn't even get out of the car.'

'Well, you haven't,' said James. 'Your face looks lovely.'

'Thank you,' said Gina, smiling. It was nice to be in an exciting place, on the arm of a handsome man who paid compliments.

They walked onto the Prom, then along, gazing at the

sea, which looked cold and grey, and then went down some steps onto the sand. There was hardly anyone there, just a few people packing up for the day and a dog walker or two. A chill wind blew off the sea. James and Gina walked on the sand, their feet sinking in. Gina pulled her cardigan tightly around her and stopped to admire the view and breathe deeply.

'It smells different here,' she said.

'Certainly smells different from Blackburn.'

She laughed. 'I meant from Little Grindle. The air has a different feel to it somehow . . . fresher, mebbe.'

'Now, Little Grindle hasn't a lot to offer, for all it's my parents' home, but it does have a lot of fresh air,' James said.

'You're right there. And sheep. And fields. But it doesn't have owt else really. There aren't many folk there,' Gina remarked.

'Do you mind that? Would you prefer to be where there are crowds?'

Gina thought about what she really wanted. 'I reckon once you've seen all of Little Grindle, and know all the folk there, then you've got to the bottom of it. It's never changed and I reckon it never will. And I'm stuck there, never changing with it, whether I want to or not.'

'And do I deduce that you would like a change?'

'Oh, yes.' She almost surprised herself at the wholeheartedness in those two words. 'More than anything I'd like to see summat of life.'

James didn't reply. Instead he was staring out towards the grey horizon, a thoughtful look on his face.

'Mm, I can understand that,' he said after a while. 'I'm beginning to think, Gina, that you and I have a lot in common.'

'Do we?'

'Oh, yes. Trust me, I know.'

'Why do you think that?'

'I shall tell you later . . . probably. In the meantime, shall we go and find somewhere to eat? What would you like?'

'Doesn't everyone eat fish and chips when they go to the seaside?' asked Gina.

'Only if they're having them outdoors,' laughed James. 'It's the rule with fish and chips: on the seafront, out of a newspaper, and usually with a Force Eight gale blowing.'

'So shall we . . .?'

'The wind's not strong enough. Let's go and find somewhere we can sit down in the warm.'

~

James took Gina to a hotel on the front that had a restaurant. Gina was pleased with the white tablecloths and being waited on at table, and delighted with her gammon and chips, though she noticed James was less enthusiastic about the place and the food. This was what it must be like in Pimlico, she thought, where James lived: eating out in restaurants or hotels. He was so used to this that he couldn't see how special it was. It was a life she could get used to, as well, she decided. Perhaps she would, if she played her cards right. After all, he'd already said that they had a lot in common, and that was surely the first step to a happy relationship . . .

When they had eaten James said, 'I have in mind a little club we can go to, if you like?'

Gina didn't care that it was late: she was having a lovely time. James had been very amusing while they ate, telling her stories about the various cars he'd owned and their unreliability. He made exciting adventures of being stranded at the side of the road in winter, when anyone else would have thought it an ordeal, and the rescues all seemed to involve having to spend lonely nights in creepy isolated castles. Gina didn't really believe a word of it, but she enjoyed the tales. He could certainly tell a good story.

'How do you know all these places?' asked Gina, linking arms with him as they stepped out into the street.

'Maybe I've just been here a few times before,' he said.

James led her down the road to where the lights were brighter, then round a corner to a side street. There were some steps down into a basement and a discreet sign, 'Tom and Tabby', outside the door at the bottom. When he pushed open the door there was a thick curtain, which a woman in a black dress and very red lipstick drew aside to admit them. The club was dimly lit, and Gina was disappointed to see there was no music or dancing, though there was a bar at the back.

James found a table, drew out a chair for Gina, and then, without asking her what she wanted, went to the bar. He came back with two glasses of gin and tonic. Gina had thought it a strange drink when she had asked for one almost as a joke, remembering Mrs Thwaite and her stolen bottles, but now she had begun to acquire a taste for it.

'This wasn't quite what I was expecting,' said Gina, looking round. 'I thought it'd be livelier, like, with dancing and that.'

'I'll take you dancing another night,' said James. 'I've got to see someone.'

'What, here?'

'Yes.'

'Who is this person?'

'Just someone I do business with from time to time.'

The club was smoky, of course – everywhere was – but it wasn't unpleasant like that nasty pub in Preston, or awkward like waiting in the car in that street in Blackburn. But it was a disappointing end to what Gina had thought was her treat. She really had imagined a little dance band, a dance floor with couples, the ladies in pretty dresses, moving gently to the light, romantic songs. She sat there feeling mutinous and wondered if she should just get up and go. But that was a ridiculous idea. How would she get back to Grindle Hall? It was miles away and, although she had a little money in her handbag, it was probably far too late in the evening for her to get a train to Blackburn, then to Clitheroe and then . . . well, something – anything – to take her the rest of the way home.

'What's the man's name?' she asked sulkily.

'Who?'

'The man you do business with.'

'It isn't a man, Gina,' said James. 'Look, I can see

you're fed up, but it won't take very long and then we'll go home, all right?'

She pursed her lips and sat back, looking away. She knew she was behaving like a naughty child but she couldn't help it. She felt she was being let down, that the promised evening was just an excuse for James to have company while he did whatever this 'business' was. He'd even asked her if she wanted to go to a club, when all the time he had arranged to see someone here anyway.

'James, there you are.' A tall woman with jet-black hair, big earrings and a coat with a fur collar approached their table. She looked at Gina with a raised eyebrow.

'This is Gina, a friend of mine,' said James, who had risen to his feet when the woman arrived.

'Hello, Gina,' said the woman. 'James, shall we . . .?'

'Excuse me, please, Gina. I'll be back soon.' He stopped a passing waiter. 'Another gin and tonic for the lady, please,' he ordered, indicating Gina.

'I don't want—' Gina started to say, but it was as if she were an infant and the grown-ups were ignoring her.

James and the woman disappeared through a door at the back of the room and Gina was left alone, sulking. She had taken risks on many occasions in her life – mainly shoplifting or stealing money; and certainly she had told more lies and made up more stories than she could remember – but here she knew she was completely out of her depth. She had no idea who this woman was or what she wanted with James in the back room, and she knew little of what James had been doing at the pub in Preston or anything about the visits to Blackburn and now here. Not only that, but she was tired, she was bored, and she felt sidelined and used.

James came out of the room alone after about five minutes.

'Right, Gina, shall we go?' he asked, so it was clear to her that – as she'd suspected – the whole visit had been about the mysterious 'business' and not about taking her for an enjoyable evening out at all.

'Do as you want,' she answered and got to her feet. 'You know you're going to anyway,' she couldn't resist adding.

'And that, my dear Gina, is why you and I are so alike,' said James.

They went through the curtain, up the stairs to the street, and then Gina looked about, uncertain which way they'd come.

'This way,' said James. 'Don't be cross, Gina.'

She shrugged off his attempt to take her arm, but half-heartedly, then, with a show of reluctance, went with him back to where he'd left the car.

They got in and he drove back towards Little Grindle, the roads quiet and the headlights of the car showing only a tunnel of yellowish light in the pitch-blackness ahead of them.

'You know, you could have told me you only wanted to see some business folk, and not try to make out you were taking me out for summat special,' said Gina after several miles of silence.

'Would you have come?'

'I might. I don't know.'

'But I wanted you to, Gina. I didn't want to risk you turning me down when I so wanted you to come out with me this evening. You remarked about the air at the seaside earlier and that's exactly what you are like to me: a breath of fresh air, a proper woman with backbone and opinions, and courage, most of all. If I'd told the truth I wouldn't necessarily have got what I wanted. But then you know that, don't you?'

'What do you mean?'

'I mean what I was saying earlier – that you and I have a lot in common.'

'You're talking nonsense. We've nowt in common, really. I can see that now, despite what you said. You're from Grindle Hall and I'm from a little cottage that doesn't even belong to us. It just comes with Dad's job.'

'Ah, but you're mistaking circumstances for character, Gina.'

'I don't understand,' she said quietly.

'All right, so tell me this. Why did you take that ten-shilling note?'

Whatever Gina had been expecting, it wasn't that. Found out already! But why had he not said anything earlier? Denying it was pointless: he knew.

'How . . . how did you know?' she whispered.

'Because,' he said, 'I know a thief when I see one.'

In that moment, everything that had happened became completely clear to her and her hands shot up to her mouth in shock. Then she started to laugh.

'What?' asked James, smiling as her infectious laughter overcame him.

Gina laughed long and loud, remembering Mrs Thwaite's bitter and envious face when she had been deposed as housekeeper and exposed as the thief she was, and what she and Gina had said to each other.

It takes one to know one.

Exactly!

Gina stopped laughing and they continued home in companionable silence, the tension and Gina's bad mood dissipated.

'So what are you going to do about it – about the money I admit I took?' she asked eventually.

'I've been wondering,' said James. 'I could, of course, tell my parents and have you dismissed . . .'

'But you're not going to do that, are you, James?'

'No. What would be the point? It would only stir things up and I like things to be settled; I like to know just what to expect, though you're a little unexpected, Gina. Whatever else I thought to find on this visit, it certainly wasn't someone quite so interesting. You and I, we're from the same mould, Gina. It's my amazing good fortune to have met someone who is like me in so many ways, but so lovely, too.'

'Like you? I don't understand.'

'Yes, you do. You've already shown me how you and I are of one mind. We can do very well together, Gina, very well indeed. What I do takes me away from London sometimes, so if you're here, seeing to a few things for me, it'll save me that long, long journey up north a time or two, for which I would be very grateful to you, Gina.'

'James, stop the car!' said Gina. 'Stop here, right now.'

'What?'

'I said stop the car.'

He pulled over to the side but kept the engine running. They seemed to be in the middle of nowhere, not a light visible in any direction.

'Gina?' He looked worried. Maybe he'd misjudged everything.

Gina shifted round in the uncomfortable seat so that she could look straight at him. 'First of all, James, I don't think you can just assume I'll help you out of the goodness of my heart, and secondly, if I'm to be a part of whatever your business is – take any role in it at all, however small – then I need to know exactly what it is that you do. No pulling the wool with vague explanations and the like. No pretending summat's a treat or a nice evening out when it's all about this business of yours. No treating me like a green lass who'll wait about while the grown-ups get on with it.'

'So you're saying, if you're in, you're all in?'

'You've got it, lad. And that means I'm to be paid for owt I do, too. As I say, you can't assume I'll be doing owt 'cos I'm nice. I'm not that nice.'

'I know that, Gina. That's why I think you'd be perfect for what I have in mind.'

'So, James, I think you'd better start explaining exactly what it is that you do. And then you can tell me where you reckon I fit in.'

'Gina, you're priceless!'

'Oh, no,' she breathed, 'far from it. Now, get talking.'

~

Tom, Dora and Ellen set off up the gravel drive of Grindle Hall. They'd had such an enjoyable evening at the Lodge that Dora was almost able to forget about her troubles for an hour or two.

'You're a grand cook, Dora,' said Tom. 'I'm used to doing for myself but it's pointless cooking for one. Some nights I go down to the Lamb and Flag for a pint and a pie, game of darts with the lads, but I've enjoyed our evenings and your shepherd's pie made today extra special.'

'Aye, cooking is about giving and sharing, isn't it? I can see why you'd think there was little point in the effort just for one,' she sympathised.

'Hardly worth getting the pans out,' he agreed, wrapping one arm round Dora and the other around Ellen.

There was a rustle in the shrubs alongside the drive.

'What was that?' Dora asked, looking nervous. She'd felt anxious since her trip to the village shop earlier. The villagers had been so kind and supportive, but they obviously thought she needed protecting, and she was unnerved to think Phil was spouting lies about her, even if no one was taking any notice.

'Don't know, love,' said Tom, not dismissing her concerns. 'Wait here,' he said quietly, and stepped light-footedly over to the dark shrubs, peering into the shadows in the half-light of an overcast late summer evening. After a minute or two he came back to Dora and Ellen. 'I reckon it were nowt, just some roosting bird or mebbe a rat. We'll get the traps out tomorrow, Nell; make sure they're not thinking of moving into the sheds now the days are getting shorter.'

'I know what to do. Ed showed me once at the farm.' Ellen had a thoughtful look on her face and as they continued down the drive she looked back, searching the shrubs.

They went round the side of the house, past the kitchen door, now locked up, and Dora produced the key to the door leading from the courtyard backed by the outbuildings, and let herself and Ellen in. They exchanged good nights and then Dora and Ellen went inside and Dora locked the door, leaving the light on in the corridor, as always.

'I'll just get myself a glass of water,' said Ellen as Dora turned for the narrow stairs that led straight up to their rooms in the attic. 'Give me the key and I'll hang it on the hook.'

'Here, love . . .'

Ellen made sure Dora was off up the stairs before she ran back to the outer door, unlocked it, quickly locked it behind her and rushed out into the courtyard. She'd definitely felt the presence of someone along the drive, and who would be hiding in the dark except someone up to no good? She opened the door of the building where Gina played with Coco on wet days, and grabbed the broom handle she used for the puppy's high jump, then ran as fast as she could back round to the drive. There was no one in sight on the gravel and, ahead of her, she could see Tom briefly silhouetted by the light from his sitting room as he opened then closed his door.

Mebbe it were nowt. Mebbe, like Mum, I'm just feeling a bit jumpy.

Ellen slowed her breathing and stood quite still, looking all round, clutching the broom handle in white knuckles. All was quiet. There was no one there but her.

Suddenly there was the distant but unmistakable sound of breaking glass. At first Ellen thought it was one of the house windows, but all were closed and dark, at least at this side. The Stellions would be in bed by now.

I'll get Uncle Tom and we'll go and check together. I can't leave it . . .

She turned back towards the Lodge and saw, through the little latticed window by the side gate, flames dancing up.

'Uncle Tom!' Instantly Ellen was racing down the drive to the Lodge. When she got there she could see Tom and her father struggling in a vicious fight as the flames leaped beside them.

Ellen barged open the door and, with the advantage of surprise and having seen where in the room her father was, she set about him with the broom handle as hard as she could thrash, hitting him over and over as he left off his struggle with Tom and tried to evade her blows.

'That's from Gina, you beast! And that's from me! And this . . . and this. . . and these are from Mum . . .'

Philip sank to his knees under the onslaught of her attack, cowering and covering his head as Ellen rained down more blows, pitilessly, regardless of the fire, which Tom was now dousing with water from the flower vase Dora had filled for him earlier, then a pan of water grabbed from his tiny kitchen.

Eventually Philip collapsed on the floor and Ellen stood over him, breathing hard.

'Oh God, Uncle Tom, do you think I've killed him?' she gasped, seeing her father lying battered and still.

Tom stamped out the last flame that was flickering in the smouldering rug and bent to examine the man on the floor. Seconds went by and Ellen stood helplessly, her hand to her mouth in horror at what she had done.

'No, love. He lives,' Tom muttered eventually, mopping blood from his nose. He gathered his arms around her and held her close as she sobbed into his shirt. 'There, there, love, don't take on. There'll be no trouble for you from this, I promise. Dry your eyes, Nellie. You're a brave lass . . .'

'Oh, Uncle Tom, I just knew – I don't know how but I sort of guessed that summat was going to happen and I came back to see if you were all right, and then . . . and then . . .'

'Shush, love. You've been that brave. Where's your mum? Is she safe?'

'Yes, she's inside. I locked the door when I came out. I couldn't risk an intruder getting in.'

'No, love, not an intruder. A rat, as I said earlier. Now, you go up to the house and get Gina to phone for the police and an ambulance.'

'Will I be arrested?' Her eyes were wide.

'No, love. We'll tell the truth and there'll be nowt to worry about.'

'I think Gina's out this evening.'

'No matter. Go and telephone yourself. There's a

telephone in that little room where we saw Mr Stellion on your first day, remember, near the conservatory? Go now.'

'Yes . . . yes, I'm going.' Ellen backed out of the door and ran as fast as she could back to the Hall, knowing even as she ran that this was a turning point; that from now on her life would be changed for ever and, more importantly, so would her mother's.

PART TWO

Ellen
March 1957–November 1957

CHAPTER FIFTEEN

THE POSTMAN, ARTHUR Smollett, pedalled up the drive of Grindle Hall and round to the courtyard where he rang the bell at the back door. Gina knew what time he came by and she was there ready to take the parcel she was expecting, delivered safely into her hands and unseen by anyone else at the Hall.

'Some letters for Mr and Mrs Stellion and another parcel for you, Miss Arnold,' said Arthur. 'You're very popular lately.'

'Just a few bits of shopping that caught my eye in a magazine,' said Gina. 'I like to stock up with birthdays and the like in mind.'

'Very wise,' said Arthur. 'I wish my wife was as organised as you.'

Gina smiled and wished him a good morning. A few seconds later the brown paper wrapping with her name and address on it had been ripped off and burned in her little fireplace, leaving only a plain cardboard box, which Gina hid under her bed. She knew the kind of things it would contain. Not birthday presents, exactly – though some might eventually make someone's birthday treat – but the small items that James Stellion dealt in: jewellery, miniature paintings, little ornamental boxes, that kind of thing. All stolen.

James called this 'redistribution', meaning the items, which were sold to James quickly and cheaply by the thieves, were then sent, or brought by James himself, to Grindle Hall, many miles from where they had been stolen in London and the south of England. Then they would be sold on to people who would put them back on the market at something like their true value, leaving him a decent profit margin. Sometimes James had had to deal with what Gina thought were rather shady characters who acted as go-betweens for him and the northern dealers, such as that rough-looking fella at the Duke of Clarence last year, but since coming in on his business, Gina had objected to sharing the profit with these intermediaries, and, as she said to James, the fewer people involved, the safer the business. So now James made very few visits to the Duke of Clarence or Providence Street, Blackburn.

Now the goods were disposed of via the pawnbrokers of Manchester, Preston and Blackburn, and, of course, there was always Bella Bertolli, the tall, dark lady at the Tom and Tabby in Blackpool.

Bella, whose real name was not Bertolli and who was not Italian, had a sister with a little shop somewhere in the Lake District, where visitors could browse the pretty pieces of jewellery and pay decent money for souvenirs of their holidays. Bella's sister knew nothing of where the items Bella brought to her originated, and nor did she enquire. She bought jewellery and other artefacts from many sources and chose to think that all were legitimate.

Gina took the letters Arthur had brought up to Mrs Stellion, who was sitting in the morning room, looking pale. Coco got out of his basket to say good morning, his stumpy tail wagging madly.

'How are you this morning, Mrs Stellion?' asked Gina, patting the dog.

'Oh, Gina, dear, I could hardly get out of bed. I find the mornings so dark now and it's quite exhausting. It'll be dark still until Easter.'

'Well, it's a way to go yet, true – it's only the beginning of March – but it is getting better.'

'Oh, don't, dear! How can I bear all those dark weeks ahead? It's worse every year, I'm sure of it. By the time it's 1960, I think it'll be dark most of the year.'

'I don't reckon it works like that, Mrs Stellion,' Gina said drily. 'And anyway, Diana will be coming at the weekend for the birthday celebrations, so you've every reason to be cheerful. You hadn't forgotten?'

'No, of course not, Gina. Something lovely to look forward to. I don't know if James is coming, too. I hoped he might make it for his father's birthday, but he says he's very busy at the moment. There's a concert in Manchester I'd like us to go to, if I can still get tickets.'

'Show me and I'll telephone to see what they have, after I've taken Coco for his walk, if you like.'

'Thank you, dear. You're such a help. What would I do without you?'

What indeed?

'How are your mother and Ellen settling back into Highview Cottage?'

'Thank you, they're really happy – not that they weren't grateful for the rooms here, of course, but it's nice to have your own space, isn't it?' Gina glanced ironically round the morning room, which was larger than the whole of the downstairs at Highview Cottage.

'If there's anything stored upstairs that you think they would like, let me know,' said Edith. 'Not from the nursery, though,' she added quickly.

'Thank you, Mrs Stellion. I'll take a look and ask Mum, too. Now, Coco, time for us to be out,' said Gina. 'Come on, boy,' and the well-trained dog obediently followed her from the room.

Gina decided, as it was a beautiful sunny day, despite what Edith had said, that she would take Coco for a walk into the village. They set off down the drive, Coco meandering between interesting scents along the way. When they got to the Lodge, Gina allowed herself a peek through Tom's window, as she often did.

All trace of the fire had long since been removed or made good. It hadn't done much damage, thank goodness; Ellen had intervened too quickly, freeing Tom from Philip's assault to douse the flames before they spread too far.

Gina remembered arriving back with James in the car on that most momentous of evenings to find the drama almost over, though the presence of the police had sent James and Gina, with her new knowledge of his activities, into a tailspin for a moment. Luckily they'd just about kept their nerve, and soon found the police weren't in the least bit interested in them. Her father had been taken away in an ambulance. He'd never gone home again. Now he lived at Calderstones Hospital, a vast mental asylum near Whalley. There were regular, though infrequent, reports on his progress, apparently, but Gina didn't trouble herself with them. She was just glad to have her father out of her life – all their lives. Ellen and Tom had acted entirely in self-defence and Philip had been declared the instrument of his own downfall.

Gina's thoughts turned to James; how close they had become since that evening when he'd told her everything of his business and invited her to join him. Now she thought she was in love with him. He said he felt the same about her, but sometimes she wondered . . . He could be so wonderful, so loving and kind when he wanted to be. He'd mentioned taking her to join him in London once or twice. Nothing had come of that so far, though she had high hopes of it still. He was waiting until the time was right. He had made no suggestion that he should move north to be with her, however, although he claimed to miss her when they were apart, and she felt there were times when he seemed only to think of her when he wanted her to hide some items or sell them on for him.

'It's very useful having you here to keep an eye on things,' he'd said last time he visited his parents, at

Christmas, removing a couple of silver gilt cups she'd had hidden under her bed and stowing them in the boot of his car, parked near the back door. She'd seen there were two cloth bags in the boot already. 'It's good to keep a distance between supply and demand. I'll drive over to see Bella tomorrow – do you want to come . . .?'

Of course, she liked the money that came from the sale of the items, and a few times, on afternoons off, with James's permission, she had taken some of the smaller pieces to various pawnbrokers' shops herself. She always went by bus and liked to play a part and make up a little story about the necklace or brooch she'd brought and why she needed to pawn it. She knew better than to offer information, but it was always a good idea to have a story in place in case anyone ever quizzed her. She even kept a diary of which pawnbrokers she had visited, what she had left there and for how much, and what she had said, if anything. She was nothing if not thorough.

She wanted so much for James to turn up for his father's birthday. Edith would stop being so peevish for a few days and, with luck, there would be the chance of a drive out 'to the seaside'. Gina was keen to get rid of the stolen items she'd received in the parcels as quickly as possible. James always cleared it with his mother when he took Gina out; he remained Edith's darling boy and, though Gina didn't know exactly what was said, she got the impression James could wind his mother around his little finger when it suited him. Gina was careful never to speak affectionately of James to Mrs Stellion, in fact never to speak of James at all, so there was no danger of any questions being asked.

And then there was the pleasure of James's company. She thought of how he liked to drive the little car so fast, sometimes with the roof down, even in winter, his fair hair blowing untidily – oh, but so boyishly – in the wind, a rather flash pair of sunglasses on his nose . . . his handsome profile . . .

Coco was snuffling and woofing around her feet, eager to get on with the walk.

'All right, you little beggar,' she said affectionately. 'I haven't forgotten you. Come on . . .'

~

It was a Wednesday afternoon and Ellen and Sally were free to go to see Mr Shepherd in Great Grindle. They knew their elderly friend also looked forward to these visits and they tried to go as often as their limited free time would allow.

'Come in, Nell, love,' said Mrs Mason as Sally opened the door to their cottage to admit her. As ever, the place was chaotic with noisy infants. 'David, Frankie, shut up and say hello nicely to Nell, like the little gentlemen you are.'

'Lo, lo, lo,' shouted David, or was it Frank? Ellen didn't know; the twins were identical and always dressed the same too.

'It saves having to think about the unimportant things,' Sally's mother had once explained. 'All the clothes are blue, all fit both boys, and if I see owt they need I buy six of it, 'cos you can bet your life it'll be covered in summat unmentionable within an hour of being put on. They can choose what to wear themselves when they're buying their own things. If they grow fast enough they can share with Polly, too. That'll save a bit more messing about in a morning.'

Ellen had looked at Polly, wearing a pink gingham frock at the time, and burst out laughing.

Today Polly was wearing blue rompers, so Ellen thought Audrey Mason was planning ahead.

'How's your mum, Nell? I haven't seen her for a week or so. Polly, pipe down a bit, love, will you? I can hardly hear myself think.'

'She's very well, thank you, Mrs Mason. She's been busy with getting the Hall ready for Mr Stellion's birthday at the weekend, and we've been making new curtains and other bits for the cottage of an evening.'

'I might walk over with the kids in the pram before it gets dark and have a look.'

'She'd love it if you did. You're welcome any time.'

Audrey Mason lowered her voice. 'Not heard owt new about your dad?'

'We have not. I think Mum would rather not be thinking about him at all,' said Ellen.

'Aye, don't worry, lass, I'll zip my lip on that subject then. But you both know where to come if you're worried about owt, don't you?'

'Thanks, Mrs Mason.'

'Looks like a nice afternoon for your walk over there.' Sally's mother changed the subject. 'Frankie, David, shush a minute, will you? Give my best wishes to Mr Shepherd, won't you?'

'Aye, Mum. We will that,' Sally said. She raised her voice over the noise her siblings were making. 'If you're not in when I get back, I expect you'll have gone to Highview. Leave me a note and I'll put the tea on.'

'Good lass. Off you go then.'

Sally kissed her mother, Polly, David and Frank in turn, and she and Ellen went out into the quiet of the village street.

'Crikey,' Sally muttered.

Ellen and Sally walked on in companionable silence for a few moments.

'So, you're pleased to be settled back at Highview?' said Sally eventually.

'Of course. The attic at the Hall – it was kind of the Stellions, and helped us out when things were bad, but it wasn't a home. Mr Beveridge's new man already lives in the village – Nathan Prentice, you'll know him, I expect – so he and Mrs B have let us have the cottage for not much rent, and they even bought the paint; said it was helping them if we kept it updated. They've been so kind.'

'They are. And you'll be pleased to be at the end of the lane from Ed, I reckon,' Sally suggested, looking sidelong at Ellen.

'It's long been our home and now Mum's made it all bright and beautiful instead of gloomy and dark, like it had got over the years 'cos Dad didn't see the point of improvements. It's like a different place and she's like a different person.'

'I'm right glad, Nellie. So what's happened to . . . to your dad's things?' Sally's curiosity could sometimes get the better of her.

'Oh, Mr and Mrs Beveridge have stored them in the back of one of the outhouses. Mum's removed the lot. I reckon she hopes she won't need to think about him coming back ever.'

'And what do you think, Nell?'

'Same as Mum, same as our Gina: I never want to set eyes on that monster again.'

Sally reached out and silently gave Ellen's arm a squeeze and they turned off the road and into the fields to cut the corner from the journey.

When they reached Great Grindle Main Street, there was an unusual amount of traffic backed up along the road, moving slowly.

'Mebbe an accident,' suggested Sally, 'though I can't see any sign . . . Oh, it's a funeral! That explains it.'

The funeral cortège was already ahead of them and they followed it up the road. At Bookworm Cottage they opened the gate and went up the path to knock on Mr Shepherd's door. There was a long wait. Just when the girls were beginning to get anxious, the door opened and there was Mr Shepherd with his walking stick.

'Come in, Sally and Ellen. I'm a bit slow today, with my hip, but I'm glad to see you.'

The girls went in, each giving him a hug.

'We saw a funeral procession just now on Main Street,' Sally announced, bursting with curiosity. 'Do you know whose? I hope it wasn't a friend of yours.'

'No, not a friend exactly, Sally, but someone I was acquainted with from the library van: Mrs Thwaite. Ellen, you'll remember her, as I reckon you must have crossed over at the Hall. Widow, nice enough in her way, but no sense of humour.'

'Oh! Yes, of course. Goodness, I'd no idea she'd died. She wasn't *that* old, was she?'

'Younger than me,' said Mr Shepherd with a slight smile. 'Heart attack, I was told. I wonder you hadn't heard, Ellen, what with your sister taking over when the lady broke her arm last year.'

'I've heard nowt about her, I'm afraid. Oh dear, I wonder if they know at the Hall. But why wouldn't they? Yet . . . oh, I'm a bit confused. I'm sure I would have heard, though not necessarily from Lucas Hillier in the library van.'

Ellen and Sally exchanged looks.

'He's not chatty,' Sally said.

'So I gather,' said Mr Shepherd, drily. 'Ah, well, there we are. It'll come to us all in the end . . . and in the meantime there's more books to read than any of us'd manage if we lived to be a hundred.'

'True,' smiled Ellen. 'Shall I make a pot of tea, Mr Shepherd, and then you can tell us what you think of *My Family and Other Animals*? I can hardly believe we managed to recommend a book to you that you hadn't already read!'

~

On the way home the girls discussed the news about Mrs Thwaite.

'What if Mr and Mrs Stellion haven't heard she's dead? It seems such a strange thing after she worked for them for all that time – you'd have thought her nephew would have let them know – but they'd have wanted to be at the funeral, surely, and I know they weren't there. Gina told me earlier that Mrs S was going to Whalley to see a friend.'

'I don't know, Nell. Had she fallen out with them at all, do you know?'

'Like what?'

'Well, she did leave with her broken arm and never went back. And your Gina was made housekeeper quite soon after Mrs Thwaite's accident.'

'She retired, that's all. I expect she was glad to go and live with her sister and not have to work.'

'I expect so. I'll get Mum on to it next time the library van comes around and let you know.'

~

'By heck, Dora, you've made this a little palace,' said Audrey Mason, going in through the back door of Highview Cottage and looking around the kitchen.

'Thank you, Audrey. We've been busy but we've had a lot of help: Nancy and Albert couldn't have been kinder, and Ed's a grand lad and painted all the ceilings. Truth be told, I think it was half to impress our Nell, but I don't mind. And then Tom, of course, shifted all the furniture up- and downstairs for us. Even Gina helped by washing the front windows downstairs when we were finished.'

'David, Frank, you two sit there and don't touch anything,' instructed Audrey, pointing to the hearthrug. 'Polly, you and Teddy on that chair, please, love, and do try not to suck Teddy's paws. You'll get fur in your stomach.'

'Come and sit on my knee, boys,' said Dora. 'There now, that's grand . . . So you see, we're very lucky.'

'Well, you deserve a bit of luck, Dora. And how's things between you and Tom?'

Dora smiled. It wouldn't be like Audrey Mason not to say what was passing through her mind. 'Thank you, we're just fine. Tom's a good man – the best – but I'm still married to Phil.'

'No one would blame you if you were to divorce him, love, what with him being like he is. It's not as if you haven't got grounds.'

'I know, but *divorce*, Audrey. I don't know anyone who's divorced.'

'Nor me, but I bet we could point to a few with unhappy marriages.'

Dora sighed. 'True enough, lass, but it feels like kicking him when he's down. Besides, I have to wait five years after he's been certified insane, and that's a long time yet.'

'Well, you must do as you feel's right, love. But you don't have to sacrifice your whole life, you know. Everyone deserves to be happy, and I fear if you were still together he'd be kicking *you* when you were down.'

Dora looked shocked, though she knew Audrey spoke the truth.

'And don't forget Tom deserves to be happy, too,' Audrey added for good measure. 'Now, let's have a look at your sitting room, Dora. Come on, Polly, and don't touch anything.'

'Would you like a cup of tea, Audrey, and summat for the little 'uns? I've dandelion and burdock.'

'No, thank you, Dora. I'll just have a quick admire of your handiwork and then get these babes out of your way before you're mopping off sticky fingermarks. I said *don't* touch, Polly . . .'

Audrey Mason stayed to admire the pale colours on the walls upstairs and down, and the floral curtains, 'a bit like Mrs Stellion's bedroom,' confided Dora, 'but less flowery, like, and made of remnants from the market, of course.'

'You've a real talent, lass,' said Mrs Mason as she left, stowing all three infants into an enormous, well-sprung but shabby pram that resembled a small boat in shape.

Dora waved them off down the lane and then noticed Ellen approaching at a distance, walking slowly with Edward, their arms wrapped around each other. He made a habit these days of meeting her in the village after she and Sally had been to Great Grindle to see Mr Shepherd. Edward was saying something, and Ellen looked up into his face and laughed as he pulled her to him and kissed the top of her head. They stopped to greet Mrs Mason and the children.

Dora watched, smiling. That's what she wanted for her

darling Nellie: a fine man who adored her, to love and protect her, and who Nell loved in return; a life of laughing together; and maybe, eventually, a pramful of beautiful babies. What more could a woman want?

It seemed that Nell might have found the right man to share her life. Dora hoped so.

And what of Gina? She worried about her younger daughter, who could be so naughty and wayward. What Gina needed was a good fella to keep her on the straight and narrow. Dora hoped it wouldn't be long before she found such a man.

CHAPTER SIXTEEN

Ellen watched Ed until he reached the turn in the lane and was out of sight. Such a dear man, so gentle and kind, always considerate about how they spent their time together, always meeting her if she was out without him, and walking her home. Today he'd been full of news about his Herdwick lambs being born. She loved to hear him talking about the farm and all his plans for it. He was so cheerful, so full of hope for the future, despite being a farmer!

From where she was standing, she could see just how badly overgrown and untidy the cottage garden had become since she and Dora had fled Philip's violence that evening after the village fête all those months ago. Although he had been there alone for only a few days after Ellen and Dora had left, the cottage had been beyond filthy by the time he was carted off, first to hospital and then to the asylum, having been officially declared insane. Returning only to visit it weeks later, when all the formalities had been dealt with, Dora had seen it with new eyes and had been appalled at its shabbiness. Having worked so hard on the house, she and Ellen now needed to tackle the garden before the weeds took over entirely. Ellen felt the stirrings of excitement within her when she thought of restoring this patch of ground, not just to its former glory but *beyond* what it had even been before. It could be their special project for the spring: a little garden with which they could do whatever they wanted. There was so little in life where they had such freedom!

She went inside where Dora had a pot of tea ready.

'Hello, Nell. How was Mr Shepherd this afternoon? I saw you pass Audrey Mason a few minutes ago – she came to admire the decorating.'

'She wouldn't be admiring the garden, though, Mum. I've just noticed how bad it's got. It's grown up since even last week. Let's see if we can do a bit each week and get it back in shape by Easter. What do you say? Uncle Tom can mebbe lend some heft – I know he wouldn't mind – and Ed, too.'

'Thank you, Nell. Good idea – I've been feeling a bit down about it – but we mustn't take advantage of our menfolk.'

Ellen beamed. '*Our menfolk,* Mum – yes.' They exchanged smiles. Neither pried into the other's private life but discreetly looked out for each other. It was Ellen's greatest wish to see her mother happy, but she and Uncle Tom would have to find their own way in their own time. She wouldn't interfere.

'Oh, and I have some strange news,' Ellen went on, looking serious. 'Mrs Thwaite has died. A heart attack,

Mr Shepherd said. Sal and me saw the funeral procession – not many mourners – and we wondered if Mr and Mrs Stellion knew about it. Seems odd if no one saw fit to tell them after all the time Mrs Thwaite worked for them.'

'Aye, it does. I'm sorry to hear of the lady's death. She wasn't my particular friend, but I saw no harm in her. I shall mention it to Gina tomorrow. She's the one to raise it with Mrs S. I can hardly go barging in with the news and upsetting folk. I wonder Mrs Bassett didn't mention it. I thought they used to be friends of a sort, but mebbe I read it wrong.'

~

'Mrs Thwaite dead?' Gina said.

Dora could see she was trying to compose her face into something resembling solemnity, but a smile was definitely playing at the corners of her mouth.

'Gina, you needn't look so pleased about it,' Dora snapped before, God forbid, Gina shamed her by breaking into the laughter that was so obviously threatening. 'For goodness' sake, Eliza Thwaite was an employee of this house, just the same as we are, and worked here for a lot longer than you have. Have a bit of respect, lass, and try for once to behave in the right way.' Dora was shocked and furious at Gina's suppressed mirth. What could possibly be funny? Sometimes the girl just didn't know when she had overstepped the mark. How had she raised a daughter who could be so heartless?

They were in the little library, where Dora had taken

her cleaning things and then quietly asked Gina if she'd come in. She had planned to break the news to her privately, then maybe speak herself to Mrs Bassett while Gina told Mrs Stellion. Now she wasn't at all sure she could trust Gina to act appropriately.

'Sorry, Mum,' said Gina, composing herself. 'It must be the shock. I'd better tell Mrs Stellion.'

'Not if you're going to laugh you hadn't. You'll upset her terribly.' Dora sighed heavily. 'What is it, Gina? Did you have summat against the woman?'

'Mum, she was housekeeper here and now I am – what could I possibly have against her? It was only a short time when we were both here . . . before her accident.'

Dora gave Gina a long look. 'So, are you going to tell Mrs Stellion nicely, assuming she doesn't know already, which I reckon she can't or she'd have said summat?'

'Yes, I'll tell her.'

'Then make sure you do it properly and that you're kind to her.'

'Yes, Mum.'

~

Mrs Stellion was indeed upset, especially to hear that Mrs Thwaite was not only dead, but to realise that her sister hadn't written to tell her former employer, and the funeral had taken place without the Stellions' knowledge.

'It was Eliza who chose to retire after her accident. I thought she was living happily in Great Grindle with her sister,' Edith lamented. 'Oh, Gina, dear, it seems as if she might somehow have held a grudge against us – or her family did, to cut us out of their lives so completely – and I can't think why.'

'There's no knowing . . .' said Gina vaguely. 'I'll bring you up a pot of tea, Mrs Stellion. Try not to be upset.'

'Oh dear, I fear there's been a dreadful misunderstanding,' Edith went on, tears in her eyes. 'Perhaps I should write to her sister.'

'Why don't you leave it until after Mr Stellion's birthday celebrations?' Gina suggested. 'I'll find out what I can and then we'll decide what's the best thing to do.'

'Oh, Gina, you're right, of course. Thank you, dear.'

Edith leaned back in her chair, patting her forehead as if she felt a headache coming on, and Gina went to make the tea.

It was, she decided that night, tucked up in her bed above the boxes of stolen goods, extraordinary how everything had worked out so well. The book of spells was gathering dust on her shelf these days. It had proved so effective that she was wary of it, and had long since decided to consult it only in emergencies. The spells were both extremely powerful but also far reaching. Who'd have thought that it would take so long to get rid of her father, from the little cursed bottle hidden in the wall last spring to his being incarcerated in the asylum at the end of summer? And now Eliza Thwaite was not only out of Gina's way, which had proved to be sufficient, but out of the way of everyone!

Gina turned over in bed, laughing quietly. James had telephoned his parents to say he'd be here 'at some point' for his father's birthday, so there was much to look forward to. Gina remembered that she'd recited one of the incantations and performed a little ritual in connection with James, too. Well, she now knew better than to be impatient: these magic spells didn't necessarily bring instant results, but they certainly were effective in the end.

~

James slouched into the house late on the Saturday morning, just as the mist was lifting from the fells. Gina had been looking out for him from an upstairs window, and her heart fluttered with excitement when the little car, the top up this morning against the damp, crunched up the drive. Always one to announce his presence, James parked prominently at the foot of the front steps and unfolded himself from the driver's seat.

Gina rushed out to the corridor and was taking the stairs two at a time when she saw Edith, George and Diana were in the hall to greet him already, so she slowed and tiptoed silently to join them at a distance.

'Happy birthday, Dad,' James said, and he and George shook hands. Then James turned to kiss his mother and hug Diana.

'Nice to see you could make it,' said George drily. He'd said the same thing at Christmas, Gina remembered. 'Diana came up yesterday.'

'Not at the office yesterday, Di? Doing important typing?' teased James.

'Been working my socks off to get the early train up, actually,' she said. 'Not that you'd know about working.'

'Or trains,' smirked James. 'But I do know about socks.' He raised the turn-ups of his trousers to reveal bright orange socks.

'Good heavens!' said Edith, laughing. 'I've never seen anything like them.'

'I shouldn't think you have in Clitheroe,' said James. 'I'll get you a pair if you like, Dad; cheer up your meetings at the brewery.'

Everyone was laughing then, and Gina felt a pang of envy at the happiness of this family. She wished she was one of them: a Stellion, in on the jokes, a proper part of their lives at the Hall; wearing nice things that Stellion money could buy. She shot an envious look at Diana's smart trousers, soft, fine jumper, and her shiny hair tied with a knotted silk scarf – a rich girl's look, she knew instinctively; a father who didn't snarl or belt her, a strict but kind man who wasn't in a lunatic asylum.

'Gina . . .?'

'Oh, sorry, I was . . .'

'Would you mind just popping my bags up, please, Gina?' said James. He grinned and winked discreetly at her as he turned away.

Gina went down to the car and opened the boot. There was his little weekend case and also a zip-up holdall. She lifted them out and shut the boot. The holdall whispered with the sound of crumpled newspaper: *treasure.*

It wouldn't surprise me if we took a trip to the seaside.

Gina buried her jealousy and looked forward to the part of James's life that she was in on, and of which George, Edith and Diana knew nothing.

~

It was Sunday before Gina and James had a chance to make any plans.

'I need a breath of air,' James said languidly at breakfast. 'Gina, may I join you and Coco for your walk?'

'You may, James,' smiled Gina.

'I might come, too,' said Diana.

'What time's your train, darling?' asked Edith. 'You mustn't risk missing it. Dad will take you to the station, of course, won't you, George?'

'Oh, after lunch, Mum.'

'And what about you, James? How long can you stay, darling?'

'Thought I might hang around for a few days; drop in at the brewery, show willing. What do you say, Dad?'

'Excellent. It's about time you took an interest there. I shan't live for ever, you know, and then the business will be yours. Heaven knows what you get up to in London, working at that art dealer's, but it seems a bit of a come-and-go kind of job. You'll need to take over from me at Stellion's Brewery at some point, so you might as well begin learning what's what now.'

Art dealer's? Is that what James has told them?

Gina hadn't thought through that James would have had to lie to his parents about what he did – make up a whole alternative life – but how could he not? Yesterday, when the family had gone to Manchester for the concert Edith had chosen, George had been sporting a very nice pair of gold cuff links, which James had given him for his birthday. Gina would have bet almost anything that they hadn't been bought in any jeweller's.

Gina, James and Diana walked Coco through the gardens. The little dog was endlessly entertaining and provided a talking point for the three of them, although Diana addressed most of her remarks to James, rather side-lining Gina.

'What's he up to now?'

'I think he's scented a rabbit or summat,' said Gina, as Coco raced into the herbaceous border, snuffling among the spring bulbs.

'Ridiculous creature, but I do love him,' said Diana. 'Piggy sends her regards, by the way, James. I meant to say earlier. She wants to go to see that film *Bus Stop* and I said I'd ask if you want to go, too.'

'I might.'

'Well, let me know, though I realise you have a heavy social life in London these days.'

And she's making it quite clear I'm not a part of that. Gina began to feel left out, which she knew was Diana's intention.

'Right, well, it's chilly out here and I think I'll go and get my stuff together before lunch,' said Diana.

'Lightweight,' laughed James. 'You're turning into a soft southerner.'

'So what?' Diana answered, twirling round and heading towards the side of the house, her hands in her pockets.

'I thought she'd never go,' said James, directly she was out of hearing range. 'I've been dying to speak to you alone since I arrived.'

'Me, too. I've got the parcels in my room and I gather you've brought summat else in your luggage.'

'A few bits and pieces I thought Bella could shift for me . . . for us.'

'I've got a few pounds from the pawnbrokers I've been to since you were here at Christmas, from taking in the small pieces. I'm having to be careful and not go to the same ones very often, or take too much.'

'Clever girl. We can't afford for them to get suspicious. Not that they really care, provided they can shift the goods, but we don't want anything traced back to us. We'll go to see Bella on your afternoon off, if you like. Remind me when that is.'

'Wednesday.'

'Right, so I'm here until at least then. That'll give me the chance to earn a bit of credit with the parents, especially Dad, if I can bear to visit the brewery in the meantime – what a yawn – and perhaps I might reacquaint myself with the Duke of Clarence.'

'Oh, James, why go there and be paid less by another fella, who'll sell on the stuff himself, when you can sell it directly to Bella?'

'Well, I've tried sticking with Bella, but there's a limit to what she wants to take – I mean, the kinds of items.'

'I don't understand.'

'She doesn't take watches, for instance, though there's a nice little market for some makes of watch.'

A watch was a watch to Gina. She hadn't really looked at any watch closely except to tell the time.

'Well, you know best. But I'll be glad to go to Bella's on Wednesday. Then we'll tot up how we're doing.' Gina had so far been upfront with him about what she got from the pawnbrokers and she expected James to be straight with her about the items he offloaded.

'I'll look forward to it,' said James, giving her his most charming smile.

'I have missed you,' Gina said softly, leaning in to him.

'And I've missed you, too. Where would I be without my clever girl looking after my interests here while I'm up in London?'

'I wish I was up in London with you.'

'Well, then you wouldn't be here looking after my interests, would you, sweetheart? Maybe in the summer. Business picks up at holiday time and we could work together. Let's see how things are then.' James laughed lightly and bent to kiss her.

Gina wrapped her arms around him and the kiss became more passionate.

'Missed you so much,' she repeated softly as they eventually drew apart.

'Darling girl. Now, where's that crazy little dog? Coco, here, boy. *Good* boy. Why don't you and Coco go on without me, Gina? I've got a couple of things I need to see to before lunch.'

'Oh, all right.' Gina felt she had been dismissed, but

James wasn't here for very long and he might well have plenty to do. And she did have the trip to Blackpool to look forward to, even if she wasn't sure whether or not she liked Bella Bertolli.

~

After lunch, Diana said she ought to be thinking about getting her train.

'Gina, please would you give me a hand with my things?' she asked.

'Of course.'

Gina followed Diana upstairs to her room. When they got there, Diana shut the door.

'What are you up to, Gina?'

'What do you mean?'

'I saw you kissing James in the garden this morning. I don't know what your game is, but it had better stop now. I just hope Mum and Dad didn't see you as well, pushing yourself forward, trying to worm your way in.'

'It were nowt—' Gina began, unable to deny what Diana had seen all too plainly.

'It didn't look as if it was nothing,' Diana snapped. 'Just remember, Georgina Arnold, you're an employee of my parents, that's all. This is *not* your home where you can do as you please, and you are *not* one of us.' She gave Gina a severe look.

Gina felt furious. She should have seen this coming, with the cold shoulder Diana had been giving her. It was cheap, too, of the beautiful daughter of the house to pull rank when she had all the advantages and Gina had no grounds on which to defend herself. But she quickly gathered her composure and raised her chin. She was still close to James, and Diana knew nothing of their 'business' together, so let Miss Diana Hoity-Toity Stellion think what she liked. She didn't know the half of it.

'No, Diana,' Gina said quietly, facing down Diana's fierce stare. 'I'm not like *you.*'

'Now, please would you bring my case down for me?' Diana scooped up her handbag, coat and gloves from the bed and went out of the room without looking back. Gina followed, trying to rally her spirits but feeling like a lowly porter.

When she got downstairs, Diana was kissing her mother and brother goodbye, George standing at the door ready to stow the case in the boot of his car.

'Bye, Mum. Thank you for a lovely time. Such a good concert . . . You take care and try to keep cheerful. It'll be warm enough for you to sit out and enjoy the garden soon.'

'Bye, my angel. Thank you for coming to see us. Come again soon, and bring Piggy, if you like.'

'Will do, Mum. Bye, James. Do try to behave. Maybe I'll see you in town . . . that film . . .'

'Yes, I'll see you, Di.'

'Goodbye, Gina. Thank you for everything you've done for me this weekend,' said Diana, then leaned in closer to murmur, 'and remember what I said.'

'Yes, Diana. I won't forget,' Gina said, meaning it. It occurred to her that she might have a look through the long-neglected book of spells and see if there was a suitable one to wipe the superior sneer off Diana Stellion's pretty face.

~

'Do you have any plans for this afternoon, Gina?' Edith asked as Gina poured them each a cup of tea.

'I thought I might go and see a friend in Preston,' said Gina. 'Would you like me to post your letter?'

'Yes, please, dear.'

Edith had spent a long time writing to Mrs Thwaite's sister, Mrs Hillier. It wasn't a lengthy letter, but it had taken some care to get the wording right.

Gina had learned from Ellen, who'd learned it from Mrs Mason, who'd very quickly managed to extract it from Lucas Hillier, that Mrs Thwaite had not really wanted to retire at all. She'd cut off all communication with the Hall and asked Mrs Hillier never to contact the Stellions again either.

'Seems like she'd been thrown out and she thought she'd been hard done by,' Ellen told Gina. 'It doesn't sound like Mrs Stellion, does it, to do something so unkind? I wonder if there was some misunderstanding.'

'Mebbe,' said Gina. 'P'raps Mrs Thwaite was embarrassed about the gin Mum and me found.'

'What gin?'

Gina told her the official gin-discovery story as Dora knew it, and Ellen was taken aback.

'I never had her down for a thief. Well, if Mum found

it and reckons it was stolen, I'd believe her, wouldn't you?'

'We both thought the same. Mum hid it in the cleaning cupboard and after a bit I sort of added it to the tray in the sitting room and no one noticed, so at least Mr and Mrs S got their gin back – or what was left of it. Who knows how much she'd drunk over the years? Anyway, I reckon Mrs Thwaite must have known she was rumbled. She was quite a bitter old woman, I found out when I came to work here, and just the kind to take umbrage.'

'Mm . . . difficult. Have a word with Mum. She'll mebbe know what you should say to Mrs S.'

So Gina had done so, although already she knew it didn't really matter what she said so long as Edith was satisfied she was doing the right thing: her letter was not destined to reach Mrs Hillier. It was Gina's ultimate revenge on the former housekeeper that even in death she should be regarded as an outcast from the Hall.

~

Gina pulled the boxes James had sent from London out from under her bed and opened them with a pair of kitchen scissors.

'See, I didn't even have a nose through them,' she said.

James laughed. 'I wouldn't put it past you to have a look and then seal them up again,' he said, 'but it's all the same to me. I know exactly what's there.'

'Well, I don't,' said Gina. 'At least give me sight of them before we show Bella.'

She rummaged in the crumpled newspapers and extracted a pretty little silver box, then a second with a different pattern on the lid, and finally a necklace of purple stones.

'Garnets,' said James. 'Some people like them and they can fetch a bit of money.'

'Ooh, rings – I know what these green ones are,' said Gina, lifting out from the second parcel a couple of gold rings with tiny emeralds set in them.

'They're a bit small but perfect for Bella's purposes,' said James. 'Nothing too big or too precious.'

They looked through the rest of the items, Gina asking what each was made of and whether it was especially valuable. Then they wrapped them all up in the newspaper again and put them into two cloth bags that James had brought with him. Gina asked James to show her what he had brought with him in the car. They were supposed to be working together, and she felt sidelined whenever he showed Bella items she herself had never set eyes on before. Reluctantly he nipped out to the car and fetched the zipped holdall, which he'd stowed there earlier, and they went through everything. These items were much the same size and of the same kind as those in the parcels Gina had received, but she still wanted to see them.

'So that's fourteen pieces altogether,' Gina said, when they had rewrapped them.

'Correct, Gina,' said James, giving her a long look.

'Now you make sure old Ma Bassett is about her cooking pots, and if the coast is clear I'll take this lot out to the car.'

Gina unlocked her sitting-room door, had a quick look down the empty corridor and James had the loot in the car boot within moments.

'See you in the lane beyond the gates at two o'clock,' said James, kissing the top of her head. 'Be on time or I'll go without you.' He winked and turned away to the front of the house.

Gina was learning to be a very strict timekeeper since she'd joined James in his 'business'.

She made her preparations for the afternoon, laying her clothes ready on the bed: her coat and hat, her handbag; the scarf of Diana's that she'd admired the first time she'd ever gone into Diana's bedroom and found it in the dressing-table drawer. In revenge for Diana's angry words she'd decided to take it. It was a small and rather feeble act of vengeance, Gina knew, but nonetheless it was significant: she would not let snooty Diana Stellion tell her what to do.

She slipped Mrs Stellion's letter to Mrs Hillier in the fire in the sitting room before she left that afternoon.

~

Gina and James arrived at the Tom and Tabby, the stolen goods in the cloth bags.

'James, good to see you. Come through to the back, darling,' said Bella, appearing immediately, dark hair so neat that it could have been a wig, and, as always, a coat with a fur collar. This afternoon's was a fox fur, the head and front paws hanging down on one side, the tail on the other. Gina looked at its glass eyes. *Revolting* . . .

'And Jenny, too,' said Bella, giving Gina a thin smile. Gina didn't bother to correct her; she knew Bella hadn't really forgotten her name. She did feel a moment's disappointment that James hadn't chosen to correct her, though.

Bella sashayed ahead of them to the door at the back of the club, opened it, then closed and locked it behind them. The little room was furnished like a room in a house, with a desk in the middle. There were a couple of glass-fronted cabinets against the walls, and a bookcase. The shelves of these pieces of furniture displayed ornaments such as silver boxes like those among James's current hoard, a pair of candlesticks and some silver photo frames, but not so many that it looked like a shop. Gina thought Bella must have other places where she kept most of the items she bought.

Bella carefully looked through the pieces James and Gina had brought her, switching on a desk lamp and peering through a loupe at one point. She didn't say anything, which Gina knew was her way. Eventually she named a price for the lot, James talked her up, she suggested a compromise and they shook hands on the deal. Gina knew Bella always offered low and was prepared to be talked up, but that it was only a token compromise and Bella left herself a good margin of profit. James had told her they both expected it and, in the end, he had to deal with Bella or take the loot back to the Duke of Clarence, Providence Street or a pawnbroker's shop.

'If we offer her stuff we know will suit her, we'll be pretty certain she'll buy the lot,' James had explained to Gina the first time they'd visited Bella together. 'That way we're shot of it and we don't have to look for an alternative buyer. It's worth it, even if Bella is meaner than a witch's curse, provided I make some kind of margin.'

'Stay and have a drink – on me,' Bella invited James, when the formalities were completed, the cash had been counted into his hand and she was showing them both back into the main room. 'And you, too, Gina, of course,' she added as an afterthought. 'Not quite your bedtime yet, is it, sweetie?' she smiled.

Gina smiled thinly back. 'Thanks, I'll have a gin and tonic, Bella,' she said, just as James started to say they ought to get back.

'Long way to go, have you, love?' Bella asked. 'Remind me where.'

'Only as far as Preston,' said James. 'Yes, OK, thanks, we will stay for a drink.'

Bella showed them to a table and ordered drinks. She sat and chatted for a minute or two about 'business'; how her sister had had a lean time with her shop in the Lake District over winter. 'We can't afford to pay out top prices until things pick up a bit, love,' Bella said. 'But if the market improves over summer, you can be sure we'll be interested when you bring us summat a bit special.'

'I'll bear that in mind, Bella,' said James.

Bella glanced up as a shifty-looking man came through the thick curtain at the entrance. 'Please excuse me. It's been lovely to see you James, love . . . Jenny.' She sauntered over to the newcomer on her red high-heeled shoes. 'Max, love . . .'

Gina drank her drink, determined to finish it because it was at Bella's expense, but not really wanting to be here any longer.

'Heck, she's annoying,' she said as she and James emerged into the stagnant air of the Blackpool side street. 'What's she keep calling me Jenny for, when she knows darn well what my name is?'

'Take no notice,' James laughed. 'It's just a little power play, that's all. She's all right really. Tighter than a duck's eyelid, but we all know the game, and at least she pays cash up front.'

'Yes, and I hope you've not forgotten my part in this business,' Gina laughed. 'You've made a few pounds today and I don't want to find you've headed back to London and forgotten to pay me.'

'As if I would.'

'Well, make sure you don't. And I heard you saying we had to get back to Preston. You don't trust her, do you, James?'

'It's just better to be careful . . .'

'She doesn't know you're James Stellion of Stellion's Brewery, does she?'

'Gina, for goodness' sake keep your voice down,' James hissed. 'There's no need to even say it, never mind broadcast it to half of Blackpool. Of course she doesn't know.

Do you think I'd lay myself open to blackmail? You've got a lot to learn, my girl.'

Gina thought that perhaps she had, but she would make sure she was a fast learner.

~

Edward had invited Ellen to come up to Highview Farm for her tea when he met her on the way home from seeing Mr Shepherd. All afternoon Ellen had looked forward to this treat. Nancy was a very good cook, although the food was plain, and the Beveridges always made her feel very welcome. Dora said Tom had invited her and Betty and Reg Travers to the Lodge to play cribbage after work, so Ellen didn't feel obliged to turn down the invitation in order to keep her mother company.

'Tom will walk me home and Ed will bring you back safely, so we've nowt to worry about,' said Dora, who was nervous on her own these days, even though Philip was locked away.

When it came time for Ellen to go home, Edward took up his big torch and Ellen had her own to light the way down the lane. It was pitch-dark but not especially cold. Their torches made two companionable yellowish beams of light in the black lane.

'I sometimes see all sorts down here if I'm quiet,' said Ed. 'Once I saw a badger, and once a wild sort of a cat, like a domestic cat but bigger and fiercer.'

'Weren't you frightened?' asked Ellen, taking his free hand.

'Nah, it weren't interested in me. Shot across the lane and stopped only a moment to look at me before it went through the hedge and away. It had huge yellow eyes.'

'Spooky. I'm not sure I'd want to see one when I was alone,' said Ellen.

'You'd be all right. But you're not alone. You're with me, Nell, love.'

'But I might be by myself one time.'

'But you needn't be, lass.' He paused and she heard him swallow as if he were nervous. 'You needn't ever be alone again if you don't want. If you like, we could be together always.'

Ellen's heart did a little flip, but she was anxious not to misunderstand. 'What are you saying, Ed?'

He stopped and put an arm around her. 'That I'd like us to be together for ever, love. That I'd like you to marry me . . . if you'll have me, that is.'

'Oh, Ed . . . I'd like to marry you, but . . .'

'But what? I'd love you and take care of you for ever, Nell, and I'd never treat you badly. You've seen how good my mum and dad are together – respectful of each other and that – and we'd be like them.' Edward was worried that Ellen had seen a far-from-perfect pattern for marriage with her own parents, and maybe she thought there was a risk all marriages could turn out like that.

'Oh, my love, I know you would take care of me. I would never doubt that. It's just that I'm getting on with the gardening at the Hall so well now, and really loving my work, and I wouldn't want to have to give it up. Of course we'd want to have children – you'll want a little boy to leave the farm to eventually, like generations of Beveridges before you – but I'm only twenty and I'd really like to carry on at the Hall for a while before I have to give it up.'

'Why would you have to give it up? I'm that proud of what you do, Nell. I've seen the way Tom's given you more responsibility and how much you've learned, even though you've not been there quite a year yet. I don't see why a woman with a talent like yours should waste it by giving up her job just because she'd got married. I know you hear of it, in the towns, like, with some kinds of work, but country women have always worked. There's no reason why you shouldn't be a gardener and a mother.'

'Oh, Ed, I'm that glad you understand. I'd hate for us to get off on the wrong foot with any kind of misunderstanding.'

'I reckon you and me understand each other all right, Nell. You know what the farm means to me, so why wouldn't I think the Hall garden meant the same to you?'

'Dear Ed, thank you. You are the dearest man in the whole wide world. I do love you so much and I do want to marry you.'

'So is that "yes" then, Nell?'

'It's yes, Ed. Yes, please.'

They celebrated with a long, long kiss and then continued silently down the lane.

Suddenly Ed stopped. The sky was clear and the stars bright.

'What is it?' whispered Ellen. 'Not a wild cat?'

'No, my love. Look ahead, look up. Shooting stars!

You've got to be quick to see one, but if you do you should make a wish.'

They stood in silence, their torches switched off, eyes trained on the black starry sky. Suddenly: 'There!' breathed Ellen.

'I saw it, too. Did you wish?'

'I did. Did you?'

'Oh, yes, love. There's only one wish I could make tonight, though.'

'Me, too,' said Ellen, kissing him again.

CHAPTER SEVENTEEN

'SOME LETTERS FOR Mr and Mrs Stellion and another parcel for you, Miss Arnold,' said Arthur Smollett, putting the little brown-paper-wrapped box in Gina's hands. 'I'm sorry, I don't know what's happened with this one. Looks a bit like someone's sat on it. Let me know if there's owt missing and I'll bring you a form to claim for it.'

'Thank you, Mr Smollett. I'd be very angry if that were the case,' said Gina. 'Folk expect to get their post intact, not smashed up like this.'

'It's hardly smashed, love—' Arthur began.

'It's bad enough,' said Gina. 'Please make sure it doesn't happen again.'

'I didn't—'

'Thank you, I'll let you know if I need the claim form,' said Gina, shutting the door in his face. She knew she'd been rude, but the parcel from James looked as if it might well have been opened and her stomach was dancing with anxiety.

She sped into her sitting room, locked the door behind her and ripped off the already torn brown paper and put a match to it in the hearth. Then she opened the misshapen box and rummaged through the crumpled newspaper to find the jewellery. For a moment she thought there was nothing there but paper, but then she unearthed a rather creepy mourning brooch with some dead person's plaited hair in it, and a couple of long slender hatpins with pearls at the ends. That was all. There did seem to be a lot of newspaper to wrap up so few items. She stood back, trying to think clearly, her heart pounding.

Then she looked through the small cardboard box again, more carefully this time, taking out each piece of newspaper and straightening it to make sure there was no jewellery hidden within the folds. Nothing.

Maybe there had only ever been these few items in the parcel, but they hardly seemed worth sending. James usually sent more than this at a time. Gina looked carefully at the hatpins. The pearls were big, although of course they might not be real, and the tops of the pins were embellished with tiny stones, which might or might not be rubies. The brooch was a ghastly thing, the skinny plait of grey hair surely of no value to anyone except a sentimental relative of its original owner.

What if there had been more pieces and someone had stolen them? Gina paused a moment to consider the irony of that. But the person who had stolen them might have noted her address, might even know the items had been stolen once already, and connect her with them. They knew her name and where she lived!

Gina closed her eyes and took a few deep and calming breaths. It was pointless guessing and speculating; there was only one thing to do and that was to ask James. She had never telephoned him before, but now she would have to do so, and make sure no one overheard. Maybe there was nothing to worry about, but this was the only way to be sure.

She tidied her hair, which had got a bit wild during her frantic search through the parcel, and composed her face, then unlocked the door and went down the corridor, remembering to take the letters for Mr and Mrs Stellion with her.

'Gina, love, would you like some lemon barley?' asked Mrs Bassett as Gina tried to get by the kitchen without being seen.

Actually, a cooling drink would be nice. It was a hot June day and Gina's panic over the parcel had left her feeling heated and uncomfortable.

'Thank you, Mrs Bassett. I'll take a jug up for Mrs S, too. I had hoped she'd be feeling a bit better today, but she says there's nowt right about her at the moment.'

'Oh dear, poor lady. I wonder if she could stomach a little lemon junket. Would you ask her, please, Gina? I'm using that many lemons at the moment, it's a shame Tom and Ellen don't grow them in one of them greenhouses.'

'I bet Ellen would have a go if she thought you'd want them,' said Gina vaguely. 'But I'll take the jug of barley water and go and find Mrs—'

'And would you ask her if she and Mr Stellion are in for dinner this evening, please, Gina? I'm wondering if she'd manage to eat a chicken pie. I know Mr S always likes my pies. In fact, I remember him saying that—'

'Yes, Mrs Bassett, I'll ask. And now—'

'And I've been wondering whether Tom might have some more of those new potatoes like he dug for me last week. They'd be just the thing to go with—'

'I don't know. You'll have to ask him, Mrs Bassett.'

'With carrots and spinach, I reckon. All new baby vegetables to tempt Mrs S with her sensitive stomach. Build her up a bit when she's feeling fragile. What do you think, Gina, love?'

'Lovely. And now—'

'Of course, I could always just poach the chicken in a little light broth with the baby carrots. She always likes that when she's feeling a bit under the weather. With mebbe a tiny bowl of the junket to follow. What do you reckon, Gina? And then again—'

'Mrs Bassett,' said Gina, rather too loudly, backing towards the door with the barley water on a tray, 'I'm sure whatever you decide will be grand. Now *please*, can I just get on?'

She fled before the well-meaning cook had a chance to say anything more. Mrs Bassett had a heart of gold, but sometimes Gina just wished she'd shut up, especially now, when her mind was in turmoil about the opened parcel.

Edith, too, seemed to want to try Gina's patience to its limits with her fussing and her numerous requests. Would Gina please take Coco for a walk? Please would Gina pass this morning's letters, and where was the letter opener? Please would Gina telephone Fowler's shop and ask for some of those plain biscuits to be delivered with this week's order? Please would Gina sort through those magazines and see if she could find that picture of the dress with the sailor collar that Edith had in mind to have copied . . .?

It was on the tip of Gina's tongue to snap back, but then she realised the impatience was all of her own making and these simple tasks were exactly what she was employed to do. And as for telephoning Fowler's shop, that was the perfect opportunity to be making another phone call.

'I'll make the phone call to Fowler's first, shall I?' said Gina, getting up to look for the book in which Edith had noted down all the telephone numbers she used.

'Oh, no hurry about that particularly. I think Coco would like his walk now, dear,' said Edith. 'He's been quite noisy this morning and it's set my head pounding. Please take him for a good long one and he and I will both feel better for it by lunchtime.'

Gina was beginning to think she'd never get to telephone James, especially as she'd just spotted Edith's personal directory on the little table beside her. There would be no sneaking it out unnoticed. Then she had to ask about the food so Mrs Bassett could get on with preparing it, and go down to deliver the answers. By the time she set out with Coco on a long walk, she felt as if she had been wrung out, and she still hadn't even had a chance to speak to James.

If something was missing, would he even believe her

that the parcel had been damaged, possibly deliberately? Maybe he'd think she had taken the things herself and made up the story. Gina felt even more anxious now. James Stellion was so attractive, but there was an unknown aspect to him. He certainly couldn't be trusted, of course. As it was, she thought they needed each other equally, although she suspected he knew a lot more about her than she did about him, which gave him the upper hand. And he was the Stellions' son and always would be, whereas she could be replaced at the Hall. For her own sake, she wouldn't want to fall out with James.

~

Ellen, standing on a ladder, secateurs in hand, saw Gina striding quickly through the rose garden, completely ignoring her, then veering off to the front of the house as if to go down the drive. Poor Coco was trotting along beside her, being pulled to heel and not being allowed to stop to explore all his favourite interesting places. Gina looked like a woman on a mission or, more likely, a woman in an extremely bad mood.

Now what? There was always something unsettled about Gina. She was amused by the strangest things, such as the sudden death of Mrs Thwaite – Ellen still felt shocked when she remembered what Dora had told her about Gina's reaction to that news – and was never entirely happy with her own lot, always casting an envious eye over other people's lives. The current object of her bitterness and envy seemed to be Diana Stellion, although

Ellen couldn't imagine why on earth that should be. Diana was way out of Gina's league. Ellen recalled it was envy of her own new job at the Hall that had inspired Gina to come to find work here. She seemed no happier for it really, though, despite the work being cleaner and easier than helping at Highview Farm. There was a wildness about Gina that was unpredictable. She was like a creature that could not be entirely tamed; perhaps like the wild cat Edward had told her about that evening he'd proposed: a loner, shy of company, yet with the potential to be fierce and dangerous.

Ellen felt her stomach do a happy little skip at the thought of Edward and that lovely evening with the shooting stars. He worked well with his father at Highview Farm, and he was that proud of his own little flock of Herdwicks. The first of the lambs would be ready for market in the autumn, and he was so excited, it did her heart good to hear him.

She tried to imagine, as she did so often, what it would be like to be married to him and have the pleasure of his gently cheerful, loving company all the time. They'd discussed where they'd live. Albert and Nancy had said they could live at the farmhouse – there was plenty of room and Ed's parents could not have been kinder to her – but Ellen really wanted a place of their own. The obvious home for them would be Highview Cottage, but that would mean Dora having to move out, and Ellen would not make her mother homeless, especially after she'd worked so hard to make it beautiful. The cottage belonged to the Beveridges, though, so ultimately it must be their decision. Then Edward had had the idea of building another little cottage on Highview land, but that would take time and effort, and the farm itself took as much time and effort as any man could give in a working day. Well, she would just have to see . . . There was plenty of time. They hadn't even set a date for the wedding yet, although Edward had bought her a pretty little ring with three sapphires set in gold. She didn't wear it often, though, because her work in the garden was not a place for delicate jewellery. She loved Ed with all her heart, but she didn't want to rush into marriage. After all, the garden needed so much attention. The deadheading alone was an almost full-time occupation in June . . .

She sighed to see so many of the rose heads falling into the wheelbarrow as she snipped away. If only the best of the roses could last for ever; if only the best of life could last for ever, too: happy moments she never wanted to forget, always bright and complete in every detail instead of fading into the past. So much of her time lately she wanted to remember all her life: not just that magical evening when Ed had proposed beneath the shooting stars in the dark lane, but simple things, like finishing the decorating with Dora and celebrating with a well-earned cup of tea; the bookish conversations with Mr Shepherd; jokes with Sally on their walks to see him and back; the day Uncle Tom had first allowed her to set some new annuals in the herbaceous border entirely to her own planting scheme . . .

Then there was the little garden at the cottage, all tidy and flourishing now, with a new climbing rose, a present from Tom to Dora, growing beside the back door, and rows of flowers and vegetables. There was always a pretty jug of flowers on the table these days and Ellen knew her mother was happier now than she'd been for years. She'd put on a bit of weight, which suited her, and she was smiling much more, and singing as they cooked their tea together or pottered about in the garden.

'You and me, love, we get on just grand, don't we?' she'd said only the previous evening when she and Ellen had taken their cups of tea outside to drink them sitting in the sun. 'You know, Nellie, it's so good not to have to worry all the time, to know when I come home that it's going to be a nice evening.'

Ellen had hugged her mother. She understood exactly what Dora hadn't said. No one was missing Philip.

This summer felt like a welcome respite from the unhappy summers of previous years, thought Ellen, snipping back another cluster of browned flowers on Mrs Stellion's favourite red rose. Why would either she or her mother want anything to change – at least for the moment?

~

Gina closed the door of Mr Stellion's study. She laid Edith's book of telephone numbers down on the desk, picked up the phone and dialled.

The telephone rang at the other end once, twice, three times . . .

Come on, come on . . .

Gina was just thinking James must not be there when the phone was picked up and a woman's voice said, 'Hello?'

It had not occurred to Gina that anyone other than James would answer. Who was this woman? Suddenly she realised she knew nothing about James's life at 'his place' in Pimlico.

'Good afternoon,' said Gina. 'May I speak to James Stellion, please?'

'He's not here,' said the woman.

'Oh . . . when will he be back?'

'I've really no idea,' said the woman, unhelpfully. While Gina wondered what to do next, the woman seemed to relent because she said, 'I'll take a message for him, if you like. Who's calling?'

'It's Gina. Please would you tell him Gina called and . . . just . . . I need to speak to him.'

'Yes, all right, Gina, I'll tell him,' and she put the phone down.

Who was that? Gina's mind was racing. James had certainly not said anything about a woman. Gina had always imagined he lived alone in his big house with his big garden. He might have a housekeeper of his own and maybe someone like Tom or Ellen to look after the garden. If she really examined her imaginings, she would have said that he lived alone because he was just waiting for the right time to ask her to come up to London to join him. Maybe that abrupt woman *was* the housekeeper . . . though her attitude had rather suggested she wasn't a paid employee.

Gina walked up and down beside the desk a while, thinking and worrying. Now she had not only the opened parcel to worry about, but this mysterious woman as well. What if she was James's girlfriend? Oh, good grief, it was possible. Gina had thought *she* was James's girlfriend, but maybe that was only while he was in Lancashire. His life in London was entirely separate, she realised, and she knew she didn't – couldn't – trust him. That was rather the whole point of James Stellion and the business he was in: he was entirely untrustworthy.

Gina sank into James's father's chair and put her head in her hands. All she could do was wait until James telephoned and asked to speak to her. Then everything would become quite clear . . . or at least clearer. There was nothing she could do until then except hide the horrible brooch and those stupid hatpins in the box under her bed beside the contents of some other, rather more promising, parcels she had received lately.

She picked up the phone again and dialled the number for Fowler's shop, hoping it would be Sally Mason who answered, and not Mr or Mrs Fowler. Gina had had enough awkward conversations for one day.

~

It was three days later that James telephoned the Hall. It was late morning and Gina had just come in from taking Coco for his walk when she heard the telephone ringing in George Stellion's study. Luckily Mr Stellion was at the brewery and Gina, still keen to speak to James, knew that and rushed to get the call, barging into the little room without even thinking of knocking.

'Grindle Hall.'

'Gina, thank God it's you. Listen—'

'James! You got my message, then?'

'What message? Never mind. Gina—'

'No, it's important. You see, that parcel—'

'Gina, shut up and listen. The police have been to my lodgings and searched the place. They may be on their way to the Hall now. You have to get rid of the stuff.'

'James, what are you talking about? Lodgings?'

'What? Oh, shut up and *listen*, Gina. Take the stuff I sent you to Bella. You have to go now, before the police arrive. If they find it in your room, or with your prints on, you'll be arrested, and if you squeak then I'll be arrested, too, and we could both end up in prison.'

'What, now? Go *now*?'

'Yes! I said so, didn't I? There's no time to lose. Go straight away and put the stuff in a bag – some of it's worth quite a bit and the police are looking for it – then take it to Bella.'

'Why would the police come and look in my room? They know nowt about me.'

'I'm . . . I'm not sure . . . they just might, but I'm certain they'll come to the Hall and have a look around and ask questions, so just get rid of it to Bella and we'll both be quite safe. If they were to question you and you slipped up, then they'd search your room, and if they were to find the stuff then you'd be in serious trouble, and that means that I would be as well. *Serious* trouble, Gina.'

'James, where are you? Are you still in London, at your place in Pimlico?'

'No, I told you, the police were there. I'm lying low at a friend's place.'

'James, when I rang the other day, who was that woman?'

'What? What does that matter? Just go and get the stuff and take it to Bella and do it now.'

'James—'

'Please, Gina, just go and do that, for both our sakes. I'm not joking: the police could turn up any time. Can you do that for me, please, sweetheart? Just go and do it now, please.' He was pleading and Gina felt suddenly breathless and very frightened. This was really happening and she could be arrested; they both could.

'Right . . . right, I'm going now. I promise I'm doing that now, James, as soon as I've put the phone down.'

'Good girl. I'll come up and find you as soon as I can and I promise I'll be very, very grateful. Now go!'

'Yes . . . yes . . . I'm going.' She put down the phone and stood trembling, her heart pounding.

Right, I've got to go now . . . with the stuff . . . to Bella.

She rushed out into the corridor and along to the door at the back of the hall. Coco, hearing her footsteps, gave a little bark and Edith called, 'Gina, dear?'

Gina ran through the door and down the steps, past the kitchen, where Mrs Bassett was rolling out pastry and the delicious smell of chops grilling for lunch hung in the air.

'Gina, love, is that you? Would you be able to . . .?'

Gina didn't stop to hear what it was Mrs Bassett wanted. She rushed into her sitting room and grabbed her handbag, in which she kept the money she had taken from Mrs Thwaite's dead husband's jacket pocket all those months ago, and the money she had made fencing the loot, visiting the pawnbrokers and taking the better class of items to Bella. Someone of Gina's status had no business having that much stashed away: she needed to take it with her now. She raced into her bedroom, threw herself down beside the bed and pulled out the boxes from underneath. There was a shopping bag hanging on her door and she grabbed it and tipped the contents of the boxes into it, shaking them roughly down. She needed something to put over the top, to stop anyone seeing and to keep them safe. There was Diana's silk scarf on the dressing table. Gina tucked that over the jewellery, took her coat and hat and rushed out to the corridor, locking her sitting-room door and pocketing the key.

'Gina, is that you, love?' called Mrs Bassett again, but Gina was through the back door and into the courtyard in a moment.

She was just hurrying round to the drive when she saw a black car coming up towards the house. In it were two men in police uniform. She leaped back and flattened herself against the side wall so they would not see her, desperately trying to silence her gasping breath. It was exactly as James had said. The police were here to search the house.

She heard the car stop in front of the Hall and the policemen slamming the car doors. Then there was the sound of their footsteps crunching on the gravel. Oh Lord, they were coming round this way! Desperately Gina looked for somewhere to hide. If she was caught with her coat on, a large amount of cash in her handbag and a bag of stolen jewellery, too, there would be no story she could invent to save herself that they would believe. Quickly she ran light-footed across the courtyard to the outbuilding where she played with Coco. As usual the door was open and she nipped inside and stood behind the door, making herself as flat as she could, the incriminating bag of jewellery resting between her feet. She hardly dared breathe as she strained to hear if the police were coming to find her.

There was the sound of approaching footsteps and the two men said something to each other that she couldn't hear. Then, after what seemed an age, their footsteps receded and she thought they must have gone round to the front of the house. Fortunately for her, she would not be available to answer the bell when they rang. They'd have to wait several minutes for Edith to rouse herself to go to the door, or for Dora to do so. But unfortunately for Gina, this meant she couldn't escape down the drive because they'd see her.

Gina remembered a little path to the side of the outbuildings that ran parallel to the drive, then petered out not far from the gates. It may well have had a use when the Hall was built and the courtyard had been surrounded by stables. She crept out, past the bricks and the broom handle she had trained Coco to jump over, and sidled between the two buildings to the side of the courtyard, onto the old overgrown path, then fled down it in a swift kind of tiptoe, her footsteps almost silent on the weedy grass. When it got to the point that the path ceased, she crept to the camellias that bordered the drive and shouldered her way through. She was almost at the foot of the drive, and the policemen had left the big gates open. From the scratchy shelter of the dark shrubs she glanced up the drive and saw their parked car, but there was no one in sight. She'd have to be quick in case anyone noticed her from the windows. In seconds she was through the gates and into the lane.

As she set off at a fast walk in the direction of Great Grindle, she heard a bus approaching from the Whalley direction and she hurried to the bus stop just in time to hail it. What luck! Within minutes of leaving the Hall she was on her way, ultimately to Blackpool, by bus and then by train. She worked out the journey in her mind, not knowing the timetables but hoping to get to Blackpool by the end of the afternoon.

It was only as she sat waiting for the train at Preston railway station that Gina had a chance to catch her breath and think about what she'd done. James had said, 'I'll come up and find you as soon as I can,' but find her *where*? Not at Grindle Hall. By now the police would have told Mrs Stellion the reason for their visit, and Gina's absence would be sending out its own message loud and clear. She could not just go back when she'd sold the stolen items to Bella and pretend that nothing had happened.

She imagined returning to find the police still there and, worse, Mr Stellion himself questioning her in his study, asking very, very difficult questions . . . learning from her all about what his son really did in London and when he came to stay at the Hall. She could imagine George Stellion getting stricter and angrier the more he learned, and Edith would be sitting to the side of his desk patting her aching head and having the vapours. And then the police would descend on Gina with handcuffs and escort her out to their big black car. There would be Dora, standing at the door, watching her go past, weeping on Tom's shoulder, and Nell beside her, looking stricken but brave, and as the officers drove away to the police station, to lock her in the cells, Coco would be watching her shameful departure through the windows, and whining . . .

'Are you all right, love?' It was a grey-haired woman asking.

'Oh! Oh, yes . . . I'm all right, thank you.' Gina sniffed and realised she'd been crying.

'Not bad news, I hope?' asked the woman. 'I don't want to pry but you look that sad it set me wondering if mebbe you could do with a cup of tea or summat.'

'Oh, yes, please,' said Gina.

She'd had nothing since fleeing the Hall and was now very thirsty. The lady seemed kind and, apart from taking the stolen items to Bella, Gina had nowhere to go and nothing to do. She had no job now – that was a certainty – and, really, she needed to think about her situation and make her own decisions, not just go along with whatever James had said. Look where that had landed her so far!

'What time is your train?' asked the woman.

'I was thinking of going to Blackpool so there are

plenty of trains,' said Gina. 'It doesn't matter; I've nowt to be there for, really.' She sniffed again and delved in her pocket for a handkerchief.

'Ah, love, don't you fret yourself,' said the woman. 'Come on, let's have a sit-down and a cuppa and you can tell me all about it. A trouble shared and all that.'

Gina followed her to a little station café where she sat at a round table while the woman bought a pot of tea. All the time Gina was working on her story.

'So, love,' said the woman, as she poured Gina a cup of tea, 'have you come far?'

'From out Skipton way,' said Gina. 'I've just come from my mum's funeral and now I'm alone in the world.'

The woman looked at Gina's black dress and coat and nodded. 'What, asked to leave, were you?'

'Aye, by our landlord. We lived in a little cottage but now Mum's gone I can't afford to rent it by myself.'

'Ah, you poor love. Here, drink your tea. My name's Mary, by the way, Mary Hathersage.'

'I'm Diana . . . Thornton,' said Gina. The name Thornton flew into her head and she realised she must have seen it on a destination board. It was safer not to announce she was Gina Arnold in case her name hit the headlines in the next day's newspapers.

'Well, Diana, what are you going to Blackpool for? Do you know someone there you can go to?'

Gina shook her head. 'Not a soul, but I thought, what with it being a place with a lot of visitors, I might be able to get a job there . . . in a shop or a café, mebbe.'

'I reckon you might. It's the beginning of the holiday

season. But where would you stay, love? I take it you've not made any plans for that?'

'No, Mrs Hathersage. I thought I'd see what I could find when I got there.'

'Mm . . .'

They drank their tea in silence and Mary poured Gina a second cup.

'The thing is, love, I'm not sure it's safe for a pretty young woman like you to be finding her own way in a vast metropolis like Blackpool. You come across all sorts of chancers and the like.'

Gina suppressed a smile. *Vast metropolis?*

'What do you mean, Mrs Hathersage?'

'It's Miss Hathersage, but call me Mary, please, love. I don't stand on ceremony. I mean folk go to Blackpool to have a good time and there's other folk only too willing to relieve them of their hard-earned wages while they're there. You know, landlords and landladies who offer cheap rooms and it's not as nice as they advertise. Too late then when they've got their hands on your money and there's nowt for breakfast but stale toast and a filthy bathroom shared with ten others.'

Gina nodded. Mary Hathersage sounded as if she might have been taken for a ride herself at one time and was speaking from bitter experience.

'Now, I'm not saying there aren't plenty of honest folk in Blackpool, too, but it's not allus easy to tell the good 'uns from the bad 'uns straight off, if you get my drift. When accommodation's in demand, that's when standards drop or chancers move in.'

Gina was impressed. 'I reckon you could be right, Mary. It's lucky for me that I met you and have fair warning.'

Mary patted Gina's hand. 'Well, I couldn't let a little lamb like you wander where there might be wolves, could I, love?'

Gina nearly spilled her tea choking back her laughter, and had to cover it with coughing.

'So, what you do think I should do, Mary?' she asked.

'Why, I reckon you should come home with me, love. I can put you up and you'll be quite safe while you look for a job for yourself.'

Crikey, I never saw that coming. This could be the luckiest break of my life . . . or a really bad idea.

Gina studied Mary Hathersage, the upward creases round her kindly eyes, just like Uncle Tom had; her respectable hat and light coat over a flowered frock – the sort of garments Dora would call 'good'. She appeared completely genuine.

Aye, but so do I and the police are after me. But what better place to lay low than in the company of a respectable elderly lady?

'Have you room for me?' Gina asked. 'It's that kind of you, but I wouldn't want to put you out.'

'Oh, it's no bother, love,' said Mary. 'My sister, Ruth, and me, we have a little guesthouse in St Annes. We can accommodate you, no trouble.'

'Well, that sounds lovely,' said Gina. 'I'm that grateful.'

'Come on, then, Diana. Where's your stuff?'

Gina gripped her shopping bag with the stolen items in it. 'What stuff?'

'Why, your luggage, of course, love. You weren't thrown out with nowt but what you stood up in, surely?'

'Oh, no . . . I . . . it was stolen. It was stolen between Skipton and here. Someone must have got off the train and taken it with them.'

Mary gave her an old-fashioned look. 'Right . . . I'm sorry to hear that. So you've only that?' She nodded at the shopping bag of stolen items.

'Yes. I'm afraid so.'

'Oh dear. We'll have to see what we can do. Our train will be here directly so come along, Diana.'

Mary set off towards the platform for the St Annes train and Gina followed her, still wondering if this really was a sound move or absolute madness.

CHAPTER EIGHTEEN

'I DON'T THINK I shall ever forgive Gina,' said Ellen. 'I think she must have gone mad.'

'Aye, it's hard to believe,' said Tom. 'Your mum is that upset. She's taking it very much to herself, like it was her who brought up Gina to be so bad.'

'Gina's always been trouble, but that's not Mum's fault. And now she's on the run from the police, possibly in possession of stolen goods. Oh, Uncle Tom, I'm very worried. What if she's fallen in with other criminals, folk like – I don't know – like bank robbers, with guns?'

'Don't fret, love. I think the police will find her before long and stop her getting into anything worse. Really, that would be the best thing – if she were to be arrested. After all, it's what's going to happen eventually anyway. The sooner she's found, the sooner we can all sort it out. We've yet to hear her side of the story.'

'True, I suppose. Oh, I'm that angry, I could slap her, I really could.'

Ellen took a calming sip of the tea Tom had put down

in front of her. They were at the Lodge, having had a very unpleasant afternoon in the company of two police officers. Mr Stellion had been summoned from the brewery, and he and Mrs Stellion had been interviewed as well. If the police thought they'd learn anything new they must have been disappointed, as it quickly became apparent that no one had the slightest idea what had been going on.

The Stellions thought that James worked for an art dealer, but it turned out that the only dealing he did was in stolen goods.

'I don't understand,' Edith had said, weeping and flapping her hands. 'We gave him the best education we could afford; everything he wanted, made sure he had enough money to establish himself in nice, respectable lodgings when he went to London. He's going to take over from my husband at the brewery eventually – why would he be dealing with burglars and thieves?'

'It seems Mr James Stellion has had a bit of bad luck at the races of late, madam,' the more senior police officer said. 'We've spoken to some friends of his in London and it turns out he's very fond of a bet on the horses. Seems his stakes were rather higher than his income. We suspect he thought this was an easier way to earn money quickly than working at a proper job, but then he started to lose more often and turned to crime to raise some cash.'

Poor Edith put her head in her hands and gave herself up to sobbing, while George asked questions about the kind of items James sold on.

'Small pieces, mainly,' said the policeman, 'though that

doesn't always mean small in value. We found several items of jewellery and some watches in James's lodgings. They answer the descriptions of pieces taken in various burglaries in the south of England. There was also a parcel packed up ready for the post, addressed to Miss Georgina Arnold at this address. It was found to contain a few more such items. James's landlady said someone called "Gina" had telephoned a few days ago to speak to James. We think James has been sending some of the stolen goods to Georgina.'

'But what could she have done with them?' asked Dora, white with shock. 'She wouldn't know who would want to buy them. She's just a country lass and has lived all her life in Little Grindle. Mebbe she's not been sent owt so far and that parcel would have been a first.'

'Possibly. We're looking into whether she may already have received some goods and stored them here for James until he visited. It would mean the items were well out of sight of the police down south. Now Georgina Arnold seems to have disappeared, which is suspicious in itself, and we are very keen to speak to her and find out what she knows about James Stellion's activities,' said the officer.

Dora started to cry then, so there were two weeping mothers, lamenting that their children had gone so entirely off the rails. Ellen sympathised, but she wished they'd be a bit quieter so she could think what on earth could have happened to Gina and where she could have gone.

'I think we should look in Gina's rooms and see if she's left a note or summat,' Ellen suggested. 'I'm still hoping this is all a mistake and she'll be back any moment, or summat's happened – nowt to do with this – and she's had to go to see to it.'

The policemen looked incredulously at each other and Ellen felt foolishly optimistic, but she didn't want to give up on Gina so easily. There was still hope, wasn't there?

'Good idea,' said George. He looked at the wailing mothers and saw there was no point asking them to help. 'Would you show the officers downstairs, please, Ellen? Tom and I will come too.'

Gina's sitting-room door onto the corridor was locked and the key was missing from its usual hook in the kitchen.

'I heard her going past just before lunchtime,' said Mrs Bassett, eyeing the policemen nervously. 'I called out, but she can't have heard, I reckon.'

'Is there a spare key?' Ellen asked her.

'Not that I know of, love.'

In the end, Tom forced the door open with the help of the police officers. It was a violent act that brought home to Ellen just what serious trouble Gina was in. She rushed into the room calling, 'Gina! Gina! Are you there?' She could see no note, so she went into Gina's bedroom and had a very quick search around.

'Her coat and handbag are gone,' she called.

She looked to see what else, but couldn't be sure. Then she trod on something hard on the bedside rug and bent down to see. It was a hatpin with a large pearl at the end and a tiny red stone on the pinhead. To her certain knowledge it didn't belong to Gina. The red stone might even be a ruby and the pearl was huge. For one crazy moment she thought about putting it in the pocket of her breeches and telling no one, but what if it was a vital clue to where Gina had gone – besides being a dishonest thing to do?

'I've just found this,' she said, coming back into the sitting room, where the policemen were looking in the cupboard, and handed it over to them.

~

When the police had gone, having found some empty cardboard boxes but no other items they believed to be stolen, either in Gina's rooms or in James's, the Arnolds and the Stellions felt awkward and subdued. Neither wanted to blame the other for James and Gina's dishonesty, but each was very disappointed in both. In the end George suggested Edith went upstairs to lie down, then he saw the Arnolds out through the front door.

'It's a bad business,' he said. 'But if we hear anything, we'll let you know.'

'Likewise, Mr Stellion,' said Tom.

'And you're not to worry about your jobs here,' George added gravely. 'I know this is nothing to do with you and you're no more to blame for this than Mrs Stellion and I are. Let's carry on as best we can. There'll be gossip, but it will affect you in the village more directly than us, though we'll have our own share of it to face elsewhere, you may be sure of that.'

'We'll not be fanning any flames against James,' said

Tom, reading the subtext correctly. 'We know nowt about owt for certain, and we'll not be speculating either.'

'Thank you, Tom. Now I think you should all go home and recover from this terrible shock.'

'Yes, Mr Stellion . . . yes, sir . . .' they murmured, and set off slowly down the drive.

When they got to the Lodge, Dora said she wanted some time to herself to think through all that had happened; she ambled off home up the lane, her shoulders bent under the weight of her worry, leaving Ellen and Tom to discuss what they could do.

'Just when all was going right for Mum,' said Ellen furiously, taking another sip of her tea. 'She was only saying the other day how happy she was now she's back at the cottage. I know it's made a right big difference to her to have your friendship and support now Dad's gone,' she added shyly.

'She's made a difference to me, too, lass,' said Tom. 'Oh, if only Gina could behave herself, the little witch. I'd like to think she's the innocent party in this and it's all down to that scallywag James Stellion, but we both know Gina . . .'

'Mm,' said Ellen, as a strange idea began to seep into her mind, some half-remembered event she couldn't quite pin down.

~

The next morning was a Saturday. Ellen worked in the garden on some Saturday mornings but, before she went to the Hall, she walked down into Little Grindle village to call on Betty Travers.

'Hello, Nell, my love. I can see summat's the matter. Come in and tell me,' said Betty, opening her cottage door wide. 'Reg is out the back already with Fred Hardcastle, working on the rota for the fête, so we'll have some peace and privacy.'

'Thanks, Mrs Travers. It's Mum and it's also our Gina . . .' Ellen told the whole sorry tale so far as she knew it, leaving out nothing. Betty was a good listener and didn't interrupt.

'. . . so you see, Mum could really do with some cheering up and a bit of company this morning – someone she knows she can trust,' finished Ellen.

'I'll go over now and see her.'

'Thank you, Mrs Travers. I hardly like to leave her alone, she's been that upset. After all Mum has had to put up with, with Dad, you'd have thought that Gina could at least have tried to behave herself.'

'Aye, you're right there, Nell. But your father and Gina are surprisingly alike, for all they didn't get on. Still, best to see what Gina has to say when she turns up.'

'Do you think she will turn up, Mrs Travers?'

'She will if she's run away, Nell. She can't run away for ever. Now you get off up to the Hall and I'll go and tell Reg where I'm going and then I'll follow you up the road. Have courage, my love.'

'Aye, Mrs Travers. Thank you, I'll try.'

~

Ellen and Tom worked silently all morning at separate tasks. It was warm, a good day for gardening, and neither of them wished to talk about the awful events of the previous day, yet what else was there to talk about when it filled their every thought?

Early on, they heard the familiar low roar of Mr Stellion's car and the crunch of the gravel as he drove out, then Ellen was weeding along the front when he returned with Diana in the passenger seat. The car disappeared round to the courtyard and the house remained quiet. It felt to Ellen as if someone had died.

All the time she worked, she tried to think what it was that had hovered on the edge of her memory the previous day. If only she had the slightest clue where Gina had gone she would go and look for her, she vowed.

She remembered what Betty Travers had said: *Your father and Gina are surprisingly alike.* Dad was in a lunatic asylum – was Gina mad as well?

Suddenly she knew what she had been racking her brains to remember. It was that weird afternoon last year when Gina had said something about a magic spell and stopped her picking that strange little bottle out of the stone wall on the farm; how Gina had looked so odd and . . . mad. For a moment she had been quite frightening.

But no, Gina wasn't really mad . . . was she? She'd always been naughty and wilful, but that wasn't at all the same as being insane. She could be cruel and envious and bitter, too, but that was just her character, not insanity. Ellen loved her sister and would do anything she could to make things right about the stolen items, but she had to acknowledge she sometimes didn't really *like* her very much.

Just the morning to get through and then she'd go and see Edward and his parents and tell them what little she knew before they heard a different version that had circulated three times round the village until it was unrecognisable as the truth.

~

Gina woke up in a comfy bed with beautifully laundered sheets on the Saturday morning and lay thinking about all that had happened the previous day. It had been quite exhausting and for a few moments she wondered if she had imagined some of it. But no, this quiet little hotel room was real enough.

She went to the window and opened it. She couldn't see the sea but she could smell that lovely sea smell that she'd remarked on to James the first time he'd taken her to Blackpool. Now Blackpool was just up the coast and she had a decision to make. Should she take the stolen jewellery to Bella, as James had asked, or should she stay here and be Diana Thornton, orphan from Skipton, at least for the time being? Being Diana Thornton bought her some time to think things through, and after all, James had made no arrangement to come to find her.

The more Gina thought about James, the angrier she felt. He had not cared that she'd lost her position at the Hall, lost the trust of her employers – and probably everyone else by now – not cared about her at all. He'd done a runner and sacrificed her to try to save what he could of the stolen items not at his home in London. He'd got in a panic and had got her into a panic, and now they were both on the run.

On the run from the police! How quickly that had happened!

No doubt if she took the stuff to Bella, Bella would be expecting her, and James would have made some arrangement already whereby she, Gina, would be paid only a small share of the money for the loot and he would be collecting the rest when he chose to turn up. Gina didn't much like Bella and she didn't trust her. Now, thinking about all that had happened, she decided she didn't like James and she didn't trust him either. Look at the way he'd made her believe he cared for her, even talking of her going to join him in London this summer. He'd also told her that he lived in a big house in London, when all the time 'his place' in Pimlico was lodgings.

And to think she had thought she was in love with him! What a fool she'd been. It was clear now there was only one person he was in love with, and that was himself. Well, there was a lesson to be learned and, by heck, she'd be learning it. The lesson was: look after yourself and trust no one else.

So, that was decided: she would not be taking the loot to Bella, if only to spite both her and James.

She glanced down into the little side road off the wide main street that ran down towards the sea. An old lady with a little dog was walking slowly along towards the shops. The dog was brown, like Coco, though not a spaniel. Gina thought of Coco, of the fun they'd had, and how she'd trained him to walk so nicely to heel and to amuse Edith with his tricks. She sighed; those days were gone. She'd wanted a life of fun, filled with interesting new people, to get far away from the village of Little Grindle, where nothing ever happened. Well, something would be happening in Little Grindle now, and she would be a big part of it, though not there to witness it. She'd certainly livened things up there, she'd be willing to bet.

She turned and looked at the little hotel room, plain but very clean. She thought of Mary Hathersage, and her sister, Ruth, who last night had been puzzled by their new guest, Diana Thornton, but welcoming and kind nevertheless. Maybe she'd lie low here for a day or two until she'd decided what to do.

She could, of course, just go back to the Hall and tell Edith and George Stellion what had happened. The police would be called and she'd be arrested. That was certain. She'd lost her job at the Hall the moment she'd left with the loot. But the Stellions were important people in that part of Lancashire and maybe they had influence with the police. Perhaps they might even hush the whole matter up with regard to James by blaming her and having her locked up while he would be spared prison. As Diana had said, *You are not one of us.* Or they might know someone clever to represent James, who could persuade a jury in a court of law that Gina was solely responsible for selling the stolen items. After all, she was the one who'd gone to several pawnbrokers with various items over many months, and she'd even kept a record of the stories she'd made up. It didn't look good, she knew.

~

'We've been wondering – if you've nowt else planned and no one to go to – if you'd like to help us out here for a bit, Diana,' said Mary, when Gina, the only guest in the hotel, had eaten her breakfast of mushrooms on toast. 'We've got three visitors coming to stay with us this weekend, and we sometimes get others turning up during the week.'

The hotel was a bit off the main route to attract passing visitors, Gina thought, but Mary and Ruth must know their own business.

'Thank you, I think I'd like that,' said Gina. 'It's quieter in St Annes than Blackpool, and it might suit me better, me not knowing the place. What would you want me to do?'

'Well, there are the vegetables to peel, and the tables to set and the rooms to clean and tidy,' said Mary. 'Could you manage that?'

'I reckon I can,' said Gina, 'though I don't know much about cooking.'

'We do the cooking,' smiled Ruth, a shorter, younger version of her sister. 'The hotel is for vegetarians and we have our own favourite recipes.'

'Vegetarians?' said Gina, racking her brains. 'Folk that eat only vegetables?'

'That don't eat meat or fish,' corrected Mary.

'Heck. Are there many? I mean, it's a bit of a small market to run a hotel on, isn't it?' asked Gina.

'We are in the vanguard, I admit,' said Ruth. 'But folk do seek us out and I can proudly say we even have a few who come to try it and are converted.'

Gina laughed. 'You make it sound like a religion.'

'Oh, no.' The sisters looked shocked.

'Although it is about respecting all the creatures of the earth, sea and sky,' Mary added.

'Crikey . . .' said Gina faintly. 'Well, I reckon I can do veg and tidying, and I'm grateful you asked me.'

The sisters each extended a hand and shook Gina's. 'Welcome to the Merrylife Hotel, Diana,' said Mary.

'You'll need a few things,' said Ruth. 'Mary told me you'd had your bag stolen. Is that right? We can give you a little advance on your wages to get some essentials, if you like. It won't be much but it would help if you've nothing.'

'That would be lovely, thank you,' said Gina. 'I've very little money.'

This is the perfect place to lie low for a bit, she mused: a side-street hotel with hardly any visitors, and certainly no one who's likely to have seen me at the Tom and Tabby in Blackpool. And it's run by a couple of trusting old biddies who believe everything I say.

~

When she had finished her morning's work, Ellen decided that Betty Travers, with her knowledge of old country lore and the more mysterious ways of life, was the person to ask about that strange event of last spring. With luck, Betty would still be at Highview Cottage with her mother.

Betty was just preparing to leave when Ellen arrived home.

'That time already?' Betty said when Ellen went in through the back door. 'Your mum and I have been talking that long, I've lost all track.'

'Hello, Mrs Travers. Hello, Mum. Oh, Mrs Travers, I'm right glad you're still here. I've remembered such a strange thing about Gina and I'm wondering what it means; whether it's connected in some way with what's happened. You see, it was just before she got her job at the Hall, and look at the trouble that has brought her to. I've never told anyone this and I know it sounds mad, but it was summat Uncle Tom said yesterday that half reminded me.'

'Tom? Does he know whatever it is?' asked Dora.

'No, I'm sure he doesn't, Mum. He just made me think.'

'Go on then, love,' said Dora.

'Well, it was last year, in the spring. I saw a little bottle, like a medicine bottle, half hidden in one of the stone walls up on the farm, and I was going to pick it out to see, but Gina knocked my hand away and then she started talking nonsense. Said it was a spell and I weren't to touch it. Then the next time I said owt about it, she said it were nowt and she'd made up the spell story just to frighten me. I don't know why. I thought it was mean.'

Betty nodded slowly but she didn't look surprised. 'What did it look like, love? Can you remember?'

'Just a little bottle with summat dark in – dried blood,

mebbe, or some other liquid – and I think the stopper was tied round with what looked like hair. I've never seen owt like it before or since.'

Betty nodded again and looked thoughtful. 'Was that all, Nell?'

Ellen thought hard. 'I think so. Sometimes I thought Gina was up to no good when we shared a room, and she could be secretive, but I never saw owt else like that. 'Course, soon after that, she went to live at the Hall.'

'And about the time you found the bottle, did owt unusual happen?'

'Like what?'

'Oh, to you or anyone who was on the farm, mebbe.'

'Not anyone, but I do remember a few of the sheep died and Dad got all worked up about it and was in a mood for days.'

'I remember that,' said Dora.

'And did he know why they'd died?'

'No, it was all a mystery, but he reckoned the sheep were always thinking of new ways to die. That's what he used to say, wasn't it, Mum? Honestly, Mrs Travers, I can't think why he worked with sheep. They seemed to fuel his misery and make him all the worse.'

'So it could have been anything?'

'I reckon so.'

'So why are you worried about this now, love? Do you think it has owt to do with Gina's disappearance and this business with the burgled things?'

'I don't know. I can't quite get my head straight about it.'

'I don't understand,' said Dora. 'Why would Gina talk about casting a spell? She has no special powers.'

Betty was thoughtful as well, as if she, too, was trying to remember something.

'It was all very odd,' said Ellen. 'Gina can be envious and bitter if she thinks other folk have what she wants, though she isn't such a hard worker that she is prepared to take the long road to get on in life. If she tried a spell, like whatever it was I found, and it seemed to work because she saw what she thought was some kind of result, might she start to believe she has special powers? Might she be . . . *deluded* – is that the right word? – even though it wasn't real?'

Betty's face was grim. 'I feared summat like this.'

'What do you mean?' asked Dora, looking worried.

'It was at the village fête last summer. You remember, I did a bit of fortune-telling, and who should come in but your Gina. Well, I foresaw straight away that she was going to be leaving Little Grindle and there'd be money involved, though not how it came about. But then I saw – clear as day, it was – summat I've never seen before. I saw she'd been messing about with magic spells. 'Course, I warned her off. I were that angry with her for dabbling in summat she knows nowt about. She scarpered pretty quick, so I thought she'd heeded my advice. I didn't say owt to you then because, well, the fortune-telling is private to each client.'

'I don't understand, though,' wailed Dora, looking tearful. 'Gina can't do magic, can she?'

'No, love, of course not,' said Betty. 'No one can cast

any kind of spell unless they have the gift, but Gina didn't know that. If she thought she'd cast a spell and owt happened – nowt to do with the spell at all, but just summat that took place and that always was going to take place – she might think she'd brought it about, do you see? She could be getting into a right muddle in her head if she thought she had the power to make owt happen.'

Dora and Ellen looked at each other, aghast.

'It's not healthy to be thinking you are able to decide what happens in other folk's lives,' said Betty. 'I was worried then that it might be fostering ill-wishing and envy.'

'Oh dear,' said Ellen. 'It all sounds a bit mad, but if Gina's got things all out of proportion, and if owt's happened and she's understood it all wrong, then there's no knowing what she's thinking. Mebbe it's all led to her dealing in stolen goods and being on the run from the police.'

'Oh, don't, love,' said Dora, rocking backwards and forwards on her chair, her hands to her mouth in distress. 'What can we do to help her?'

'I don't know, Mum. We can't help her until we find her.'

'I'm just wondering . . . where might Gina have got the spell from?' asked Betty.

'Oh, I never thought. She couldn't have made it up. She would have to have had some instructions,' Ellen said. 'How do you know all the old lore and the fortune-telling, Mrs Travers?'

'It's passed down from mother to daughter,' said Betty with a smile. 'But not everyone's got the gift. In some families it just dies out and that's why there are fewer "wise women" these days than in the days of yore.'

'Well, Gina didn't get any daft ideas about magic from me,' said Dora crossly.

'No, Dora, love, no one's blaming you. I reckon she's found some old documents or some such and has followed those, not realising that without the gift she's harming no one but herself.'

'Oh . . .' Dora started to cry again. 'I'm sorry, Betty, but I just can't stop crying since Gina ran away.'

'If Gina had some written instructions, I can only think they'd be in her room at the Hall,' said Ellen. 'I'll go and see what I can find – anything at all that might help us know what she's up to or where she might have gone – and if there is owt, we can decide between us what to do. What do you say, Mum?'

Dora gave a watery smile. 'Yes, love, thank you.'

'And we'll get Uncle Tom in on this, too.'

'Yes, Tom's always such a help,' Dora sniffed.

'Right, that's decided.'

'And you can rely on me and Reg for any help we're able to give, Dora,' chipped in Betty.

'There you are, then, Mum. Let me see what I can find this afternoon and I reckon between us we can work summat out.'

And I just hope there's summat there to give us a few clues, 'cos I haven't the slightest idea where to start.

CHAPTER NINETEEN

Ellen went up to the farm to tell Edward and his parents what had happened to Gina. Nancy Beveridge shook her head sadly and Albert kept silent altogether, so Ellen felt their disapproval of her sister, who had been such a hopelessly unreliable employee for them.

'And now we're desperate to find out where she's gone and bring her home safely, if only to help her face her punishment and try to ease her way into an honest life,' finished Ellen.

'Well, good luck with that, love,' said Nancy, which Ellen couldn't take as wholehearted encouragement.

Edward offered to come down with Ellen to the Hall to see what they could find that might help to trace her.

'I think it's best I ask Uncle Tom to come with me, Ed, but thank you,' Ellen said. 'They're feeling a bit fragile at the Hall, what with James being in trouble, too, and Uncle Tom is known to them.'

'Yes, you're right, of course,' said Edward. 'You just

come and say if you need me, though. You know I'll do anything I can to help you.'

'I know,' said Ellen, giving his hand a discreet squeeze.

Ellen went up the lane to the Hall, stopping at the Lodge to explain to Tom what extraordinary news she had learned from Betty earlier and what she planned to do.

'Of course I'll help you,' he said. 'We'll go in through the kitchen and not bother the Stellions at all. They've no reason to mind you going into Gina's rooms. The police have already been through them and they took away only that hatpin.'

Mrs Bassett had already left for the afternoon, but Tom had a key for the back corridor and so they went in that way. The door to Gina's sitting room was unfastened, of course, with the lock smashed after Tom and the police had forced their way into it the previous day.

The rooms felt deserted and already dustier than the day before.

'What are we looking for?' asked Tom.

'I don't rightly know. Anything that might be a clue to where Gina has gone,' said Ellen.

They looked around but the sitting room was strangely impersonal considering Gina had used it for a year. There were just two things on the shelf: her basket of knitting and a book.

Ellen took them down. The book had a worn red binding and looked very old and shabby. It struck her as odd that Gina should have a book at all; she'd never been known to borrow anything from the mobile library.

Tom was thinking along the same lines. 'What's it about?' he asked. 'I'm surprised to see Gina's been reading.'

Ellen opened it to the title page and realised immediately this was exactly the kind of instruction book she had been talking about with Betty earlier. 'It's called *A Booke of Spelles and Diverse Incantations for the Domestic Student of Witchcraft*,' said Ellen, hastily putting it down on the table as if it were burning her hand. 'So Gina really did think she could cast spells! How on earth can she have decided she could do that, I wonder. I don't even want to touch the thing.'

'It's only a book, Nell,' said Tom, taking it up and flicking through, then reading a page or two. 'It's kind of like recipes, but the result is a spell rather than a cake or a loaf of bread.'

Ellen leaned over gingerly to take a look. 'I wonder which one Gina tried.'

'Or which ones. There are mebbe twenty here, although the old-style spelling makes them difficult to follow. I can't think Gina used this regularly. It'd take a while to work out what it all means and to find the things to use.'

'Betty might know summat about this kind of book.'

'Or Mr Shepherd.'

'Aye, I could take it to show him. I doubt there's any clue as to where Gina has run away to, though.'

'No,' said Tom. 'There's nothing here at all, really. I wouldn't show the book to your mum just yet, though, love. It's a nasty old thing and she'd be right upset.'

'I'll keep it hidden from her, at least until I've found out more about it.'

'Good girl.'

'It's sad,' said Ellen, looking around. 'I never thought of it before, but Gina had no friends. There's no letters, no invitations to anything; she never joined in the things we liked to do in the village.'

'Like your dad, then.'

Ellen gulped. 'Yes, I keep coming back to that, Uncle Tom. Mrs Travers said that Gina is like Dad and I just wonder now whether she's a bit mad, too. It's scary, but . . . what kind of madness is this?' She pointed to the strange book. 'Who in their right mind would have a book of spells and think they could do anything worthwhile with them?'

'Well, Gina did.'

Ellen sighed and lifted up the knitting, which looked as if it was a half-finished cardigan. 'She'd have been better getting on with this,' she said crossly. 'It's nice. I wonder what it's meant to look like when it's done.' She rummaged in the bottom of the basket, beneath the unused balls of wool, and pulled out the knitting pattern and, with it, an exercise book. It looked like the kind of book both girls had used at school. At the front Gina had made a note of how many rows she'd worked of her knitting pattern, but as Ellen flipped through, she saw some different notes recorded upside down at the back. She turned the book over and saw her sister had used the back of the notebook to record dates and places, and a few words of description, like part of a little story.

'Oh, Uncle Tom, I think we need to look at this properly,' she said. 'Listen.'

Wednesday 19 September

Joshua Hellman, Blackburn

Mrs Eliza Thwaite, war widow. Pearl necklace. £4.

'Mrs Thwaite? Surely not. Why would Gina write down what Mrs Thwaite sold?'

'Because it wasn't Mrs Thwaite, Nell, it was Gina. She was just using the name.'

'Here's another for the week after.'

Wednesday 26 September

Alfred Barker, Blackburn

Mrs Nancy Beveridge, husband left her. Rent to pay. Garnet earrings. £2.

'I think we can safely say that is not Nancy from Highview Farm,' said Tom.

'The cheek of it, using the names of real folk, well known round here, in whatever it was she was up to. If we find out who these fellas are whose names she's written down, I think we'll know for certain what she was doing. There are a few of them, and not all are in Blackburn. There are some in Preston, too. The days are all Wednesdays and there are always a couple listed close together and then a gap.'

'I reckon I can guess already,' said Tom. 'It wouldn't surprise me if these weren't the names of dealers in second-hand jewellery, or mebbe pawnbrokers, and Gina's taken summat to each of them, on her afternoon off, with a little story ready in case they were to ask.'

'So she was selling items of jewellery as long ago as

last autumn!' Ellen was shocked. 'And all the time she was working here for the Stellions, as innocent as you like, walking Coco and looking after Mrs S and so forth. Using this house – her employers' house – to store the things she was selling, no doubt.'

'I think we may safely assume that the items Gina sold were sent to her by James Stellion and that the parcel the police said they had found addressed to Gina in his lodgings was far from the first he was to send to her. If Gina has behaved badly, then James Stellion is a disgrace, using her to sell on stolen goods. She's just a lass and knows nowt of the world, whereas he's older and has the benefit of education and opportunity.'

'But Gina's been that stupid I could shake her,' snapped Ellen. 'She knows right from wrong – or was brought up to. Now I don't know what she believes.'

'If James Stellion walked in here now, I'd knock him down,' Tom said fiercely, then added: 'But we need to keep clear heads and think if there's owt we can do with what we've learned.'

'The right thing to do would be to give this exercise book to the police, wouldn't it?' said Ellen. 'They will want to trace the jewellery and give it back to its proper owners, if they can. But I don't think they'd be interested in the book of spells.'

'Me neither. It was right there on the shelf if they wanted to look at it when they were here. I'll take the exercise book to the police station this afternoon.'

'Uncle Tom, I'd really like to find Gina, if I can, before the police do, and try to understand why she's been up to no good – what with trying out spells and selling stolen stuff. I'm worried that she'll put herself in some terrible danger with all her wrong-thinking, but if she'd just listen to me and see sense I can mebbe help her.'

'But this might be evidence, and it could lead to the stolen things being recovered, love. I have to hand it over, though I think those two policemen are pretty useless that they didn't find it themselves.'

Ellen sighed. 'You're right, of course. But I'll just copy down a few of the entries and try to follow them up, just to see if this is really what we think it is. These fellas may remember summat Gina said that could help us find her.'

Tom thought hard for a few moments. 'Yes, Nell. We're only guessing so far, though I reckon we're right. You do that, but don't go by yourself.'

'No fear, Uncle Tom. I'd be terrified in case they were ruthless criminals.'

'I'll go with you.'

'No, I'll copy out a few entries and you take the notebook to the police straight away then. I'll ask Ed if he'll go with me this afternoon, but I promise I won't go alone.'

~

Ed borrowed his father's Land Rover to take Ellen to Whalley, where they caught a train to Blackburn.

'I don't know much about Blackburn beyond the main shops,' said Ellen, when, after the short journey, they emerged from the station to a busy late afternoon as people bustled around to finish their shopping before the shops closed. 'I have only the names of these fellas: Joshua Hellman, Alfred Barker and Sidney Simmonds.'

'Well, if, as your uncle Tom reckons, they are pawnbrokers or dealers in second-hand jewellery, I'd say we'll need to look off the main street, away from the big shops. They'll be modest and discreet premises, I reckon.'

'Yes . . . Oh, look, there's a policeman over there.' Ellen sped away down the street after the uniformed bobby.

By the time Edward had joined her, she was noting down directions and nodding. 'Thank you . . . yes, thank you.' She smiled and the constable looked charmed.

'Oh, Ed, we're in luck. That helpful policeman knew of two of these people and their premises are just round the corner. Come on. We want to catch them both before they close.'

They went to the nearer place first, following carefully what Ellen had written down. Three golden spheres, the sign for a pawnbroker's business, were suspended high up on an ornate bracket, visible from the end of the narrow street, and Ellen hurried to the door of the place, Ed jogging to keep up with her.

'Alfred Barker: Loans' said the sign over the front window. The window, grimy in the sooty air, was filled with an assortment of items: jewellery, small pieces of furniture, a dinner service, candlesticks, a stuffed squirrel and a fur coat among them.

Ellen turned to Edward and pulled a face and he shrugged.

'We'll just have to ask nicely,' he said. 'I've no idea how to go on at these places.'

He went ahead and opened the door, and a bell jangled. Inside, the dim premises were untidy, with items piled up and every surface covered. Some of these surfaces were large pieces of furniture with labels attached, and there was a glass counter dominating the small space in the middle.

'Good afternoon,' said a man's voice. Ellen and Edward looked around but could see no one.

A rather short man stepped out from behind a dress-maker's mannequin. 'Can I help you?'

'Yes, please,' said Ellen. 'Are you Mr Barker?'

'I am, miss. What can I do for you?'

'I'm looking for a lady who I think might have come here, most recently in February – Mrs Beveridge . . .?'

'I'm afraid I don't know her,' he said.

'Oh, but she's been here a few times. She looks like . . . a bit like me,' said Ellen. 'She's . . . a friend.'

'I'm sorry, I have so many customers that I've long since given up looking at the faces. It's what they bring here that I tend to notice more.'

'Oh . . . oh, I see,' said Ellen, disappointed.

'Are you sure?' pressed Edward. 'A tall lady, aged less than twenty, long dark hair?'

'As I said, I don't notice the people any more. They all look the same to me, the folk that come here: like they need money. Do you know what she came in with?'

'Last time it was a jet brooch and a jewelled tiepin. I think she might have brought in a gold charm bracelet and a pair of garnet earrings last autumn.'

'I see . . .'

Ellen's eyes were fixed on the man, willing him to remember something about Gina, but she was disappointed.

'No, I'm sorry. I did have a gold charm bracelet, but someone came in and swapped it for a very nice camera. Here, I'll show you . . .'

He went to the window and took a posh camera out from the display.

'I'm sorry, Mr Barker, I'm not here to buy owt,' said Ellen. 'Just to see if my friend might have said summat about her plans.'

He was starting to lose patience now. 'Plans? What would I know about the *plans* of folk who come in hocking things?'

'Nowt,' said Edward, firmly, not liking the man's tone. 'We just wondered if you could help us. Our friend is out of touch and we'd like to find her, that's all.'

'I don't do missing persons, young man,' said Mr Barker with finality.

'Well . . . thank you for your time, Mr Barker.' Edward took Ellen's arm and escorted her to the door. He could feel she was about to get cross with the unfriendly pawnbroker. He pulled the door shut firmly behind him and led Ellen down the street.

'Horrible little man . . .' she was muttering.

'Darling, he was just being careful, that's all. As were we. Mebbe he thought we were after claiming stolen stuff, or mebbe he thinks "Mrs Beveridge" is in trouble with the police, which she definitely is.'

'He was shifty and horrible.'

'Nellie, what did you expect?'

'Oh, I don't know.' Ellen flung her arms down in exasperation. 'Some kind of clue. Something Gina might have let slip so we'd know where she might have gone.'

'It was always a long shot, love. Even if the man remembered owt, he might not want to tell us.'

'Aye, you're right. Do you think it's even worth trying the other fella?'

'Well, we're here now and we've nowt to lose by asking. You never know. Where did that bobby you were flirting with say the other fella is?'

Ellen smiled. 'I was not flirting, as well you know. It's back to the main street and along a bit, then turn off,' she said, consulting the directions she'd written down.

They soon found the premises of Sidney Simmonds. Like Mr Barker's, it had the three golden spheres sign above the door, and also a window full of a muddle of items of many kinds.

'Feels like the same place,' said Ellen. 'I hope we have more luck here.'

'Me, too.' Edward opened the door and they both went in.

There was a young woman a little older than Ellen behind the counter to the side of the shop. She was wearing a strange combination of clothes that looked as if they might have come from the stock: a tea dress with a gaudy brooch pinned on it; a short navy-blue jacket that might have been worn by a very small sailor in a different life; a little straw hat with a bunch of artificial cherries attached to one side of the brim.

'Good afternoon,' she smiled. 'How may I help you?'

'Is Mr Simmonds in, please?' Ellen asked.

'No, I'm afraid he isn't today. I'm his daughter. Can I help at all?'

Ellen didn't want to repeat the encounter she'd had with Mr Barker, and she'd already made up her mind to just ask outright about Gina.

'I'm not here to buy owt or raise a loan,' she said. 'I think my sister may have come here in February and brought a pair of pearl earrings. If she gave her name she mebbe said it was Mrs Travers.'

'Oh, I'm afraid I don't remember that name. Now, let me have a look if I've got the earrings . . . Would you recognise them, love?'

'No, but I'm hoping you might recognise my sister. She looks almost exactly like me,' said Ellen, offering a straight-on view of her face. 'She's bit younger but we look the same.'

Miss Simmonds gave Ellen's face proper scrutiny. She frowned. 'Sorry, I'm not sure I do. It might have been my father who dealt with her, of course. But pearl earrings, you say . . . and in February?'

'Yes, that's right.'

'I'll look 'em up,' she said, and pulled a huge ledger out from under the counter. 'All right . . . when in February, do you know?'

'The twentieth, a Wednesday,' said Ellen.

'Mm . . . yes, here we are, just as you say. My father bought them from Mrs Travers, and it was a pair of earrings, but we sold them on after Easter.'

'Well, at least we know she came here,' said Edward, when they had thanked the woman and left the place. 'Now we know her mission was to sell small items to different pawnbrokers.'

'Pearl earrings indeed!' huffed Ellen. 'As if Gina would have pearl earrings of her own to sell. I know it was a small chance we'd learn owt, but all we have learned is that Gina really was involved in selling on the stolen items. Uncle Tom and I guessed that when we saw the entries in the exercise book that he's taken to the police this afternoon.'

'We know she sold some things; we know she's got some others with her because she'd obviously dropped the hatpin you found in her room and gave to the police – at least it means she's not without money, wherever it is she's gone.'

'That's a comfort, I suppose, even if she's living on ill-gotten gains,' Ellen conceded. 'At least she won't be sleeping on the street with nowt to eat.'

'Don't even suggest that to your mum, Nell,' warned Edward. 'We'll have to think where else she could have gone.'

Ellen shrugged dejectedly. 'Do you think it's worth trying to find this last fella, Mr Hellman, while we're here?'

'Might as well. Then we'll have done all the names in Blackburn,' said Edward. 'We don't know where he is, though.'

'I'll go back in and ask Mr Simmonds' daughter, as she was so helpful. You never know.'

Ellen and Edward re-entered the pawnbrokers and asked.

'Joshua Hellman?' said Miss Simmonds. 'He's over the other side of Blackburn. It's a fair walk but not difficult to find. But he's closed on Saturdays. Look, why don't I take a telephone number, and if I think of owt I can let you know? Or if Mrs Travers, your sister, comes in again, I can tell her you've been looking for her.'

Ellen was just about to thank her and leave, having no telephone, when Edward jumped in.

'It's Grindle 413,' he said. 'Ask for Edward or leave a message. But please, would you not tell Mrs Travers we're looking for her?'

'Oh? But I thought you were.'

'We are, but Mrs Travers is rather a troubled person and is having a lot of difficulties at the moment. She won't let us help her, though. We really want to find her before something nasty happens to her or she gets into serious trouble.'

'I see . . .'

'I'm not sure you do,' said Ellen. 'I don't want to burden you with owt that's not your problem, but "Mrs Travers", as she's calling herself, has taken summat that's not hers. We'd like to find her and make everything right – as right as we can – before she gets beyond our help.'

'Stolen goods?' asked Miss Simmonds, nodding slowly. 'It wouldn't be the first time I've seen that. We try to be honest here, but sometimes dodgy stuff comes in and there's nowt you can do to recognise that.'

'Then you do understand why we want to keep my sister safe from that path. There's folk who love her back home and we'd give owt to make sure she's safe. If she comes in, please would you telephone Edward as quickly as you can? We could be here within twenty minutes.'

Ellen's heartfelt plea convinced the pawnbroker's daughter. 'I'll do what I can. I'll write down what you've told me so I won't forget, and I'll tell my father, too.'

'Thank you . . . thank you so much, Miss Simmonds. I'm very grateful.'

'I'd better take your number, please, Miss Simmonds,' said Edward.

She gave it to him and then Ellen and Edward left and walked to the station to get the train home, feeling that their afternoon had been largely a complete waste of time, with only the merest glimmer of hope at the end from the helpful Miss Simmonds.

~

The following day Ellen took the books of spells to show to Betty Travers.

'How's your mum, love?' asked Betty, showing Ellen in. 'I was right glad to be able to lend an ear yesterday. It's a hard time for her – and for you – what with your father and now Gina.'

'She's trying her best to keep cheerful, but she'll be back at work at the Hall tomorrow and that'll be hard for her, what with James Stellion . . .'

'You're right, Nell. It's a bad do.'

Ellen went into the little sitting room and sat down on the sofa as Betty indicated.

'Reg is bell-ringing at the church so we won't be disturbed,' she smiled.

'Thank you, Mrs Travers. After I saw you, Uncle Tom and I went to see what we could find in her room yesterday afternoon that might tell us anything at all. We found summat we thought the police should see, but also this book. I haven't shown Mum because I know it'd upset her.' She pulled the book out of her satchel. 'It's exactly what you said about Gina needing to follow some instructions to cast a spell. Here's what looks like a whole book of instructions.'

'Let me see, love.'

Betty took the book and read the title page very carefully, then turned the page and read slowly and thoroughly. The spelling was obscure and she was a practical rather than a scholarly woman. Ellen sat silently and waited.

After many minutes, when she had read quite a few pages at the beginning and then a few in the middle, and then more towards the end, Betty looked up at Ellen.

'Absolute rubbish,' she said. 'It's just what I guessed. Gina hasn't the gift, and this messing about with candles and bits of paper, and wishing and hoping, and cutting up and burning plants is of no use to anyone except someone foolish enough to believe in it, and they are deceiving themselves.'

'So not magic at all.'

'No, Nellie, love. Just nonsense. Oh, plants have a special place in healing and can be powerful, make no mistake, but only if you know what you're doing. My mother passed to me the gift of healing with plants –

tisanes and poultices, what's good for easing childbirth and what for indigestion and a whole host of ailments besides – but it's just an ancient form of medicine, widely used before folk had proper doctors to go to, and is to be used only for good. These instructions here – well, it's nothing like that. It can't possibly make a difference to anyone. It's just foolishness.'

Ellen was nodding. 'So Gina couldn't just read the instructions and perform some kind of magic?'

'No, love, of course not. That's what I'm saying. It'd be like her trying to look into my crystal ball or do the palm reading: she doesn't know how because she hasn't the gift. I can only do that because I was fortunate enough to inherit the gift from my mother. It is never to be used for my own good, and always for the good of others. I like to cheer folk up a bit if I see summat nice is going to happen, and set them back on the right path if I think they're going astray.'

'Well, I'm just anxious that Gina's been led astray by this nonsense.' Ellen flapped her hand disdainfully towards the book on Betty's lap.

'Aye, love, I'm afraid that's the danger. It's what I saw at the fête last summer when I warned her off. It's like I said, she can't do the spells but she mebbe thinks she can. If owt happened, she might think she'd brought it about when it was allus going to happen and was nowt to do with her.'

'I wish I knew which ones she had a go at and what she thought she'd get from them,' said Ellen. 'It might help us to see what Gina wants and mebbe even where she's gone to get it, though I can't help but think she's just run away.'

'I know, love, and I wish I could help you with that, but I can't. I foresaw a journey for Gina but not where she would go. But I'll call over and see Dora again this afternoon and take a little calming brew of freshly picked camomile to ease her anxiety before she goes to bed, if you like.'

'Oh, I'm sure she'd like that, Mrs Travers. Thank you. And thank you for your advice. I might take the book and show Mr Shepherd – you know, who used to be in the library van that comes round – and see what he makes of it.'

'Good idea, love,' said Betty, handing it back to Ellen. 'Mebbe I'll see you later.'

Ellen left Betty's cottage and wandered up to the turn in the lane that led to her own home. She heard the sound of an approaching car and moved to the side as Mr Stellion's unmistakably splendid vehicle sped towards her. Mr Stellion was driving, and in the front next to him sat Diana. Ellen held her hand up and gave a friendly wave. Mr Stellion acknowledged her but Diana looked straight ahead, her facial expression turning to one of fury as the car passed Ellen.

Oh dear, she's obviously blaming us for what's happened. So unfair!

Ellen walked slowly home, the book in her satchel. She felt half tempted to take it out and hurl it into the hedge bottom, so furious was she with Gina.

'It's no use getting cross, love.' It was Edward coming

towards her, reading her mind; he knew her so well and cared for her so much.

'I know, Ed. But I've just seen Diana Stellion go past in the car and she made a big point of ignoring me even though I waved. She used to be so friendly.'

'Aye, love, but she's fooling herself if she's being mean now. Her brother, James, and Gina are both wanted by the police – which of them does she really think started this lark with the stolen things? If she gives it any proper thought, she'll see it's not your fault what your sister gets up to with her brother.'

'Dear Ed, how did you get to be so wise?' Ellen said, cheering up. 'I reckon you know everything.'

Edward threw his head back and laughed loudly. 'Mebbe a bit about sheep, love, that's all.' He turned Ellen to him and wrapped his arms tightly around her. 'I wish I were so clever I could tell you where your sister is, love,' he whispered into her hair. 'If only I did know, we'd get into the Land Rover and go and get her right now.'

'Yes, love, I know we would. I just hope that day comes when we can.'

'It will, Nell, I'm sure of it. Whatever happens, I'll be there with you and we'll face it together.'

CHAPTER TWENTY

GINA WAS GETTING bored of the Merrylife Hotel and of the relentless good natures of Mary and Ruth Hathersage. Nothing seemed to annoy the sisters or put them out of sorts in any way. Gina had attempted a few acts of rebellion just to add a welcome note of friction to her days and vary the monotonous cheerfulness of hotel life, but the sisters hardly seemed to notice, or if they did they dealt with it so cleverly that it took away any pleasure Gina might have derived from her antics.

She took to dropping items of crockery or forgetting to set the tables properly for dinner, but the sisters just treated her like a rather slow child.

'Never mind, Diana. No harm done,' said Mary when Gina smashed a plate.

'Don't worry, Diana. You'll soon get the hang of it,' smiled Ruth when half the cutlery was missing from the place settings.

One day in July, Gina pretended to forget that a small party of Dutch people were booked in; she left the rooms unprepared, taking herself off for the afternoon for a solitary picnic on the beach, but when she returned the Dutch were there, all was well, and Mary didn't even mention it.

'Ah, Diana, there you are, dear,' she said. 'I hope you've had a good afternoon? Would you mind, please, just peeling these potatoes while I roll out this pastry?'

In the face of Mary and Ruth's smiling kindness, Gina felt a little mean-spirited at playing such petty tricks, but would her life ever be more than peeling potatoes, she wondered. She might as well be at Highview Cottage, preparing tea with Mum and Nell.

In the first few weeks of employment at the Merrylife, Gina had hoped – in addition to lying low – to meet some interesting people, just as she had when she went to the Hall but, exactly as she had discovered at the Hall, she had misjudged the situation. The guests at the little hotel were, on the whole, far from glamorous or exciting. Many were middle-aged or elderly couples. The women tended to look a bit like Mary and Ruth, while the husbands wore sports jackets and ties all day, even though they were on holiday at the seaside. Often the couples sat and read books while they ate, even though they were eating together.

Despite the lack of interesting people at the Merrylife, Gina rather liked St Annes, with its long, wide main street, smart shops and sandy beach. But while she was there, working at the hotel, she felt she was biding her time, waiting for something to happen. There had been no photograph of her emblazoned across the newspapers, and by the middle of July she'd given up looking out for unwelcome publicity or, if she were out, feeling a tap on her shoulder in the street followed by her prompt arrest by a policeman.

In the meantime, the stolen items she'd brought with her from Grindle Hall were still in the shopping bag and hidden at the back of a drawer in her room. She wasn't quite sure what to do about them now, and was putting off making a decision. It wasn't too late, surely, to take them to Bella, but she was still angry with James and reluctant to do as he'd asked when he was so selfish. She could never forgive him for losing her her job, or for speaking of 'my place in Pimlico', deliberately misleading her into thinking he lived in a splendid mansion when it turned out to be nothing more than lodgings.

She wondered whether to look around and see if there was someone else – an antiques dealer, maybe – who would be interested in buying the stolen things, but with no idea of their value, she would be entirely in the hands of the dealer and, she couldn't help thinking, probably cheated out of their true worth. It wasn't that she needed the money, but she didn't like the thought of being cheated. She still had all the cash she'd brought with her and her weekly wages more than covered all her needs. Even so, it might be a good idea to get rid of the things. They were no use in a drawer and the longer she kept them the more chance there was of someone discovering them and asking awkward questions.

~

In August a couple and their daughter came to stay at the Merrylife. Mr and Mrs Hanson looked quite old to have a child of about twelve, Gina thought, and their appearance was old-fashioned and staid. Their daughter was called Mavis, and Gina felt sorry for her, with her unstylish clothes, more suitable to someone five times her age, and her unfashionable name. Mavis sat sullen and silent between her parents at dinner the first evening, pushing the vegetarian food about her plate, looking as though she was in custody and wanting to escape.

The food at the Merrylife was, to Gina's amazement, delicious, but she knew it wasn't everyone's idea of tempting when the very idea of a dinner without meat or fish was an oddity to most people.

Breakfast on the Hansons' first morning was a repeat of the evening before, with Mavis looking as if she was enduring the experience, and her parents tense and nervous, as if they weren't used to eating away from home.

Of course, Mary and Ruth were kindness itself.

'Have you plans for the day, Mrs Hanson?' Ruth asked.

Mr and Mrs Hanson looked at each other. 'Er, no, not really. We thought we might look round the shops a bit,' Mrs Hanson said, 'and maybe sit and look at the sea.'

'Lovely!' cooed Ruth. 'And what about you, Mavis?'

Mavis evidently wasn't used to being consulted and was tongue-tied.

'Diana, love, I don't think you're very busy today, are you? Do you think you could take Mavis off to have a little fun?' asked Ruth.

Gina wasn't given to acts of kindness, but even she felt she could do better for the poor girl than the shops and sitting looking at the sea.

'Yes, all right. We'll think of summat fun, won't we, Mavis?' She gave Mavis a little wink and the girl smiled shyly.

When Gina was clearing away the breakfast plates, she said quietly to Mavis, 'Make sure your dad gives you plenty of pocket money if we're to have a fun day out.'

Mavis nodded silently and smiled again.

Ruth arranged that Mavis should be in the hallway at the time Gina finished her breakfast duties.

'Right,' said Gina, 'where d'you fancy going?'

'Dunno,' whispered Mavis.

'Ah, love, there's bags to do,' said Gina. 'Have you ever been to Blackpool?'

Mavis shook her head but her eyes were shining.

'Then you haven't lived,' said Gina. 'C'mon, let's go and live a little!'

~

The bus took the girls along the seafront, north to Blackpool. They travelled on the top deck and Mavis was delighted to see the sea all along their journey.

'There's no sea in Coventry,' she volunteered after a largely silent journey.

'We'll go on the beach and have a walk on the sand if you want,' suggested Gina.

'Yes, please, Diana.'

So they went down onto the beach, and then Mavis wanted to paddle in the sea.

'It smells strange,' she said. 'Sort of like fresh air but more so. It's nice.'

'You'll have to tuck your frock in the legs of your knickers,' suggested Gina. 'And we haven't got a towel so you'll have to dry your feet in the air.'

By now Mavis was more talkative. 'It's freezing!' she yelled as a big wave rolled in and slapped her goosepimply legs.

'It's always cold in the Irish Sea,' laughed Gina. 'They should call it the Coldish Sea instead.'

Mavis laughed at the terrible joke. Then, by the time her feet were dry, she was cold on this overcast day, so they headed off to a café to have hot chocolate to warm up. Then Gina suggested they went up the Tower, which she had once done with James.

All the time, Gina was keeping an eye open for Bella and also for James. She didn't think she'd see James here, but she thought it wise to keep a lookout. Bella was unlikely to be at the places where visitors went, but she did work in Blackpool and so Gina was being careful.

'It's amazing!' Mavis yelled into the wind, when they got to the top of the Tower and could look out over the sea and along the coast for miles. 'If I had a telescope I could probably see Mum and Dad sitting on a bench in St Annes.' She hadn't had a lot to say for herself so far, but at least she wasn't whispering shyly or looking cross and sulky now.

When they came back down to the ground, Mavis said she was hungry.

'All right, we'll go and have summat to eat,' said Gina. 'What would you like?'

'Not vegetarian food,' said Mavis. 'Mum and Dad went to a meeting where someone was preaching about vegetarianism and now we have to eat it all the time.'

'When was this?' asked Gina, feeling sorry for her all over again.

'Only just before the school holidays. They got all keen and had to book the Merrylife for our holidays. Usually we go to look at some ruins.'

'Crikey, whose idea is that?'

'Dad's interested in history and likes to go round ruined castles. Mum and me aren't bothered about them, but it's what we do on holiday. Now I'd quite like a day without ruins, or vegetarian food,' Mavis added sadly.

'I thought it was weird at first,' said Gina, 'but Ruth and Mary are such good cooks that I don't mind not eating meat or fish. Try it this evening and I bet you'll think it's nice.'

'It's not nice when Mum cooks it,' said Mavis.

'Well, why don't you ask the ladies to give your mum a recipe or two to get her started?' suggested Gina.

'Oh, Diana, you're so clever,' gushed Mavis. 'But let's have something not vegetable now.'

'How about fish and chips, with masses of salt and vinegar, eaten in the open air out of a newspaper?' suggested Gina. 'It's the only way to do it.'

Mavis grinned. 'Mum says eating in the street is common,' she said.

'It isn't in Blackpool,' Gina said. 'Folk'd think you were odd if you didn't. We'll find a bench, though, not wander about the street.'

As they ate their fish and chips Gina thought, as she had done the first time she'd come to Blackpool with James, of that long-ago day out here with her parents: how Dora had tried to make it nice for her and Ellen despite Philip's refusal to enter into the holiday spirit. Funny, she never thought about her father much at all these days, though thoughts of Dora and Ellen would often flash into her mind: mainly of these past few months, since her father had gone, when all three of them had worked at the Hall. Gina wondered how Ellen was getting on now with the responsibility of the rose garden . . . That got her thinking of the times she'd walked around it with Coco, on his lead, trotting along beside her so trustingly . . .

'Diana, do you have any brothers and sisters?' asked Mavis. It was as if she'd picked up on Gina's thoughts.

Gina pretended not to hear and looked away.

'Right, when you've drunk your pop we could go to the Aquarium, Aviary and Menagerie, if you like, Mavis,' she suggested brightly after a few moments.

'Yes, please, Diana.'

~

It was as the bus back to St Annes pulled away south that Gina saw Bella Bertolli. Gina and Mavis were seated upstairs, near the front and on the seaward side so that Mavis could enjoy the view. There, on the Promenade, was the unmistakable figure of Bella in her fur coat, a dead racoon's pelt fastened around her neck, despite this being an August day. Bella was talking to a weaselly-looking man in shabby clothes and the expression on her face was serious. Gina had never seen Bella outside the Tom and Tabby before, and in the harsh light of a summer afternoon she looked hard and sour, her glamour tawdry and false, her black hair shining bluish.

Gina shuffled down in her seat a little but there was no real danger of Bella noticing her on the top deck of the bus. As the bus gathered speed, Gina looked back over her shoulder and, as the figure of Bella receded, she decided she was right not to trust Bella to give her a fair price for the items still hidden in her room. The woman was no more to be trusted than James Stellion. In fact, she remembered, James didn't really trust Bella either; he'd never told her who he really was in case she ended up blackmailing him.

Gina took a long hard look at herself as Mavis gazed in wonder out of the bus window. Were those really the kind of people she wanted to be involved with: James Stellion and Bella Bertolli? She wished . . . she wished she had done things differently – or some of them, at least. She really wished she hadn't got the loot in a drawer in her room, still to get rid of.

~

When Gina and Mavis returned to the Merrylife Hotel, Mavis looked like a different child.

'Hello, girls. You've obviously had a nice time,' said Mary, seeing Mavis's glowing face.

'Oh, Miss Hathersage, it was the best day of *my entire life*,' grinned Mavis. 'We've been all over, up the Tower and everything, and I saw some birds and polar bears, and I paddled in the sea, and Diana said it was all right if I drank some pop, and we ate fish and chips—' She clamped a hand dramatically over her mouth at that point and Mary burst out laughing.

'It's all right, Mavis. I know people do when they go to the seaside. Mebbe your parents have done so, too.'

'Perhaps in a café, but probably not out of a newspaper,' smiled Mavis. 'And I think they're trying their best to be vegetarians.'

'Well, they're already back and in their room, so why don't you go and tell them about your lovely day before dinner?' suggested Mary.

Mavis ran off upstairs and Mary turned to Gina.

'And what about you, Diana? Did you have a good time?'

'Mebbe, Mary . . . mebbe it was the best day of my entire life,' smiled Gina. 'But I'm not quite sure.' Then, for a second, the cheerfulness fell from her face and she looked stricken.

Mary gazed at her with a serious, interested face. 'I hope you'll tell me about your other days sometime, Diana. I'm a good listener . . .'

'I'm fine,' said Gina, and went up to take her outdoor things off and get ready to help prepare the food.

~

One Wednesday afternoon, Ellen and Sally took the strange little books of spells to show Mr Shepherd, just as Tom had suggested.

'What have we here, I wonder,' Mr Shepherd said, taking the book out of the paper bag Ellen had wrapped it in and looking at it with interest. 'Not the kind of thing we usually discuss, eh, girls?'

'I'm sworn to secrecy,' said Sally. 'Nell knows what it's like at ours: nowt's private and everything's up for discussion.'

Ellen grinned at her trusted friend.

After Mr Shepherd had examined the book inside and out, he handed it back to Ellen.

'It's a pretty binding, or used to be when it was new, mebbe a couple of hundred years ago, but the content is nonsense – you know that, don't you, Ellen?'

'I certainly do, Mr Shepherd. I showed it to Mrs Travers in the village. She's a kind of wise woman; delivers babies and sorts out ailments with her recipes. She knows all kinds of strange things that the rest of us might find hard to understand, and she said it was rubbish.'

'Well, there you are, then, Ellen. You'll have no need to waste your time reading it.'

'Oh, no, Mr Shepherd, it wasn't me who was reading it. I found it among my sister, Gina's, things.'

'Well, let us hope Gina didn't waste *her* time with such nonsense then. It's the kind of book that was published by a charlatan and sold privately in a small number. The binding is nice, which makes it look like a serious book, but think of it as being like a cure a snake-oil salesman might peddle: all for show and profit, with no basis in truth at all. Highly illegal, too. Everyone round here knows what happened to the Pendle witches and they were just wise women, not real witches at all. I suppose a museum might be interested in it as it's so old, but for valid information it's entirely useless.'

'Yes, Mrs Travers thought so too.'

'I take it there is no news of Gina?'

Ellen sighed heavily. 'None at all. I've been to places I thought she might have been seen in Blackburn and Preston, but no one could help. It's been a few weeks now.'

'Well, if she's half your sense, Ellen, I reckon she'll turn up safely before too long.'

Ellen was not convinced, but it was nice to have the encouragement of her respected old friend.

~

Summer was waning and the evenings had a dimmer, more golden light about them now, towards the middle of August. The shadows were long and the air was damp with the hint of autumn.

Dora went along the lane towards Highview Farm with a little basket, hoping to find some blackberries that might have ripened already in the places where they would have caught the sun. A robin sang in the hedge alongside her and accompanied her on her walk. Ellen had gone ahead to the farm to see Edward, and Dora said she'd follow her up, share what blackberries she'd found on the way with Nancy, and they could discuss plans for the wedding.

Dora smiled; Nancy was keen to see Edward married to Ellen, but Ellen herself seemed in no hurry. It was as plain as it could be that she loved Edward, but she was also in love with gardening. When she wasn't at the Hall, digging and planting and pruning and weeding, she was in the little garden at the cottage, doing the same but on a much smaller scale. Dear Nellie, such a funny girl. Any other lass would be up to her neck in wedding preparations with the prospect of a good man like Edward Beveridge putting a ring on her finger.

Ellen hadn't said, but Dora just knew she was waiting for Gina to come home before she could settle down herself.

As ever, Gina was not far from Dora's own thoughts either: her difficult daughter. If only she knew whether Gina was all right; if only she'd come home, explain her part in the business with the stolen items and face her punishment. How could Gina herself rest easy with this mess and uncertainty hanging over her?

Mrs Stellion was lost without Gina. Dora suspected that, despite doting on her scallywag of a son, Mrs S had a lot of affection for Gina and didn't blame her at all for what had happened. It was sad to see the lady so listless and frail. She had grown very thin and she seldom went out at all these days, even to see her friends in Whalley. The village fête this summer had reverted to its alternative venue and a pall of misery hung over the Hall.

The previous week Dora had plucked up the courage to ask Mr Stellion if there was any news of James.

'Nothing that I know about, Dora,' he said carefully, 'but I just have a feeling he may have gone abroad.'

'Ah . . .' said Dora, 'I see. Well, I hope wherever he is, he's safe, and you and Mrs Stellion soon have certain news to set your minds at rest.'

'Thank you, Dora. No news of Gina, I take it?'

'No, sir.'

Now, as Dora walked towards the turn in the lane, a cloud drifted over the setting sun and took the heat from the day. Abruptly the robin stopped singing and flew away, and the lane was plunged into a gloomy and foreboding silence. Dora shielded her eyes and looked up. What a strange shape that cloud was, like a misshapen figure, a dancing goblin . . . She shivered. Then, sensing the silent presence of someone behind her, she turned sharply.

There, standing in the lane the way she had come, was a man. She had not heard his approach. Her stomach did a little flip of fearful surprise and shock to see him. He was dressed in dark clothes, and his face was oddly shadowed. Her heart pounding, she peered carefully at him. He seemed half familiar and yet a stranger, like a person might seem whom she had known years ago. She took half a step towards him, straining her eyes to make out the shadowy face. All the while he stood perfectly still, just staring at her.

'Phil . . .?' she whispered.

He did not speak but raised one arm towards her and beckoned her to him.

Dora gasped as an ice-cold grip of terror enveloped her. She took a step back, then another, then turned and fled towards Highview Farm as fast as she could, screaming over and over, 'No! No! Leave me, leave me alone!'

She dared not turn to see if he was following, because at any moment she knew that his arm could be around her neck, much as a dog might go for the throat of a lamb, and she would be brought down . . . brought down and strangled.

Jute, Albert Beveridge's dog, was in the yard and he rushed towards Dora, barking loudly. Suddenly the yard was filled with people: Ellen and Edward, Nancy and Albert.

'Mum! Oh, Mum, what's happened? What was it?'

Dora fell into Ellen's arms, weeping uncontrollably, while Jute, his hackles raised, stood at the gateway to the farm, barking and barking into the empty twilit lane.

~

Nancy, Albert and Edward could not have been kinder after Albert had telephoned the asylum to ask why Philip was out and frightening his wife in the lane, only to be told that Philip had died an hour or more ago.

'A stroke,' Albert said to Dora, as Nancy rubbed her back gently and plied her with sweet tea.

'But I saw him. I know it was him.'

'Some strange thing that I can't explain, Dora,' said Nancy, sensibly not attempting to give it a name, 'but he's gone now, love, and can't hurt you. You've nowt to fear, though every reason to be sad.'

Dora mopped her face with a handkerchief while Ellen sat, stunned, unable to give words to what she thought or felt.

After a while, Nancy suggested that Tom should be told the sad news and Albert went down to the Lodge in the Land Rover to tell him and to bring him back to the farm.

'Oh, Tom,' was all Dora could say as she fell into his arms.

They held each other tight.

'Let's go and make us all another pot of tea,' suggested Nancy, and Albert, Edward and Ellen followed her out of the sitting room, leaving Tom and Dora alone.

'Albert told me what you think you saw,' said Tom. 'Oh, lass, he can't hurt you now. He's gone.'

'But he was there . . . he was so real,' wept Dora. 'The Asylum can't have made a mistake, can they?'

'No, love. There will be no mistake. I reckon what you saw was Philip going on his way. He'll have moved on by now. You'll not see him again, have no fear.'

Dora shivered and he hugged her close.

After a few minutes she said, 'I need to tell Gina, but I don't know where she is.' Tears started from her eyes again. 'I wish my little girl was here,' she wailed. 'I can't bear to think of her all alone and no one to tell her that her father is dead.'

'Mm, it's a bad do,' said Tom. 'But don't take on so, lass. We need to put our heads together and see if there's owt we've overlooked. She's not been far in her life and I can't think she's travelled that far now.'

'Mr Stellion reckons James has gone overseas,' sniffed Dora.

'Well, I'd be amazed if Gina is with him,' said Tom. 'I think, whatever she thought of James Stellion before the police came looking for him, she's got a clearer picture of him now.'

Ellen put her head discreetly round the door and then brought in more tea, the Beveridges following behind. It had been planned as an evening to discuss the wedding, but now there would be a funeral to prepare.

Ellen, too, was thinking of Gina. If only she could find her and persuade her to come home. But it seemed too much to hope that, after all these weeks, she'd be home in time for her father's funeral.

CHAPTER TWENTY-ONE

Ellen wondered whether to give visiting Mr Shepherd a miss, it being the day after her father's funeral, but Dora was keen she should go.

'It'll do you good to get out of the house and think about summat else, love,' she said, handing Ellen a cup of tea. Both of them were going to work this morning, trying to get on with their lives, though today was Ellen's usual afternoon off. 'And you know Sally is always a cheery sort. You love your bookish talks with Mr Shepherd and, don't forget, he looks forward to your company now he doesn't get about so much.'

'You're right, Mum, of course,' said Ellen. 'I'll ask Uncle Tom if I can take Mr Shepherd a bunch of those asters. They're very vigorous this year . . .'

Ellen felt sad that her father had died, but in a detached way, such as anyone would feel to learn that any person they knew was dead. He'd been out of their lives for a year now and she'd long since ceased to think about him. She hadn't loved him – she acknowledged that now – and her memories of him were overwhelmingly of his sulks, his silences, his ill temper and his outbursts of violence against his wife and daughters.

The visit to Mr Shepherd was a real tonic for Ellen after the horrible funeral, attended by her friends and Dora's, keen to support them, but none of Philip's because he'd had no friends. Ellen felt so pleased she'd made the effort. She knew how Mr Shepherd valued his 'young visitors'.

It was as Ellen and Sally were walking home that, near to where they turned off to take the short cut across the fell, they saw a car at the side of the road. The bonnet was up and a man was leaning down into the engine, while a woman and a girl stood nearby, looking fed up.

'Hello, have you broken down?' called Sally.

The woman and child turned and the girl broke into a huge grin when she saw Ellen.

'Diana! Fancy seeing you here.'

Ellen looked at Sally and shrugged. 'I'm not called Diana,' she said. 'You're mebbe muddling me with someone who looks a bit like me.'

'Oh . . .' The girl frowned and looked carefully at Ellen. 'Not a bit like you – *a lot* like you!' she said. 'In fact, just like you.'

'Shush, Mavis. It's not Diana; the lady's just said.'

'And sounds like you, too,' said Mavis.

'Shush, Mavis . . .'

Ellen and Sally exchanged looks.

'This Diana,' said Ellen carefully, her stomach doing a little flutter of hope, 'where is it you know her from?'

'The Merrylife Hotel, with the Misses Hathersage,' said Mavis.

'Never mind that,' said Mavis's father, preoccupied with his car crisis. 'Is there a garage in Great Grindle, do you know? I can't think what's wrong with the car. I might have to go and get someone to come out to look at it.'

'There is a garage,' said Sally. 'My brother Roger works there. It's not far for me to go back and get him, if you want?'

'Oh, would you, dear?' said Mavis's mother gratefully. 'Thank you.'

'I'll come with you,' said her husband, 'and explain what's wrong.'

'I thought you said you didn't know what's wrong,' said Sally.

'I don't, but I might be able to explain the noise it's not making,' he said confusingly.

As Sally set out with him on the short walk back to Great Grindle, Ellen said to Mavis, 'Tell me about this hotel and Diana.'

'It's in St Annes. We stayed there a couple of nights last week,' said the woman. 'We're touring Lancashire and Yorkshire. I'm Mrs Hanson, and this is my daughter, Mavis. I must say, you do look very like Diana.'

'Just like,' reiterated Mavis. 'Miss Ruth Hathersage asked Diana to think of something nice for me to do one day and she took me to Blackpool. We did all sorts of things and she was really fun. We did the Tower and the zoo part underneath, and ate a fish-and-chip picnic, and Diana let me drink pop, and I even went in the sea, which was freezing cold!'

'She was very kind. I don't really approve of drinking pop, but I think Mavis had a lovely day and Diana was very patient with her.'

'It was the best day ever!' piped up Mavis, and her mother looked pleased and then, briefly, hurt.

Kind and patient . . . this doesn't sound much like Gina, yet who else would look just like me?

'Tell me about this hotel,' said Ellen, trying to keep any sense of excitement out of her voice. 'Merrylife, you say?'

'That's right. Mary and Ruth Hathersage own it. It's in St Annes, just off the main street. We went because it's vegetarian.'

'But the food's really nice,' volunteered Mavis. 'Miss Ruth gave Mum a couple of recipes. It was Diana who suggested that.'

More and more peculiar . . .

'Anyway, this girl who looks like you, but maybe a little younger – Diana – she helps at the hotel,' said Mrs Hanson.

'Do you know how long she's been there?' asked Ellen.

'No. She was there when we stayed, that's all I know.'

'I really thought you were her at first,' Mavis said excitedly.

'Does this Diana live at the hotel?'

'Yes, she lives in. She seems to do a bit of cleaning and helping in the kitchen and dining room,' said Mrs Hanson. 'Why? Is she a relative of yours? I suppose she must be to look so like you.'

Ellen smiled. 'I think she might be. Now, let me write down the name of this hotel and how to find it. You don't happen to have the telephone number, do you . . .?'

Soon Sally and Mr Hanson returned with Roger in the van from the garage and, as Mr Hanson walked around the front of the car scratching his head, Roger set to work to try to fix the engine.

'I hope it won't take long,' said Mrs Hanson fearfully. 'My husband is determined to see Clitheroe Castle this afternoon, and then we're on to Skipton to view the ruins there tomorrow.'

Sally looked taken aback. 'Lovely . . .' she murmured, catching Ellen's eye.

The girls said goodbye and Ellen thanked the Hansons for the information about the Merrylife Hotel and Diana. On the walk across the high fields, she told Sally what she'd learned.

'Do you really think it might be Gina?' asked Sally.

'It must be. That girl Mavis thought I was her, and who else would look so like me but Gina?'

'And – it's obvious – she's pinched Diana Stellion's name.'

'Well, she's Diana something, but I doubt it's Stellion; Mrs Hanson didn't know her surname.'

'So what are you going to do?'

'I'll go up to the farm and ask Ed's mum if I can use the phone. I won't tell Mum until I know more.'

~

'Good afternoon, is that Miss Hathersage?

'Mary Hathersage, yes.'

'Is it possible to speak to Diana, please?'

'Oh dear, I'm afraid not. Who's calling, please?'

'My name's Ellen Arnold, Miss Hathersage, and I think Diana may be my sister.'

'Oh! Oh, no, I'm so sorry, Ellen, but Diana is no longer here.'

Ellen felt her spirits plummet. She would know whether this Diana was indeed Gina the second she spoke to her, of course, but now that eventuality, on which she'd built all her hopes, was not to be.

'Hello? Are you still there?'

'Yes, Miss Hathersage. Do you know where Diana has gone?'

'I'm afraid not, dear. She's just disappeared; taken her things and left.'

'What, for good?'

'It would seem so. We're quite upset. We guessed she was troubled, but we hoped we could help her in some way, or at least her job here was a help to her . . . whatever it was that was wrong. She said she was an orphan and had no one, but I rather guessed there was more to it than she was saying.'

Ellen was thinking hard. She could not let this be a dead end, and the word 'troubled' reinforced her belief that this Diana was Gina.

'Miss Hathersage, would it be all right if I came to see you, please?'

'Of course, dear. Come tomorrow . . . I think there's no time to lose.'

~

'. . . So I'm going to St Annes to talk to Mary and Ruth Hathersage tomorrow, Mum.'

'Do you want me to come with you, Nell?' asked Tom, who'd spent the afternoon at the cottage.

It was on the tip of her tongue to refuse, but her uncle was such a strong and calming presence that Ellen knew she'd be glad to have him there if the news was bad or the situation became awkward. And it was always better to go anywhere with a companion.

'Oh, yes, please, Uncle Tom. Ed offered, but Nathan's ill and I know Mr Beveridge can't really spare Ed just now.'

'I'll let them know at the Hall that we've been unexpectedly called away. They'll think it's to do with your dad, I reckon. We'll set out early. Don't worry, Dora, love, we'll find Gina and bring her safely home.'

Ellen felt comforted by her uncle's positive attitude but, when she lay in bed that night, thinking over what Mary Hathersage had said, she felt full of fear for Gina. Just why had she left the hotel in such a hurry?

~

Gina woke up feeling cold, stiff and itchy. The bed smelled unclean and she thought it might be full of bugs. She didn't dare lift the sheet and look at the state of the mattress. This hotel was grubby inside and out, and a disgrace when compared to the bright and cheerful comforts of the Merrylife, but it was cheap and the woman on the reception – if the dusty and cluttered desk by the door could be called that – had not shown any interest in Gina herself at all. All she was concerned about was that Gina could afford the little that the room cost.

Gina eased her stiff shoulder and examined the scabs on her legs where she'd been pulled over in the street. Mary and Ruth had patched her up nicely, but she could really do with changing the dressings on her knees, and the huge bruise on her thigh was black.

She stood up, putting her feet straight into her shoes to avoid treading on the stained carpet, and went to lean on the windowsill, ignoring the dust and a couple of dead flies. The view was the back of a row of terraced houses, the stone walls black with soot. Was the whole of Blackburn covered in soot she wondered.

She'd thought life with the Hathersage sisters at the hotel was settling down into a boring routine, albeit with different guests to be bored about every few days, but now her life was suddenly in turmoil again and she wasn't quite sure what to do for the best. Fleeing to Blackburn to try to sell the loot had seemed to be her only course of action after what had happened in Blackpool, but now she was here, alone, and she felt so unsure of herself, so lost. She'd dreamed of a life far away from the Lancashire fells, but even when she'd had the money to go far away

– maybe down south to London; maybe to Liverpool and then on to America – she'd gone only as far as the Lancashire coast. It was as if Little Grindle and Grindle Hall would not let her go, and if she wandered too far, they twitched her leash and she would be drawn back in, just as she used to pull Coco to her to train him to walk to heel.

She'd have done anything to get away in the spring of last year, when she was working without making any effort at the farm, feeling resentful of anyone who seemed to be getting on in life or had money or things that she wanted, but the truth was that when she had got away, she'd felt lost and unsure of what to do with herself. Little Grindle was all she knew. Now when she wanted to escape in her head to a better place, it was to Highview Cottage, with Mum and Nell, sitting round the kitchen table, laughing and drinking strong tea, or the rose garden at Grindle Hall, a perfect paradise of beauty, with fragrant flowers clustering around the bench she'd liked to sit on, and Coco at her feet, looking up at her adoringly.

Oh God, Gina, what have you done? Why did you think that was not enough for you?

How had she taken this wrong turn from the Merrylife to a horrible hotel in Coalhouse Terrace, Blackburn so quickly? It should be called Chimney View, she sneered miserably. The horizon was dominated by that gigantic chimney she'd seen from the passenger seat of James's little car – the Audley Destructor, she'd learned it was called. Amazing and awful at the same time.

Was it really only the day before yesterday that she'd decided to go into Blackpool for the afternoon by herself? What an idiot she'd been . . .

~

The day out with Mavis had given Gina a taste for the gaudy delights of Blackpool and she felt ready to risk the very small chance of bumping into Bella Bertolli; she'd keep a lookout, she resolved. St Annes was so much smaller than Blackpool and could be a little too quiet, in Gina's opinion.

Gina had window-shopped along the main commercial street and then come across a more run-down row of small shops in a side street, including some selling antiques. She looked in the windows, wondering if this would be the right place to try to get rid of the loot still hidden in the back of her drawer.

She chose one shop, which sold small items, including jewellery, and went in to look.

The man behind the counter didn't greet her. He seemed to be reading a newspaper and Gina browsed the displays, trying to decide what to do. She saw some beads very like the ones stashed in her drawer and held them up to examine the jewelled clasp.

The man looked up from his paper and gave her a hard stare, and Gina put the necklace down and moved on to a display of brooches. She hardly even knew what happened next. Maybe old habits died hard with Gina, and she hadn't consciously meant to steal the little pearl brooch at all, but the man behind the counter was there with his hand around her wrist before she knew it.

'I saw you trying to nick that, you little thief,' he snarled. 'I know your kind.'

'No!' said Gina, trying to shake him off. 'Leave me alone. I never—'

'You never what? Put that in your pocket? I saw you and now I'm going to call the police.'

'No, I never meant—'

'Never meant to be caught?' He tried to drag Gina behind the counter, calling, 'Dave, Dave, give us a hand. Here's another of 'em trying to rob us.'

The door at the back of the shop opened and a hugely fat man lumbered out. He was smoking a cigarette and wheezing noisily.

Gina knew she had to get away now. There was no chance she would be able to escape from the two of them together. She aimed a kick as hard as she could at the groin of the man who held her and he let go of her wrist immediately, crumpling to the floor with an agonised yell. Luckily for her he blocked the advance of the fat man, and Gina fled from the shop, out into the street, desperate to disappear from sight before either of them could pursue her. She ran along and then down the first side road she came to, then down the next off that.

There was no one about here and she listened out for any sign the men were following her. She waited a few minutes and heard nothing. She was just about to move off, back to the busy streets, when a voice in her ear made her jump in fright and she gave a little cry of shock.

'I'll have that, thank you, lady,' said a man, as he made a lightning-quick grab for Gina's handbag over her arm.

'No you don't! Get off!' she said, not letting go, trying to wrestle her bag from his hold, but the man was stronger than her and, with a violent jerk, he pulled her to the ground, dragging her along as she fought to keep possession of her bag. Within seconds he had pulled it from her grasp, twisting her shoulder, and then sped away from her, leaving her where she lay with bloodied knees.

'You bastard . . . bastard,' yelled Gina, helpless to do anything more than hurl insults.

The really galling thing – the thing that made her blood boil at her own stupidity – was that the robber would be thinking he'd won the jackpot when he eventually inspected the contents of the handbag. All the money she'd saved from her wages at the hotel, plus her share of the money from the sale of James's loot, *and* the money she'd stolen from Mrs Thwaite, who'd stolen it from Mrs Stellion – all of it was in that bag. He'd got the lot, leaving her with only the small change in her pocket and not a penny in the world besides. Thank God she still had the jewellery in the shopping bag, hidden safely in her room at the Merrylife, though that was no use to her until she'd sold it on.

Eventually she rose stiffly to her feet, feeling her shoulder and arm – not broken, just sore – and brushed the street dust off her frock as best she could. Her knees were badly scraped and bleeding. What to do? She hobbled off to the main street and went into a chemist's shop. It smelled a bit like that smart chemist's in Great Grindle where she'd bought Mrs Stellion her special soap and had stolen a lipstick. That seemed like a lifetime ago.

The pharmacist and his assistant were all good sense and kindness, washing Gina's grazes and applying some dressings. Gina told them she hadn't any money to pay them, but they waved that concern away and even gave her the bus fare back to St Annes.

'I just tripped on the steps down to the beach,' Gina insisted when they asked. The last thing she wanted was the police on the scene.

When she arrived back at the Merrylife, Mary and Ruth were not so easy to deceive.

'Diana, you've come back all damaged and without your handbag – what else are we to think but that you've been robbed?' said Ruth.

'Tell us what happened, Diana, please, and we'll go to the police.'

'No, not the police,' said Gina, a little too quickly.

'But your handbag, dear . . .'

'I don't want a fuss. There wasn't much in it . . . just a few coppers.' She couldn't admit to just how much she'd been carrying around. Why had she even done that and not left the money stashed away in her room in a sock or something? Why did she ever think it would be safer in her handbag in the street?

'But the man who robbed you – he needs to be locked up. Other women are not safe while he's loose,' said Mary indignantly. 'We'll go with you, Diana, and you can explain.'

Explain to the police? Gina reflected that probably the police would very much like her to go to them with some explanations! It was the very situation she was in St Annes to avoid.

‘Please, Mary and Ruth,’ she said pathetically, ‘it’s all been very trying and I think I’d like to have a lie-down.’

‘’Course, love. I’ll just see to some fresh dressings and bring you some nice hot chocolate, and we can talk about it again in the morning,’ said Ruth.

The next morning Gina rose very early. She’d already gathered her things together ready for her flight from St Annes, and she helped herself to a few one-pound notes that the Hathersage sisters kept for emergencies in the sideboard in their little sitting room before letting herself out of the Merrylife Hotel for the last time.

~

It was mid-morning when Ellen and Tom arrived at the Merrylife Hotel.

‘Ellen! I know it’s you because you look exactly like Diana,’ said the lady who answered the door. ‘I’m Mary, and it was me who came across your sister at Preston station one day in June. Come in, both.’

‘Thank you, Miss Hathersage.’

‘Mary, please, love.’

Ellen and Tom were shown into the Hathersage sisters’ little sitting room behind the hotel dining room. All the hotel guests had already departed to go sightseeing for the day.

'This is my uncle, Tom Arnold,' said Ellen. 'We've left my mum at home. We're all the family Gina has . . .'

'Gina? Ah, Diana's real name. I did wonder. And when she said her name was Thornton, I guessed that wasn't real either and she'd just read it on one of the departure boards at the station.'

Ruth came in with a pot of tea, and news of Gina and explanations were exchanged. Ellen and Tom had discussed on their train journey how much to tell the Hathersage women and, finding they were so sensible and down-to-earth, Ellen was relieved not to have to hide anything from them.

'. . . So now my father, Uncle Tom's brother, has died. We had hoped to find Gina before the funeral, which was two days ago, but we were all out of ideas about where to look until I just happened upon Mavis Hanson and her parents and their broken-down car. Mum is very anxious to have Gina home, not only to break the news of our father's death, but to give her the chance to explain her part in the business with the stolen goods. We think she was led on by James . . . by James, the man behind it all. He's older and, well, we think Gina might have been taken in by him.'

'Mm, that's not impossible,' said Ruth. 'It's a terrible disappointment that you and your sister can't be reunited here and now, but she took herself off very early yesterday morning, before we were up, and we haven't seen her since. She's taken everything she brought with her . . .' *and one or two things she didn't*, '. . . and has gone without leaving a note or anything.'

'It was after that robbery in the street the day before . . .'

'Robbery?' Ellen was alarmed. 'Good heavens, surely Gina wouldn't—'

'No, don't worry, dear, she hasn't taken to street robbery, I'm certain of that. She was the victim on this occasion. She had her handbag stolen.'

'Oh, no! Is she all right?'

'A bit grazed and bruised but nowt that won't soon heal. We tried to get her to go to the police but she completely refused. Now, of course, we understand why. The police would have been very interested indeed to meet her.'

'And did you never guess she was a fugitive from the law, Mary?' asked Tom, also including Ruth in his question with a kindly look.

'We guessed straight away that summat was all wrong about her: a story that didn't hold water about her luggage, and she seemed not only to have no family but not to have anyone at all in her life,' Ruth answered.

'It was as if she had been suddenly cast adrift from all human relationships when I came across her at Preston station, but now I know she was on the run I can see that there was no one she felt she could go to,' said Mary.

'She could have come to us,' said Ellen, and Tom reached out and squeezed her arm. 'We know she can be bad, but we'd have stood by her and . . . she *should* have come to us. If you can't go to your family, where can you go?' Ellen sighed heavily.

'True,' said Ruth. 'We tried to look out for her, guessing, as I say, that she might be in some kind of trouble, but in the end we are not her family and there was nowt we could have done to keep her here if she felt she had to go.'

'She can't run away for ever,' said Ellen, remembering Betty Travers telling her exactly that. 'We were so nearly here in time to find her after Mavis told us about you, but Gina can't have gone far, surely? I can't think she's going to leave the country like James— Well, she'd have gone abroad straight away if she was going to, I reckon.'

'Yes,' said Tom. 'Lancashire is all she knows and I reckon she's gone no further. Now, I think we'd better go to the police and tell them everything we know. We can't save her from the law, and it would be dishonest to try when we know she's done wrong, but we can't help her either if we can't find her.'

'Yes, you're right, of course,' said Mary. 'We'll get our coats on and we'll all go together now; get it over with.'

~

The police were interested to learn that Gina was still on the run in the county and had been hiding out in a very respectable, if somewhat eccentric, little hotel in St Annes.

'The last place we'd have looked for her really,' said the sergeant to whom Tom, Ellen and the Hathersage sisters told their story. 'She could have stayed with you for ever, Miss Hathersage, and we'd never have found her. As it is, she's broken cover, so to speak, and we'll alert our colleagues in the Force to keep a lookout for her.'

'You won't hurt her, will you?' said Ellen. 'She's younger than me – only eighteen – and not violent or anything. She's just . . . naughty, really.'

'Dealing in stolen goods is a great deal more than "naughty",' the sergeant said severely.

'Yes, yes, of course . . .'

'She's a sweet girl who's lost her way,' said Ruth to the sergeant, using the same tone as he had. 'She's been misled by a scoundrel, as I understand it. I won't say she was a good worker at our hotel, because she tended to laziness, but she has the potential for great kindness, and the world needs a little more kindness, wouldn't you agree? Same for all the creatures of the earth, sea and sky.'

The sergeant looked taken aback but Ruth's viewpoint was inarguable.

Outside the police station, Tom and Ellen said goodbye to the Hathersage sisters, hugging them and promising to keep in touch.

'I just thank God you found her, Mary,' said Ellen. 'Who knows what trouble she'd have fallen into otherwise.'

'Well, let us pray she's not fallen into bad trouble now,' said Mary. 'We'll telephone your young man, Edward, at the farm and leave a message if we hear owt of her.'

'And we'll let you know, too.'

'Good luck, love, and goodbye,' they called as Ellen and Tom made their way to the train home.

Ellen and Tom sat on the train from St Annes to Preston, feeling defeated. Gina was somewhere close by, they were sure, but just where?

CHAPTER TWENTY-TWO

GINA LEFT COALHOUSE Terrace and was glad to go. With a little luck she wouldn't have to spend another night in such a wretched place, but she was eking out the money she'd stolen from the Hathersage sisters until she sold the rest of the loot, just in case there were any difficulties. She'd got rid of the nasty mourning brooch and the hatpin – where had the other hatpin got to? – at a pawnbroker's in Preston the previous day, but she was finding it difficult to remember what she was supposed to be called and what her story was at each place. She'd left the notes she'd made at the back of her old exercise book at the Hall when she fled, and now she wished she'd brought them with her to remind her. Mostly it didn't matter, but at one pawnbroker's the man remembered her better than she remembered herself, and he became suspicious. That was when she decided to move on and try her luck in Blackburn. She recalled for certain that she was Mrs Travers at Sidney Simmonds' shop.

The breakfast at Coalhouse Terrace had been as

horrible as the room: congealed eggs like rubber, strangely grey underneath, accompanied by thin toast spread with a tiny spot of sour-tasting margarine. Being a country girl, Gina was used to good food. Even though there had never been any luxury at Highview Cottage – far from it; potatoes featured most days – the food always tasted wholesome and had been well cooked. Now she had an idea how really poor people lived, people who had lost hope and given up caring because they couldn't afford to. When she'd gone back upstairs after breakfast to collect her things, she'd seen a rat running down the corridor. That explained the vile smell around the wardrobe in her room.

She'd tried to leave the squalid hotel without paying, tiptoeing down with her things, but the woman on the desk was too quick for her and Gina had handed over the money for her room and the inedible breakfast with ill grace.

She went out into the overcast late-August day. Rain threatened and she had no umbrella and didn't fancy a soaking. She made her way to King William Street, where there were plenty of shops. By now it was spitting with rain. At a hardware shop she saw the inevitable bucket just inside the door for shoppers to put their wet umbrellas in, and she waited outside, pretending to look in at the window, until someone with an umbrella went into the shop. No sooner had the woman left her wet brolly in the bucket and turned away than Gina picked it out and was off down the road with it. Luckily for her it was not a distinctive colour, and within a few yards she was mingling with other shoppers holding black umbrellas.

Now, if she remembered rightly, Sidney Simmonds' shop was along a bit and then down a side road. She'd be glad to sell the last of the stolen items. There were a couple of metal fruit dishes that might have real gold on them and the necklace similar to the one she'd seen in that antiques shop in Blackpool where the man had grabbed her after she'd pocketed the brooch.

It was raining quite heavily by the time she saw the familiar three golden spheres. She gathered her courage and went in.

Behind the counter was a woman only a few years older than herself, wearing an unusual combination of clothes: a cream satin dress with a low waist, such as Gina had seen in wedding photographs dating from the 1920s, with a black tailcoat over it. On her head was a headdress made out of feathers set into a jewelled hair slide. The effect was odd but strangely attractive.

'Good morning. Can I help you?' asked the young woman. She looked closely at Gina.

'Yes, please, I wonder if you'd be interested in buying a few little items I have here.'

The woman leaned over the counter in the dimly lit shop and fixed her eyes on Gina's face. Gina took a step back.

'I'm sorry,' said the woman, hastily straightening up. 'The light is poor today with this rain and I've left my glasses in the back. I'll just go and get my father, Mr Simmonds, to help you. Please take a seat. He won't be long.' She hurried away through a door at the back of the shop, closed it behind her, and Gina, her sore knees stiff, perched herself on the high stool beside the counter and waited.

Mr Simmonds was taking rather a long time to appear. Gina wondered whether to just go, but she remembered he had been very kind to 'Mrs Travers' when she'd come in in February with a pair of pearl earrings, and she wanted to get rid of the dishes and the necklace without any fuss. James had been impressed with the amount she'd been given for the earrings so Gina was hoping her luck would be in today. She really did need some good fortune. It had been a very bad couple of days . . .

How much longer is he going to be? Is that woman suspicious? She did look at me a bit oddly but she said she hadn't got her glasses. Mebbe she wasn't wearing them when she got dressed either . . .

A few more minutes passed. Gina wondered again about leaving but the rain was tipping down now, running in torrents off the sill above the door outside and splashing noisily into the street. Even the umbrella would be of little use in this weather.

At last, Mr Simmonds came out through the door behind the counter, leaving it open. He was a small, thin man with white hair and a kind face. He looked nothing like his flamboyantly dressed daughter, though there was a similarity of gesture, Gina saw as he greeted her.

'Good morning – although I see it isn't with regard to the weather,' he smiled. 'How may I help this morning?

Mrs Travers, if I'm not mistaken?' he spoke quite loudly and gave her an old-fashioned little bow.

'Yes. I'm surprised you remember. I've got summat I thought you might be interested in buying,' said Gina. 'Some dishes and a necklace.'

'Just let me close this door, Mrs Travers, and I'll have a look,' he said, going to do it. 'Well, let's get the items on the counter and we can see them properly.'

Gina took the fruit dishes out of the shopping bag and put them on the glass counter top.

'Now, they'd be easier to see against a good surface,' he said. 'I'll just find the velvet . . .' and he disappeared through the door in the back for a couple of minutes.

Gina glanced out at the teeming rain and decided she was in no hurry to leave anyway, which was just as well, as Mr Simmonds was taking his time.

'There we are. Sorry to keep you waiting, Mrs Travers,' he said, placing a black velvet mat on the counter. 'Now let me see what we have here . . .' He picked up each of the fruit dishes in turn, very slowly, and inspected it from all sides.

'Mm, very interesting. These are sterling silver and finished inside with gilt. Very nice . . . very nice indeed. I remember seeing something similar in . . . oh, it must have been about 1935 . . . and they fetched quite a lot of money. I'd gone to an auction in Manchester . . .'

He was off on a long tale that didn't really interest Gina, except that the dishes in question had been worth quite a bit.

'I shall need to look very carefully at the hallmark,' he

said when he'd recounted the tale of the previous dishes at some length. 'Now, what can I have done with my loupe . . .?' He felt in his pockets, then searched the counter, then disappeared into the back again. Eventually he reappeared with the eyeglass and inspected the hallmark on each of the dishes, then declared he needed his callipers and had to go to look for those as well. After a while he came back with them and measured the dishes to see if they were a matched pair.

'I'd better note it down,' he said, as if this were a novel idea. 'Now where can I have put the ledger, I wonder.'

'Try under the counter,' said Gina, a touch impatiently.

'Yes . . . yes indeed. How observant of you, Mrs Travers.'

Gina said nothing. She didn't recall Mr Simmonds being so absent-minded last time.

'While I've got my ledger out, I'll just remind myself what you brought in last time. Do you remember when that was, Mrs Travers?'

Oh, for goodness' sake, what does it matter?

He smiled at her kindly and she felt a little mean at her impatience.

'Early this year,' she said. 'Before spring, I think.'

He turned the pages very slowly, beginning right at the start of the year and looking carefully.

'Here,' said Gina, reading upside down when he got to the right page.

'Ah, yes, those pretty earrings. Yes, very good . . . very good indeed . . . Now, I'll just note down all the details of the dishes. They're not rare but they are in excellent condition. I'll need to make careful note of this decoration. It'll take me a few minutes. May I offer you a cup of tea?'

Gina glanced out again at the pouring rain. Her stomach rumbled loudly; she'd been unable to eat the nasty breakfast at the hotel.

'Yes, please. That would be nice,' she said, deciding she was here for the morning. And after all, she had nowhere else to go. She just needed the money from the sale of these things.

Mr Simmonds called through to the back, 'Sadie, a cup of tea for Mrs Travers, my dear, if you will?'

'Yes, Dad. I'll put the kettle on.'

'It won't be long, Mrs Travers,' said Mr Simmonds. 'I'll just make sure the door won't blow open. It can do when the wind gets up and it really is raining fast.' He went over to the door and made a show of securing it.

Gina didn't notice him flip the 'Open' sign to 'Closed'.

'Now, I shall note all the details while you just sit there comfortably out of the rain,' he said, and began to write down everything about the dishes in a very slow longhand.

Sadie brought out a cup of tea and a sugar bowl, then went away and came back with a plate of chocolate digestive biscuits. She put them down in front of Gina with a little wink and went away again and Gina busied herself with stirring sugar into her tea and eating the biscuits.

'Now, then,' said Mr Simmonds, glancing outside through the glass in the door. 'No let-up in this rain, I see. Did you say you have a necklace, too?'

'Yes, here,' said Gina, pulling it out of her shopping bag.

She'd just got it arranged on the velvet when there was a noise at the door. Gina turned to see, to her complete astonishment, Ellen rushing in, with Edward and Tom just behind her.

'Gina! Oh, thank God you're safe!' Ellen threw her arms around her sister. 'Oh, I thought I'd never see you again. We've been so worried.'

Gina pushed Ellen away, her face showing amazement as she looked from her sister to Tom and then Edward.

'What . . . what are you doing here? How . . .?' She made to rise from the stool as her look of surprise turned to an angry frown, but Ellen was holding her so tightly that she was unable to move, unable to get away.

Tom was shaking Mr Simmonds by the hand and telling him who they all were, while Sadie came round the counter to speak to Edward and Ellen. Ellen continued to hold onto Gina, and Edward was grasping her other arm so that, supposing she was thinking of getting away, she was going nowhere. In effect, they had her prisoner.

'I thought you weren't going to get here before she left,' Sadie said. 'Even I was wanting to leave, Dad went on so . . . He was magnificent, though. I've never seen him move so slowly.'

'Thank you, thank you,' Ellen kept saying, wiping away tears with her free hand. 'Oh, our mum will be made up to have found Gina. She's been that worried. We all have.'

'There's no need to make a stupid fuss. I was about to do a bit of business with Mr Simmonds,' said Gina indignantly, trying to shrug off her captors. 'Just let me go, can't you?'

'Come on, Gina, time to go home,' said Tom. 'I suppose we'd better take these things with us and hand them over to . . . the interested parties,' he added quietly, collecting the dishes and necklace into Gina's shopping bag. 'And I'll be sure to let those interested parties know how helpful you've been,' he added to Mr Simmonds. 'Thank you for everything you've done for us.'

The farm Land Rover was parked outside the shop, and Tom escorted Gina out to it and made sure she was shut safely in the back, while Edward and Ellen thanked the pawnbroker and his daughter again and promised to let them know what happened to Gina.

Ellen climbed in the back of the Land Rover and sat next to her sister. 'Mum's at home, love,' she said. 'She can't wait to see you.'

Gina shrugged and turned away with a furious look on her face.

~

Gina told her story first, Dora sitting next to her on the sofa, with Ellen and Tom in the saggy old armchairs in the little sitting room that was so seldom used at Highview Cottage. Edward went home and, with a significant look at Tom, said he'd come back in a while.

Gina grew angry as she told how James Stellion had persuaded her to help him sell on the various stolen items he'd sent to her in parcels.

'He completely took me in, Mum,' she said indignantly. 'He told me he lived in a big house in London, something like the Hall. I thought he'd have a housekeeper of his own, and mebbe gardeners like you, Uncle Tom and Nell, but it turned out he lived in lodgings.'

'Shameless, taking in a young girl like that, blinding her with stories of wealth,' tutted Dora.

'I never thought he lived in a place like that,' said Ellen, puzzled. 'Are you sure that's what he said? Diana shares a flat with a friend in London, not a big place at all. It's Mr and Mrs Stellion who own the brewery and have the deep pockets. What did James actually say?'

'He called it "my place in Pimlico",' Gina said. 'What was I to think?'

'That he *lived in lodgings*, mebbe, Gina. I reckon you wanted it to be a grand place and you hadn't got a clue. You knew all along that the things he sent you were stolen and you just liked the money.'

'*Nell*,' scolded Dora. 'Be kind.'

'Be daft, more like,' muttered Ellen. 'Gina, you've taken yourself in, you know you have. He used you to help him, but it was you who agreed to it, knowing what you were doing was wrong. You could have said no.'

Gina looked sulky and mutinous.

'We know you went to live at the Merrylife Hotel,' said Tom, 'to hide from the police after they came to the Hall. It was lucky for you, and for us, that you found Mary and Ruth Hathersage.'

'What do you know about them?' said Gina, sorry her story wasn't to be a complete revelation and her family gripped by her adventures. She wanted to put her own slant on events, too.

'Uncle Tom and I went to see them the day after you left the Merrylife. That was bad luck. Had we been a day earlier we'd have found you there. The Hathersage sisters could not have been nicer. They didn't seem to mind that you told them terrible lies about being an orphan, cast adrift and penniless in the world,' said Ellen, 'instead of a criminal, on the run, with stolen goods that you stored on their premises, just like you hid the stolen things at the Hall.'

'I worked there for several weeks. I earned my keep,' said Gina, indignant again.

'And then you had your handbag stolen—'

'It was awful. Look, I'm covered in grazes,' said Gina, showing her knees. 'The man took all my money.'

'All your money, Gina? How much was all?' Tom asked.

'Every bit,' she said evasively. 'I had to beg my bus fare back to the hotel from the chemist who bandaged my knees.'

'So how did you pay your train fare to Blackburn, when you ran away from the Merrylife because you thought Mary and Ruth might call the police over you being robbed?' asked Tom with a severe look on his face. 'How did you pay for a place to stay before we came to get you from Mr Simmonds' shop?'

'Well, I . . . sort of borrowed some money from Mary and Ruth . . .'

'"Sort of borrowed"? You mean you stole it, you wicked creature,' said Ellen. 'After all they did for you, you took advantage of their kindness and their trusting natures. Mary suspected you were "troubled", she said. Well, Gina, you're not *troubled*, you're just *trouble*, and the way you repaid their kindness goes to prove it.'

'No, I meant to pay it back when—'

'When you sold those stolen items to that nice Mr Simmonds? Gina, I despair of you; you're just a liar!'

'Nell, please . . .' murmured Dora, looking stricken that her girls were quarrelling so soon after Gina had come home.

'Mum, I think you need to tell Gina our news now,' said Ellen.

'Yes, you're right, love. I needed you home, Gina, love, to make sure you were safe and because you have to face up to what you've done, but I also need you here to tell you some sad news. I'm afraid your father is dead.'

Gina looked puzzled, as if she couldn't understand what her mother was saying. No one spoke and eventually she said, 'When? How?'

'About two weeks ago, in the asylum. He had a stroke and died, love.'

Gina put her hands to her mouth. 'Oh! Oh, no. I'd kind of forgotten about the spell. Once Dad was gone to the madhouse, I thought that was it and we were rid of him that way.'

'W-what do you mean?' asked Dora, remembering what Betty had told her had happened in the fortune-telling booth at the fête, but keen to learn the truth from Gina. 'Rid of him how? What spell?'

Gina was looking very serious. 'I didn't really mean to kill him,' she said quietly. 'I knew the spells took time to work, and sometimes they worked not always in the ways I thought they would, but when . . . when the sheep died, I thought that was the end of that one. And then when he hit you, I was that cross and I made another . . . and now he's dead.'

'What are you talking about?' snapped Dora, frightened. 'Talk sense!'

'I was going to make a new start after I'd sold the last of the stolen things: start again somewhere and try to be good, and now . . . now I've killed Dad as well as Mrs Thwaite.'

'Killed them? What nonsense is this?' demanded Dora, losing patience completely.

'I wanted to put all that behind me and now you're bringing it up again,'Gina said, her face contorted. 'It's so unfair!' She started to cry, making a lot of noise and flapping her hands dramatically, and Tom led her into the kitchen before she became hysterical.

'Ellen, do you know what she's on about?' Dora was angry and upset.

'Yes, it's just that Uncle Tom and I found a silly old book of spells among Gina's things in her room at the Hall. We told you about the exercise book, but not about this book. We were sure she'd been trying them out. You know Mrs Travers foresaw Gina's future in her crystal ball at the fête and warned her off messing with magic spells – not because she could really do them, but because she might do herself harm believing in such nonsense and it might lead her down the wrong path. Gina can't possibly have killed Dad – he died of a stroke in the asylum – and she can't have killed Mrs Thwaite either.

Didn't Mrs Thwaite have a heart attack? Gina was nothing to do with that.'

'What had Gina got against Mrs Thwaite, anyway?' asked Dora, at a loss.

'I don't know, Mum. You'll have to ask her.'

'But she did laugh when I told her that Mrs Thwaite had died,' Dora remembered. 'I was so ashamed, but I just thought it was Gina being heartless.'

'That's all it could have been, Mum,' said Ellen patiently. 'She wanted Mrs Thwaite's job at the Hall, and somehow she got it, and then the old lady died and Gina must have thought it was to do with some stupid spell she cast.'

'Why does everyone seem to know so much more about this than me, her own mother?' asked Dora. 'Even Betty, from what you say.'

'Uncle Tom and I know because we found the book and I took it to Mrs Travers. I didn't want to worry you, and I reckon she didn't either. The spells aren't real, just Gina's imagination after reading the daft book. I took it to Mr Shepherd, too, and he said it was just lies and the book was a fancy way of getting people to part with their money.'

'And now the silly girl thinks she's got magical powers. Betty told us she'd warned Gina about that at the fête. But I can't even say it without thinking it's madness.'

Dora and Ellen looked at each other, both thinking the same awful thought: Philip had been declared mad and locked up, and they'd never seen him again.

'It's rubbish,' said Ellen resolutely. 'That's all. You know how Gina always wants summat more than she's got, and she's the last person to put in a bit of honest graft to get it. I reckon she saw this stupid magic idea as a short cut to getting summat without making an effort, and she believed it because it was easier than hard work.'

'Aye, lass, I hope it's no more than that. I can hardly credit the nonsense I've heard from her this afternoon.'

'Oh, Mum . . .' Ellen hugged her mother. 'You know the police need to know we've found her, don't you?'

'Of course. I wish it wasn't so, but she has to face up to what she's done, even if it isn't her who thought up the business with the stolen goods.'

'The real villain is that James Stellion, but Gina helped him and she may even know where he is.'

'I don't think she does. He's gone abroad, his father thinks, and left Gina to face her punishment.'

'Well, if he's not here to take his punishment, she ought to place all the blame on him,' said Ellen. 'He led her on good and proper. I reckon he flirted with her and made her think she was special to him and then used her in his dodgy dealings. I saw them together at the fête last year and it looked to me like she was a bit in love with him even then.'

'More fool her, thinking herself equal to the Stellions,' said Dora sadly. 'Gina's not one of them, nor will she ever be.'

~

Gina had dried her eyes and drunk yet another cup of tea.

'You know what you said earlier, when Edward was driving us back: that whenever you wanted a lovely place to escape to in your mind, it was the rose garden?' said Ellen.

Gina nodded.

'Why don't we go there now? It's looking very pretty – I'd like you to see how hard I've been working – and Mr and Mrs Stellion are away today so not there to mind.'

'Yes,' Gina said quietly. 'That would be so nice. I'd like to see if it smells as lovely as I remember.'

Ellen, ever the gardener, shook her head. 'Not as strongly, and not so many flowers, but it's still very pretty. It's stopped raining so shall we go now?'

'Yes, let's. Just you and me.'

They walked up the lane to the turn into the Hall drive, and let themselves in through the little gate beside the Lodge.

'I never thought I'd come back here,' said Gina as their footsteps sounded in unison up the gravel to the front of the house. 'Do you remember the bicycle?'

'I do. Really, Gina, did Mrs S lend it to you or did you pinch it?'

'It was about the only thing I didn't pinch,' said Gina.

They went round the front and into the rose garden behind the hedges. It looked blowsy and end-of-season but still beautiful.

'Let's sit here,' said Gina, choosing a bench.

They sat together but not looking at each other.

After a while Gina said, 'I once sat in the vegetable garden and I overheard Uncle Tom and Mum talking. They love each other, you know.'

'I do know, Gina.'

'I think they should get married now Dad's gone.'

'Mebbe they will. I'd like that. I don't know why they didn't get married in the first place, all those years ago.'

'Summat to do with Uncle Tom already going to marry that girl that was killed,' said Gina. 'Ask Mum about her.'

'P'raps.'

A soft breeze wafted the fragrance of some roses that had been trained to climb alongside the bench, and each sister took a deep breath.

'Heaven,' murmured Gina.

'Gina, about the so-called spells . . . did you try any others?'

'Yes, yes I did. I tried one against Diana – she was so horrible I wanted to wipe the stupid sneer off her snooty face – and I tried an incantation to make James fall in love with me.'

'And what do you think happened?'

'Nowt with either of them. Probably it was me that did the falling in love, but I don't think even that was real. Yet James told me to go and take the stolen things. He gave me a chance to get away and get some money for them. I thought he was panicking but now I think the police must have found summat in his lodgings that pointed to me and he was helping me. So he wasn't entirely selfish.'

'We heard there was a parcel addressed to you with some stolen stuff in it. It was obvious he was sending things to you. So mebbe he did care for you a bit and wanted you to get away,' Ellen told her. 'I don't know if he was in love with you really, though, Gina.'

'No, I reckon it was that I just wanted it to be real, to become a part of the Stellion family. I just wanted to be like them.'

'But, Gina, you're part of our family, the Arnolds. That's good enough, isn't it?'

'It is now, Nell. I don't want anything more than that now.'

They sat on in silence. After a while they heard distant footsteps. The sound grew louder – there were people coming up the drive – and Ellen took Gina's hand.

'Be brave, Gina,' she said. 'Remember, you've always got us – Mum and Uncle Tom and me.'

'Yes, the Arnolds, my family,' said Gina. She took Ellen's hand. 'My sister.' She leaned over and kissed Ellen's cheek and then stood and faced the policemen as Tom led them into the rose garden.

CHAPTER TWENTY-THREE

'I DON'T REALLY think it would be right for me to have a happy ending,' said Dora, 'what with our Gina being in prison.'

'Ah, love, it's not right that you should be punished as well,' said Betty, pouring Dora a second cup of tea as they sat in Betty's warm kitchen, autumn leaves descending gently outside. 'You didn't bring her up to take what's not hers.'

'I know, Betty, but it's . . . I don't know . . . like I'm turning my back on her, somehow, if I'm happy and she's locked up and miserable.'

'I can't see how it's better that you're all miserable, Dora,' said Betty. 'What's Tom done wrong? Why should he be made unhappy because of Gina selling some bits and pieces that didn't belong to her?'

'I don't know . . .'

'I think it's time you thought of Tom in all this, love. He deserves to be happy.'

'That's what Audrey Mason said one time.'

'Well, then Audrey and me are both talking sense. Tom's devoted to you. Don't forget he rescued you from Philip's violence when it got so as you had to flee your home. How much longer are you going to make him wait? Neither of you's getting any younger. And have you thought that Tom may not wait for ever? There's many a single woman in Little Grindle who'd be glad to take on Tom Arnold. He's good husband material, and you'd be daft to stand by and watch him being snapped up by . . . well, someone less deserving, but with sharper elbows.'

'Like who?'

'Well, Florence Birch, for instance.'

'Miss Birch! Don't talk daft! She's eighty, as she's always telling anyone who'll listen! Oh, come on, Betty, you can do better than that.'

'Renee Fowler's sister, then.'

'Tom's friendly with everyone, Betty, and well you know it.'

'Quite, love. That's my point. Don't take him for granted, that's all.'

~

Ellen swept the paths of the rose garden free of the dead leaves that had blown in. The garden at Grindle Hall had a different kind of beauty in autumn from its summer splendour, with berries on the holly trees and drifts of autumn crocuses and cyclamen at the edges of the paths and under trees. It was a shame Mr and Mrs Stellion were not here to enjoy it this year. They'd gone abroad – to Italy, it was said, where the air was very clean and good for Mrs Stellion's health – and a manager had been put in to run the brewery, which made it sound to Ellen as if her employers meant to stay in Italy for a while.

Diana had taken Coco to London, to live with her. Ellen looked around, seeing in her mind's eye Gina walking the little dog along these paths, then running with him into the village. The outbuilding had for weeks held the piles of bricks and the broom handle she'd set up for his entertainment, but the sight of it had saddened Ellen so much that she had stacked everything away and the door was now closed on a bare floor. She wondered if Coco was now a town dog, or whether he was still a country dog at heart, missing the peace and the stark beauty of the Lancashire fells as he walked the crowded London pavements with Diana. It would take a lot to make Ellen give up Lancashire, but little Coco had had no choice.

She closed her eyes and took a deep breath. Ah, that lovely smell of frosty air and bonfires . . .

'Gets me like that, too, lass,' said Tom, coming down the path with a wheelbarrow.

'It's the smell that means it's time to put the garden to bed for the winter,' said Ellen. She sighed. 'I wonder if we'll even have jobs here in spring, when it's time to get it going again.'

'I haven't heard that Mr Stellion is selling up,' said Tom. 'We're needed to keep the place ticking over, even if Mr and Mrs S are away. They don't want to come back and find the garden has gone to rack and ruin, do they? Although it's not as it was between them and us now Gina's in prison and their James has got away scot-free. I know your mum feels the same. Might be less awkward for all concerned if we looked for jobs elsewhere.'

'True, yet we'll all be sorry to go. It can't ever be as it was now, though. But even if we're not doing new planting and making changes here, I've got plans for the garden up at the farm,' Ellen told him. 'When Ed and I get married, I thought I'd try summat new. Nancy is keen, too. Mebbe some herbs; get a little business of our own going . . . Mum says she'll help. There's little for her to do now the Hall is empty of folk and she also felt it was difficult working there after Gina was arrested. She told me she tried to avoid even seeing Mr and Mrs Stellion, and she thought they felt the same about her.'

'Your own herb garden sounds a good plan, love. Yes, I'd like to see your mum having summat new in her life. She misses Gina and worries about her. A little business would give her summat else to think about.'

Ellen took a deep breath. Now was the time to say to Tom what she'd wanted to say for months.

'Uncle Tom, I know what would give her summat else to think about; what would make her really happy after all that's happened over the years.'

'Oh, yes?'

'I think you know, too. Why don't you ask her to marry you? You must know that she loves you.'

Tom looked thoughtful but not at all surprised. 'Mebbe

I do. I don't want to crowd her, though. She's had a lot on her plate.'

'And that's the very reason you should ask her, Uncle Tom. She deserves to be happy and so do you.'

'So you wouldn't mind?'

'Mind? Why would I mind? Don't tell me you haven't asked her 'cos you thought I'd mind. You must know that's not true. Anyway, this is about what Mum and you want, and not about me. I'm marrying Ed and we're going to be happy ever after,' Ellen beamed. 'I reckon you and Mum could be happy ever after, too. You've waited long enough; you must know it's the right thing to do.'

'Aye . . . aye, Nell, I reckon you're right. I was going to marry a lovely lass – Sarah, she was called, Sarah Swaine – but she was killed. Road accident, it were. I was away learning gardening at a big place in Northumberland at the time. I already knew your mum, of course, from the village, and I liked her a lot; we all knew each other in Little Grindle then, just as now. All friends together. Anyway, after Sarah died I kept on with my training and then came back here to work in the Hall. I never planned to come back here especially, but the chance came up and I took it. But by then Dora was married to my brother, Philip. He was always a bit of a miserable bugger, though he wasn't so bad in his youth as in later years. I reckon Dora thought she could make him happy, but he hadn't a happy nature and he just got worse and worse.'

'It was an illness, wasn't it?' said Ellen. 'We tried but he couldn't be made cheerful because a kind of blackness had overtaken him. Then he got as he couldn't cope with the bad feelings and he was so envious of normal, happy folk, and I suppose that fed his bleak moods even more. He just grew worse and worse.'

Tom nodded. 'Aye, you're right there. He couldn't seem to pull himself out of it.'

'But,' she smiled, 'we're looking to the future now, Uncle Tom, and in particular, your future. Yours and Mum's. It would make her so happy to take care of you and to have you taking care of her, too. I think,' Ellen added shyly, 'she'd like to be married to a really nice man.'

'Well, if you think I could make her happy—'

'I do! I do!'

'—then I'd best get on up to Highview Cottage.'

'Go, go now,' laughed Ellen, almost dancing on the spot in excitement and flapping her hands to urge Tom on his way. 'Here, take these . . .' She produced her secateurs from her jacket pocket and quickly snipped off three of the very last roses, binding them together with a spare length of twine. 'I know they're not mine to take, but no one's here to mind. Now go!'

Tom hugged her, taking the roses, then, laughing, went off to find Dora. Ellen listened to his fading footsteps and smiled.

She sank down onto a bench, realising it was the one she had sat on with Gina that afternoon when the police came and took her away. Gina had gone with them quietly; she knew that the game was up and she must face her punishment.

Ellen leaned back and closed her eyes, thinking of all that had happened since she'd first come to work at the Hall, choosing to remember only the good things and closing her mind to the rest. First of all there was everything she had learned in the garden under the careful and patient tutelage of her uncle, and how he had eventually trusted her with the rose garden as her own responsibility; then there was falling in love with Edward and how he understood why she should want to continue working at what she was good at, and not give up a career that had once looked as if it could take her to the position of head gardener here or at another garden one day; there was the morning of the flood and poor Mrs Thwaite breaking her arm, and how everyone had worked together to prevent the house being flooded; the Wednesday afternoon visits to Mr Shepherd with Sally, and the old man's kindness and generous sharing of his bookish knowledge; the village fête held in the garden and the fun of all the preparations . . .

Ellen opened her eyes and in the clear autumn sky before her she saw a curiously shaped cloud. It was like a pair of white birds with long, elegant necks and massive, powerful wings. As she watched, one of the bird shapes broke away and sped off across the sky, while what remained changed more slowly in the winds, growing rounder until it resembled not a bird but a beautiful rose.

There were footsteps on the gravel of the drive. For a moment it was just like that afternoon when Gina had been arrested; Ellen's heart thudded at the sudden terrible memory. Then Edward appeared, with his cheerful smile and his adorably ruddy farmer's complexion.

'Thought I'd find you here, Nell.'

'I'm just thinking of going home. There's nowt much to do here now.'

'I'll help you pack your tools away and we'll walk back together?'

'Yes, please, Ed. And I think – I just *know* – there's going to be some good news when we get home.'

'Are you allowed to tell me now, lass?'

Ellen laughed. 'I have just two names to give you, Ed: Mum and Uncle Tom.'

Ed was laughing then, too. 'And about time. My mum will be made up about that – Dad, too.'

'So will Gina. She may have been envious of a lot of people, but she wanted only the best for Mum and Uncle Tom. She'd known for a long time that they loved each other, she told me. And I realise she never betrayed them or sought to take advantage of what she had overheard. I'll write to tell her this evening that Mum and Uncle Tom have their happy ending.'

'Aye, you do that, love. Do it straight away.'

'Yes. This is the very best news and I can't wait to share it. I'll never give up on Gina. She knows that, but just in case she ever forgets in the horrible place she's in now, I always sign my letters, "With love from your sister, Nell".'

CHAPTER TWENTY-FOUR

'. . . With love from your sister, Nell.'

Gina folded her letter from Ellen and put it back in the envelope. So, Mum and Uncle Tom were going to get married. About time. She herself had wanted that all along, right from the first spell she had cast, when she wished for her father to disappear from their lives. Now, at last, the future she'd plotted would come about, although Dora would be living at the Lodge with Tom alone before long, when Ellen married Edward. Doubtless *they* would go to live in Highview Cottage, as it belonged to Edward's parents.

Gina sat on her high, hard bunk bed and examined what she really thought about the news of the forthcoming marriage.

The answer was, in truth: not very much. She tried to conjure up a picture of Mum wearing a pretty new frock and hat, Uncle Tom smiling down at her, outside a registry office, Nell and Edward showering them with confetti – tried to be pleased about it all – but it seemed like some strange dream about people she used to know a long, long time ago, and about whom she now felt indifferent. They could do as they wished; she didn't begrudge them their happiness but she wasn't there to be a part of it and it was pointless to try to work up any enthusiasm. That would lead only to disappointment, and Gina was careful to guard against any raised hopes about reality while she was serving her punishment.

She wouldn't be home for Nell's wedding to Edward, which was scheduled for the spring, either. Did she care? Not really. She wished them well in a detached way, but her family were now part of an old life to which she'd decided she would never return, even when she was released from prison.

No, Gina Arnold was gone. When she got out of here she would be a different person – a new person – and incarceration afforded her almost unlimited time in which to think about who this person might be.

She lay back on the thin blankets and closed her eyes, wondering what this new woman was to be called. She'd had a few names already: Gina Arnold and Diana Thornton, and also, amongst others and for a brief time, Eliza Thwaite and Nancy Beveridge, both on their uppers and needing to pawn their belongings in Blackburn and Preston.

Gina laughed then. Eliza Thwaite – it would serve that old crone right for all eternity if her name lived on into Gina's new life, but no, on second thoughts, she'd rather not be saddled with that woman's name.

What else could she be called? Mary or Ruth Hathersage?

No, those ladies had already 'lent' Gina some money; they could keep their names. They'd been kind and deserved no part in Gina's future adventures. Besides, Gina thought superstitiously, she didn't want, by taking one of their names, to become like them, taking waifs and strays under her wing and spreading sunbeams over 'all the creatures of the earth, sea and sky'. That would be far too much like hard work, especially for her!

A bell rang and Gina climbed down and prepared to be let out of the cell to go to her job in the prison kitchen. She'd bluffed her way into this employment, saying she'd worked in the kitchen in a big house, which was almost true. She had learned a lot from watching Mrs Bassett, and Grindle Hall *was* quite a big house, no matter that only two people lived there most of the time. Once in the prison kitchen it hadn't been difficult to follow instructions from the cook to stir porridge, mash potatoes and boil up stew, along with preparing all the other unappetising, beige-coloured food that was dished up. Frankly, Gina was certain she could do a lot better alone, without anyone telling her what to do. Mrs Bassett could have told this cook a few things about making decent gravy.

While at Grindle Hall Gina had thought she'd never want to make any kind of career of cooking but now she could see it might be a way forward in life – not permanent, but something to get her where she wanted to be.

As she stood peeling yet another bucket of potatoes, her hands red from the cold water, she allowed her mind to wander. She tried out the name 'Hannah Bassett', whispering it to herself. Would it suit her? This new Mrs Bassett was a widow, and had been a cook in a big house. But the family she worked for had gone abroad and closed up the house, and she wasn't needed there any more. It would be very difficult to contact them as they were travelling around Italy, although their daughter, Diana, would be happy to give a glowing postal reference for her 'favourite cook' to secure a new position, Gina was sure. She'd work out how to manage that when she had to.

This new Mrs Bassett was going to look in one of those posh newspapers in which 'Situations' were advertised as 'Vacant'. A job outside Lancashire would be best. Mrs Bassett was a Lancashire lass through and through but had now reached a point in her life when she was keen to see other parts of the country. Ideally, the new position would be in a very quiet house, cooking only for an elderly widow or a widower. She could manage that kind of work easily. In fact she meant to do that job so well that before very long she would become indispensable. It didn't really matter who the person was, provided they were old and trusting . . . and rich, of course.

Gina dropped the peeled potato into a second bucket to rinse, then dived her hand in for the next, thinking what kind of house she'd like to go to live in and where she'd like it to be. There was plenty of time for her to have it all worked out before she left here . . .